Hellish Beasts

Brian Carmody

Black Rose Writing | Texas

ISBN: 978-1-68433-335-6
PUBLISHED BY BLACK ROSE WRITING
www.blackrosewriting.com

Printed in the United States of America
Suggested Retail Price (SRP) $19.95

Hellish Beasts is printed in Chaparral Pro
Cover art courtesy of Nick Pitarra

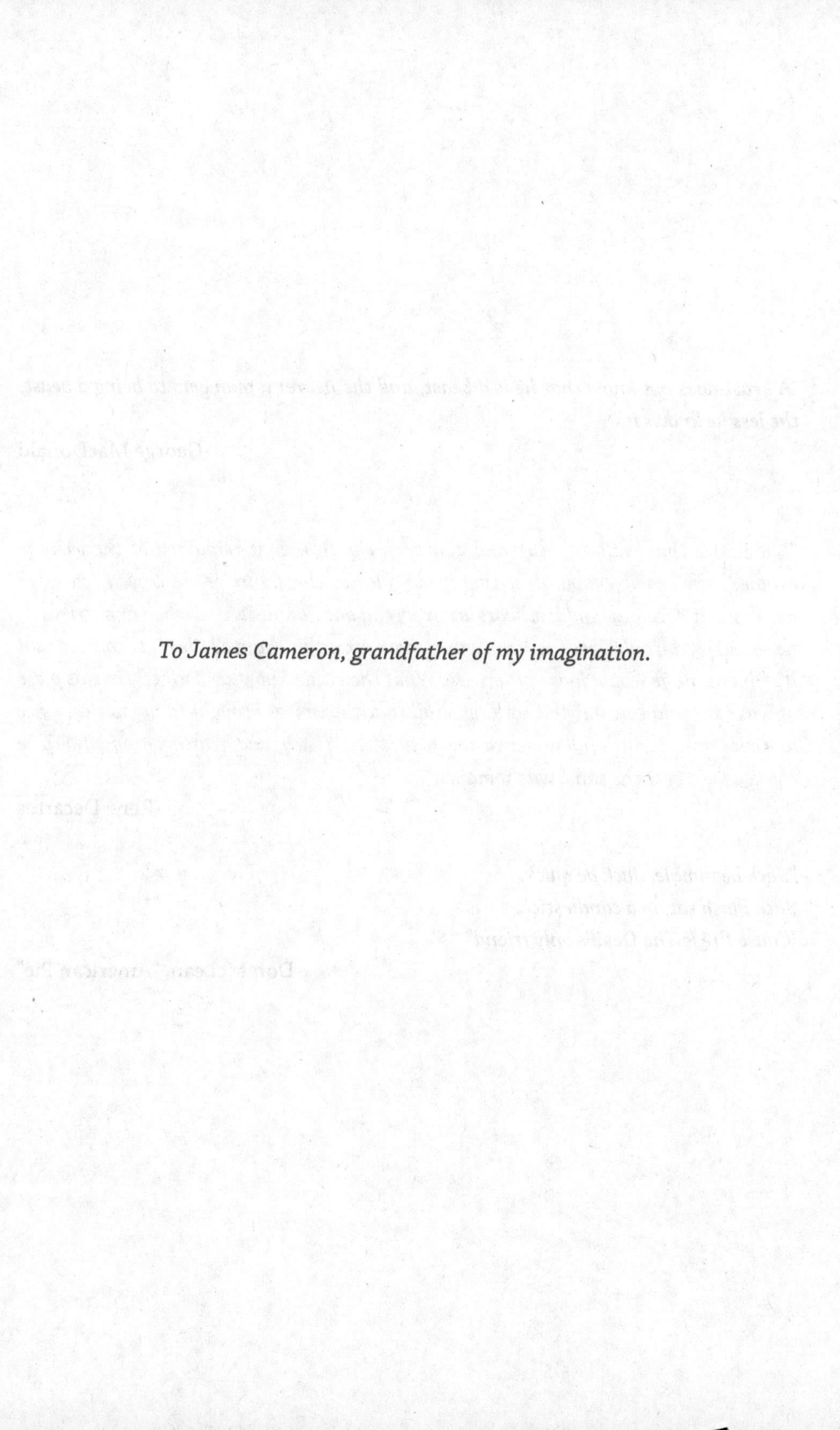

To James Cameron, grandfather of my imagination.

"A beast does not know that he is a beast, and the nearer a man gets to being a beast, the less he knows it."

-George MacDonald

"But notice that while I speak and approach the fire what remained of the taste is exhaled, the smell evaporates, the colour alters, the figure is destroyed, the size increases, it becomes liquid, it heats, scarcely can one handle it, and when one strikes it, no sound is emitted. Does the same wax remain after this change? We must confess that it remains; none would judge otherwise. What then did I know so distinctly in this piece of wax? It could certainly be nothing of all that the senses brought to my notice, since all these things which fall under taste, smell, sight, touch, and hearing, are found to be changed, and yet the same wax remains."

-Rene Decartes

"Jack be nimble, Jack be quick.
Jack Flash sat on a candlestick,
'Cause fire is The Devil's only friend"

-Don McLean, "American Pie"

Hellish Beasts

Chapter 1: The Buddy System

I don't expect you to believe. It would certainly be easier to write the whole terrible experience off as fantasy, and God knows that'd be preferable. That if the entire, fevered, haunting ordeal was merely a scary story to tell in the dark, and shelve when Halloween is done, and it comes time to move on to November and the more familiar time and warm holidays that come with it.

You do that, and God Bless you, and God smiles upon you. Myself, I cannot forget, and I know that it is vain to even try and perhaps ill-advised to desire. The nightmare haunts me still, perhaps not as it did when the danger was fresh and real and my breath still short, but the haunting is there. There are some nights, fewer now and far between, but tiring and terrible when they do come, where I still find myself awake in wane hours, paralyzed to move, not daring to make a peep, and wondering if all the king's horses and all the king's men may charge in and take me to some fresh Hell, the likes of which I'll describe presently. As is, I don't hear the sonorous buzzing of the piper's tune, nor is my nose plagued with the scent of burning flesh, and it's been a good long while since a bee stung me in the privacy of my own quarters. Yet the memory persists, and I hesitate to write it down. It may be that by typing it out, putting the whole wretched thing to paper, at last, I'll have exorcised some demon. Or at the very least, told a story.

It wasn't all bad though. There were sights seen, lessons gleaned, and a new look at Los Angeles. Love and friendship, even in such a twisted yarn like this, can be appreciated. Lilith was a heavenly creature, and even Mike turned out okay in the end.

I don't expect you to believe, but I'll ask you to read. Indulge me in that, if you will. It is, by my own estimations, something of a great quest.

And like many great quests, it started with a question. And that question was this:

Do you think our way of life will ever be caricatured as a historical theme park? When I was a kid, we would go on these field trips to colonial days attractions, where they have people dressed, acting, and talking in a simulation of what life was like in the 1700s. It'd be weird if 300 years from now tourists are going to, I don't know, "21st Century Village" or something.

I mean, those places are pretty weird already. Colonial Williamsburg was one we went to. A "living museum." Field trip in 6th grade. It was fun to ride the horses and play with the 17th-century toys, but not everything was always on the level. We used The Buddy System. I was partnered up with Mike Kripke; we were both kinda class clowns and sort of lagged behind.

Mike Kripke. There was a kid. The kind of guy you loved to bring around because he made your parents uncomfortable. No filter and he was always saying the weirdest stuff. He told me that earthworms tasted "milky." Dared me to try it one time, but I chickened out.

Mike played soccer and basketball. Which we all did-but he also played football, indicating he was of a tougher constitution than I was. Keep that in mind, as it will come up later. He wasn't a very tall or bulky boy, but he was a force to be reckoned with on the field. He was very casual about it, however, acting like getting knocked around when he was still in grade school was no big deal. Nor were his preponderance of merit badges anything he would brag about, nor thinking the machete collection his Dad let him keep in his bedroom anything more than rote. Never before and rarely since had I known a guy so nonchalant about his own distinction.

It wasn't the first time any of us had gone colonial. Virginia history was very big in Virginia and a constant part of our primary curriculum. So, we had the treatment, read the books, gotten visits from in-character historians who told us about chamber pots and pre-revolutionary medicine. Madame Goodrich, I'll call her because I don't remember her name, and her servant Tabatha gave an assembly. The petticoated lady held a glass ball to Samantha Smeaton's arm and told her that ordinarily, it would be superheated, so as to create a vacuum effect when pressed to bare flesh. Suck the blood out. They were crazy about blood-letting back then. Tabatha matter-of-factly told us, "Most of us wouldn't be like Madame Goodrich. 98% of people back then lived in ordinary houses. Only a few owned plantations."

I always thought that was odd, because she said "us", as if it would be *us*, and not other people 200 years ago. I wouldn't have lived in a shack or owned a plantation. I wouldn't have lived anywhere back then because I didn't live back then. It was a stupid hypothetical. I don't believe in reincarnation.

But I did like time travel.

By this point though, maybe it was a little lame. Or perhaps it was just a result of overexposure. I still got a kick out of it. Mike said it was boring, and I didn't challenge him on that.

"What's the point?" he asked, kicking at the dirt. "These people didn't like living back then. Why do we have to pretend it's so neat?"

"What do you mean they didn't like living back then?"

"They used, leaches, remember? They won't shut up about the leaches."

"They didn't know any better."

"And their babies all died, and people only lived to be like 50. It sucked."

I don't know why I felt the need to defend the quality of our ancestors' lives, but I argued. "They didn't know things would be better though. It was the most advanced technology, and medicine had ever gotten."

This gave Mike pause. "So is today. This year. Never been better."

"Do you think that's the way it goes?" I asked. "Things just get better?"

"The better the future gets, the worse the past looks." He gazed up at the sky, contemplating the futility of progress and retrospect. "Maybe someday they're looking back at us like barbarians. Right now they're calling us uncivilized and stupid."

"Right now?" His timing was confusing, but his point was prescient.

"Yeah, like in the future, they think we're a bunch of cavemen!"

"'Cause we don't have flying cars or robots?"

He shrugged. "Yeah, and other stuff too. I mean, they had slavery back then." He gestured around to the theme park emulating that "back then." "1800, they had slaves."

"Yeah."

"1900, they don't have slaves."

"No. Ok?"

"But white kids and black kids still have to go to different schools. And in 2000, we know that's bad, but in 1900 they thought that was okay."

"And they were wrong."

"Yeah, but they think they're good because they're better than 1800 when there were slaves."

"Well, we're better than 1800 and 1900." I wanted to defend our year, though I could see where he was going.

"Are we good though? What are they saying about us in the year 2100?"

• • • • •

One thing I always loved was the candle maker. I thought it was neat to see them dip the wick into the hot vat of wax and take a perfect candle out. Mike wanted to go to the well, but that didn't take too long-I mean, it's just a well - so then we went to the...what do you call it, a candle shack?

It was different this time. I guess by the time you're 12, you're not as easily impressed by simple stuff. The candle maker-the "Chandler", was this big sweaty guy with a dirty shirt. I mean, he's dressed in the colonial clothes, so I guess they were pretty dirty back then, but it was still off-putting.

There was just something...wrong with the guy. Maybe it was his bulbous cheeks, sweaty and puffy (ruddy?), or his beady little eyes, blackish pinpoints in a bowl of baby flesh. He never quite looked you in the eye, but perhaps I preferred that with him.

And it really smelled in there! I didn't remember it smelling that bad before. I asked the Chandler what that smell was. He said it's the tallow. (It turns out, it wasn't the tallow)

He was sweating profusely, and he asked us, "You boys want to see me dip my wick?" Mike sniggered at that. I didn't get it at the time, but now I can see the double entendre. Seems a bit inappropriate of a joke to make around kids.

We gathered around. He dipped the wick in the vat and sort of stirred it around. Did it usually take this long? Then after a minute, he took out the wick. Not the best I had ever seen at that or any other colonial establishment, I can tell you that. It was all crooked and uneven. Bulbous at the base like the guy's puffy cheeks, and then coming out to a thin, spidery tip, like a witch's finger.

I was unimpressed but too polite to say anything. Mike, on the other hand, had a mouth on him.

"What a crappy candle!" he said. Chandler turned red, either out of anger or embarrassment. I think he knew it. The boy was challenging his craft. So he challenged the boy. "Think you could do any better, kid?"

And it was really smelling bad now. Hog fat left out in a rotting pumpkin bad.

Mike cocked a smirky grin, stepped up to the vat. "Yeah!" He reached for the wick.

Chandler bellowed, "FEEL IT!" He grabbed Mike's right hand and shoved it in the wax.

Mike screamed.

I ran.

His screaming was ringing in my ears, but as piercing as that shrill shriek hurt to hear, at least it masked the nefarious, the horrifying, the unspeakable sound of Mike's burning flesh. Bubbling and melting in the fiery wax. Sweat must have been pouring down the Chandler's face as he punished the boy who embarrassed him. I could hear Mike crying. But I was powerless. It wasn't *my* hand in the wax. So what could I do?

So I ran.

I wasn't proud of that. He was my field trip partner, and I left him behind. That was the whole point of The Buddy System. You watched out for each other. Accounted for the other guy. Everyone back on the bus.

But there I was, a scared little boy, running across that stupid little theme park, huffing asthmatic, looking for an adult to make everything all right. Only my eyes were wet. Mike's whole world was melting.

I found the Town Crier. My class had gone on to churn the butter, and by then Mrs. Linne still hadn't noticed we were missing. But then that's the irredeemable flaw intrinsic in The Buddy System. Both for one and one for both. "Does everyone have their buddy?" Yes ma'am, but what if they're both missing? We were.

The Town Crier was a middle-aged man with anachronistic glasses and balding hair. His sneakers, clumsily visible underneath his smock, relieved me. This was the present, and he knew it.

He was alarmed by my tears even before I told him what happened. And I wouldn't stop crying for a while. I didn't have to tell him much. Just saying the words "Candle Shack", as inarticulate and inaccurate as that may have been, was enough to cue him in. He knew what was going on before I did.

Speaking of candles at all raised an eyebrow. Because at that point they had no candlemaker. Least of all that beast in the shed.

I received more of an explanation later. I was waiting in the police lobby for my parents to come pick me up. I had already told the Crier, teachers, and the police what happened. The facts, such as I had them, had been conveyed, and now I suppose it had come time to console the boy and tell him what happened.

"I know you're scared," I heard a soft but commanding voice tell me. A large man with brown shoes and a dark tan suit was standing over me. I didn't look him in the eye. All I could stare at was his suit, the color of which I would associate with beeswax. Couldn't get my mind off it. I could still smell it, stronger now that I was confronted with a similar color (to my eye and mind).

Somewhere between honey and burning flesh. "It's alright to be afraid. You should be in these times, but you have to know there's nothing you could do."

He put his hand on my shoulder. It was meant to be comforting, but I jerked back, so quickly that it might be rude, but he didn't object. He understood I was on edge, even if he didn't know that being touched right now felt like a bucket of ice water. Truthfully, all but one of the adults I met today had been kind, helpful, gentle people. But that experience was tainted, and I was seeing my elders through frightened lenses, exaggerating their traits as if through a funhouse mirror. Madame Goodrich with her thin neck and creaky voice. The Town Crier who might look like Santa on a brighter day but now his glasses had a sinister glare, and his wispy strands of white hair creeped me out. The officer in charge with his buzz cut and super-serious demeanor seemed like he could yell to me at any moment if I didn't give the right answer, and I kept staring at his gun, black and cold in its holster. I bet it was heavy. Loaded. Now this would-be friend with his deep, yet effeminate voice, and suit that evoked that old smell of wax and therefore animalistic pain with tinges of sweetness. It wasn't his fault, I tried to tell myself. He couldn't have woke up this morning, put on that suit, and known there would be the victim of a wax incident to talk to.

"There's nothing you should have done, either," he went on. "You shouldn't think you should do anything but run when there's a...sick man like that."

"Who-who was he?" I asked.

"You've lived a charmed life," he said gently as if this would explain. "There are people you can't understand."

The "Chandler" didn't even work there. He was just some guy who was obsessed with colonial times but didn't get hired because he wasn't any good at anything. Couldn't shoe a horse or bake a shoefly pie. Couldn't even recite Governor's Names in The King's Old English. And I knew he couldn't make a candle worth a damn. But he loved this place. It was his own personal Fairyland. Didn't want to leave. Wouldn't take no for an answer. They rejected his application. They turned him down when he tried to get another interview. Finally, they banned him from the park. That didn't work.

He had snuck in two days before. Slept in the barn, hid from passing by officials. Poked his head out and plied his trade to the unknowing tourists. I guess nobody complained about the shoddy workmanship on his candles, but when you're a 21st-century simpleton visiting an insane artisan gracious enough to bless you with his craft, what recourse do you have? Take your candle and shut up.

Then my parents came, whisked me away, the police psychiatrist/child caseworker or whatever he was, vanished, and I was taken to Wendy's for an extra-large Frosty and Blockbuster for two Adam Sandlers and a Jim Carrey.

John Henry Bowers was his name. He was promptly arrested and subsequently incarcerated. There was no trial or anything, so I guess he took a plea. I didn't really hear anything about him after I gave my statement to the police. Talking to the detectives was possibly scarier than the encounter with Bowers himself. Because I knew from the start, it was a bad situation. And I was so ashamed. The police, the teachers, and my parents kept telling me it wasn't my fault, wouldn't stop telling me what a good job I had done, how brave I was. That made it worse.

One thing that always confused me was, where did the wax come from? They told me that their actual Chandler, a man who had worked at the park for over 40 years, had passed away two months before and they had yet to replace him. But the candle shack was defunct then. And surely there was no residual wax. Yet he had a vat filled. Where did he get it? Nobody answered that.

There was an explanation for the smell though, partially at least. The man who burnt my friend's hand had not left his little shack for two days. He had soiled himself, repeatedly, not wanting to expose himself, or, which was worse, leave the sanctity of his wax.

Mike missed the next couple days of school, which was no surprise. I was dreading his return, and shamefully hoped it would be prolonged because I did not relish the conversation, the necessary and agonizing apology all the adults told me I didn't have to make. Trent, this was not your fault, you did the right thing, buddy. You're a hero. I didn't want to see the look in his eyes. Because whatever the teachers and our parents said, we knew the truth, he and I. I left him in a lurch. He got burned, I got out, and yeah, sometimes life is that simple. On an intellectual level, yeah, the grown-ups were right. I couldn't have done anything against the big crazy man and his hot bowl of wax. He could have shoved my face in the tub, and what would that have helped? But at the end of the day, you're in that moment, and you're seeing yourself, 12 years old for the love of God, but you know what? So was Mike. He stayed. He stayed and took it all, and I didn't do a damn thing about it. We were Buddies.

•　•　•　•　•

Mike got second-degree burns on his hand. They said that's less painful than third-degree burns, but I dunno, sounded pretty bad to me. He came back to school with his hand bandaged up. Completely in gauze, like a mummy. Gave me a little wave, which I returned with the slightest of nods. We didn't interact until lunch, and then, what, was I not going to sit at our table? Was he?

Kevin Furley and Tom Eisenbraun were already sitting in their customary spots. Mike wasn't there yet, so I sat down. Now he would have to make a mistake.

"I hate it," Kevin was saying. "It tastes like cardboard."

"What tastes like cardboard?" I asked.

"The stuffed crust pizza. It's so gross."

"You're crazy," I said. "It's the best thing they have here."

"Pizza Hut has the best," Tom countered. "They- "

He shut up, because there was Mike, standing in front of the table, holding his tray. Fish sticks and chocolate milk and bandaged burnt hand and the world kept spinning.

"Scooch over."

Scooch we did. But conversation lagged. Finally, Kevin addressed the elephant in the room.

"Did it hurt, man?"

Mike shrugged. "It was pretty hot."

Who wanted to keep this topic going? Thank God for Tom.

"Miami's hot," he volunteered. "I visit my Nana there in the summer. It gets so hot outside my balls stick to my leg like Krazy Glue."

And that was it. We didn't talk about the incident again. Mike and I went to the same middle school where we sort of stuck with different crowds. He invited me to a couple of his parties, but then we went to different high schools and lost touch after that.

Chapter 2: Renewal

This all came back when I renewed a book from the library. I didn't finish it before the due date, and when you're going all the way, you want to finish what you started, so I got an extension.

Going All The Way by Dan Wakefield. A funny and stirring novel about the quarter-life crisis of two Korean War vets as they struggle with sexual frustration and the general malaise of 1950s Americana. I quite liked it.

The guy at the counter ripped out my previous receipt-which I was using as a bookmark-and threw it away. He printed out a new receipt with my updated due date, but I told him I wish he hadn't taken out my placeholder so quickly. He said he could get it back for me from the trash, but it's a moot point then. It wasn't that specific piece of paper I wanted, but my place, which took me a few moments to find again.

I was there looking to find a good Harold Lloyd biography. Wanted to bone up for a symposium we were hosting at The Egyptian Theater. Maybe work some interesting details in my introduction.

It's a nice library, the one downtown. 6 stories of books. And such a fascinating design. Recall City of Angels.

But it's not always the most quiet. I was in the fiction section, sighing once again over all the Russian literature I might never get around to when I heard it.

A cat. Mewling somewhere. Sounds hauntingly close yet unreasonably far away. As if it is within the walls itself.

Weird. I thought, who let that in? It wouldn't be unusual to see a cat walking around a used bookstore, but a library?

I walked through the stacks, and the cat got louder. It wasn't meowing either. It was yowling, screeching like I said like it just got stepped on. What on Earth was going on?

I was in the large sci-fi section now. Surely, I wasn't the only one who heard it

Across from me was a tall guy holding the latest Robert Chambers in his gloved hand. He wore one black glove on his right hand, but I doubted he was going for a Michael Jackson look. His face was at once weathered yet youthful. He perused the pages of the book he was holding with only mild interest. It was as if he was seeing the words and understood, the story itself had little consequence.

I decided to get his attention. I wasn't going mad here, was I?

"You hear that?"

Guy nodded, swallowed. "Maybe it was the birdbath," he said with a matter of fact swagger. His eyes don't even leave the page.

"What birdbath?" I asked. "What are you talking about? That's a cat."

He agreed, expanding, "I know, but maybe it got in because there are birds-the cat was chasing the birds in the birdbath."

"Ok? But what birdbath?"

Finally, he looked up and continued this bizarre and frankly irrelevant train of thought.

"Maybe there's one outside-by the window. They could have left the window open a little. The birds bathe, the cat jumps in, then crawls in..."

Nah. We were on, what, the fourth floor of a government building essentially. They don't leave windows open in LA. But now we were committed to this mystery.

His eyes darted around. Intent and manic, but not nervous. *Focused*. Like a caffeinated rat. My impression of the cat was auditory, but it was as if he was smelling it out.

With his eyes.

"Kitty's over there." He pointed one black leathery finger towards mystery. I didn't know why he was wearing one glove like that. Did he think it made him look cool?

Well, I trusted his sensory perception more than his sense of fashion, so I followed him. I've never liked that, by the way, this segregation of books. Mystery over here, sci-fi/fantasy here, then general fiction. It's all fiction, isn't it? This isn't a video store. Just do alphabetical by author, let us sort it out.

"How do you think it got in?" I asked as we pass from the fantasy into the west. Remember The Pagemaster?

"There was an old lady who swallowed a fly," he crowed melodramatically, a sick joke. "Yeah," I answered flatly. "I heard that one too. When I was 5."

"Well you hear them, don't you?"

I stopped. He stopped. We listened. Yes. Buzzing.

"Flies in the library." I shrugged aggressively. "Flybrary. So what?"

"You're not surprised at their presence?"

"No man, what are you talking about? There's always flies in here, by the window sill. They get in through the cracks."

He threw up his hands, stupid glove and all. "That's it."

"That's what? What's it?"

He sang again, under protest. *"There was an old lady who swallowed a fly. I don't know why she swallowed that fly."*

"Perhaps she'll die." I wasn't singing.

"You know what happened next?"

"Sure. She swallowed a spider to get to the fly inside her."

"And then?"

"She swallowed a bird to get at the spider inside her. She swallowed the spider to get at the bird. I don't know why she swallowed the fly. Perhaps she'll die." I spouted this off mechanically, rote, with no sensibility for fun or nursery rhyme good humor. This was an irrelevant trifle.

"And then?"

Dude, where's my cat?

I sighed, "And then the old broad swallows a cat."

He smirked, triumphant. Repeated himself, as if he had won some argument with this Mother Goose absurdity. "That's it."

"I still don't get this. I don't understand-" I stopped myself because that phrasing is an admission of shortcoming. As if I'm somehow at fault for not following this schizophrenic digression. So I turned the tables. "Because you haven't explained it very well."

"Look at it this way? The birds and the bees, the cats and the spiders, they're all like us, right?"

"Ha!"

"Of course, they are. They're either hunting or playing. The Old Lady swallows them to hunt. If they're not occupied so, what are they doing? Bathing maybe?"

Again with this non-sequitur. "I hate birdbaths," I muttered. "They're gross and get dirty easily." I still remember my grandparent's birdbath, and how much that stunk. "They're more like bird toilets. You seen one of those? They are so full of bird crap!"

It didn't vex my partner.

"Bird baths have never been-excuse me-for the birds," he began, "Like all statues and gardens of stone, they are built, they exist, they persist as the most opulent and magnanimous of man's monuments to himself. He thinks that by constructing an artifice, a pond by his own hand, make the birds drink here and not in their natural watering hole, he has somehow exerted control over nature. Like most imperfect acts of insecure men, the only thing the artisan's artifice bathes is his own fragile ego."

I scowled. I didn't think I liked this guy. "So, you don't think it does? We manipulate where the birds drink, and that's not control?"

"Not by a damn sight," he smiled smugly. "In our hubris, we apes fail to see that we are but part of the machine ourselves. Birds bathe, men mason. And the cycle begins, and so it has been since time immemorial. It's all happened before. It will all happen again.

The shrieking was really getting unbearable now. We were so close to it. And maybe the window was open, because there were a few flies now, buzzing around with their own sound and little wings.

No-not flies. Bees. So odd.

"So why do we do it?" I challenged, "It's the 21st century, we got philosophers like you, why are we still making birdbaths?"

He swatted a bee away nonchalantly. It may sting his face, and I know it could sting me anywhere it damn well pleased, but there's no way it was getting past that thick black glove. Maybe that's the reason. If they came in handy even just this once, there's a justification. "Because birdbaths are the last vestiges of an ancient and dying epoch. An antediluvian era when giants roamed the Earth and tributes were made to harpies in pools of marble. You think it's a coincidence, so many resemble pillars and cherubs? The bird bath is the last acceptable temple in our modern age. Sanitized, deprived on sanctity and sold in an aisle at Sears between bags of manure and weed whackers, but temples still."

I had about had it with him, and that mewling was getting to me, so I'm curt. "Word of advice, friend. Next time you feel like bringing up such a dazzling insight, keep it to yourself. Please."

"Hey. You brought it up."

"Misanthrope," I growled.

"Existential Realist," he countered

We'd reached the end of the stacks. And suddenly, just as it began, the shrieking stopped. There were plenty of those bees buzzing around, but no sound from the cat.

We stopped. Dead still. Listening.

"What's that?" I whispered.

"Absolutely nothing," he spoke in room tone. Indoor voice, but classroom, not library, as if he hadn't a thing to hide. He wasn't keeping quiet for anyone, for any reason.

"Do you think it heard us coming?" I asked imperatively because nothing was no kind of answer.

"I don't think it heard much of anything."

He was pointing to the corner. Sitting right under a row of red leather books, there was a dead cat. Bees buzzing around. Fully dead. Its gut open, like a tire track on a burst stomach.

I wanted to hurl. "But it was just shrieking."

"True."

It looked like it had been dead for some time. Well, it was quiet now.

I backed up against the wall, sticking my face in my shirt up to the bridge of my nose, the way I do when I want to sneeze inside. "Oh God," I heard myself saying, voice slightly muffled by cotton and the Hawkman logo on my chest. "What happened? What is happening? What's going to happen?"

"Easy, friend." My supposed friend was slowly walking towards the feline corpse in the corner. He was curious but unafraid. Puzzled, but not horrified. He crouched down, hunched over, knees bouncing up and down on top of springy heels, as if jumpy at such a neat discovery. And he had to assure me. "I don't think it's of threat to you." He looked back at the cat as he said this, eyebrows cocked as if it's a joke in itself. And maybe it is. Road kill not in the road, but four stories high in the City of Angels book depository. Maybe that is some joke. But I wasn't laughing. "Threat?!" I coughed twice. "Yeah, no, but rabies? Plague! Germs! Come on dude, what happened?"

He shrugged. "Cat died." And that's all she wrote, huh?

I backed up further. I was closing in on the wall. I wished I had more space, but it wouldn't budge, no matter how much I forced. "Are you being funny?!"

"I'm being factual." He was showing traces of annoyance himself now. "Conveying, with simple pragmatism, all that we do know to be true."

"Okay, no kidding it's dead! But how?!"

"Don't know."

"It was torn apart man! And what did that-could do that to us?!" I stopped to consider my own raving statement, as it confused even myself.

He stood up. Turned to face me. "'What did that'?" He mulled over the phrase, chewing it and finding its taste unpalatable.

"Well...yeah." I was uncertain. My voice was shaking. Could you blame me? Could any of you honestly blame me?

He walked a little closer to me. Lowered his voice, because now he was thinking about what he said. Turned it over again. Maybe there was something to it. Maybe I could offer insight. "What do you think did it?"

I was baffled. "Well, I don't know! Like a rabid animal?! Or maybe...some crazy homeless guy with...with a knife?"

He considered. "It's possible. What did she swallow next?"

"I'm sick of your games, man!" I looked around. I was nervous and now very self-conscious of my volume. So, I dropped my voice, quieter than I needed to be. Now, unfortunately, I sounded like a little scared kid. "Could we get in trouble for this?"

He shook his head, irritated at something. "Take your nose out of your shirt, man. You look ridiculous, and I can barely hear you."

That offended me. Take my nose out of my shirt? That's the weird action? Why don't you have your nose inside your shirt? "No! What about the smell?!"

He closed his eyes and took a deep breath in. "The smell," he repeated serenely. "I've always loved that. Book bindings, old pages and the like."

With my free hand, I pointed to the monstrosity in the corner. "There's a dead cat right there!"

He strolled over and stuck his face right in it, inches away from the opening. Took a whiff. That made ME gag.

He turned back to me.

"No smell," he said simply, but with such unshaking conviction, I had to believe him.

I slowly peeked out from my cotton fortress. Took a tentative sniff.

Books. Binding. Paste. Those familiar scents I loved so much. The olfactory is the most evocative sense, and I was back in every warm library memory I had ever known when I smelled that.

And nothing, not a single hint of rot from that unspeakable pile.

"What does that mean?" I asked in a tiny surprised voice.

He stood up again. "I don't know. But it's not really the weirdest thing about it, wouldn't you say?"

I looked around again. In the distance, there was an Asian girl with glasses and headphones on her computer. Blissfully oblivious to what we were witnessing. A man with broad shoulders trudged by her, Tom Clancy audiobooks in hand. He paid no attention either. But still, there were concerns.

"Seriously, man, could we get in trouble for this?"

"Why would that happen? I didn't kill the thing."

"Well, neither did I!"

"So, what's to worry about?"

Besides everything?

"Good point."

He turned to the cat and patted me on the shoulder. It's a gesture I found oddly reassuring. Telling me we're in the real world, and people are still here. You don't have to go mad. "Listen, you go get somebody. I'll watch the cat."

I nodded at him, keeping that subject out of my peripheral. "Sure. Sure."

* * * * * *

I went to get someone. Pete, the scrawny college kid manning the fiction section. He was quite aghast and called the security guard, who in turn calls animal control.

The security guard, Roger, was a large black guy with a deep voice. Perhaps he was a tad shaken himself, but he maintained a cool and collected face. "Thank you." He told us. "We'll clean this up."

We take that as all we need to go. Good riddance to this whole affair.

What a mess. What a horrible.

I said that out loud, because I think it is a simply eloquent turn of phrase appropriate for the situation. Like that Victorian mainstay, the Parade of Horribles.

"What a mess. What a horrible..."

The Man in the Glove turned to me. "You're right there, brother." He patted me on the back again, and again I felt awash with relief, this time more complete because I felt this ugly incident was wrapping up and soon we could put it behind us. There was something comforting in that. And I was warming up to him, out of necessity. We had been through something nobody else had, like strange veterans of the War of the Dead Cat. We were in this together.

He flipped his head up, in the direction of the library's East entrance.

"Lunch." It was as much a statement as an invitation.

"Lunch," I repeated the word as if it was in some dead foreign language.

He swung around, started walking. "Don't even have to leave the building to get some Panda."

And it was weird-well, the whole thing was weird. But more than fear at this moment, I was feeling touched. The horror was over – that, I was hoping.

But now we were going to lunch. I don't know. New friend. Despite the grotesquerie of that afternoon, still lying on the floor behind us, I felt welcome. I had just met this person, we talked a little, underwent an experience, and now it was so easy-he was taking it for granted that I'd go have lunch with him.

If only it were so simple with women.

• • • • • • •

We got coffee at the Panda Express, conveniently under the same roof. I had little appetite, needless to say. Maybe I could stomach some frozen yogurt, but they got rid of the TCBY they had there years ago. He, on the other gloved hand, ate voraciously.

"I just don't get it," I said over and over again. "Those weren't death cries. That cat was alive and well one second, then it's dead and rotting for days the next."

"There's no explanation," he said casually. "No use looking for one either."

That steamed my hams. "If it happened-and it did happen-we both heard and saw - there must be an explanation."

He wiped his mouth and opened his fortune cookie. Took the thin white slip out. Read it. "Accept with simplicity that which comes to you."

Think on that. I realized we haven't made a proper introduction.

"I'm Trent, by the way."

"Mike," he tossed me the fortune, "Mike Kripke."

Chapter 3: The Misfit

I journeyed across the City of Angels to the only theater in LA showing the new Arnold Schwarzenegger movie, *Aftermath*. Laemmle's Monica Film Center in Santa Monica. I'm reminded of that other time I went all the way to Santa Monica to see a movie that wasn't playing anywhere else. 2011, for Joel Schumacher's *Trespass*. That was an alright movie, but I really made a day of it. Went to the beach, paid a visit to St. Monica's Catholic Church, which was the Schwarzenegger family's home parish, flirted with a blonde nurse over a Pimm's Cup and took a lot of pictures.

Aftermath was an even better movie. It was great! This may come as a surprise to you, but it shouldn't: Arnold can totally do drama! This might actually be the first straight drama of his career, and he brings the gravitas and pathos from lead up roles like *Maggie* into a subtly moving performance of anguish and grief here. His character, Roman, is a loving husband and father who loses his wife and pregnant daughter in a tragic plane crash. A collision caused in part by the irresponsibility, a moment's carelessness of air traffic controller Jacob (Scoot McNairy). What follows is the story of two men, both extremely devastated by this tragedy in very different ways, as they try to cope with the grief and the guilt. I was reminded of *The Crossing Guard* and *The Place Beyond the Pines*. Despite his name, Scoot McNairy is an actor we can now take seriously. He's previously played schlubs and patsies, in movies like *Killing Them Softly* and *Batman V Superman*. Here he's a vulnerable, complex deuteragonist. His shock can't stop the numb tears from falling as he asks the airline over and over "How many people died?" He walks through life half-awake, only asking his psychiatrist for more drugs rather than opening up, and arguing with his wife Maggie Grace as he was about to serve their son raw eggs. It's little touches like that, forgetting to turn the stove on, that the film and its director Elliot Lester use to portray a man who doesn't want to show he's been turned inside out by guilt.

Indisputably the biggest action star of all time, Arnold's post-political cinematic come-back has been a little less than stellar. I've enjoyed it though. *The Last Stand* was a fun return to form and *Terminator: Genisys* was at least better than *Terminator: Salvation*. His best post-gubernatorial film until now though was probably *Maggie*, the most dramatically affecting zombie movie I've ever seen. *Aftermath* continues the thread, lets Mr. Universe flex his dramatic muscles as the bereaved father looking for answers and justice. Listen to the insistent calm fury in his voice as he shows the photo of his family again, and again to the airline executives who would rather just pay him off and wrap the whole thing up. See the man falling asleep by the grave of his wife, daughter, and unborn grandchild. One of the most chilling shots has Roman, the mourning contractor, standing on the edge of one of his buildings in progress. Spreads his arms like wings. Juxtaposed with a quick shot of the plane's wings it's one of the movie's most effective motifs. Is he going to jump? He's got nothing left.

This isn't *Death Wish*, a pulse-pounding revenge thriller. The story is based off true events, and the filmmakers are mature enough to respect that, to know that the human drama of death and aftermath can be more exhilarating than any number of car chases or bullets. One of the most brilliant things about the movie is how abrupt the climax is. It's rushed, violent, and senseless. There aren't grandiose speeches, exaggerated fights, or melodramatic flair. It's like the real violence of real life, followed by the sudden and irretrievable realization that actions have consequences. The denouement is quiet and potent and goes to show that with this kind of story, nothing ends. Nothing ever ends. Closure? Does that even exist in real life? I don't know. But there are people, and they can make decisions. Maybe even learn things. See it.

• • • • •

After the movie, I hung around Santa Monica for a while. I had been here a couple times since 2011, especially since they expanded the Expo Line last year. Downtown to the beach by train in less than an hour. Who could argue with that? So, I had visited a few times last year and this year, going to the pier and the boardwalk, getting some stupendous ice cream at that indoor carousel that was in the young Dennis Hopper movie *Night Tide*. Even had a couple dates there, even rode the Ferris wheel with one, but it wasn't as sweet or as romantic as it is in the movies. Hell, is anything?

Wasn't piering this time, as I was trying to recreate my previous trespass in 2011. Santa Monica is such a beautiful city. Sure, there are homeless street performers, plenty of panhandlers, but can you blame them? It's such a clean and sunny city, so warm and fun-if you've got to live on the streets, you could choose a worse place. And giving them the bum's rush, putting bars on benches so they can't sleep there, forcing them out doesn't alleviate their situation. It just makes them easier to ignore. They have to live somewhere. The homeless don't just disappear just because you can't see them. *Won't* see them.

• • • • •

I played in the water a little bit, though it was cold and I was worried about leaving my clothes unattended.

I looked across the way as I trudged out of the water towards my sandy pile of clothes. The pier jutting out divided the beach into North and South, like the 38th Parallel. I was on the North side, Ventura in the distance. I decided to cross over. Towards Venice.

Cross *under*, rather. Yeah, instead of going all the way up to the parking lot, or bustling past the crowds up the stairs, across the pier, and down the other staircase, why not skip all that noise and pass underneath?

My first thought as I crouched (yes, the overhead was increasing low) through that cavern of rough wooden pools in the sand was *dank*. How did this wood last in the sea breeze and exposure to the elements? It looked like these poles could collapse at any moment.

My second thought was *illegal*. Nobody else was walking through here. They knew better. Was I "trespassing"? I got nervous, but when you're halfway through the tunnel, you really have no other option but to keep going. What, you're going to turn around and go back, mea culpa? It's the same length through the same place, forbidden or not.

I was alone right now, but I wasn't the only one who had been there. Clearly. Look at the graffiti.

End DAPL in stenciled letter. Someone had been in a hurry, so they just spray painted the frame. Smart. Sure. Pipeline on Native American land. I can dig it. Or not dig it, rather. Get behind the movement, rather.

Burns The King of Wax scrawled across in sickly white…paint? I guess so, what else would it have been? But I couldn't be sure of the substance or even the color (it was a pale, almost greenish white, and recall that such a languid green was the medieval meaning of "pale") let alone the meaning. Who was The King of Wax? Some gang figure? Did beautiful Santa Monica have those?

18C. Orange decal. Actually, I don't think this was graffiti. It looked too official. Probably meant something. Designation of the area maybe, city instructions. This is the 18th Quadrant...or "Cector".

I didn't get up to Arnold's church, but I did go to find a Pimm's Cup.

That was one thing I really did want to reenact, but how? It's a liqueur some bars have, and some don't. What, could I just Google "Pimm's Cup", "Santa Monica"?

Yeah.

Yeah, that's exactly what I did. And somebody had uploaded a photo of their Pimm's Cup to the Yelp page for a place called "The Misfit". I take a look, see the red stools surrounding the old-fashioned bar, and this is it! Six years later, only the city and one beverage they carried to guide me, and I had found the place.

Place was crowded. Bartender asked me what I wanted, knew immediately what I meant, so that was nice. No blonde nurse in sight, but that's...whatever. It's not like this was some great romance I was trying to relive. I had just chatted her up long enough to exchange pleasantries and find out that she was a nurse. And this gentleman prefers blondes. Maybe if I was a sailor on shore leave, like Dennis Hopper in *Night Tide*, that would have been a nice pairing. Whatever. Everything's affected. You can go to the same places, even order the same drinks, but you can't meet the same strangers.

But I wanted to talk to somebody, so I gave Mike a call. He was living in a garage in Santa Monica now (not HIS garage, understand), so he could be right over.

• • • •

I still couldn't get over the coincidence. He'd led an interesting life since NoVa. MFA in Philosophy, followed by a professorship and a couple years in the army. Toured in Afghanistan, for crying out loud. He was seeing combat while I was watching Batman cartoons in my parents' basement. Before his military service, Mike got an associate teaching position (semi-professor? I don't know) at the University of Nebraska, Omaha. Didn't work out, he said curtly, one night, when the beer was making my tongue looser than his and I attempted the stupidest joke I've made since I made my cousin flip a coin over her marriage:

"What happened? Did you have sex with one of your students?"

"Yep." He said it matter of fact, and my heart sank into my stomach. What was I thinking? And there was no "Just joshing!" or "Nah, I just wanted to spread my wings." So, we let that lay.

Still. Military service? Professorship? Kind of put my stagnant screenwriting career, risible bids at private investigating, and part-time work as a program researcher for The Angeleno Film Archive to shame. But then again, so did everything. And if anyone ought to be shamed, it should be the man who took sexual advantage (too harsh?) of his student.

But I held my tongue.

I was there a good 45 minutes before Mike showed up. Already on my second Pimm's which was CONSIDERABLY cheaper than I anticipated. I was half-regretting inviting him as I got more lubricated and comfortable with the feminine presence. Mike was always better than me at that kind of thing. I mean, there was that rumor about him in 6th grade. Or I should say, a rumor that surfaced in 9th grade about an alleged *rendezvous gallant* alleged to have occurred near the end of grade school. It went that Sharon Kerry gave him a blow job in the boy's room. And this was supposed to have happened in SIXTH GRADE. I wasn't sure if it was to have happened before or after the wax incident. Mike did stand out after that. Admittedly, we gave him a bit of distance, and the teachers treated him with kid gloves for the remainder of the school year.

Jeepers, oral sex in public was literally elementary school for this guy. And I didn't even have my first kiss till 22.

Then Kate Brewster, Lana Russian-name, Mia Brodsky, the list went on, all the way till high school and the parting of the ways. Ladykiller and he didn't even care. Good thing there wasn't a blonde nurse, I thought in an admittedly less than Christian sentiment, he'd probably scoop her up.

But he was there for me. Waved as he entered, and I got us a booth in the back.

"The Misfit," he let his lips run over the title. "I never been here before. Been in Santa Monica a month, but I never been here before."

"Well I've only been to Santa Monica twice, and I've been here twice."

"Why do they call it The Misfit? It's stupid. Everyone's out of place in a bar anyway. It's why we're all in here, getting drunk enough to look each other in the eye."

I had a theory that was more about showing off my literary insight than a plausible guess. "Maybe they're evoking the Flannery O'Connor story, you know, *A Good Man is Hard to Find*?"

"Spill it."

"Well the villain is called The Misfit, and my professor called him a singular character in all of Western literature. He kills an innocent family in the story, he's one of the most evil characters, but he's not a true sadist, maybe not even a nihilist. He doesn't get any pleasure out of it, has no philosophy to impart. All he says is 'No pleasure in it.' "

Mike considered that a good long while. "Well he was lying then, or wrong at least. Anyone articulate enough-conscious even to describe their experience to another sentient being, gives up a part of themselves, lays it bare, and he does so of his own volition. True selflessness being a philosophic absurdity, there is some enjoyment, even if only on a molecular level, experienced by this man conveying his own sorry state."

"Even if it's only to make the others feel miserable and like their meaning is meaningless?"

"Especially. He is defining a purpose."

Hmm.

"Check it, check it, check her," Mike was saying, changing gears.

Black hair in a red dress. Well, that's a weird way of putting it. I mean, she had black hair and was wearing a red dress.

Mike nudged me, grinning, as I looked at her. "Snow falls in Manhattan."

I looked at him blankly. "I-I don't know what you mean. Are you talking about cocaine?"

He rolled his eyes. "Lips red as the rose. Hair black as ebony. Skin white as snow."

All true. And all tantalizing. I wanted to kiss her lips. Smell her hair. Caress her skin.

Caress is a stupid word, now that I come to think about it. It's a pretentious term for a desire we all know is not refined in the least. A primal, animalistic urge to paw, to grope, to fondle.

To devour, perhaps, because drool is drool, and the intense hunger I feel at seeing a beautiful woman is not unlike hunger. But it's an insatiable and futile appetite, isn't it? There's no satisfaction in it. You grab and squeeze all you like (that they let you), but second base offers no end, no answer. You're a blind dope fumbling in the dark, trying to cup as much pleasure as you can out of as much flesh as there is, but it never reaches a point of completion, and there's no real purpose. It's no real pleasure in life.

Going all the way though? Well...

"Uncanny," she smirked, not glancing up at us after Mike finally cajoled me into coming over with him.

"What's that?" Mike asked. The X-Men, I drolly wondered to myself.

"Snow White," she said plainly.

That threw us both for a loop. Mike was the first to recover.

"So, it's your hearing that's uncanny."

"And your perception." She turned to him at last, challenging. "You knew that I was Snow White."

Mike slid into the stool next to her, now properly intrigued. "You typically shack up with dwarves like us?" he asked slyly. Which really pissed me off, not only because it was a corny and suggestive line, but because Mike was easily 6. 6'1, and thus was never prone to the pains of traditionally short kids like me. I mean, I had grown up. I'm a decent 5'9, maybe even 5'10 now, but I was always one of the short kids in class. He never was. So, what did he know?

Besides, it was a nonsensical thing to say, especially if you're trying to get into a girl's pants. Even if she was Snow White. I mean, dwarves like us?

But she smiled. Or half smiled, anyway, which is just as good with a line like that. "I mean I literally am Snow White."

Mike frowned-but only for a half second. He didn't want to show that this confused or perturbed him in any way. Guy like Mike, he couldn't afford to lose his composure, especially over just a glib little line.

And it was, wasn't it? Like when a girl on Tinder says "I'm basically just a puppy in a human body". Aw, how endearing.

But Mike wouldn't leave it at that. "Why don't you refresh my memory of what 'literally' means exactly."

She persisted. She was having fun. "It means that. Exactly."

So was he. "Mirror, mirror, at the bar…" We all looked up at the mirror hanging over the bar. Mike, Snow White, and me, the odd man out. "…How I wish upon a star." Mike was a poet now, romantic handsome jerk. "I wish I may, I wish I might, find out what she means tonight."

She was impressed. And finally, straight. "Disneyland." She smiled with a satisfied finality.

Mike threw up his hands in triumph, glad that he had solved the mystery, and using charm and wit at that. "So, you work at Disneyland!"

"I *perform* at Disneyland," she corrected with a sweet smile. "I'm a Princess."

"You certainly are." He took her in appreciatively, now that he knew just who he was dealing with. "Freshen your *Sauvignon Blanc*, your highness?"

Mike put such a ridiculous French flourish to that, so I was secretly pleased when her answer contradicted him. "It's a Chardonnay, actually." Ha. "And I'm fine for now, thanks."

"I like Coppola," I volunteered, apropos of wanting to wedge my way into this conversation. I knew I had no chance with her, and especially with Mike around and already laid this foundation, but gee, I didn't have to just stand out in the cold.

My "contribution" didn't even elicit a response, and why should it have? I added nothing. It was barely even true. As you might guess, I liked Coppola movies, and was more or less indifferent to his label. I'm not a sommelier, but I am a cinephile, so there's that.

"Disneyland, huh," Mike promptly ignored the third wheel. "The Magic Kingdom!"

"Happiest place on Earth!" She was chipper. "And back when I lived in Florida- that's where I'm from- I used to work at Disney-WORLD!"

"Snow White gets around," Mike remarked, raising his eyebrows.

"Actually, I was Ariel."

"I love mermaids!" Maybe I was a little too eager. But that got my attention.

And I had hers. "Oh yeah?"

"There's this bar in Sacramento-"

"Where are you from?" she asked, suddenly interested in what I had to say. But I didn't want to go there now.

"Dive Bar it's called. They have real live mermaids swimming around in the tank above the bar. It's awesome."

Mike frowned. "What are you talking about, Trent?" The idea of actual mermaids seemed beyond him. I had the upper hand. For once.

"It's true. I've seen them. Flippers and everything. One swam right up to me and touched my hand through the glass."

"I believe him," said Ariel, which made me feel nice. "But I didn't swim in a tank. I sat on a giant seashell, and there's sort of this animatronic flipper in front of me, so it looks like it's mine and I'm flipping it up and down."

"A good magician never reveals her secrets."

She looked at him slyly. "Who says I'm a good magician?"

"Aren't all mermaids magical?"

"I'm not a mermaid anymore."

"You're still a princess, Snow."

This had gone on long enough. So, I decided to throw a cold shower of

Godwin on their flirtation by bringing up black Nazis.

"Um, can I ask you something?"

"Sure." She was less playful with me.

"It might be inappropriate, but..." Mike was looking at me, cross, and Ms. White was a little weirded out, but she indulged.

"Shoot."

"Well at Disneyworld, I heard, at the Indiana Jones Adventure Show...do they deliberately cast African American actors as the Nazis? So, it's less offensive somehow?"

She immediately knew exactly what I was talking about and was not offended, which I will always count as a triumph. She was even amused, in a way that was good for me, and it was all the sweeter that for once Mike was the lost boy. "Well, they're not Nazis. Officially. The cast sheet calls them 'German Soldiers'. You know, there's no Swastikas or anything."

"Right," I said while Mike obediently bobbed his head as if he had a frame of reference.

"But everyone knows what's up. I mean, they're guys in black uniforms and jackboots fighting Indy. Come on."

"And the casting?" That was Mike, not me. I had decided not to pursue that question anyway because it was racial.

She giggled. "It's not like it's a *rule* or anything. They can't exactly put that in the casting notice."

"Wanted: Black Nazis," I jumped back in. We were already in it, so why not?

"Right. But there were plenty of black guys there, a couple 'German Soldiers' who'd be out of place in real life. Whatever. It's a fun show."

I edged closer, subtly. I could smell her perfume. Plum scented. Sexy, but then so was every perfume. And everything a woman wears. Mike and I were standing on either side of Snow White, so she was between us, and I was pleased and already mildly aroused that I was contributing more than Mike. She was paying attention to me now. Mike's stupid crack about us being dwarves was forgotten in favor of my more provocative talking point. Maybe controversy is sexy. Who knows?

So I went on, "One of my film school professors told us that back in the 60s, at the studio commissary, all the Nazis used to eat lunch together."

"All the Nazis?" Mike furrowed his brow. But Snow was bemused.

"They were mostly from *Hogan's Heroes*. But there were a couple from movies being filmed at the same time. They had to eat in uniform for time."

"Swastikas in the cafeteria," she chuckled.

"And here's the kicker: They were all Jewish."

That did it for her. "Here's to shared interests." She raised her glass, and we klinked.

So did Mike.

(And let's leave that typo. In the context of the conversation, it's unintentionally brilliant.)

Snow White left after her healthy glass of white wine. We tried to get her to stay for one more, but she simply and apologetically said that she had a long drive back to Anaheim. That led to Mike asking if she was working tomorrow. No, but later this week. That was the smooth segue he used of let's exchange information (the us in "let us" being her and Mike, of course), so that this 30-year-old Afghan war veteran with a burnt hand and a series of sexual malfeasance could coordinate a time to come see Snow White ("Miranda", in fact) at work. Work being pretending to be a cartoon princess, posing with children, and waving to her at the job would be the next step in Mike getting laid. I hate so much about so many things.

"Yeah, you guys should totally come see me sometime!" Miranda (what magic left) flashed a cheery smile and touched Mike's arm before walking out, favoring "us" with a little wave before she walked out.

Yeah, I was ostensibly one of "you guys" she invited to come see her.

But not really.

How do you stay in the bar after that? The evening had clearly peaked. We had our drinks, and we had met a girl, chatted her up, and I thought we both did pretty well. Mike did better, naturally. I rarely ever had illusions about actually taking a woman home (and to be fair, no Catholic should) but there were points in that discourse when I was hopeful about the chance for an exchange of business cards, a "find me on Facebook", something like that.

And contact information had been exchanged. Hers for Mike's. They programmed their numbers into each other's phones. I probably could have injected myself into that exchange, gotten her number as well, for the same ostensible purpose, and she would have gone along with it. She'd have given me her number and taken mine to avoid that awkward moment when you make crystal clear to two strangers you've known for half an hour who you prefer to know and who you could do without. I could have done that, but what on Earth would the point be?

To that end, it was kind of a bust for me. Miranda was clearly the best prospect that was going to come along that night, and Mike got her.

Geez, I sound bad writing this. I probably am.

At any rate, I didn't really feel like staying. What, have a couple more drinks, get a little sloshed, pretend to listen to Mike's various philosophic ramblings while I reminisced about the one that got away? It was all a little depressing.

But I wouldn't be alone.

So we stayed. Mike was three beers in, I was nursing yet another Pimm's, and that suddenly got his attention.

"It's particularly sad, is it not, when a man can't admit why he's drinking-or else isn't man enough to drink it straight." There was something between scorn and humor in his voice. He pointed at my glass. "What is that?"

"That I'm drinking?" I rose the cup. (Crimson more accurately, but I'll allow the pun)

"That red fruity, what is it, Planter's Punch?"

"Pimm's Cup."

"The Hell is Pimm's Cup?"

"It's...Pimm's No. 7? I think? And 7Up. Only they probably use Sprite."

"What's Pimm's No. 7?"

"I don't know."

"Come on."

"Well, it's like, an herbal liqueur I think? Kind of like Campari. Sweet but not too sweet, and it goes great with soda."

Mike was actually almost annoyed. "Well, why are you drinking it if you don't even know what it is?"

I was reticent at first. "I always have a Pimm's Cup when I come to Santa Monica."

"WHY do you always have a Pimm's Cup whenever you come to Santa Monica?"

He was persistent in pressing on, and I actually appreciated that. It was strangely flattering. Like someone was paying attention to me and cared about the answers to the questions they were asking, no matter how seemingly trivial. I was finding I could be honest with Mike. About anything.

So I indulged him. "I saw it in a movie," I admitted.

"Yeah? Which movie?"

"*Ghost Town.*"

He smiled. "Yeah, I liked that one. That was one of Scarlett Johansson's first, wasn't it?"

"No, you're thinking of *Ghost World.*" Mike was wrong on two counts, in fact, because *Ghost World* came out in the year 2000. Post *All the Pretty Horses* and *Home Alone 3*, and more than a lustrum after she would have made Elijah Wood's too-perfect-to-be-acceptable adopted sister. Not that any of that mattered.

"Oh. Right. So which one was *Ghost Town*?"

"Eh, just some rom-com where a guy can see ghosts, and they won't stop bothering him."

"Hmm."

I didn't have the energy or inclination to talk about that mediocre Ricky Gervais/Greg Kinnear outing in any detail. What passion or discussion could it provoke? I was embarrassed to even mention it.

"And they drink Pimm's Cup in it?"

"No. Gregg Kinnear's the ghost, and he's encouraging Ricky Gervais-who I think was a dentist - he's saying he should be more manly or something. They go to a bar, and Gervais wants to order a Pimm's Cup, but Kinnear shoots that down. Says it's a fruity, girly drink."

Geez, this was awful. I got that burning sensation in my nose that occurs when I give too much of myself away. And the annoying thing was, I knew Mike wouldn't be giving any back.

"So, you drink it because in some stupid movie they say it's a stupid drink?"

"No, it's just, that's the first time I heard about it. I mean, it's a famous drink. I think they drink it at horse races in England."

That was enough for him and thank God we could drop the origins of my appetite for the drink aside and get to it.

"You wanna try some?"

"Sure do."

To even his own surprise, Mike liked the Pimm's Cup, this fruity and somewhat obscure herbal liqueur I claimed, with little authority, was enjoyed by English gentlemen at horse races.

"Not a bad choice, Malloy." He savored his sip. "Not bad by any measure."

"I'm not going to say 'I thought you'd like it,' because I didn't think you'd like it."

He shrugged. "I'll drink anything that gets the job done."

"I'm not sure it will though," I admitted. "I don't think the alcoholic content is very high."

"You drink enough of anything, it'll get you wasted. I seen guys smashed with Shandy. You know what pruno is?"

In fact, I knew exactly what pruno was. I knew about prison wine from the internet, and I met another Afghan vet at a bar once who told me the method used by American servicemen in Muslim countries. But I wanted to hear Mike's version.

"It's prison wine, right?"

"I ain't never been to prison. Jail, a couple times, but no, not a serious lock-up. No penitentiary pruno for me."

"But you know how to make it."

"I had to. We're on Pacific Time out here? Kabul's on Medieval Time. Sharia law. No booze allowed. Talk about the horrors of war, right?"

I chuckled. Then I got serious.

"I just wanted to say, Thank You for Your Service."

"Shut up. Don't say that again." He seemed oddly indignant like he was annoyed with the gesture.

"No, I mean it. I come from a big military family. I would have joined up myself."

"Why didn't you?" he asked flatly, not really caring.

"My asthma."

"Oh."

"You know I thought about trying to get a waiver, or uh-"

"-Whatever...What was I saying?"

"Pruno."

"But we're out there in the sun all day. IEDs, snipers. Damnit. And not a whore for a thousand miles. Give us something to drink, damnit."

"So, you make your own."

"A man's got to have options. Orange juice. Orange juice and a lot of sugar. Throw a couple of slices of bread in the bag for the yeast. Bury it in the desert bag for three days, and bam!"

"Sounds disgusting."

"Hot horse piss. But it works."

"Are you sure you're even getting drunk? What if it's just...poison? You know, brain damage."

"Friend, what do you think getting drunk is?

"Good for two things: Degreasing engine axels and killing brain cells."

"No sir. The sugar gets sticky. That's a terrible idea."

"But it's a quote. I was quoting The Matrix."

"You take a lot from the movies, don't you?"

"Sure do." It was just a simple fact, and I wasn't embarrassed.

"But you do have good taste." He slurped. "On occasion."

"Thank you."

"Let's get some more."

He suggested we order the entire bottle, which I thought was a neat move, like something from the Old West. Our waiter, who looked like he wouldn't be out of place in Mumford and Sons, gladly acquiesced.

But when he brought over the bottle, not only was it NOT Pimm's but some off-brand imitation. *Pin's Brew*. The drink itself was a paler shade of green, rather than red, and the label...I've always thought with Evan Williams, that cheap well whiskey, that the bottle was deliberately meant to look like Jack Daniels, either to trick or evoke. The mockbuster of liquors.

So it was with the lettering of Pin's Brew, I think. Only underneath that large, reminiscent PIN'S, there was a distinct logo. An actual pin, I guess, standing like a maypole, around which some stupid piebald harlequin danced. Who was that guy? The whole thing was oddly medieval and irksome.

I wanted Pimm's!

Not only was it not that, what do you think we saw? Or saw us, perhaps more accurately.

A human eye. Just floating in the liquid, staring right out of the bottle, right back at Mike and me.

Chapter 4: First Impressions

I was supposed to go on a date to the Aquarium of the Pacific in Long Beach, but she had to cancel at the last minute. Ah well. I was looking forward to it. The aquarium part anyway. Dating, as I've said, recalling Roy Cohn, can be tedious and disheartening. Especially online dating just for the sake of it. Why do I travel all over town to be bored and nervous at the same time? That's why I stopped with the lunch/coffee dates. Those are dull. I do museums now, or Santa Monica. Or yeah, aquariums. I've always loved aquariums. The one in Baltimore, when I was a kid, was PHENOMENAL. My saying about aquariums is that they're like if a zoo and a museum had a baby. There's something relaxing and intellectually stimulating about it. Those big blue tanks, the swimming animals, all the knowledge they drop on you.

My last aquarium date wasn't great. For all its finer points, Santa Monica's aquatic zoo isn't one of the highlights. It's small, and it doesn't take long to exhaust the whole thing. My date left rather abruptly. She said she had to pick up her brother from soccer. This is only 40 minutes into our meeting, and I'm thinking, well you knew about soccer when we set this time didn't you? Maybe she was just making up an excuse to leave. We didn't really click. It happens. To me.

Then a friend invited me out for drinks and/or karaoke, but he also had to cancel. I was already at Union Station. Contemplated riding the Red Line up to Universal Studios, finally checking out the VooDoo Donuts, then spend the night in Hollywood. Nah. I'd go back to Glendale, where I live.

Walking through Union Station, I noticed the fish tank. I wasn't done with my aquarium experience after all! So, I spent a couple of minutes looking at those fish. Had a staring contest with this bulbous fella with eyes on the side of his head. I wasn't sure if he even had lids so it might not have been a fair fight. But I still won. He looked away.

"Candle fish."

I turned around. This Metro employee, a cute blonde with the pressed blue uniform Rick Santorum vest was standing surprisingly close to me. Snuck up on me. Startled me in an embarrassing way. I actually jumped. What a doof.

"Sorry, did I startle you?"

"No," I dissembled. I noticed her name tag. CHIP. Wasn't that boy's name? No, it's not anybody's name. I don't just mean it's not anyone's full, legal, Christian name. I mean nobody in real life is named or nicknamed Chip. Doesn't happen. That's just in movies and the like.

Nonetheless.

"What, uh, you said it's a candlefish?"

"That's right!" She grinned wide, a mouth full of too many teeth that were far too white. "Eulachon. A Pacific smelt."

Smelts and a Coke? Mark McKinney's harsh voice ran in my ears.

I was confused. "But it's not...it's glowing-or does it have to be deep in the ocean? Can we just not see...?"

She knew what I was getting at, and explained with polite condescension. "No, they're not luminescent. They're called candlefish because they're so high in body fat that sailors used to actually burn the fish as a candle once it had been dried out."

Sorry buddy, I thought as I looked at the little guy, who didn't respond favorably to that news.

Startled once again when I saw Chip's chipper reflection in the glass of the tank. She was hovering right over me. It was unnerving. I think I felt her breath on my shoulder, though that may have been just my imagination, running away with me.

"Don't burn me!" A pathetic, high pitched cry, childish yet morbid.

Egad! She was doing a cutesy fish impression about not being burnt, and it was ghastly!

"Heh, heh," I laughed dutifully, turning from the fish to her. This was awkward. I'm not a vegetarian, but maybe I should be. Thinking about animals getting killed always made me sad. Especially when you anthropomorphize them, give them sentience. A fish crying out that he doesn't want to be burnt. What sick person would find that funny?

"But, um," I tried to get serious, make small talk. Felt oddly obligated. "He's not-they're not actually made of wax."

"Uh-huh. Nobody's made of wax," she grinned again. Those teeth. Was Chip a shark? Maybe she belonged in this tank. "Nobody but The King!"

"What? What king?"

"The King of Wax!" And she threw her head back, endless teeth on full display, laughing like a water-hyena.

"Who's The King of Wax?"

She sighed, as if out of condescending pity, and touched my arm. Her nails were fire truck red, and her grip was simultaneously entreating and unsettling. "I've got to check the trains. Enjoy the fish." She walked away, descended to the Red Line.

What kind of joke was that? No context to it. No rhyme or reason, sense or meaning. No real pleasure in it. What, so this fish has a lot of fat, but he's not a king made of wax, and I'm supposed to laugh at that? Impossible! Meaningless! Maybe there was something I was missing. Like your old pal Mortdecai, I didn't have the necessary frame of reference. The whole exchange left me unsettled and annoyed. Intellectually, I should have been thrilled. She was pretty, right? And blonde. She was a woman paying me attention, breath on my shoulder, touching my arm, telling me jokes. But those jokes were creepy, and her teeth, and her name, and her King...

Whatever. I went to Glendale, bar hopped a bit, and got some late-night breakfast from Conrad's. The day was a wash. No date, no Karaoke, just fish jokes, pancakes, and Netflix.

Then Mike called me at 3:00 in the morning.

"If this isn't an insanely beautiful woman, I'm hanging up." He didn't dig my Erik Avari impression. Or didn't get the reference more likely. Anyway, he told me he had a "lead" on the Pimm's Cup incident. A lead like we're detectives now or something, which is fantastic, and tells me to meet him in Highland Park.

Chapter 5: Into The Little Cave

Now here is what had happened back in Santa Monica, to catch you up to speed.

When that atrocious bottle of "Pin's" arrived with the ocular surprise, naturally Mike and I were horrified. Apoplectic.

My heart fell into my stomach. I felt like I was going to vomit pure fear. After the cat, maybe I shouldn't be surprised anymore. By any of it.

Mike was angry, righteously so, and he tried to disguise his fear with sheer volume.

"WHAT THE HELL IS THIS?!"

The waiter, fortunately, was not a demonic and malicious imp as Chandler and Chip seemed to be and responded to this unexpected horrible as a decent and sane human being. First, paralyzed with shock, then frightened, and then stuttering apologetic.

"I'm-I'm-I'm...." he reached for the bottle, hands shaking, as if by removing it from our sight he could banish the foul memory from existence.

"Never mind that!" Mike roared savagely, ripping the bottle out of the waiter's reach. "Just get out of here!"

"It was supposed to be Pimm's! We-" The Waiter was having trouble grasping the concept in this context, and so was I. Get out of here? Where was he to go?

"Leave!"

The Waiter backed up slowly, his eyes darting around, not sure where to look, before fleeing completely and disappearing into the back.

The bottle lay-

The bottle

That DAMNED FOUL BOTTLE...

Lay on the table, still. Mike crouched down to face it level. He looked it in

the eye. He looked IT in the eye. The grotesque, disembodied eyeball barely floating in the murk near the bottom of the bottle, staring out at him. Lidless, soulless, it looked at him. And Mike looked back.

Perhaps undead cats and unaccounted eyeballs are not, contrary to aghast first impressions, the oddest things on this little blue dot.

· · · · · ·

I saw this reality show once about a pair of Siamese twins. They were just entering high school, and the narrator was talking about the experience. What they'd do if they were taking different electives and all that, I suppose.

Then there's footage of them talking to a boy in the hall, and the narrator said something like, "They are interested in dating...but they're not going to tell us about that."

The show cut to talking heads of the sisters, agreeing. One of them said something like, "Yeah, we don't have to tell you everything about our private lives." The other nodded.

At the time it irritated me to no end. Part of it was my curiosity, of course. How DID they plan to date, to romance, to sex, to marry? I wanted to know logistically, physically, morally. I was annoyed that this informative documentary was filling us in on one twin playing the sax and the other takes to her art, but they won't tell us how many vaginas they have or what arises when one wants to date a boy the other doesn't approve of.

Then there was the perceived hypocrisy, as silly as that sounds in retrospect. You've invited a documentary crew into your lives, probably for profit, and millions of viewers are seeing NEARLY every aspect of your lives, and you balk here? Now you have privacy concerns? We've seen your custom-built bed, you might as well drop the pretense of privacy and inform us what you plan on doing in it.

I realize now that's a less than compassionate, Christian response. First of all, everyone is entitled to their own privacy, especially on affairs of the heart. Second, wasn't I assuming that these teenage girls made the decision to greenlight the documentary? Surely their parents, and could we really blame them? Conjoined twins are special needs with special costs, I imagine, so turning a medical drawback into an economic asset by utilizing our modern-day appetite for REALITY in all its oddities is a solid plan. Were the girls pushed into it by domineering parents under protest? I don't know. Was it exploitative? Absolutely. The show-runners would likely sing you a line about empathy and education, but let's be honest in our cruelty: We were watching a freak show. And admitting that is as cruel, barbaric, and dehumanizing as it is truthful. Sure, there may have been some doctors in the audience, but the natural human response to gawk at curiosities is not necessarily rooted in worthy sentiment.

Finally, I also realize how untoward it is to fixate on the potential sex lives of underage teens. Grotesque at any age, but this curiosity was surely creepy.

So go older. Years earlier I saw another show about another pair of conjoined sisters. Safely in their forties. One worked in a factory, the other wanted to be a country singer. They were franker about their dating. One had a boyfriend and said, rather curtly I thought, "When I'm on a date, she's not there." or something to that effect. It sounded firmly exclusionary, which I suppose is the point, but how could she simply not be there? It's as if the girlfriend wanted her single sister to simply shut down, cease to exist when she was on a date. They are literally attached (at the head, if I recall correctly), but it seems like loneliness was possible.

Chang and Eng, the original Siamese twins, did get married...perhaps to a pair of sisters? And they had children.

Well, we all try to have normal lives, whatever that means. People are the same, I guess, an extra arm here, dry fish skin there. Maybe the real oddities are twisted souls. Mike, at times like these, did seem like one of God's own curiosities.

Because he didn't blink.

Eyeball in the drink and he accepts it. Reality is still open for business. He's just indignant is all.

"What is the intention here?" he grumbled, while my mouth was still agape, the abyss falling in.

"I'm...gonna throw up" was all I could manage, and just saying those words felt like vomit itself.

He frowned as if my sickliness was the night's real crime. "No you won't, either."

"Should we talk to the manager?" If he could play cavalier, so could I, I decided.

After a good long moment, Mike shook his head. "Nah," he said, deep in thought. "Nah, they aren't doing anything."

"Why not!?" I said that louder than I intended to, but I was upset.

"Snow White. Sure, she's gotta go home alone..." He was drifting.

"Mike."

"Trent," he began patiently. "What do you think they would know?"

"Well, I'd like to think they could tell me what an eyeball is doing in our bottle of Pimm's." I sounded crosser than I intended, or maybe I didn't. Crossness was justified, even for Mike, who was being deliberately obtuse.

"Pin's."

"Whatever! I want them to tell me why!"

"Trent," he leaned in, "they'd be as confused as us."

"But they're the ones who served it."

"They thought it was Pimm's. Take a look up there." He pointed to the bar. Above the bar, in its own distinct section was a row of red accurately designated for the Pimm's. Like I said, this junction was known well enough (via Yelp) for its Pimm's to display it prominently.

"Yeah. So? They got the wrong bottle." And that was putting it lightly!

"Not just the wrong bottle, my friend. The wrong level of reality."

"You getting at here?"

"You see any other bottles of Pin's Brew on that shelf?"

I did not.

"Maybe we got the last one." A (gross) thought occurred. "Ugh! You think we were drinking eyeball juice the whole time?"

"Absolutely not. That was Pimm's."

"Well, how do you know? How could you know?"

"Pimm's is red, isn't it?"

"Yeah," I answered, unnerved for some reason. "And..."

"And?" he challenged, holding up the bottle of Pin's Brew.

Ahem. The *pale green* bottle of Pin's Brew.

I was confused and mortified.

But you know something? This time it was a different type of horror. Cat ripped open, that was gross. Now, what was unsettling me on a deeper, more cerebral level was not the eyeball floating in the drink, but the fact that the drink had somehow changed color, instantly- or not changed. It had never been red, had it? It was always that sickly light green, and now I had to question my entire perception and sanity.

There is just something you can't put into words about that. And I know it's not much. Trick of the light? Mistaken memory? Mandela Effect? Whatever. But if something as simple as the color of a drink was wrong or could shift without shifting from one second to the next, what else about the universe doesn't make sense?

"It was red," I said flatly, at last.

"Yes, it sure was," he offered no opposition. "It was red, and it's always been green."

"Merry Christmas," I mumbled.

"It's an odd thing, I agree, when you realize it is not the drink that's changed, but you."

"Skip the bend the spoon crap."

"Alright. But it was red. And it was always green."

"Schrodinger's Pimm's. Okay."

"That's the thing! It was Pimm's! It was when he set it down, and it definitely was when he took it off the shelf. Yet it's always been Pin's Brew."

"Mike," I groaned. "You're giving me a headache."

"Of cosmic proportions, I'm sure. But the thing is, they'd have the very same headache here, and there's no help for it. Not from them anyway. Not from that waiter, not from the bartender, and not from the manager. Answer is Pin's itself."

I didn't have the energy to ask what he meant. Or maybe I dreaded the answer. Anyway, the conversation sort of dragged to a lull after that. Finding an eyeball in your drink tends to have that effect. Not much more to say, is there?

The waiter never came back with our tab. Mike stood up, bottle tucked in his armpit under his coat, and gestured towards the exit with a cock of his head. I followed him out, warily, careful not to look at the bar, or any of the waiters, or any of the other patrons who presumably still lived in a sane reality.

We were skipping out on the bill, but decency had skipped out on us, so fair trade? No, Catholic guilt was abundant, as per usual. I figured our tab had to be near a hundred at least, including the bottle-but perhaps The Misfit would be glad to be rid of it. And of us. If our vanishing meant no lawsuit, then we could very well take the evidence as well, thank you and goodnight.

It was cold outside. We stood on the sidewalk, shivering in the beach air. We didn't make eye contact. Stared at each other's shoes.

After a brief eternity, I peeped, "I'm gonna...get going."

"Trent," his voice was strong. I looked up. "I've got this," Mike said with calm command, as he touched my arm with one hand and tapped the bottle with the other (keeping it mercifully out of sight) that I believed him.

I accepted that, nodded, and went on my sweet way. I didn't ask him what he meant.

• • • • • •

So, then I get that cryptic Kripke call in the witching hour.

"If this isn't an insanely beautiful woman, I'm hanging up," I groaned.

"Never mind that." Mike, humorless as always, was in no mood for jokes or obscure references to a throwaway line from a 20-year-old movie. "I cracked the case."

I sat up, somewhere between amused and annoyed and still quite drowsy. "'Cracked the case', Mike?"

I heard his sigh on the other end. A pause.

"Mike?"

"I'm here. Listen. Yeah. Cracked is too far. Some things still need to be done. Many things. All things."

"I'm going back to bed." I held the phone up so I could see where to press the end function.

"Trent, no!" his voice, so recently relaxed, was now frantic, audibly so, even when I was holding the phone away from me.

"Okay," I yawned. "I'll bite. What's up?"

"Listen. You-thanks, by the way," he expressed genuine gratitude to me for staying on the line, and I was slightly touched. "You remember that bottle?"

"What?!" This wasn't funny.

"You know, in Santa Monica-"

"Mike-"

"Pin's Brew, the eyeball-"

"Mike! Jeepers, man!"

He stopped. I think he realized how absurd it was to think I could have forgotten. "Right. Sorry. Of course."

"So, what's up?"

"Like I told you. It's the bottle. It's a brand maybe. I mean, that's what I thought," his voice trailed off. "No. No," he whispered solemnly. "I can't do this over the phone, Mike."

"Trent," I corrected.

"Hah." Nervous laugh. "Just meet me."

"Now?"

"No. No, that's fine. It's closed now anyway. But I got it. It's halfway between you and me. So that's convenient. Tomorrow evening?"

I held the phone away from me. Stared at the time.

"You really mean today?"

"Trent. Please."

• • • •

"Halfway" turned out to be a dive bar called La Cuevita in Highland Park, which I thought was exceptionally generous of Mike. What, 8 miles from me, 20 from him?

That wasn't the point though. What we were seeking, as I would soon learn, was not about geographic convenience but of a mystery ripe to be solved.

Mike said 5. I've always been a punctual guy, so I strolled in around 4:35. That's a thing about me. But I'm generally the only one. Everyone else shows up late.

Today though, Mike surprised me by stopping me outside. He was waiting by the entrance, had been for some time, it seemed.

"Hey Mike," I stopped, a little unnerved (but then this was an unnerving mission wasn't it?) by his posture and harried expression. "We going in?"

"Yeah. Yeah, let's go."

"The Little Cave" was a basic translation and indeed the bar's own signs (adorned with a painted bat) indicated this. It was a roomy establishment, dimly lit by candles for ambiance- an effect more effective, I'm sure, during the night hours. When Mike and I strolled in, there was a vastness to the atmosphere, like we were in a large empty warehouse. Three other civilians present. One blue-collar middle-aged man at the bar soaking his head in suds, two older women sipping wine in the corner. Chandeliers hung from the ceiling, which could hardly be said to be cathedral size, but I guess we were okay, as far as getting hit on the head goes. Nobody under Richard Kiel would have to worry about just walking into one, but if you wanted to be a kid and see if you could touch it, you probably could.

"Sup guys." Sitting on an absurd little wooden stool was a tall (ungainly so) guy with a ponytail and a scruffy goatee. His arms were inked, but I didn't care about his tattoos because he was a dude. He gave us a little head flip. The reverse nod thing.

"Hi," I answered politely while Mike looked around the place.

"You got IDs?"

"Sure." I had mine ready and out. Mike was still gathering wool in this mundane little cavern he saw as rich with mystery.

"Cool," The Bouncer bobbed his head up and down while looking at my license and handing it back.

There was an awkward pause as we waited for Mike to stand to attention and produce his. This annoyed me. Be as serious as you want, Mike, be a cryptic mystery, but for the love of all that is weird, just show him your ID!

"How about you, man? You got your ID?"

Mike didn't look at him. Just stared out at the bar. "We're gonna sit..." he started to point but let down his arm lethargically, lacking purpose. He didn't even finish his sentence.

"Yeah, but," Neil (as I would later learn) was a patient guy, but this was tiring him. It was such an absurd little trifle. Clearly, Mike, a 30-year-old veteran, was old enough to drink. But rules are rules, and routine is routine, so "Come on man, just show me-"

Then it was in his face. He studied it for perhaps a moment longer than necessary, but to be fair, Mike gave him no choice.

"Okay," he said slowly, handing the card back to Mike and giving the slightest of nods. The casual affability was gone from his voice. I almost felt like apologizing, but that'd be a ridiculous act itself. Mike was distant, not curt. Whatever.

I followed Mike to the bar, took a seat next to him. The bar itself was wooden, and Mike soon busied himself by digging his fingernails into it. In the shelves over the bar were the glass bottles, lots of them, but plain and unwashed. Wasn't like The Misfit. This place was not catering to the Santa Monica smart set. This was a bar, plain and simple, take it or leave it, have a drink. I liked that, and the ambiance was neat, and.

And.

And there she was.

Lilith.

• • • • •

For a long time, I've had an unfortunate habit of seeing certain women, to quote my inner thoughts, as "oppressively beautiful". It's sick, sad, and gross, but I can't help it. Sometimes I see a woman so gorgeous and sexy that my first reaction almost skips straight lust entirely and heads right into despair. They hurt to look at, the knowledge I have no chance with her, and all the more depressing because I know every guy is staring at her, all day long, hopefully with more confidence than me maybe. It frustrates me that gawking and lusting after her is expected, is predictable, but that doesn't mean I can stop. So, it's one long futile cycle of seeing a woman so stunning and scantily clad that I feel bad.

To quote Sal Paradise, seeing a Mexican maiden, wrote

A pain stabbed my heart, as it did every time I saw a girl I loved who was going the opposite direction in this too-big world.

Or even Portnoy, the chronic liver-screwing masturbator that he was, beautifully articulated his unrequited lust for the shiksas at the ice rink.

I have no resentment towards the women, so that's good. But sometimes I see one who looks so good it brings me right down.

Such was Lilith.

How to describe her? My angel in the rough, my demon, my raven-haired bewitcher?

Smoky.

We'll get there, and you'll soon see why, but that's the one word that sticks with me, perfectly. Aesthetically and thematically, she remains...smoky.

But first impressions? Fishnet legs, riding all the way up to tight cut-offs. Full jean shorts. Exposed midriff. Copper skin. Pierced navel.

Her top. God help me. Black tank top, low cut, lots of cleavage. MISFITS atop a smug skull (it's a Punk band I'm aware of, but not too familiar with on a specific level), but I'm not looking at the music.

Sleeve tattoos. A tapestry of death roses, simmering snakes and los Muertos covering both those long arms.

Her face. Full pouting lips pierced by an apathetic ring. Her eyes were brown pools-or black, I might say. Smoky. Yes, here. Black mascara and eyeliner created that effect, or maybe just accentuated the intrinsic smokiness buried beneath her surface.

"Hey guys," she said casually as we took our seats. "You want to see the menu?"

I glanced at Mike, an act of servility I instantly regretted in Lilith's presence. What, I couldn't even order a drink without his approval and guidance?

At any rate, Mike gave only the slightest of nods-and not the least indication of what we were doing here.

Not that I minded. "Sure," I said as Lilith slid the menu (scrimshaw on thick paper) across the bar. Black vines down her wrist. I liked looking at her.

"Any recommendations?"

"All these..." she stuck a long polished nail (black, of course), onto a rectangular box at the bottom of the menu. "are $5 on Happy Hour."

I resisted, thank God, the urge to pull out my phone and confirm the time.

"And is it?" I asked, "Happy Hour?"

"Well..." she rolled her tongue lackadaisically, considering my banal question. "Are you happy?" Her tone was as flat, yet there was still a hint of playfulness that perhaps only such a sexy Goth could pull off. That silly response would be irritating from a man, and if he raised his eyebrow in that manner as she did-almost as punctuation-well, that'd be a punchable face, wouldn't it? But on her, it was an arousing micro-expression. Dr. Trent Lightman, keep it in your pants.

I perused to the menu, paying special attention to the Happy Hour selections.

CALIFORNIAN
VODKA, GRAPEFRUIT, ORANGE JUICE, BITTERS

Was that Californian? Certainly, citrus was represented, but I don't know. The vodka made it sound relatively banal. Grapefruit must be very healthy because it tastes bad and has negative calories. It's good for disguising the taste of alcohol. I recalled a bit from Wakefield's <u>Going All The Way</u> about a more appealing cocktail "The Seabreeze", which was gin and grapefruit or something to that effect. Gunner said it was good to take on picnics and it got you drunk without realizing it. I thought was a more appetizing title anyway, and while I loved being a Californian, I had little interest in drinking one.

PIRATE AND COKE
WHY NOT?

Why-first of all, that's not a list of ingredients. Second, hardly a prized distinct cocktail to be proud of, is it? Making the natural assumption that Captain Morgan was the pirate (a bartender once told me a "Skinny Pirate" referred to a rum and diet coke), this was clearly nothing but garden variety Rum and Coke. Pish posh. And you're advertising it? What else?

SMOKEY MARGARITA
JAVIS MEZCAL AND FRUIT JUICES
Fascinating. Especially the mezcal. But more on this later, because

(SPOILER ALERT!) this is the one I choose.

SINO PALOMA
SINO SILVER, LIME, GRAPEFRUIT JUICE, SODA

I dig the silver. It is naturally metallic, and thus classy. And it kills werewolves. My Dad says that silver got that reputation because it's actually really good at killing germs. Or germs can't live on it. I forget. I don't know if it's really effective against lycanism, but I do remember Dad putting drops of silver iodine in our water when we were kids. Good for our immune system, I think. Though I doubt you'd get the same result from tequila. And silver in that case probably just refers to the color of the label. Nothing else-though it does imply there's a gold label maybe? How about the bronze, huh? Some of us are strapped for cash!

OLD FASHIONED
YOUR CHOICE OF EVAN WILLIAMS BOURBON OR SINO IRISH TEQUILA

I resent, on a primordial level, the idea of substituting tequila (IRISH tequila?!) for whiskey and calling that an Old Fashioned. Just no. My friend/collaborator back at USC, Dan Miller, loved to drink Old Fashioneds. Cause he saw it on Mad Men. I reckon he felt like a black Don Draper. Nonetheless, it was a weird notion. Tequila. Nothing old fashioned about messing with a cocktail like that. For that matter, who drinks tequila in cocktails anyway? What's a tequila cocktail? You either put it in a margarita, or you get smashed off shots.

COLD GIN THYME AGAIN
GIN, CUCUMBER, THYME, FRESH LIME JUICE

I'm...I'm not sure what is being referred to here? I mean, clearly, some punnery is afoot, but to what aim? What are we quoting? Cold=Old. Obviously. And Thyme is Time. But gin? Good?! Old Good Time Again? Is that a phrase? It's dubious, especially because gin is not a great substitute for good. And I hate cucumbers.

SAZERAC
OLD OVERWROUGHT RYE, PERCHAUD'S, SIMPLE SYRUP AND A KISS OF ABSINTHE

Ah! New Orleans! This is a storied drink, is it not? And I dig the absinthe, even though absinthe is overrated. I'm old enough to remember when it was illegal in America. It has this great big reputation, unearned-The Green Fairy, and all that. People get caught up in the imagery and mysticism, Vincent Van Gogh, Moulin Rouge and all that. They think it gives you hallucinations. It's really just liquor. Perhaps back in the day, inferior bottles rotted with wormwood poisoned the drinker, and maybe that spread some rumors/misconceptions, but this stuff is just a strong licorice-flavored spirit. So why then am I still so allured? Perhaps romanticism cannot be unconvinced, not even by–or especially not by mere fact and logic.

IRISH MULE
TULLAMORE DEW, LEMON, GINGER BEER

Ginger beer, nice. With the lemon, all you'd need is honey to have a cold remedy that could get you plastered. And it's great to have a mule outside the Eastern Bloc. Vodka's a better mixer, but I prefer whiskey in general, and the Irish evocation spoke to my roots.

But I knew what I was getting. Look around. Look at her. Smell the air.

And that was it of course. Because how could it not be? *Smoky.*

"Smoky," I repeated, verbally this time, pointing to the menu while drinking in the smokiness of her eyes.

"Good choice," she said, which I assumed was true.

"I like mezcal." Which was truer still.

"How about you, Michael?" She asked as if there was nothing at all odd in her address.

Mike looked up as if there was something very much at all odd in her address. "What you call me?"

She smiled, pointed at his glove. "You're wearing one glove. Like MJ."

MJ would always be Mary Jane to me, but I knew what she meant.

So did Mike, evidently, because he eased up-annoyed, but no longer paranoid or alert that this bartender, a stranger in a strange place, might somehow know his name. Pure coincidence.

God's way of remaining anonymous, don't you know?

"I was in Afghanistan," Mike grunted, a little more aggressive than I would have liked.

Why bring that up? Irrelevant and deliberately misleading. I suppose framing your scalded hand as a war injury was more impressive than letting everyone know the real truth about a field trip gone sadistic. I wonder if that's what he told everybody.

"Cool," Lilith said with a shrug and, electrifying, a glance at me.

She was fascinating, this new woman. No apology, no backtracking. If she saw a vet with one glove over a wounded hand (presumably) damaged in combat, she felt no obligation to retreat from her initial cute observation, that it was indeed the King of Pop who trademarked the one glove look, and that Mike was currently passing a remembrance.

"And Mike's his real name!" I contributed, not giving a care to his subtle scowl. Oh, use your real name, Mike. She can handle that truth at least, and you're in no material danger.

"Well Happy Unbirthday, Mr. Coincidence," she smirked dryly. Couldn't you just love her?

Mike didn't. "Yeah yeah," he grunted. "Just gimmie a beer. Something cheap."

"PBR's on Happy Hour. $3."

"Fine."

She pointed at us, one finger each, recounting our orders. "Smokey Margarita. Pabst Blue Ribbon."

"Yes, thank you," I said. Mike just looked down, the sourpuss. Perhaps he was already realizing that ordering a beer was a disarming act, remembering his true intentions for being here before being caught up by Lilith's mind games.

"Strong stuff, that mezcal," she said, bending over to retrieve the bottle, offering a tantalizing glimpse at her lower back tattoo, a slithery, scaly serpent with its tail in its own mouth.

Jeepers, Trent. Get a hold of yourself. I mean, how sexy is a snake? Ah, good point, but look where it is.

"Right, uh, is it like mescaline?" A stupid thing to ask, sure, but I was making conversation.

She chuckled warmly as she poured the drink. "They might be from the same cactus. I don't know. It doesn't make you hallucinate or anything."

"Unless you swallow the worm, right?"

She held up the bottle so I could see the wormless bottom. "That's only in Monte Alban mezcal. We don't carry that here. But I know what you mean."

"So, does it do anything?" I asked, glad we were in friendly waters. "If you swallow it, I mean."

She shrugged. "I dunno. I never swallowed it before. I guess if you drink the whole bottle and swallow the worm at the end, you'll be pretty fucked up. But you just drank a whole bottle of mezcal, so that's probably why."

Time for another movie reference. "They say if you swallow the worm, it doesn't know it." Willem Dafoe, *Born on the 4th of July*.

"Huh?"

"Uh, like maybe it's blind or something, can't tell the difference."

"That and it's dead." She slid me the drink.

"Right." I took the glass from her, and for that most heart-palpitating of moments, our fingers touched. Transference. Her tips gliding away as my hand took the drink. Warm skin on a cold, perspiring glass. My breath quickened. My heart beat faster. My cup overfloweth.

She unceremoniously picked up a can of Pabst Blue Ribbon from the cooler, cracked it open and put it in front of Mike. I didn't crack a Dennis Hopper reference, because why bother?

"Here you are, Michael," she said matter-of-factly. "Or should I say, Mike."

Mike grunted in reserved disapproval. She turned to me.

"I suppose that makes you Elvis?"

Sexiest thing anyone has ever said to me.

"Not quite," I laughed affably, hoping I was playing it cool. "Just Trent over here. Non-musical Trent Malloy."

"Well, I won't ask you to sing." She cocked her head to the chalkboard behind her, announcing the bar's weekly events, none of which started before 9. "Karaoke's only on Monday."

Indeed, the board indicated that Monday was, in fact, Karaoke Night. Tuesday was Open Mic. On Wednesday, bizarrely, scheduled was "Rod Stewart Live". That couldn't be real. But what was it?

(Today was Thursday, so we had a few hours until "The Rogues", a local band, I assumed.)

"That's a relief."

"And I'm Lilith." She smiled broadly, excessively cheery in ironic parody of such cheeriness. What she didn't realize, unless she did, was that I took it as warm all the same, and extra appreciated the self-awareness in her smile.

I raised my drink. "Thanks for inviting us to your garden, Lil."

She pursed her lips, going over that in her mind, not quite convinced but giving the allusion its day in court. "I know what you're referring too, but it doesn't really work." She leaned over the bar, eyes wide, tone mock-serious, loud and faux-aggressive. "It's a cave, dude!"

"Right."

A coarse voice from the end of the bar called for a refill.

"A demon's work is never done." She rolled her eyes, giving me the slightest of (what rapture!) winks and crossing to the drunken vulgarian taking her from me.

"She wasn't a demon," I said, too late and quiet for her to hear.

"Trent," Mike's voice was cold, impatient. "What are we here for?"

That irritated me, the interruption of my delusions of flirtation, as well as that nagging question. Why were we here? You tell me. "Yeah, what's up? You called me, man."

"Sure, sure." Mike nodded, back on track. "Yeah." He lowered his voice. "It's about Pin's Brew."

Of course, it was. I didn't allow myself to show panic. "Go on."

"We weren't setting foot back in The Misfit, and maybe that was a mistake, but nonetheless, we are here."

He let that sit.

"Here?" I asked, looking around.

"I did some...detective work."

"Nobody asked you to do that."

"Shut up. Anyway, I did a search for Pin's Brew."

"And?"

"Nothing. No website, no BevMo listing, no social media presence. It's a drink that does not exist."

I furrowed my brow. "So, it's obscure. Or maybe it was brewed in house. You ever think of that? The Misfit-"

"It's not The Misfit, Trent. You know that. They thought they were serving Pimm's. Guy was shocked, scared. He didn't know anything more than we did. It *was* red, but it's always been green, remember?"

"Yeah. What's your point? And how does that draw us here?"

"Look at my eyes Trent." Crows' feet, deep wells of insomnia. "Been up for days." I believed it. Tired days and sleepless nights. In aid of what? "I've scoured the internet. Remember Yelp?"

"Yah, I remember Yelp! That's what brought me to The Misfit! But that's how you found Pin's Brew?"

Mike thought about that. How to answer. "Yes and no."

"Mike."

"I did do a search for "Pimm's" on Yelp. You know, a few bars carry in LA. Then I went to Instagram. Girls post pix of their drinks. So, I did a cross search.

See who posted a photo of their Pimm's for all their girlfriends to see."

I was actually on the edge of my seat. "And?"

He took a sip of Pabst. "Way I see it Trent, is...after your eyes have been opened, and you can see the way it is-the way it really is-well, you're not going to shut them again. The veil's been torn. We've seen the man behind the curtain, and Oz won't come out again."

Boy, was that the truth. But what did it mean? Here. Now. In this context?

"9 times out of 10, they post Pimm's, it's Pimm's. But..." He slid me his phone, Instagram app open to BarleyWinks87's account. She was hot, as most of her beach pics attested, and she partied, as her nightclub entries showed. Mike pressed one of the photos. Enhance.

Pimm's Cup at La Cuevita! So fancy! #PretentiousCocktailNight.

"But that's not Pimm's," Mike said with quiet finality.

No, it was not. The photograph showed, clear as night, that same ghastly pale green liquid in a glass like mine, sitting on this very bar we now sat at.

"So..." I didn't know how to finish that sentence, what to say next, so I just let it drag out.

"She orders a Pimm's Cup. She thinks she's drinking Pimm's. She takes of it, posts it online, all 39 who liked that photo, I bet ya, they saw Pimm's."

"So, what makes us different?"

"Maybe we're special."

"Like we've been chosen by God?"

He mulled that over, not dismissing it outright, "Or else just a freak accident of the cosmos. Whatever it was, we can see now."

"I think I know what's next."

"Good boy." Mike raised his hand and called over Lilith. "Excuse me."

She sauntered over. Swayed. "What's up?"

"Another round. But this time, can we get two Pimm's Cups?"

Her reaction was neither horrified nor indicative of any personal affiliation with horror. Right now, it was just a drink. And she was a bartender.

A sexy, sarcastic bartender.

"Wow, Pimm's Cup. Y'all can't get enough of that, can you?" She drolled, "Day and night, will anybody ever order anything else?!" The edges of her lips curled up in a silly smile, and she retreated behind the bar to find the fateful libation.

She came back a moment later, two glasses of, yes, red cocktail in her hands.

"Drink up, governors." British accent. Horseracing.

The cocktails did look like Pimm's Cup, ordinary, appetizing red Pimm's. And not an eyeball in sight, thank God. Thank God, but how did that help our mission?

"Mike," I murmured. "They're red."

He didn't say a word. He grabbed his glass tight, staring down into the red.

And slammed it.

"It's meant to be sipped," I protested lamely after he had already drained a drink I couldn't intellectually reconcile tasting again.

He wiped his lips, savoring the taste, and declared, "'Meant' doesn't mean what it's meant to mean anymore." He raised his hand.

"Reload?" Lilith asked, impressed.

"Something like that," Mike said casually, not wanting to give himself away. "How 'bout we get the whole bottle this time?"

Lilith was a bit taken aback, but not on a preternatural level, mind. "That's $175." She said as if that three-digit number should intimidate us out of the ridiculous notion. It did for me.

But not for Mike. I hear you" he said, reaching into his back pocket and taking out a billfold. "One hundred, two hundred." Put the bills on the bar, and finished with, I hated his guts for saying, "Keep the change."

"Big spender. You sure it's not Cristal or Dom Perignon you're after?"

"Pimm's." And not another word.

I was near a sweat as she bent down to retrieve the moment of truth. Then the sweat went from cold to hot as I saw the snake staring into my soul. Girl with the Serpent tattoo. Again, it wasn't the design that heated my blood (though I admit, something was alluring about something so diabolic), but its placement. There's less of a skip than the poets and romanticists may like to admit between slutty and sultry, and the storied "tramp stamp" as much as classy men with worthy tastes like my father would insist, was and is extremely beguiling.

My eyes were still all over her in a yearning, depressed, sinful way. I think she picked up something of that, because she kept glancing at me, throwing tiny smiles my way, smiling with her eyes as well as her mouth, half winks that only the lovelorn could perceive or appreciate.

And maybe she was just doing her job. Enticing look and becoming manner for the tips. But a man can dream.

"Here you are. The whole bottle." She put it down before us, between us, seemingly unaware of the monolith she had hoisted.

Whelp, there it is. Half full bottle of Pin's Brew. A piebald jester dancing around an actual pin, for whatever that symbolized, was on the faded label of this pale green elixir.

Lilith didn't see anything out of the ordinary. For all she knew, it really was a bottle of Pimm's, God Bless Her. She leaned forward, resting her head on her hands, smiling widely, looking from Mike, to the bottle, to me.

"You gonna pour the lady a glass?" she asked, beckoning sweetly.

Mike had no time for such courtesies. He didn't even look at her, entranced as he was (as was I), by the green liquid in front of us. "Never mind that," he said curtly, with a rude way of his hand. "We got our drink."

I pried my eyes away from that haunting green to offer an apologetic look to Lilith, but it was nothing to her. She picked herself up with a shrug.

"No sweat off my sack." She walked to the other side of the bar.

"Mike, you didn't have to-"

He held up the bottle to me. "You see that."

"Green. Pin's Brew. No eyeball, thank God."

"Right but look here. On the label."

He pointed out a bit of text:

Pin's Brew is bottled exclusively at the Deakins Porthouse, 432 Stonebrooke Road in ██████████████████████ (this part was scratched and faded past legibility.)

"Pin's Brew is bottled exclusively at the Deakins Porthouse, 432 Stonebrooke Road in..."

"San Simeon, California!" Mike said with a cheer of triumph.

"I've never heard of it."

"Me neither!"

"I mean, I've heard of San Simeon, of course. That's where Hearst Castle is. I meant I've never heard of Deakins."

"I know what you meant!" He was quite excited now. "Sons of bitches make you collect the whole set!" He laughed.

"Mike. What are you talking about?"

"That other bottle, Trent, you remember, from The Misfit?"

"How could I forget?"

"I looked on that label. Also incomplete. 'Pin's Brew is bottled exclusively at the ████████████████████████████████'" he covered his mouth with his hand and mumbled into it here before finishing with "in San Simeon, California!"

"So, you already knew where it's brewed."

"I knew the town, Trent. They could be making it at Hearst Castle or San Simeon City Hall, for all I knew."

It came to me. This was exciting. "But now we know where. We know exactly where."

He slapped me on the back affably. "Exactly!" He grinned knowingly. "And that's where we're going next."

"Where?" What? No. "I can't just jet off to San Simeon on some goose chase. Are you crazy?"

"So, wait till the weekend." He blew it off. "Hell's not going anywhere."

Note: what he *probably* said is "Hell, it's not going anywhere."

"Whoo! Progress!" Mike unscrewed the cap of the bottle and raised it to his lips.

"Whoa man!" I protested. "You're not really gonna drink that, are you?"

Mike paused. "Why not." He knew why not. Come on. He glanced into the bottle. "*Eye* don't see no reason to stop." He elbowed me as he took a swig. Jerk. Cool jerk.

He stood up, bottle still in hand. "Let's split it, Trent. Got some packing to do."

"Next week," I corrected. "Don't go without me."

I still don't know why I said that. It's like, why wouldn't I want him to go without me? Did I really want to be a part of…whatever this was?

"Sure thing, Trent. I'll wait."

Bottle in hand, he sauntered out of the bar.

•   •   •   •   •

How to process all that? I stared down into my smoky margarita. Only halfway through, I was already feeling the effects. The room itself seemed to have a distinctive smoky quality by this point.

Though that could have been the smoke. I looked up from my glass, and there she was. Lilith, black eyes supreme, locked on mine, smoke gliding out the lit cigarette wedged illegally between her pouting dark lips.

"Smoke gets in your eyes," she said matter-of-factly, as smoke poured out of her mouth, like a sensual dragon.

"As long as it's not in my drink." To my credit, I did not cough. I actually found the smoke sexy, which I'm sure is unhealthy, if not perverse.

"How's it treating you?" She pointed at my glass with her cigarette.

"It's doing the trick so far. Sweet and citrusy, and yeah, smoky."

"Could just be me."

"Either way."

"Either way what?"

"I like it all the same."

She stood up, smirking. "And I thought you were going to complain about California's indoor smoking laws."

"I look like the fire marshal to you?"

"I don't know what he looks like," she said pointedly. "Or she," as a PC afterthought. "The whole point is we don't know who it is. If it's a secret inspection, they just come in, plain clothes, look around, take mental notes. I guess."

"Jeepers. What a living."

"I don't pity the guy."

"I guess you wouldn't."

"Pity's for the pitiful," she answered dryly.

I looked around. "You seem to be doing pretty fine." To her scoff, "I mean hey, Rod Stewart Live's no slouch."

"Lame!" she extolled affably. "Lame joke!"

"Yeah well the joke's on me, 'cause, that's what it says."

"And you think we really got Rod Stewart?"

I shrugged. "I'm a trusting guy. Your board says Rod Stewart, who am I to question?"

"We got Rod Stewart Live."

"That's the way he is. Last time I checked."

"And when was that?"

I had to think. Rod Stewart? When was the last time he had crossed my consciousness? I've never made a point of it, but I kind of dig him, come to think of it. Gravelly-voiced 70's rock crooner, looks like a British Barry Manilow. I guess I liked his songs, especially "Reason to Believe". My Mom certainly liked him. But if the name of this tribute band was a gag, why choose Rod Stewart, of all people?

"I don't know."

"Come back some Wednesday. You'll see."

Chapter 6: Applanation (Goldmann) Tonometry

I hate Applanation (Goldmann) tonometry. Thank God if you don't know what that is. I hate it almost as much as I love Oops! All Berries. I hate it more than Ebert hated *North*, which wasn't even that bad. It had some funny moments, Elijah Wood was in top form, and there were some cool cameos. I liked Bruce Willis. And it gave the world Scarlett Johansson. Some people say she's overrated, and maybe she is. She doesn't really add much to *The Avengers*, honestly. But there's *Ghost World*, *The Man Who Wasn't There*, *The Spirit*, and *Her*, so it's not a complete loss. I do regret lusting after her so hard in my teens and early 20s. When was she on the beach with Josh Hartnett? Maybe it was around *The Black Dahlia*, which was also pretty good. That era was probably the height of my desire. Sorry Scarlett. Sorry God. But I went to confession a bunch, so I'm ok there. But you hate her first movie so much you're gonna write a book about it? You only had to see it once, Roge! I have to have this evasive and harrowing exam once a year/18 months/whenever I want my contact lens prescription updated! Pneumotonometry is less uncomfortable but less accurate, so my "doctor" refuses to use that method. And it's so much money. I'm nearly 30 years old, I have to pay some stubborn so-called medical professional a lot of money (to me) to stick these probes right up to my cornea, almost touching. God forbid he should bump the equipment or I accidentally jolt forward. Then I lose the eyes. And I have to shell out for the privilege. Or I can't reorder new contacts. I guess I could avoid the whole uncomfortable mess if I just stuck to glasses, but I prefer contacts. Probably for shallow reasons. Probably for the worst reasons. Probably, because you know, girls. One time in high school drama class this girl asked me why I was wearing my glasses instead of my contacts. I said because my eyes hurt that morning. She said, "That sucks". In retrospect, she might have been saying it sucked that my eyes hurt, but at the time it felt like she thought it sucked that I was wearing glasses-that's the impression I got anyway. At any rate, my desire to appear attractive to the opposite sex is a factor in preferring contacts to glasses. That's why I do a lot of stuff actually. That's why I work out. Not that it works- I mean, I'm in much better shape, healthier, lost a lot of weight, feel better about myself, but I'm not sure it works at making me more attractive. And even if it did, so what? Dating is such tedious rot. How can you be bored and nervous at the same time? And if you get a second and a third and so on, but you're not sure if you're actually dating or just going on a series of platonic one-on-one outings. Jeepers. My sister says I should "DTR" (Define the Relationship) early on, but how to have that conversation? I'm no good at all that. Maybe if you meet somebody on a dating site and continue to go out with them, they'll think you're dating. Especially if you text them "Goodnight handsome" with a kissy face, but then the day after he changes his relationship status on Facebook and the voice of Mandark congratulates me, she says we should just be friends. What a fool. And Bridget asked if I wanted to be her boyfriend after I already thought I was. And this was after she asked if I would be insulted if I kissed her. Of course, I wasn't, so we're making out pretty hard and she puts my hand on her breast, and she asks if I want to be her boyfriend, so she initiated all that-then when I try to get to Third, she says "Let's save that until we're *officially* boyfriend and girlfriend." And I absolutely respect her decision to not want, you know, my finger there. That's a sin anyway when you're not married. But what's this "unofficial" nonsense? Later in the night, her friend comes out of the next room to ask us if we needed a condom. *I* was the first to say no. Or maybe we said it simultaneously, but the point was, I demonstrated that I emphatically wasn't expecting sex. Ok, but then her friend says, "Unofficial congratulations." What did they know that I didn't? Was it premediated, like "I'm going to ask Trent to be my boyfriend tonight, but it won't be official." This is also after 4 months of those nebulous one-on-one outings, by the way, but the first time we made physical contact. Maybe I should lose hang-ups about sex before I turned 30, but that's a sin, and maybe 30's just an arbitrary deadline anyway. I still think about it a lot though. Maybe Lilith... And I still like contacts. And they don't even have the Wyld Eyez anymore. When I was in high school, I mowed the lawn a bunch to save money for the Hypnotica kind. Then later the red kind that made me look like Deacon Frost at the end of Blade. I still haven't ever seen Stephen Dorff in person, even though I think I talked to him on the phone once and I've been to Skybar multiple times. Whatever. Felon was great, but I don't e-cig, so maybe we wouldn't even have much to talk about anyway. But I got those lenses back when pneumotonometry was the standard, just a little puff of air, and not this medical monstrosity, this ocular torture. I hate it so much. I would watch a thousand suns die-or wait I couldn't unless some guy measures my intraocular pressure, which apparently is the most important thing in the universe to some people. Oh tonometry! Oh humanity!

But I get ahead of myself, and that train of consciousness, filled with biographic admission, pop culture details, and Catholic guilt as it was, did precious little to fill you in on the actual ophthalmological details of the testing I was about to undergo.

We'll get to that in a moment.

The appointment was Tuesday. I called Dr. Ashbrook the Friday before.

"Hey Trent. Looks like we got you this Tuesday." His voice was flat and genial, as always.

"Yeah, I was just wondering, about the exam."

"Yes?"

Be firm Trent, I told myself. You are 29. You don't have optical insurance. You have a right to ask these questions-to, yes, to make these demands. And why not? He's not your Dad. You're his patient. He's your doctor. And more to the pragmatic, if gauche, point, you are his paying customer!

"You know the part of the exam, where you bring those blue circles really, really close to my eyes?"

Articulate guy, who knows what he's talking about and deserves to have an opinion on how to conduct a proper optometric exam, right?

Nonetheless, he knew immediately what I was referring to, did not need to pause.

"Yes, that's the tonometry. It measures the pressure of the eye."

"Well do we have to do that? I really don't like it."

"Unfortunately, yes. It's part of the standard exam." His voice was firm, yet gentle. Unintentionally patronizing-not condescending, and there IS a difference!

"Right, but..." I was desperate, hence aggressive. "Do you *have* to? Can't you do everything else? Is that part absolutely necessary? Can't you give me my contact lens prescription without it?"

"I can't. It's part of the exam."

"But you didn't always do this. Did you? The thing where the blue circles practically touch my eyes, that's new, isn't it?"

"It's not *that* new. But tonometry has always been part of the exam. We used to use pneumotonometry, that was the little puff of air."

"Yes! Can we do that instead?"

Very patient. "No, we don't have that equipment anymore. It was also used to measure your intraocular pressure, but it's not as accurate. We use applanation now." He went on, "There are three methods of measuring the intraocular pressure. There's pneumotonometry - that's the puff of air. That's less intrusive, but it doesn't give us as accurate a reading. There's the Goldmann applanation, and that's the method I'll be using with the blue circles. There's also a method where we essentially put a pen right on the cornea-"

"No!"

"Yeah, that's more invasive, so we won't be doing that. We use the Goldmann applantation."

"But are you legally required to? Is it the law?"

"Yes. It's part of the exam."

"What if you didn't?"

"That'd be malpractice."

Malpractice.

• • • • • •

Monday. I was still feeling anxious. I called the office again. Got his receptionist.

"Eye Care Family Center. This is Judy speaking."

"Hi Judy, this is Trent Malloy, I have an appointment tomorrow."

"Yes! Hi Trent."

"Yeah, so I was just wondering..." Geez, this was pathetic. "We were talking about the tonometry portion of the exam." I had done my homework. Pneumotonometry sounded MUCH preferable, thank you. "Um, and I was telling Dr. Ashbrook that I really don't like the Goldmann applanation technique."

She drew a blank. "I'm sorry?"

"The Tonometry. He usually uses the Goldmann applanation method, but I was wondering if it would be possible to go back to pneumotonometry, or just skip the tonometry altogether."

She dissembled, perhaps embarrassed she didn't know what I was talking about. "I don't know what you're referring to. I'm sorry."

I took a little satisfaction from that, in fact. If the optometrist's own employee wasn't familiar with this terrible technique, then that shot a mighty big hole in this "universal standard" dodge, didn't it, doc? I wouldn't have to suffer under the pretense that shoving glowing blue circles in my eyes was as obvious and appreciated a routine as getting your blood pressure checked. There would be no looks of incredulity from family or sneers from peers along the lines of "You thought you could actually get your contact lens prescription refilled without tonometry? You fool! And then you actually thought pneumotonometry was still an acceptable method of measuring interocular pressure? Unbelievable!"

Words never spoken. In fact, I had raised the very issue with my mother several days earlier. Opening up about my pre-exam anxiety, I confessed:

"I HATE Goldmann applanation tonometry!"

Her look was pricelessly puzzled.

"I don't know what that is."

She didn't know what that was.

And neither, gloriously, for this moment, did an actual employee of Eye Care Family Center.

So, I elucidated.

"It's when he's measuring my eye pressure. He brings these instruments really, really close to my eyes. They're practically touching. I don't like that. So I wanted to see if we could skip that part of the exam or use pneumotonometry- which is the air puff."

She was skeptical, perhaps still uneasy about her less than total knowledge about everything that went on in that house of horrors.

"I'll ask."

"Thank you."

(Well, "House of Horrors". Bit melodramatic. We haven't really gotten into it yet, Jack, have we? The scaled hand and melting skin of a poor little boy with more attitude than sense. A dead rotting cat with not stench. The erstwhile eyeball, floating obscenely in the wrong herbal liqueur. Do these strike you as unseemly? Have we crossed the line? Is this Halloween?)

I take little pleasure in reassuring you, we have not yet begun to get creepy. And if those prior abominations I just mentioned will be overshadowed by the Leviathan, the impact of their disturbance snuffed out like a candle in the infernal wind of a forever midnight, then you can be sure a moment of ocular discomfort by a professional who knows exactly what he's doing will be but a trifle, and I am, as always, the perennial big baby.

She texted me several hours later:

Hi Trent, I spoke to the doctor about not having any instrument touch your eye, but unfortunately, Doc says no, as it is part of standard care.

Right. This was insufferable. I texted back exactly what I was thinking:

Call it off then. Cancel the appointment. I'm 29 years old, and I don't have to pay what is a lot of money to me to be ocularly tortured and worried about getting my eyes gouged out if he bumps the equipment or I accidentally fall forward (THAT would be malpractice). I'm going to look for an optometrist that uses pneumotonometry, much less invasive and harrowing. Or if I can't find ANYONE who DOESN'T give me my contact lens exam without Applanation/Goldmann tonometry, at least maybe I can find one for less money and less lip.

That was harsh. As if they're the ones giving attitude. But it felt good to write.

Yes, I wrote all that. And every word true. But without waiting for a response, barely a minute later if that, I immediately followed it up with:

Fine. Never mind. I'll be there at 1:30. Get it over with. Just don't y'all laugh at my rational hang-up behind my back.

How would that sound?

Trent, Dr. Ashbrooke has examined your eyes the same way every year for over 10 years. We value you as a patient and your continued trust all these years. We are looking forward to seeing you tomorrow. Friendly reminder, bring your glasses.

She added:

Have a nice day.

And that made me feel bad.

Ok

If it's not poignant, it's at least pathetic, and there's pathos. With my luck, it's both. A man of my age, whinging over such a brief exam, one I've had at least a dozen times. And making petty threats if I didn't get my way. If you're asking me "Aren't you embarrassed?", I'll have to draw from the reference pool, back to Orson Welles and those infernal frozen peas:

"Yes, always!"

· · · · ·

But here's what I find poignant, or interesting, or whatever. This tantrum about my preference to not having my eyeballs gouged out (and shoved into a bottle of not-Pimm's? Was that a factor?) aside, I realized something about my relationship with my doctor.

I cherished it.

I didn't love him, mind, but you get used to people, even, it seems, when they charge you a lot of money to do things you'd rather they didn't. Dr. Ashbrook had been looking at my eyes since high school. My parents chose him for me. And somewhere down the line, I made the (sub?)conscious choice to keep going back. Obviously, I wanted my contacts and my glasses, but hey, at some point I could have chosen my own doctor, couldn't eye? Especially since I was now living in a different city and paying for it myself.

But when presenting myself with the idea, the threat of actually leaving Dr. Ashbrook, as antagonistic as this whole tonometry thing was, I felt no triumph in that power. Only melancholy. The man was part of my life. Genial, consistent. He knew me, and our small talk, though banal, was comforting. You could say I stayed out of routine, but what is routine but the acceptance of the familiar?

And you can't spell familiar without family.

· · · · · ·

Then there I was, sitting in the check-up chair, waiting for the good doctor to come in and do all the things he was supposed to.

Dr. Ashbrook is an affable, soft-spoken man in his early 50s with a calm, dull voice. Imagine a ginger Bob Balaban.

"Hello Trent. It's been a while," he said cheerfully, walking in with his folder and clipboard.

And I noticed two things this time about the doctor I hadn't in the past. Traits that made him come off as more conservative and traditional that I had thought. Not that I had. Politically and racially, my optometrist had been a blank. His office was a place beyond politics, without religion.

This time, however, I noticed on his white coat, a small American flag pin. Doc was a patriot. How do you like that? I liked it quite a bit, in fact.

More surprising and revelatory was his coffee cup:

Black cup, white text

ATTITUDE

Across the top, in big print font. I was expecting one of those "inspiration" quotes. You know, those posters with a stock image of a beach or mountain top captioned by stale motivational clichés.

DETERMINATION: If you don't make it, it's your own damn fault.

TEAMWORK: Because life is a team sport.

HORROR: When life gives you an eyeball, bottle it in Pin's.

But under the word attitude, instead of some generic mawkish chicken soup, there was:

I can do all things through Christ, who gives me strength.

(Which would later turn out to be a quote from Philippians 4:13. Not the Catholic translation, but it still rings true and beautiful.)

Huh. So, Doc was a Christian. How wonderful and endearing. I had never really thought about him outside the confines of this office. But he had a life. And faith. And patriotism.

I knew he had a niece. Barbara. She also worked in the entertainment industry. She came up every time we talked because he knew I was a screenwriter/USC film school graduate. Barbara had done some work at Sundance, and she had also interned for 40 Acres and a Mule, Spike Lee's company.

"She was the only Caucasian there," Dr. Ashbrook pointed out.

I looked her up on LinkedIn once, though I wasn't sure how to make my introduction. What, something like:

Hey, I'm Trent Malloy. Your uncle is my optometrist. I notice we're both in the film industry. Want to connect?

• • • • •

A tenuous connection. But then, so is everything, especially in this industry. It's not what you know, it's who you know. But I didn't know my optometrist's niece. I barely knew my optometrist. I wanted to say something about our shared Christian faith, but...what?

As you may be wondering what this routine trip to the eye doctor's has to do with this story of detective work, romance, and horror, I'll indulge the obvious connection you make. It's all in the eyes, right? So then this:

"Number one or number two? Or about the same?"

"About the same."

"Pretty close. Okay, number three or four?"

"Um..."

"Number three or number four."

"I guess number four's a little clearer."

(And as long as I had him.)

"Hey doc, you, um, you ever get any eye gouging?"

"What's that?" he sounded kind of puzzled as he still fidgeted with the various lenses.

How to put this? "Well, you ever see anyone who was missing an eyeball?"

"Number five or number six?" He thought on that.

"Number five."

"Sure. I've dealt with a few veterans from Iraq and Afghanistan. A few went blind, and yes, there were some missing eyes. Why do you ask?"

"Well, have you ever had to remove an eye?"

He sat back, puzzled by this line of questioning and pausing from our exam.

"No, I don't do the ocular surgery here. A colleague of mine, Dr. Rabinowitz, will perform corneal transplants, and when necessary, removal."

"You ever refer anybody to him?"

He gently laughed, "It doesn't happen on a regular basis for...eyeball removal. But I've done it before. There was a young lieutenant. Special forces in Afghanistan. The jeep he was riding in hit one of those bombs in the road. They're not called landmines anymore."

"An IUD."

"No, an IED," he corrected. "IUD is birth control."

"Oh yeah."

"Anyway, he took a great deal of shrapnel in his left eye. We were unable to do anything for him, and to avoid risk of further infection, I referred him to Dr. Rabinowitz, who did take the whole thing out."

"What did they do with it?"

"The eye?"

"Yeah."

"Well, they had to surgically remove it. So, they make an incision right above the-"

"No, I mean, what did they physically do with the eyeball itself? After the surgery?"

He was nonplussed. "That's an unusual question."

I shrugged. So, sue me.

"Well, I imagine they must have some form of medical waste disposal. Sometimes they outsource those to private companies. It's all very sanitary."

But really, what was I expecting him to say?

Oh, they send the eyeballs to a company up north. San Simeon, I believe. They bottle them in imitation liqueur, which is distributed around the state, only found in select venues and drank by those troubled few who dare to look into darkness.

And darkness looks back.

Nah.

"Now Trent, let's get back to your eyes."

Oh, you're wondering about the tonometry, aren't you? I mean, it only makes sense, doesn't it? That is how I started this whole chapter.

First of all, neither of us said a thing about the elephant in the room, which was my insufferable whinging, the texting tantrum I threw. We just…went through with it.

So how unpleasant was this procedure?

It's like when I rewatched *The Shining*. Or actually, watched it for the first time without skipping through the parts I thought would be extra scary (the twins and the old lady in the bath). And it's funny. It's like when I finally passed my driver's test. It's not as scary as I thought it would be.

I saw this cartoon when I was a kid. I don't remember what it was called. It was about an anthropomorphic white bear, maybe British. In the episode, I saw his friend was suffering from a recurring nightmare. The main bear (Rupert?) encouraged his friend to confront his nightmare, and somehow, they went into the nightmare. The friend actually waited through the nightmare and saw it all, and it was all okay. There was a sense of relief. A feeling of "Oh. Is that all? What was I so afraid of?" That was exactly what it was like when I got my driver's license. It was a good feeling.

So *The Shining* had already terrified me, and though I had seen the clip of the twins, I had never watched the Room 237 scene all the way through. I knew exactly what happened. Jack goes into the room, he sees a beautiful woman, starts to kiss her, and then she turns into a scary old rotting woman who I guess is evil. Although actually, I didn't know exactly what happened after he saw her become that hideous sight. When I finally did see it, it surprisingly makes it less scary.

So, Jack's making out with this hot, naked woman, then all of a sudden, she turns into this rotting corpse. He backs off, and she cackles and staggers towards him, and then he runs out, panicked.

The reason it's less scary is, after the initial shock value, so what? It's like Chucky. He was the scariest of the horror icons when I was a kid, but when you think pragmatically, he's one foot tall and made of rubber. Just kick him across the room! Chucky and The Woman disarm you with their frightening appearance but just get over that. In a physical fight, what harm do they pose?

An evil laugh?! What does this ghost find so funny? That's so cliché, and over the top, it's not even scary. She's not racing towards him with a poltergeist's speed and power. She's slowly walking to him like an old woman would. The whole threat disintegrates under the question: What would have happened if Jack had stayed? Instead of bolting, he should have said, "Okay. You're grotesque, and you're scary, and you're laughing. So what? You're also old, rotting and naked. You're dead, and the sluggishness with which you STUMBLE weakly toward me clearly shows you haven't gained any supernatural strength for it. I'm a living man, 5'10 and in fine shape, and strong enough to chop down a door with an ax. If you purposelessly insist, I can trade body blows and WIN. You hurt my son. • • • • •* you. I'm the caretaker. Get out of my hotel. I'm not afraid of you."

So, you get in the car, and you're nervous because you're being tested and you failed two times already. You've had this nightmare before, and it's tormenting you. You know how scary this scene is, and you skip it. And those things, those things, please Doc, not my eyes!

But then you actually go through with it. You pass the test. You finish the nightmare. You watch the scene in its entirety. You let him examine you. And it's not so bad after all. It all clears up, like when a fog blows away. Everything is going to be okay.

You watch the old lady in the tub. You get your driver's license. The bear's friend's dream is not what it seems. And they can touch your eyes-*almost* touch your eyes, and you won't feel a thing.

It's all so much easier, isn't it? You got to admit, it's getting better. It's getting better all the time.

Chapter 7: San Simeon Saga

In Xanadu did Kubla Khan a stately pleasure dome decree...

Skip it. We weren't going to the mythic, Shangri-La-like palace of Coleridge's Kubla Khan. Nor were we going to the decadent estate of the fictional Charles Foster Kane. We weren't even going to The Hearst Castle, the latter's inspiration, a sprawling mansion I've always wanted to visit.

"Nah, man," Mike was telling me as we jetted up the coast at ill-advisable speeds. "We don't have time."

"What's the rush?"

He gritted his teeth. "We got to do this. Have to see this through."

"Well..." Do we? I didn't voice this simple objection. I countered on his terms, on the grounds that, of course, this mission was essential, but... "Can't we visit, you know, after?"

"What do you want to go that place for anyway? Tour the living tomb of a dead tycoon."

"It's supposed to be really nice!" I objected. "Like, it's so big they have four separate tours! And there's pools and statues, and history..."

"You know, he was a tyrant," Mike said with scorn. "That guy Hearst. He printed propaganda, bribed politicians, rigged the Oscars..."

"So, what? He's been dead for half a century. We're not going there to kiss his feet."

"Trent. We're not going there at all."

Oh, of course not. We had much more important things to attend to. Like this wild goose chase.

"Just as long as we're up here..." I grumbled. "Seems like a bigger draw than Deakins Porthouse."

Deakins Porthouse, for those curious, was not an actual place. Tried looking it up online, no dice. I had pointed this out to Mike, but he retorted that putting in the address given into GPS did give a result. Stonebrooke was a real road in San Simeon, and he had charted navigation to 432. But what was there? I was dubious. Also, compliant.

For all I knew, there would be absolutely nothing there. Mad fools that we were, we were driving 5 hours north to a place that might not actually exist. I mean, why put your blind trust in the faded labels of questionable liquor bottles, man? And from an address, we had to piece together, as both bottles of this strange libation (no information of it online either) had conspicuous scratching on the address of the bottling source.

Say it was even accurate in the first place. That the bottles of Pin's Brew were indeed from Deakins Porthouse, which could be found by the curious traveler at 432 Stonebrooke Road in San Simeon California? Was there any guarantee that it was still in business? How old were those bottles? Liquor has a notoriously long shelf life, I might add, and it didn't seem like this obscure brand was doing very well. The bartenders didn't even know what they were serving.

But say they are still in business. Say Deakins Porthouse is a real place, still operational and bottling Pin's Brew to ship to parts unknown...what then? What could they tell us about the odd eyeball in one of their bottles? Did I even want to know? Didn't Mike know it was curiosity that killed the cat? I mean, not *that* cat...

•　•　•　•　•

It was a long, uneventful drive, filled with silence and unease-on my end anyway. I was stewing in my own frustration and dread. Why had I allowed myself to get dragged along on such a venture? The few times I tried to engage Mike in a discourse on our motives, his replies were maddeningly sparse.

"Well, what do we do when we get there?"

"We ask them about the eyeball."

"What do you think they're going to say, man? What can they say?"

"We'll see."

Incidentally, San Simeon is a very small town, if it can even be called that (it's unincorporated). Permanent population of under 500. It goes without saying that the biggest attraction is the Hearst Castle. I mean, who else is coming out here for a place that may not even exist, right?

The California countryside is beautiful, especially around the coast. I could imagine, preferably, taking a trip this way under less weird circumstances.

With perhaps a less aggressive companion. What about a trip to wine country with that girl from behind the bar? Lilith?

That could be something. My friend Joe said that it's not necessarily as expensive as you might think. He said they have group packages where you can tour three vineyards in one weekend. And you can make your own pace. Come and go as you like. Drink wine, naturally, and take in the beauty of the Golden State. Maybe hot air balloon. Now *that* was quite expensive, maybe $275 per, something like that. Worth it though, right? Up there, not a care in the world. Among the birds. Glass of wine in hand. Beautiful woman by your side.

Why couldn't it be that?

Why was I here now, driving up like a couple of kids on Halloween, with Mike?

Maybe because we *were* kids on Halloween, or that's how we felt, or that's how we wanted to feel. This was so cool, wasn't it? Real detective stuff. Getting to the bottom of the real depraved wickedness of the Earth.

So, there was that, even if the actual car trip was not a lot of fun. I was bored and tense. And bickering? Sure. I tried to engage Mike a couple times, but it was like talking to a paranoid brick wall. Like this:

"Hey Mike, what's your favorite breakfast cereal?"

"My what now?"

"Cereal. You know, Frosted Flakes, Honey Nut Cheerios, that kind of thing."

"I don't eat all that sugary crap."

I was annoyed. "Well, it's not 'all' that crap. It's not crap. And it's not just sugary. There's a lot of fiber and vitamins in some."

"Hmm." Unconvinced.

"Anyway, mine's Captain Crunch: Oops! All Berries. It's the best cereal in the world."

"Uh-huh."

"I mean, it's funny," I laughed out of obligation, knowing that Mike did not care. "They say Oops! Right on the box. But they've been saying that for what, 15, 20 years? It's been mass-produced, marketed, and they're still pretending it's an accident?"

Mike grunted in apathetic agreement.

"But at least it's conceivable-I mean, you can imagine how something like that would happen-the first time anyway. I don't know how those factories work," I pretended to be putting a lot of thought into it. This was a long drive.

"Like, if they have one compartment for crunches and one for berries. Then maybe there was an accident or a miscommunication, and they have a box that's filled entirely with berries."

Mike nodded, eyes on the road, mind somewhere else.

"My point is. That's possible. Conceivable, anyway, in all their factories all over the world. But what doesn't work is, I'm not sure if they still have this-'Oops! Choco Donuts'". This was a box with Captain Crunch on the cover, but instead of crunch or even berries, it's a bunch of miniature chocolate donut-looking things. It's like, how did you do that? How does that even happen? Those wouldn't be in the factor! You're expecting us to believe...." I trailed off, bored myself. I then added, "They are good though..." Almost as an afterthought, though really, it's the most important point. As dubious as the premise was, the chocolate donut variety of Captain Crunch was/is delicious and worth trying if it still exists. As of writing it, I'm pretty sure Frosted Donuts Captain Crunch is still a thing. One can only hope.

•   •   •   •   •

"Hey Mike."

"What."

"You like *Candyman*?"

"The movie."

"Yeah."

"I enjoyed it. One can see in retrospect how such a film was playing-transparently of course-on the fear of urban black America. He's a slave. He's killed for impregnating a white woman. He comes back as a monster. What does that tell you?"

"What?"

"Your sins will find you out, and that which you kill will return."

"I don't know if it's all racial, Mike. In the book he was white. Also-he was the son of a slave-in the movie-but the book was British and -"

"A thing is only itself, Trent, not that which inspired it, what came before it, or what it should be. And that movie was about a big black boogeyman, and that's the reality."

Well, I didn't want to get that dark, I just wanted to talk about the movie. But this was not mindless chatter. I had recalled a conversation we had back in grade school. One of those silly lunchtime dialogues filled with misinformation and juvenile jokes. I was about to see if Mike remembered.

"When did you first see it?"

"I don't know." Then he actually did put in the effort to think. Getting semi-nostalgic, or so I figured. "Maybe my cousin Mavis showed it to me. When I was 10."

"Right, I think I remember you telling me about it."

"Oh yeah?"

I laughed. "Yeah, and you said Candyman was actually made of candy!'

He chuckled at his own absurdity. "I did not!"

"You did!"

"Really?"

"Yeah, you were telling me what parts of his body were which candy."

"That's bizarre. Like what kind of stuff?"

"I wish I could remember more. Maybe sharp candy canes for fingers? Honey for eyes?"

"Honey for eyes doesn't make any sense."

"The only one I can remember is you said his dick was a Hershey's chocolate bar."

And the crowd goes wild.

"Wow. Wow," Mike was still laughing, and I was glad to have lightened his mood. "That's something else though. That is."

"Had you really seen it?" I asked, humorously incredulous. "Why would you tell me that?"

"Answer to your first question is yes. Answer to your second is...I don't know man. I really don't know." He smacked my chest affably. "Probably just fucking with you, even back then."

"You have a talent for it, my friend."

"Yes, I do."

So that lightened things up a bit. We stopped at this place called Astro Burger for lunch and filled up. Both literally and figuratively. Or maybe just figuratively. They had a couple gas pumps, is all I meant, so Mike's car was filled as well as our bellies. We still had a while to go, but I was in a better mood after we ate.

And hey, I was in no rush to get there, like I said.

• • • • •

"She had the sexiest fucking dress you ever seen." That was Mike, of course. I don't like to swear. Or objectify women. Granted, the descriptions of the women I was attracted to in this story are very…through a male lens, but I try to respect them as people, and describing my visceral reaction is really an attempt at immersion for the reader, convey my stream of consciousness. I know it's wrong and lustful, and I apologize.

Whatever.

"Red, and you know what that means."

"What do I know that means?"

"It means she was asking for it, friend-o! Red is a naturally stimulating color. It screams sex, like a peacock or some insect you want to fuck spreading its wings."

I recall James Woods (patriot) saying something similar about Blondie's red dress in *Videodrome*, but I didn't like the implication.

"You shouldn't make assumptions about a woman wanting to have sex based on what she's wearing." And now I said something I don't really believe. "They call that rape culture."

"The fuck it is! Don't be a white knight fag. I know about so-called 'rape culture'. I was a professor for fuck's sake. That shit is bull. You don't ask what a rape victim was wearing. You think I don't know that? But you're going too far in the other direction. You're saying a woman can't dress sexy if she tries. You're saying she can't make a conscious decision to look attractive and draw the attention of her own desires. Trent, my man, I love you buddy, but you're denying a woman's autonomy." He said this last part teasingly, especially. "So, stop *mansplaining*, 'cause you sound like a tool of *the patriarchy*!"

"Yeah, yeah, yeah."

I do get over-cautious about that kinda of thing at times. Maybe you've noticed. I'm certainly not an SJW, white knight, or anything like that. Perhaps my occasional oversensitivity is a reaction to my own reactionism and how it will be perceived. Because I'm a zealous Catholic and fanatically pro-life, that I think Planned Parenthood is a genocidal organization (look at the demographics, and where their "clinics" are) and any kind of birth control or non-procreative sex is a sin, I do understand many would consider me "anti-woman", so sometimes I tend to overcompensate.

"Anyway," Mike continued, "Roxanne was putting on the lights. And this was a sexy number, remember. Total spillage. And the slit? It was cut halfway up to her slit."

"Eww. Don't call it that."

"Are you going feminist on me again?"

"No, this is me. That term just sounds gross."

"I'm talking about her pussy."

"I know. And I don't like that one either."

"Well, what do you call it?" He was annoyed, and he made a good point.

"Her vagina?"

"In casual conversation?"

"It doesn't come up in casual conversation. Or polite society."

"Yeah but this is *locker room talk*," he said with a smirk. "Besides, 'vagina', Trent? That's so clinical, anatomical. And it probably doesn't mean what you think it does?"

"I know what you're talking about."

"Because a vagina actually just means the hole, not the...whole," he chuckled at his wordplay. "The opening, not the entire."

"Yeah, I know the technical, scientific term for what we're talking about in this crude discussion is the vulva."

"The whole KITTEN caboodle."

"But it's a culturally acceptable synecdoche."

"Do you accept that?"

"I don't know. I'm sick of this entire disgusting conversation. Frat boy vulgarity meets gynecology. I don't even like sex."

He looked at me for a long moment, loaded and ambiguous.

"Yeah," he reached for the radio. "Let's find some Beach Boys."

We passed, briefly. Hearst Castle itself. There was a bit oft traffic near the exit, and I could see that majestic sprawling mansion from the highway. Ah, to be going there.

But we didn't. Turns out Stonebrooke Road was an exit off of Highway 1, three exits after that white castle of rich men's dreams, 13 miles away. Mike turned right without comment at seeing the GPS indicate this was where we got off.

More than that, posted at the fork was a standard green road sign:

DEAKINS PORTHOUSE....5 MILES

"Mike..." I trailed off, still trying to process that those ordinary white letters on that commonplace green metal, sign indicated that we, and our destination, were still very much in reality.

"I saw it," he responded, seeming to put little significance to it as he turned.

Just like that. Like it was a normal place. Well, what did I expect? *Abandon All Hope Ye Who Enter?* Place was a porthouse!

Wait, a porthouse?

"Mike?"

"I heard you. I saw it. We're going." No son, we're not there yet.

"No. Mike."

"What?"

"What's a porthouse?"

He hesitated. I guess until now he hadn't thought about it. "Well, it's..." What? "You know, Trent."

"You don't know, do you?"

He frowned. "Well, what is this place? It's a winery, right? I guess a porthouse is just what you call the house of a vineyard."

That didn't satisfy me, but I figured it was about as good as it was going to get.

Sure enough, this was a vineyard, as we saw driving through it. There were the vines. Here were the grape presses. There really looked like nothing suspicious was in sight. If only that initial impression held true.

La Cire was a gaunt, thin-lipped man who overdressed for the occasion. This steward was not surprised to see us, but then again, why should he have been? It was just an ordinary vineyard, after all.

"The plantation was founded by French settlers in 1783," he was telling us, leading us through the vines. "There was a major expansion after the second world war. Currently, we ship thousands of bottles of wine a year."

"Just wine?" I asked pointedly. "Any ales or liqueurs?"

"Yes, as a matter of fact, we do have liqueurs. Pin's Brew is an herbal variety. Tangy, with hints of saffron. It's been compared favorably to Pimm's." Mike and I exchanged a glance.

"What does it pair with?" Mike asked.

"I've always thought it goes well with romaine salad. It's a very light, airy libation."

"Any garnishes?" I knew where he was going.

"Of course. It's a spirit used in many cocktails. Cherries are popular."

"How about eyeballs?"

La Cire rolled that over, "eyeballs?"

"You heard what I said, La Cire. A human eyeball. Floating in to say hello."

He frowned. "Your humor, sir, is not working on me."

"I didn't think it would. But it's not really a joke. Listen. A couple weeks ago, me and my buddy Trent here were at a restaurant-The Misfit down in Santa Monica."

"Yes?" He was uneasy.

"Trent orders a Pimm's Cup. So right off the bat, something's not right, because instead of his red drink they give him your green. But he drinks it anyway. And he recommends it. So, I order one. And it's not bad."

"I'm glad you enjoyed it."

"Hold up, La Cire."

"What's that?"

"Well as you may have surmised, all was not well. First of all, we didn't order Pin's Brew. Ordered Pimm's Cup. There's a difference."

He tried to smile, albeit uncomfortably. "Sometimes there are happy accidents, perhaps."

"Maybe." Mike seemed to consider. "Except this time, there was, like I said, an eyeball floating in the bottle."

He let that sit there. Nothing more to say really.

La Cire was impatient. "Sir, I really don't understand your humor – or-or what you're getting at."

"There's nothing to understand. It's very, very simple," Mike defied him.

"Yes, but..." It couldn't be that simple. This did not make sense. And in a way, La Cire's bafflement reassured me. I was comforted by his lack of comfort. It meant we were still occupying the same universe. A world where eyeballs don't just show up in bottles uninvited. Maybe he couldn't give us answers, but there was something to be said for the fact that a question was demanded. "I don't know what that means!" he sputtered. "An eyeball! In your bottle?"

"Yes sir." Mike was practically grinning, glad to have someone on the spot.

"Okay." La Cire closed his eyes and took a couple of seconds to compose himself. "Yes, alright. Excuse me. I'm sorry." There it was. That must be it. Something to latch onto. An apology. Bastion of civility and decorum, even in the face of the nakedly absurd. "I'm very, very sorry your bottle was contaminated like so. I cannot imagine how that could have happened."

"May we see?" Mike suggested dryly.

Again, being thrown for a loop. This entire episode was unpleasant and confusing to all involved. La Cire struggled to have it. "See?"

"See! Si, senor, déjanos ver...Pin's Brew."

La Cire stuck out his lower lip, chewed on it. "That is...part of the tour," he said weakly. In truth, we had sullied it, called the entirety of Pin's Brew, and perhaps this man's entire worldview into question. There was no reasonable cause to deny us entry, but now he clearly wished we were gone.

We stood there for a moment. I felt a little sorry for La Cire, who clearly was not some infernal mastermind. What could he do for us? Maybe we should just leave.

But presently, he turned and weakly sighed. "This way."

Mike nudged me knowingly. But what did he know? Guy was as puzzled as I was. He just had more swagger, and right now that was dangerous.

La Cire recovered, to a certain degree, by reciting his rehearsed tour talk. This is where that was, these were a certain variety only available at this time, etc. Mike, impatient that he was, would occasionally interrupt La Cire with a demand to see the bottle facility sooner. La Cire responded, sharply, that it was on the other side of the vineyard, and we were on our way.

Frankly, I was in no rush

The House of Spirits, as La Cire gloriously introduced it (any references to Isabel Allende were all internal, I fear), was a modest structure, two stories of brick and mortar, and nothing outwardly infernal on the outside.

We stopped. La Cire gestured around to the nearby vines. "Of the various herbal liqueurs we bottle here, most are grown right here." He stopped stiffly, "Including Pin's."

Determined, La Cire charged right in with purpose.

It was a pleasant enough hovel. Not a rapid assembly line. The line moved slow. There was a large boiling pot in the corner, only very gradually filling a bottle. It seemed pleasant enough. Or it would have.

The room was attended by 3 men in white smocks. Their gloves had greenish stains, from when they moved the herbs to the boiling pot, I assume.

La Cire gestured to the room. He was short, with little formality. "Here it is. This is where we make it." One of the attendants, I think, picked up on his curtness, but said nothing.

"Yes," Mike pressed, "but where do the eyes come in?"

"That's enough of that!" He had lost his temper. "I don't know what you're talking about-or where you got this idea, this notion-it's in poor taste, wouldn't you agree?" He was looking at me now, and I felt compelled to reply.

"But it did happen, sir. One cannot change that-as the bottle, in fact, did, before our eyes, and into its eye-or eye into it, rather. All we can do is make what's right, right. Right?"

"I'd like you both to leave," he seemed disappointed in me. That saddened me, as absurd as it is. "I think I've indulged you long enough."

But then there it was. Mike had reached into his jacket and taken out the bottle of Pin's Brew, his souvenir from The Misfit, eyeball still intact. He held it high for all to see.

You take something like that out, it tends to silence the room for a while.

La Cire was speechless. So was I, and I had already seen the infernal thing. But I didn't know Mike had brought it with him! How sick was that?

"When hearing of such absurdities," Mike elucidated, "polite society tends to ignore them. The rational thing is to dismiss."

The steward sputtered.

"Your reaction is understandable. I'd apologize for the coarse nature of this display, but it is necessary, and it is not my fault, sir. When one is confronted with such a grotesquerie, he cannot ignore it. And neither can you."

"T-that..." La Cire found words.

"Yeah, we were quite alarmed to find this in our drink," Mike was playfully rolling the bottle around as if it were a mere curiosity. "Thought maybe we'd come up here, see about getting some answers."

La Cire looked sick to his stomach, which was fair. "An-answers?"

"You know. Why is there an eyeball in the bottle?"

"I...I can't tell you," he finally said weakly. "It must be a cruel joke."

Mike strolled over towards the bronze vat where it all loaded. "Whose joke?"

"No!" La Cire, with surprising ferocity, darted across the room and in front of Mike, throwing his arms up. "Go no further!"

Mike was offended. "What, like I'm gonna contaminate it, man? I'm the problem? Where are your priorities?"

La Cire's eyes narrowed. There was a conflict inside the man between apology and aggression, and it was intriguing to watch. "I cannot imagine how...*that* got inside your drink. Our Porthouse's sincerest of apologies. Our hygienic standards are of the utmost quality." I glanced over at the attendants, who didn't seem to take any note of all this strife. "And there is nothing you may glean by looking inside."

"So then why can't we look inside?" *I* asked.

The steward threw down his hands, defeated. Mike took that as his permission to walk over and peek in the pot. Nobody stopped him.

After a pregnant moment, Mike looked up and shrugged. "Nothing but a bunch of herbs."

And that was that. Nobody knew what to say. I mean, I sure didn't.

"Perhaps we can get you a refund. Or a voucher even." La Cire was regaining his composure and his civility. He had this. The tension was deflated, the eyeball was an unpleasant anomaly, and he could take charge.

"A refund, Mike. What do you think of that?" I prodded him because frankly, it's what we should have demanded in the first place-FROM THE MISFIT!

Mike got another idea, this one inspired. "Let's walk and talk, La Cire."

We walked and talked, away from the house of Pin and through the open fields.

"It's not money, I'm wanting, I'm thinking."

"Oh? No?" La Cire was curious, and just a tad suspicious.

"See the thing that really stews my herbs is, we always find Pin's Brew by accident."

"Accident?" The idea offended him.

"Yeah. Can't find it online, it's not listed anywhere. Turns out we only run into your precious liqueur on dumb luck."

I was a stride or two behind them and awkwardly interjected, "That's not strictly true, Mike. We knew what we were looking for the second time."

He scowled back at me (I was cowed) for a glance before continuing. "Yeah, it happened twice."

"There were TWO eyeballs?" La Cire was impatient, incredulous.

"No there was only one eyeball but dig this baby. We got that eye because we had our eye on the drink at The Misfit, this bar in Santa Monica."

"So you said." How he wanted this to end! "You ordered Pimm's Cup. Ordered the entire bottle. They gave you Pin's instead. That was the bartender's failing." (Implicitly, he'd like to shrug off the eyeball on the bartender as well).

"Except the exact same thing-minus the ocular unpleasantness, of course- exact same thing happens at this bar in Highland Park."

"The *exact* same thing?" he repeated dryly.

"Yeah, we're ordering Pimm's Cups- and they're red. They taste like Pimm's!" (Note: Did he really know that?) "Then we order the entire bottle, and Pin's comes out!"

"So, the same mistake was made in two different bars in two parts of Los Angeles by two different bartenders. It's little to do with me or our operation."

"But you must respect the particular peculiarity, do you not? Because the drink changed. While we weren't looking. Red to green! Pimm's to Pin's! What does that mean?"

"I don't know what that means, Mr. Kripke. And I certainly don't know what I can do for you."

"I'm not a man who believes in coincidences ordinarily- but then a frightening and monolithic universe being what it is, one can discern patterns. Perhaps, even affect a change. And you can help."

"What did you have in mind?" he said curtly, patience at an end.

"Well, I've got something. A suggestion I mean."

"I'm listening." He bent down and picked a grape. Rolled it over in his fingers. Something to distract.

"I was thinking, instead of a refund-'cause you know, it's really not your fault, it seems, you don't know what's going on." Half letting him off the hook, half accusation of incompetence. Well played, Mike. "So, do you have-I was thinking you might, you have a manifest or something? That's probably the wrong word."

"A manifest?" La Cire looked up, and there was visible relief that he was no longer under such intense scrutiny.

"That's probably the wrong word."

"What are you talking about, Mike?" I asked. I didn't know what he was after. He was still a step ahead, and it annoyed me.

"Shush, Trent." Annoying! "Do you have like a list or-you must have a record..." He sighed, started again. "Deakins Porthouse-no offense-"

"None taken," La Cire cut off his rambling in his best line of the afternoon.

"Hah, ah, what I mean to ask is, you all aren't exactly the biggest company in the world, right?"

"We are boutique operation. We're small but proud."

"So, you're limited, is what I'm saying. You're not shipping out your stuff to very BevMo and corner bar."

"You want a list of our clients." He got it.

"He gets it," Mike smiled, turned to me. "He gets it!"

"I'm surmising," La Cire surmised, "you'd be specifically interested in which facilities and establishments order Pin's Brew specifically."

"Would that narrow it down?"

"Considerably. It is a vintage liqueur, and only requested by discriminating clientele."

I stepped forward, edging slightly between Mike and La Cire. "I know it's a lot to ask," I began apologetically, "And you probably have this customer confidentiality thing..."

"No, we don't." La Cire was slightly amused. "What do you mean?"

I was taken aback, especially since Mike also seemed to see no issue with my issue. "Isn't privacy a thing?"

"If you're talking private consumers certainly," he explained, "But I was under the understanding your associate was asking about the businesses, bars, wine shops, yes?"

"That's right." Mike and La Cire were on the same side now, oddly. Mike was going to get what he wanted- what *we* wanted, I guess, but first I had to be corrected and condescended to. La Cire went on.

"Then why on Earth would we or any such establishment want to keep that information a secret? It's on the menu. They want it promoted, and we want it known where our products are commercially available!" He made it sound so obvious. Like I was the obtuse one. Hey, at least I wasn't trading in color-changing bottles of eye juice, buddy.

"Right. Okay." I nodded.

And we went back to the house, La Cire printed out a list of the clients receiving Pin's Brew, and we were on our way.

Chapter 8: Rod Stewart Live

Mike and I stopped at a Greek restaurant off the PCH on our way back from San Simeon. Papa Giorgio's, it was called, a charming little place with white columns (cheap plaster standing in for timeless stone, I'm sure) and blue paint. To look upon it, walking across the cracked parking lot at the restaurant ahead, is to see an evocation of the Greek flag. Perhaps that's what they intended. Probably. I didn't know how faithful or credible a representation of Greek culture this place would be. I just hoped I could get a gyro with that white sauce (tzatziki?) and maybe a little baklava.

Yes, yes, and yes. I feasted on my expectations fulfilled, while Mike nursed a shawarma and perused the list.

"This is good, Trent," he licked his lips, appetite whetted more by the promise of more bars that stocked Pin's Brew than by the greasy Mediterranean fare in front of him.

"Why is it good?" I asked, somewhat annoyed. Now that we had left Deakins Porthouse, I was beginning to have second thoughts, as one does after everything of consequence. Of all the words of tongue and pen, the saddest are these, it might have been. We're always second-guessing ourselves. I certainly am, at any rate. And what I was thinking now, was...

"Why'd we leave so soon? That was too-we let him off too easy."

"Too easy?" Mike questioned.

"Yeah! That was the end of the road, wasn't it? We want to find out who put the eye in the bottle, so we go to the source. The bottling plant. Tell the steward what's up, he blusters, we look in the vat, then we leave."

"I was there," he dismissed, plainly. "Now let's look at this list."

I shrugged. Forget it.

"There's only five places, as it turns out, in Los Angeles, that stock Pin's Brew."

"Do they know it?" A fair question.

"Good question!" he laughed. "They'll know it soon! Look." He showed me the list.

TECH NOIR, The Miracle Mile
The Misfit, Santa Monica
Donovan's Dive, Long Beach
La Cuevita, Highland Park
The Pick and Hammer, Burbank

"Looks like a bunch of bars, Mike."

"Five bars. And notice anything familiar?"

I rolled my eyes. "Oh look at that. The Misfit, first place we saw Pin's Brew."

"And the eye."

"And La Cuevita. Where we got the second bottle. These are some dazzling revelations, Mike."

"You oughta be pumped, my friend. The fact that there are only five bars on that list, two of which we have already been to, makes our job a heck of a lot easier."

"Our *job*, Mike? Our job?"

"You know, the investigation."

"So, what, we go to these places, see what they know?"

"Exactly."

Now it's funny. The detective in me, and I am, relished the concept of such noirish excitement. This really could be an adventure. Something to be solved. Something to participate in. Something, at long last, to live for.

But it was dreadfully unpleasant, wasn't it? First the screeching dead cat. Then the eyeball in a bottle. Followed by confronting that poor ignorant steward. Now what, confronting three more bartenders, see if they know anything? Grasp for straws in an absurd landscape? Two grotesqueries were not necessarily indicative of a greater conspiracy (though if you're reading this, no points for deducing that it turned out to be just that).

Still, I was curious. And...(aroused).

As I am a coward, who has an unmanly degree of trouble in doing what I should do or even what I want, especially if the intention is romantic, far too often I find myself relying on pretense, prevarication, or doing something ostensibly with ulterior motives.

Here then now, I had an excuse, pitiful as it was.

"I'll go back to La Cuevita," I said off-hand.

"We already went there," Mike pointed out, not betraying any indication he realized I just wanted to go back for the girl.

"Yeah," I gave casually, "But if I go back knowing what we do know, well…that's a perspective that could help." I wasn't convincing anybody, least of all myself. But so what? I was an adult. I could go back and hope I got a woman I was interested in on her shift if I wanted to. Maybe that wasn't in service of this strange investigation, but I could think of less worthy uses of my time.

Mike was fine with it. He shrugged, wiping a piece of shawarma off his upper lip. "If you want. I think I'll take Tech Noir. I heard of that place. Cyberpunk joint."

"Sounds like a pretty cool scene.

The side of his mouth cracked up in a small, rueful smile.

"Funny the lengths people go to church up their drinking holes. Giving it a fancy theme and charge $15 for a faggy cocktail, and that really convinces people they're not just trying to get stoned and laid like all the gutter rats in every other dive bar?"

• • • • •

I went Wednesday night, of all nights, which was significant if you are, like my mother and I, a fan of Rod Stewart. Wednesday night being, of course, the scheduled performance of "Rod Stewart Live", as indicated on the chalkboard at La Cuevita, as confirmed on the bar's website, an event that actually had a photo of the rocker himself to advertise it.

Of course, being the rational man that I am, I didn't honestly expect to see the legendary British pop rocker himself performing weekly (yes, the board and Facebook page indicated it was EVERY Wednesday) at a dive bar in Highland Park. And this was all but confirmed when I Googled "Rod Stewart Live" and came upon multiple booking sites offering tickets for Rod Stewart (really) live at Caesar' Palace. That was far more likely. Of course, such an aging icon would be in Las Vegas.

I also saw a few instances of "Stand-Up Comedy Show" mentioned in connection to "Rod Stewart Live" at La Cuevita. I was therefore 99% sure I was not going to be hearing *Handbags and Gladrags* live so much as seeing a series of (to be cruelly honest) mediocre local comics giving their best, God Bless 'em.

Yet I am a Christian. Hope is our mainstay. So, if there was even the glimmer of a chance I would be seeing the English Barry Manilow (apologies) in all his acoustic glory (it was a small venue, after all), then I would have to pursue it.

And I was there for the girl.

• • • • •

Strolled in at 7:48. No trouble with the bouncer, who was not our friend Neil, but rather a stout, neckless guy who lethargically sat on a stool and only gave my ID the briefest of obligatory glances before waving me on. Clearly, there was someplace he would rather be, but I can't imagine him livelier anywhere else.

The place was dimly lit and dimly occupied. I don't know why I showed up so early. The show didn't officially start until 9, which meant that it probably wouldn't actually start until at least 9:15. Such is Los Angeles. Nothing starts on time. It frustrated me because it wasn't just special movie screenings, stand-up performances, and concerts. It was dates too, like I said. I used to joke to myself about how I would show up for a date 15 minutes later, but she would make up for it by showing up 15 minutes late.

It's unfunny because it's true.

And what would I do with that time? Well, at those previously mentioned dates, typically at a museum, restaurant or the perennial favorite coffee shop, I would just hang around. Loiter uncomfortably. Look at my phone. Feel self-conscious. Maybe order a coffee after she was 5 minutes late, because hey, I'm here already, right? Bored and nervous, like most dates always are even after she shows up.

But the beauty now, at this venue is I wasn't waiting for anybody. Well, Rod Stewart obviously, but if I really expected the rocker himself to show up in the flesh, I could foresee a Beckettesque ordeal in my future.

Here though, I was in a bar, as an adult, alone. I could do what I wanted, without any pressure of making the right impression on some woman I met online for an hour of small talk and pleasantries. I was absolutely free.

And that meant drinks, natch.

It had been a while since I had gotten good and sloshed, but now a full wallet, a working Uber app, and no obligations made it seem like fair game.

I was glad to be out and about by myself and-heck, I'll say it-without Mike. Does that sound mean? Maybe, but for some reason, I doubt he'll ever read this anyway. Not where he is now, and in that state.

I made my way to the bar. Admired the admirable collection of bottles, the endless varieties of liquors hanging above. Mezcals, especially, as was this place's wont, its notability, even though, yes, as had previously, lamentably been established, it did not contain the kind that contained the worm.

Tending bar was Paul (as he would come to be known), a large, soul-patched guy with a nature as genial as his arms with bulky. I wondered if he "lifted". If weights were just a casual exercise to him, or if he was as religious about it as my cousin Rick–the "don't skip legs day" kind of fixation. He seemed nice enough, as far as first impressions go.

Though of course, whoever he was, I was disappointed to see him. I wasn't actually fooling anybody, least of all myself when I was absolutely free from the burden of making a good impression. Like I said, I was here for the girl. Seeing this guy, as nice as I'm sure he was, was a let-down.

"What's up, man?"

"Fig and York," I said dispassionately, because that was cheap, and it got the job done. $7 for a Boilermaker, as Seabass would say, or a shot and a brew as Marv would put it. Which is a good price for two servings of alcohol, especially considering this was LA, and one of those froofy signature cocktails at a more reputable establishment might cost you twice that. This combination though was hardly the Cadillac variety. A can of Pabst Blue Ribbon, which we've already covered, and Evan Williams, likewise. Frank Booth hipster swill and rotgut Jack Daniels wannabe. But it got-

What "job"? I lamented internally, reflecting that, as my twenties came to a close, getting drunk in a bar, in addition to being expensive, bad to do, and bad for you, did not generate nearly the romantic or sexual results it was hyped up to. You take the drug 'cause you think it'll help you get the girls, but when that rarely if ever happens, you keep on the drug for the drug itself.

That's depressing. Probably why I don't drink as much as I used to. Not as horny either. Correlation?

Taking a sip of the insufferable Evan Williams shot, I noticed a bag of Cheetos hanging over the bar. Hanging in a manner similar to a row of cigarettes (the patio outside was a smoking section). I imagined you could buy the Cheetos here, couldn't you? Wasn't that the point? I recalled *The Last Picture Show* by Larry McMurtry. Sonny hangs around Sam the Lion's bar in the morning and eats a couple of bags of cheese doodles for breakfast. Supposedly some bars put out bowls of pretzels, gratis, or used to anyway. I don't think I'd ever seen that myself. A chalkboard also announced you could buy a pickle for one dollar. This wasn't a restaurant, but it seemed some non-nutritious nonalcoholic sustenance could be found. Junk food, but we were junk people.

(Nah, we're cool. But it was too good a line to resist. The real junk people don't come till later, and that's not the right way to describe them).

I requested a glass when I was ready to make a boil. Poured my beer in, followed by that whiskey. I was thinking about that pickle. Months later, the bar introduced a "Pickle Rick" special. $5 for a shot of Jameson with a pickle back--a pickle back, being, I learned, a shot of pickle juice. Not extremely appealing to the sober, but if you down an entire shot of hard liquor, there are probably worse chasers.

I checked my phone. 8:01. Well over an hour before there would be any hint of the actual show, and as my main attraction wasn't here, I debated internally whether I shouldn't just call it a night. Foregoing the heavy drinking, go home early, all the more time for Netflix, and get a start on tomorrow's work. Pretty mellow, but it's not much of a party when you're there alone, and why was I here anyway?

Why indeed? Let not your heart be troubled, because here she was, coming out of the back, bottle of Mezcal in hand, Sex Pistols t-shirt cut somewhere between her navel and her chest, was Lilith herself.

She handed it off to Paul. With a sardonic glance around the still emptyish establishment, she didn't miss a beat.

"Got it, Paul. This ought to quiet the clamoring of the restless peasants. If I hear any more mewling for Monte Alban, I'll kill myself."

She was like a sexy Latin Daria. I loved her already.

"Yeah, yeah, yeah." He stocked it with the rest. "We do get the occasional request."

"That so?" She kept her eyes on the bottle in question and asked loudly. "How about it, Trent? You still want to 'swallow the worm'?"

I didn't spit up my drink because I was too cool for that, but I did get warm in my chest and could barely keep the smile off my face. She remembered me. I had to think quick and capitalize immediately on this flirtatious energy.

"Uh." Nice start, Trent. "If it's now available, I'd be stupid not to take a shot."

It wasn't a great line, but it was quick and confident, and it built off an existing rapport, and I'd be stupid to analyze it further.

"Your funeral, kid." She pulled the bottle off the shelves, and yes, as bad as it was, I was looking, relishing the...are you familiar with the term "underboob"?

She slammed the bottle on the bar. It stood foreboding, ominous. Like the Monolith in *2001: A Space Odyssey*. There was the worm alright, sleeping forever in the golden fluid at the bottom of the bottle.

"I suppose you're going to want the whole bottle again?"

"No, that's not in my purview." Not like I could tell her about the so-called investigation. "I'd have to sample the goods before I go in so deep."

"Well nobody's going to buy the cow if they can get the milk for free." Her metaphor was weird, and I'm not sure it made much sense, but who cares?

She poured a shot and put it in front of me. I stared into that shot, the amber liquid curiously foreboding. Then I looked to my glass of beer, foul rotgut still swimming in there somewhere.

"Well, actually." I was hesitant because right now pragmaticism and romanticizing were dueling. I didn't want to turn her off with talk of queasiness, but I didn't want to throw up either. I gestured towards my glass. "Maybe I shouldn't."

"Don't chicken out on me, Trent."

"No chicken," I raised my glass, "but beer, whiskey, AND tequila seems like the first train to hangover city."

She extended her bottom lip, cocked her head, furrowed her brow. She was considering my points. Then she-

"Toot! Toot!" she took the shot of mezcal, downed it in one epic throw. Slammed it upside down on the counter. Didn't stop for air, let alone my reaction, before she grabbed my boilermaker and took a hearty sip. "All aboard!"

If the locomotive was leaving the station, I wanted to get on, fast, even though I know it would kill me.

Burns so good.

That's a good line, actually, and my stomach still settling and eyes watering, I crocked it out.

"Burns so good."

"Chase it." She was 25% impressed at this point, so I knew I had to capitalize.

I threw back the entire boilermaker, down it all in one magnificent gulp. Andre The Giant would be proud.

My stomach was nauseous, and I wasn't sure what to do with this belch. Lilith was smirking.

"Looks like you can hold your own, kid."

I did what I sometimes do in polite company, which was to burp internally. The belch when up my throat, exited through my nose and my eyes. Burnt not so good.

"It's just a drink." I shrugged it off.

"Yeah? Wanna go Round Two?"

Did I?!

No. Not like this, and not now. But I wanted to deny in a not-unattractive way. And yes, this peer pressure/thinking with your heart and your crotch instead of your liver thing was not good, but there it is.

"Probably just stick with beer for now. I don't want to get too hammered before Rod Stewart goes on."

"Oh, good thinking. You're going to want to be at the height of your cognitive capabilities when he starts belting out *Amazing Grace*."

"I'm more of a *Handbags and Gladrags* guy myself."

She looked around the bar. "So, where's MJ?"

"Having a sleepover with Bubbles at The Neverland Ranch."

"It's funny because he raped children."

"Allegedly," I returned weakly, somewhat disrupting the flow of that pleasant rapport. I didn't know if she had strong feelings about Michael Jackson one way or the other, and I definitely didn't know how she felt about rape jokes. I never made them myself, of course. They're offensive and insensitive. I'm not really a hardcore PC guy, it's just distasteful. Mean, even. But I did find myself laughing on occasion if I heard one of these controversial attempts at humor that was funny enough to get past my conscience. Tosh was a good example. As it would turn out, Lilith wasn't joking when she said, "It's funny because he raped children." Like Mike, her sense of humor was pitch black.

"'Allegedly'," she scoffed. "I'm sure that's a real comfort."

To whom?

"I'm not trying to comfort anybody," I raised my hands, apologetic (for some reason) "Just stating the facts of the laws of the case. And in this country, you're innocent until proven guilty."

"Well I'm not the US Judicial System, so I don't have to worry about the constitution."

"Reasonable."

"And in the court of Lilith Vazquez, you sleep with little boys and pay them 20 million dollars when they complain-you're guilty as sin on a highway to hell."

"I'll drink to that."

And we did.

The rest of the wait-and by wait, I mean the lead-up to the actual show-proceeded in a similar fashion. Though naturally, I didn't get Lilith to myself the whole night-she did have a bar to tend, after all, and it was getting increasingly busy-I did see a fair amount of her, welcome too. She would occasionally stop in, more frequently and warmly I daresay than the typical bartender "You doing okay?" to chat, and in my mind flirt.

I know how that sounds. I recall an online article I read talking about how sad it was when guys thought female bartenders liked them. I'm not going to quote the title of the article or the website, and I don't even remember who wrote it. That piece was as cynical and judgmental as it was cogent. Yes, valid points were made. But I'm writing this story, not some sad blogger, and what happened happened, whether he would believe it or not. This was not a strip club or a Hooters, but if some bartenders did use a certain amount of sex appeal to engage their customers and elicit tips, I could accept that. Perhaps such was Lilith's milieu as well. She certainly was sexy, and she worked at a bar. Yet, fully conscious and aware of the danger of mistaking mercenary friendliness/artificial flirtation for genuine interest (and I am, as demonstrated, a reserved and cautious fellow, self-aware to a fault and constantly second and third guessing everything I do, and especially in regard to the fairer sex), I did detect there was something there.

9:00 came, and naturally, 9:00 passed. Not that I was surprised at the lack of entertainment beginning when it said it would. That was to be expected. But I never got used to it. Still such an annoyance, minor as it was.

Since I wanted to talk to Lilith again, I thought I'd ask her why "Rod Stewart Live" wasn't up yet. I decided to wait until 9:05 to engage her, so as not to be seen as overly pedantic, God forbid dweebish.

9:05 came. Lilith was on the far side of the bar, tending to a customer. I put my phone away. Relax, Trent, stop looking at the time. It was probably 9:07 before she sauntered in my direction again. She was. I was antsy.

"What's up?"

"Yeah," I took out my phone, instantly regretting this school-teacher "Be on time!" mentality, but it was too late. "Isn't the show supposed to start at 9?"

She shrugged lethargically. "They're not ready yet."

(*They*)

"Why doesn't anything ever start on time?" She knew exactly what I meant, thank God, and was willing to engage.

"Because people are tards," she quipped sharply, deadpan. "They're retarded, and they're tardy."

"I wish I could say you're wrong."

"Give them some time. They'll show up. Have another drink."

"Might as well. I'm not going anywhere."

"What can I get you, boy?"

I thought of something. Because I did have a job to do, and I might as well do it well. I know I did far too many things ostensibly, and my presence here had evolved past the flimsiest of pretenses. But it was a talking point, and there's no harm in seeing how it might play out.

Unless it turned Lilith off me, in which case there was all the harm in the world, and Mike Kripke and his silly investigation could go to Hell.

Still, she might be cool. She made rape jokes and called people tards, so she didn't seem easily shaken.

"Pimm's Cup?"

"Oh God. Really?"

"No. But I was wondering."

"'Bout what? You want to know if we've restocked it? Is that on the top of your academic concerns? And you don't even want to drink. First world problems. Worries like yours."

"Settle down, my friend," I affected my Polite Foreigner voice, which might be offensive, but like I said she wasn't PC. And I was basing it off an Eastern European café attendant I used to know, so he was white, so that's fine. "I thought it was interesting, because last time, me and Mike, Mike and I, we ordered the bottle."

"I remember. Highlight of my week."

"Right, hah. But the thing is, and maybe I should have pointed this out at the time-"

"Hold on." She went to pour some shots for a group at the other end of the bar, then she was back.

"Not sorry. What were you saying?"

"It wasn't Pimm's you gave us."

"Huh."

"That was a bottle of...It was something else."

"What are you talking about?"

"Well, we ordered Pimm's Cup."

"Yeah."

"And you made the drinks. And they were red like they were supposed to be."

"Got a lot of customers, my friend."

I didn't want to lose her interest, so I tried to get to it. "Then we bought the bottle, but what you handed to Mike, it wasn't Pimm's."

Lilith poured a guy a beer, kept her eyes on me, and didn't spill a drop.

"What was it?"

"Pin's Brew." Was that a glimmer of recognition in her eyes? "This strange drink I've never heard of before."

"Oh. You should have told me back then I picked up the wrong bottle."

"I don't think you did. I think it…switched somehow," I trailed off, because it was absurd, and I didn't know how to articulate it.

But I wasn't boring her, in fact. Her eyes were boring into me, dead focused, like I was saying something worth hearing.

"It changed into something else." Her voice was mysterious and concerned. "And not just anything else."

"No, it was-"

"Pin's Brew!" she finished for me. "A delectable herbal liqueur." Her voice was flowery, affected almost with a British accent, but it felt like she found it more creepy than funny, "With airs of elderberry, jade, and sadness."

"What's that?" It was unsettling.

"You're not the only one with weird requests."

"Pimm's Cup isn't that obscure."

"But you and Mike wanted the whole bottle. And it turned into…"

(She had to tend to two women who ordered the house wine.)

"It turned into Pin's Brew!" she returned promptly, engaged in this conversation.

"Does-does that mean something to you?" I wasn't sure what I wanted the answer to be.

"It didn't. I had never heard of it before. That wasn't your friend, was it? This isn't a prank?"

"Who wasn't? What are you talking about?"

She shook her head. Regained her senses, or so she told herself.

"Okay, it's not a prank then. I'm overreacting, dude. It's just some liqueur I never heard of. Coincidence."

"What coincidence? What 'friend'?"

She sighed. Tapped her fingers on the bar. Nails were teal tonight, like the ocean.

"A couple weeks ago. Might have been the day after you came in, actually." She glared at me with such accusation that I felt compelled to raise my hands apologetically. "Guy comes in." I leaned forward. "What guy?"

"Weird guy."

"Weird how?"

"Like…" she struggled to describe the stranger, "Truman Capote meets The Undertaker."

What did she say? Lee Marvin and Cinderella? I tried to picture two more distinct individuals.

"You mean the wrestler?"

"Yeah, you know, big guy with the hat and long coat?"

"Nearly 7 feet tall, sure. But Truman Capote was tiny. And effete. Who are you talking about?"

She frowned, dissatisfied with her own inability to properly describe this increasingly important figure.

"Don't think size. I just meant in demeanor, like the way he acted. Those were the people who came to mind."

Still a conundrum.

"I'm gonna have to sleep on that."

"Anyway, he asked for Pin's Brew-I didn't have it, hadn't even heard of it. That's what I told him."

"What'd he say?"

"Too many teeth. That's the way he smiled. His lips pulled back, showed a lot of gums. I don't why he was happy to hear I didn't have what he was asking for, but he grinned like one of those fish at the bottom of the ocean."

"Do they grin?"

"Why don't you go take a dive and find out?"

"Ha. But what happened next?"

"I told him we didn't have it and he said, 'What a charmed life you lead'."

That stuck in my craw, I'm not sure why.

"Maybe he was hitting on you."

"Wouldn't be the first, wouldn't be the worst." I wondered how I ranked. "But no, I think he just wanted to see if we had this drink, and he was satisfied that we didn't. It was weird.

"So, what'd he do then?"

"Then he ordered a beer and left. And I mean that. He got an Amstel Light, I think it was, on draft. I put in front of him, he places a twenty on the bar. I turn to get change, and he's gone. Beer's untouched."

"You drink it?" I joked, though that really wasn't funny.

"I usually do, actually. Don't let good booze go to waste-or bad booze for that matter. But...I don't know. It felt weird."

"I think that-"

"Excuse me." She went to tend bar on the far end, and she didn't come back for a while. I think maybe I had spooked or annoyed her. Maybe both. But not my fault, surely. Who was this stranger, and how did he figure into our weird little tale-was he simply an anomaly, or something more sinister?

It was 9:34 when the show started. Yep, what a surprise.

The MC was a short guy with a white shirt and a buzz cut. He came up to the bar before he started.

"Hey Lil, I'm gonna start in a minute."

"Do your thing, bro." She was cleaning a glass, didn't really care.

I turned to this 'starter', as he was clearly alluding to the show, no?

"Excuse me, you, you're part of the show?"

"Rod Stewart Live!" he lit up, "Yeah!"

"So why do you call it 'Rod Stewart Live'?" I said it out loud, at last, accepting the inevitability that Rod Stewart Live had little to nothing to do with Rod Stewart.

He sniggered, "I call it that to throw people off, you know?"

I understood the concept of throwing people off. But why Rod Stewart?

"But why Rod Stewart? You could say Rolling Stones Live or something."

"'Cause he's Rod Stewart, you know?"

He slapped me on the back affably and ran up to stage-stage being the area of the floor next to the DJ's table.

"Alright everybody! You ready to laugh?!" Some were, some didn't care. "Tonight we got three guys who sent dick pics to Donald Trump!"

Obedient laughter from the audience, and so on.

I wasn't sure how long I should stay anyway. I had confirmed, as if there had ever been any doubt (or hope) that the one and only Rod Stewart would not be performing here tonight, replaced by a series of mediocre comics. I had seen Lilith, was ecstatic that she remembered me, even my name, we had (somewhat successfully, I think) flirted a little and perhaps I should quit while I'm ahead there. I even made some traction on the investigation, because that's a real thing. Lilith confirmed that she knew nothing more about Pin's Brew, but now there was some stranger out there, a weird cross between a dandy Southern writer and a behemoth in the ring, who had also tasted of the

Pin's Brew, and was now possibly on our trail.

•　•　•　•　•

The first comedian was an obnoxious leftist loudmouth clearly working with dusty material a few years old.

"Can you BELIEEEVE there are still people against gay marriage?!" (See what I mean?) "Gay marriage should be legal and if you disagree, I'm gonna cum on your face and lick it off!" He would repeat the line about ejaculating on his opponents' faces and licking it off several times throughout the routine, as if he had stumbled upon some great and original witticism worthy of Wilde "Like a couple months ago, I saw that RACIST ASSHOLE Mike Huckabee on Fox News" (Which I'm sure he watches) "Saying that if we let two men get married, next thing, a man is gonna marry his dog!" (He scrunched up his face and let this admittedly silly argument stand on its own. His face wasn't funny.) "I'm thinking, Mike! You're worried a man is gonna marry his dog? If he's gonna marry his dog, you KNOW he's already fucked that dog, at least 50 times!"

And so. By the way, not that I think it's the government's business who you "marry", but I will defend the Reverend Governor against the predictable and unfounded claims of racism. I read this article he wrote back in the 70s about how you must treat your black brothers and sisters equally, how it is wrong to use the n-word, because they are children of Christ, like all of us. And I agreed.

"So, it's too bad Carrie Fisher died," The next stand up was droning, his face drawing his words out, his eyes blank and probably stoned. "Yeah, it's really bad because now she can't be ALIVE!" He stretched out the last word with a shrill, gravelly voice as if the noise alone should shock and offend.

Anti-humor? I didn't get it. Also, dude. Not "too soon", too late! I know that sounds callous, but it is March. The great Carrie Fisher, may she rest in peace, had been gone for months. There was little shock value in it. Or humor.

Third guy wasn't so bad. I admired what he was doing, even if I didn't laugh too much.

He sprinted onto stage in clean red sneakers and a bright smile.

"What is the DEAL with airline peanuts?"

He was doing a hyperbolized ironic Jerry Seinfeld and/or generic 80s comic thing. Cute. I'm not sure everybody appreciated the level of meta-irony he was going for though.

"The Black Box is the only thing that survives the crash? Why don't they make the whole plane out of the black box?!"

• • • • •

All in all, their sets were a bit tame and dated. Mike Huckabee, Carrie Fischer, and aglets. I mean, geez guys, get some new material.

Lilith agreed.

"- Or I'll come on your face and lick it off!" He roared for the third time.

I felt a welcome nudge on my shoulder. Do girls realize how thrilling even the slightest touch can be?

"He's been doing this same routine every Wednesday since I started working here," she whispered. "It never gets any funnier."

I concurred.

"How long has that been?"

"That I've worked here?" she chewed her lip. "Don't ask questions you don't want the answer to."

"Okay."

The fourth comedian/first comedienne was very loud, self-satisfied, and talked about her sex life. During a particularly graphic and boisterous retelling of her latest experience receiving oral sex from her Arabian boyfriend, I decided to call it a night. I'd also wager that both the cunnilingus and the Arabian boyfriend were fictional, but why let the truth get in the way of a bad joke?

I turned from the racist yelping meant to approximate the sound of a Middle Eastern man performing oral sodomy on a woman to leave. Then I stopped. I wanted to finish things off nicely with Lilith, but I wasn't sure how. Maybe just say "Bye" or "See you later". I had already made pretty good traction, I decided, and I think she was more attentive and affectionate to me tonight than any of the other patrons I witnessed, so that was neat. But there's always the danger that a formal goodbye would be anti-climactic, and I'd get that pesky burning in my nose.

So maybe just play it cool? Slight wave, whatever type thing?

Or maybe don't be a Melvin?

I'm sure standing awkwardly in place, looking at the door, very self-aware, was not the most alpha move, but saved by the-

"No goodnight kiss?"

God Bless you, Lilith. I swiveled, and there she was, smiling. Her comment was disarming, but not cruel. There was obviously some irony in it, but definitely flirtatious.

"Yeah," I played it casually, "I'm just headed out."

"Sorry Rod didn't show up tonight. But if you come back next week…"

"Maybe." She was smiling widely and blinking rapidly (*it's called batting her eyes, idiot. Capitalize!*) "I'd like to see you before then though." Speed and volume equaled confidence, right?

"Absolutely."

She said it so matter of fact, practically like *Duh, the chemistry is palpable, of course we're gonna see each other again.*

"I meant outside the bar."

"Def," she was nodding.

"Cool," I took out my phone, "so what's your-"

"No, no." She had a better idea.

And a pen, suddenly. She grabbed my left hand and pulled it to her. The tip on my skin felt-I could imagine-like the graze of her fingernails.

Done writing her number on a place I was sure to remember, Lilith gave her signature a little kiss. "Call me!"

It's weird how things can work out, isn't it? Sometimes you just gotta believe.

Chapter 9: Starry, Starry Night

I met with Mike the following Saturday at his place in Santa Monica. I didn't talk to him about Wednesday night. I didn't see the point. But I was, frankly, walking on air.

It's not that terribly hard for me to get dates. I don't mean that as a boast, believe me. I should say, first dates, those awkward exchanges of civility with the possibility of flirtation, almost always facilitated online. That's the thing. I have a decently written profile on a popular dating site (Like I'm really going to tell you which one) with a huge pool of prospects. My photos are...moderately attractive? And I'm perfectly capable of carrying on a conversation online. The icebreaker. Rejoinder. Gentle probe. Humble brag. Cautious invitation...and if we've made it that far, chances are she'll accept.

Second date, however? Different story entirely. And where I'm going right now is, they were almost entirely women I met online. I used to feel embarrassed about that, I'm embarrassed to now admit. I told people I met my first girlfriend at a Marie Callender's, which was accurate in that that is the physical location we first met in person but deliberately misleading is hiding the fact that we first made contact on a dating website. Really, it's quite ridiculous. Very silly. Why should I be embarrassed? Millions of people do it.

Still, it was quite wondrous to meet a woman in person and then date her. That was something else. It was more spontaneous. Less artificial. Dare I say, more romantic? I'm getting ahead of myself, of course, but there is a big difference between a stale online icebreaker to a "Love dogs and Disneyland, No Hookups!" type leading to boring small talk over coffee and a sultry woman IRL writing her number on your flesh. One was more exciting. Worth writing home about. Well, worth writing in this book about.

• • • • •

Mike wanted to talk about "The Case", naturally, and I was right there with him. Not that I knew what this was at this point, exactly, if it even was anything at all. What did we have, anyway? A dead cat, eye in the color-changing drink? Yeah, it was weird, but that didn't amount to a connection. That didn't mean anything.

But I was curious. And it was something to do. Things were slow lately. I was slumping at the theater, making decent money on predictable gigs. Writing was a bit blocked up at the moment. Still waiting to hear back about my pilot, and potential investors for my next short film. Same old, same old. So why not invent an adventure?

Plus, I got to spend time with Mike, and he was an interesting individual, say literally anything else about the guy. Mike had accepted our incredible reunion after all these years apart with far less pomp and circumstance than I had. He shrugged it off as a mildly interesting coincidence, whereas I saw divine intervention. I found his underwhelming response mildly annoying, but mostly I was happy to see him again.

Correction: I met with Mike OUTSIDE his place in Santa Monica. I knocked on his door, and he barged right out, only affording me a glimpse of a small studio, bare and neat.

"Let's pick up some brews," he commanded, without a proper greeting.

We walked a couple of blocks to a nearby liquor shop. I don't know much about beer, so I let Mike take the wheel on this one.

"Let's get some Pabst."

He brought it to the counter, where a particularly hairy slack-jawed yokel, looking more band geek than Hell's Angel, took note of Mike's appearance.

"What's up with the glove?"

"It's filled with Vaseline," Mike snapped. "I'm keeping my hand soft for your wife."

The clerk rang us up without retort. We walked outside as three young women walked in. One blonde, one brunette, one Asian. All stunning.

Mike didn't make any secret of his gaze. We stood on the sidewalk looking in.

"We are surrounded by trim, my good man."

"How about you say that a little louder, Mike?"

He gently slapped my chest.

"Sack up, Trent. Just because you're not getting any doesn't mean the rest of us can't have our fun."

We started walking up the hill. I took exception to that.

"Your characterization is questionable for a number of reasons. And Mike, haven't you ever heard the expression, 'Those who talk about it the most, do it the least'?"

He stopped and turned back on me.

"You think I have any problem getting it wet?" His tone was uncharacteristically aggressive.

"That's not what I mean."

"I ever tell you Sharon Kerry sucked my dick in 6th grade?"

"No! Geez! But…I did hear about that."

"Yeah, I'm not surprised you did." He nodded, pointedly. "'Cause it's true."

We didn't talk much on the rest of the way back to Mike's place.

"Let's drink this by my truck," he mumbled, to no complaint.

Mike's apartment was about 5 blocks from the beach, a single room above somebody else's garage. He didn't want to talk much about his landlords, and I wasn't really interested, but I picked up they were an older couple whose son, a surfer like his Dad, had recently moved out from home. Mike probably wasn't an adequate substitute, but he was paying rent, and it was a place to live.

Though he lived over a garage, Mike couldn't actually use it, so he had to use a side street. Which was fine by him, actually, as he parked in an alley between a sub shop and a yoga studio. I wasn't sure if where he was parking was legal, but he shrugged off my caution.

"Haven't gotten ticketed yet." Which I suppose is something the lawless and the reckless tell themselves to justify whatever. "Drink up," he said, handing me a cold can as we lay in the bed of his truck staring up at the stars.

Now I'm quite certain drinking outside in public like that is illegal but offered no protest. I was thirsty, and he was buying.

"Pabst Blue Ribbon," I chuckled, enjoying the cold gold bittersweet foam. I'm still not an aficionado by any means, but beer has grown on me over the years. It used to be, it wasn't sweet enough. Maybe I'm growing up.

"I'm not a hipster, Trent." Mike frowned. "It's cheap, is all."

"No, no!" I corrected, as Mike would be the last guy I would accuse of that dreaded affliction of our modern age, *hipsterism*. "I just laughed, 'cause, you know, Blue Velvet."

"Didn't see it."

"It's a good one. Very weird and violent."

"They drink PBR in it?"

"Yeah, it's Dennis Hopper's drink of choice."

"Well," he considered. "'Pop quiz, hot shot!'" He affected a mediocre Hopper impression and took a gulp. "Ah. So. You went back?" To La Cuevita, he meant.

"I did." I was reticent. Nothing he needed to know.

"And?"

I shrugged. What should I tell him? I held back.

"I asked her about Pin's Brew."

"And?"

Dare I mention the stranger? He'd eat that up. How to describe this guy as Lilith described him?

"You a big wrestling fan, Mike? You like 20th Century literature?"

"What are you talking about?"

I shook my head. Whoever it was who had heard of Pin's Brew, knew it by name, and seemed satisfied that we had taken it-he might be on our trail, and he was surely relevant to this "case", if indeed there was one.

"She hadn't heard of it before now."

He nodded. Enough for him. "I didn't think she would. There are a lot of low-level players, Trent. We have to figure out who to target."

"Target?! Jeepers, Mike, what do you think this is?"

"War," he sipped, simply, matter-of-fact. "You saw the cat. You saw the-"

"I saw it all," I cut him off. "Doesn't mean there's a connection or that we're anywhere close to seeing it."

"See it!" he said fervently. "That's what it's all about. You just gotta see the whole big picture, all at once. Then all the pieces will make sense."

"Just like a puzzle."

"Just like a puzzle," he agreed.

"Except," I thought, trailing off…"What if it leads us down a road we don't want to go?"

"Hell, aren't we already there?" he snorted. "I don't usually drink eyeballs, Trent. That's not my habit."

"No, but…" But what? I tried, weakly, to indicate what I was getting at. "Maybe it's better to leave well enough alone."

"Don't be a pussy." Scornfully.

"Okay." Lovecraft. I'd seek refuge in Lovecraft. "Did you ever read The Call of Cthulhu?"

"Was that the one with the squid?"

"It wasn't a squid, exactly. It was like a facsimile, an abomination one could picture-part squid, part dragon, part man. But it was supposed to be an unfathomable horror, so you can't really draw it, or imagine it. I think you would go mad if you actually saw the guy."

"That what we're up against, you think?"

"No." I almost had to chuckle at that. Eldritch Abomination killing cats at the library? But then what was it? "Just, there was this quote at the beginning of the story, it makes me think...the narrator's talking about how the only thing that keeps a man sane is that he lives on an island in the placid sea of ignorance. If we are ever able to put all the pieces together, we'd go mad."

"The world's already mad, Trent. Seeing the whole thing at once will just make it make more sense."

"You don't worry about unfathomable horror? About going nuts?"

"I'm already here," he said simply, then crushed his can and let it drop into the bed at our feet. It was a crisp night.

I wanted to roll my eyes at that. Affected nonsense. He wasn't crazy. He was just pretentious. But then, so was I, so what are you going to do? New objection:

"Well Mike, didn't we already miss our shot anyway? Target was obvious, wasn't it?"

"How you figure?"

"You see a bottle with an eyeball in it, you go to the source. The bartender, right? Or the manager. The people actually handling the drink. We bolted out of The Misfit so quick, there was no investigation."

"They didn't know anything there."

"So, then we went to Deakins Porthouse," I continued. "It's logical. This is where Pin's Brew, that color changing, reality shifting drink comes from. We talk to the steward, it's polite until it's not, but what did we get?"

"The list-"

"What list?" I cut him off. "Now we know other places in LA that have that drink? So, what? How far removed from us is that?"

Mike was patient. "I see where you're going, Trent."

"Going? I'm there. That's it. I made my point. There's nothing-what's left?"

He continued, "And I would agree with you, were it not for one thing."

"What's that?"

"Like I said. See the connection."

"I don't see any connection, Mike. I don't see...anything."

"That's 'cause you're forgetting something."

"What am I forgetting?"

He grinned slyly, "Meow."

It came screeching back to me.

"The cat?"

"Yeah, the cat. The first part of this twisted saga. Or don't you think one has something to do with the other?"

I had to admit. "Yeah, I guess I always felt so...weird stuff, you know. But I can't really put them together. A dead cat in the library downtown. Floating eyeball in Santa Monica..."

"Freak occurrences, Trent! But maybe not so spontaneous."

"You know something I don't."

"I went back, Trent. I went back."

That chilled me a little.

"To the library?"

"The very same. I went back, all the way."

I swallowed.

"They cleaned it, right? I mean, there's no cat, no stain or anything was there?"

"What there was...was...perspective."

"Perspective?"

"Yah. I went back. To the corner. To the exact spot where the meows stopped, and we found the cat. And I saw."

"What was there to see?" I was curious now. Obviously, it wasn't something I liked to think about. I would have rather moved on. But if there was something he knew, some *sense* to be found, well...I didn't really want to know. But I couldn't help from asking.

He sipped his beer and looked up contemplatively. "Sure are a lot of stars out tonight."

I gave him that.

"Yeah. Normally there's light pollution, but it's a pretty good night. Pretty clear."

"Over in Kandahar-" he turned to me to explain politely, "that was when I was in Iraq."

"I thought you were in Afghanistan?" I was confused, but he took me away with his anecdote.

"Out there..." he drifted back. "Out in the desert. Away from the city. Away from...everything of man. It's just, it's just the Earth, you know? the Earth and the great blue sky. And at night, you're sleeping under an...ocean of stars." He cracked a joyless smile. "Felt like you'd be swallowed up. And I'm not sure I believe in...God and all that...but when you're looking up there, you're so small, and THE UNIVERSE it just...it just gets to you, you know?"

I didn't. Not really. But I appreciated the sentiment, saw where he was going, and I wanted desperately to be a part of it. Man is by his nature a creature of intellect and insight. He seeks clarity and understanding and will take it where he can get it, even in the most unlikely of sources. This half-drunken veteran's waxing cosmic about being swallowed up by a universe that may or may not be Godless was something, was it not?

"Wasn't all placid and platitudes though," he admitted. "Sometimes they set the oil fields on fire. Lit up the night." Grunt. "Not in a good way."

I had heard about that. That practice anyway, in that part of the world. I'm sure it had nothing to do with Mike's situation, but it was something that had been done before, in such another war. My father went to Desert Storm. He still liked to talk about it. Not just his own experience, but all wars. All history. He mentioned something once about burning the oil fields back in 1991. I was not sure why.

"Why'd they do that?"

"Burn the oil?"

"Yeah."

"Just because, man. That's war."

Of which I knew little. Well, nothing first hand, but actually I did know a fair amount on an academic level. But it still didn't explain the motives.

"But there's got to be some reason..."

"Sure. After the insurgents lose control of a region-a field, in this case...well, you know oil is everything, right?"

"Yeah. Lifeblood of the world's economy, blood for oil all that."

"Uh-huh. And who controls the land, controls the oil, very important. They're driven out, they no longer have that land or that oil. And so..."

I was beginning to get it.

"Spite."

"Yes, sir. They figure, we can't have it, neither can you. Let it all go."

"Some men just want to watch the world burn." I instantly regretted trivializing such war stories with a stupid comic book movie reference.

"You nerdish prick," he teased, without malevolence. "Yeah, yeah they do. 'Specially those fuckers they got now. Mohammed's Ninjas."

"Mohammed's Ninjas," I rolled that phrase over. I instantly knew what he meant, but I had never heard them referred to as such.

"ISIS, man, ISIS. You've seen 'em. They dress like ninjas."

"And Antifa dress like them."

He scowled. "Social Justice Scum. I'd like to give them something to whine about..." He trailed off.

I tried to gather my thoughts. I was buzzed. "Mike, what were we talking about?"

"Stars!" he declared with such a musical fury that I couldn't help but hearing, oddly enough, Russell Crowe.

Stars, in your multitudes, scarce to be counted. Filling the darkness, with order and light...

Order and light. We should be so lucky.

But why was I singing *Les Misérables* in my mind? Where was this going? Was there really any point to hanging out with Mike, let alone pretending this was an "investigation"? There were pieces there

No matter, another musical digression.

"Trent, you know that Don McLean song-*Starry, Starry Night*?"

"The title of the song is actually *Vincent*. But I do know what you mean."

"*Starry, starry night,*'" he crooned.

"It's about Vincent Van Gogh," I pointed out.

"Good old lend-me-your-ear Vincent."

"Tortured artist."

Mike snorted.

"He tortured himself."

"Isn't that enough?"

"No, Trent. Some of us have real problems."

That struck a nerve. I felt a need to defend the late, great Van Gogh.

"You don't think mental illness, epilepsy, poverty, everything he was going through are real?"

"Snowflake. Some of us have real things to worry about."

"Yeah, you're saying some people don't have to invent problems?"

He didn't get that I was challenging him.

"Exactly."

"Like a Scooby Doo/Hardy Boys investigation, running around California with our dicks in the air?" (Not a good insult. Didn't know what it meant.)

"Fuck you, Trent." He sat up, angry and a little hurt. "Did I kill that cat? Did I put that eyeball in the bottle? You think nothing's going on?"

"No," I had to admit. "Okay, there's something, but I don't see..." And I didn't. But Mike had an angle.

"That list he gave me, La Cire. I still have it. I looked into it."

"Yeah, we both have, Mike. You go to bars, see if they have what you're drinking?"

He pursed his lips, thinking about how to get to it.

"Are you familiar with Dr. Victor Thane?"

"Who's that?"

"Is that a yes or a no?"

The question annoyed me.

"That would be a no, Mike. That's why I asked."

"Don't get smart."

"Fine. Sorry. Who is Dr. Vincent Thane?"

"Victor."

"Who is Dr. Victor Thane?"

"Hah," he laughed dryly. "I think you said Vincent because I was singing- we were talking about that. Like a subconscious, subliminal thing."

"Damnit, Mike."

"Yeah, yeah, yeah. I'm getting there, brother. Hold your horses."

"So, Dr. VICTOR Thane?"

"He's a head shrinker out of UCLA."

"Ok."

"He's also one of the owners of The Pick and Hammer."

"Ah, right. The bar in Burbank? They have Pin's Brew?"

"Who said it was a bar, Trent?"

"What? You said-I mean, it was on the list."

"It was. But what you have to understand is, The Pick and Hammer is like The Magic Castle-The Magic Castle being the magician's club."

"I know what The Magic Castle is, dude. That's where they filmed *Lord of-*"

But he cut me off before I could reference Scott Bakula.

"Then you can appreciate the parallel. The Magic Castle is a private club for magician's only. The Pick and Hammer is for psychiatrists."

"Psychiatrists have a private club? Like with a bar and everything?" It just didn't seem right for some reason.

"Yes sir. Seems those doctors need plenty of their own medicine- or rather, a differing brand. Don't get high off your own supply, mind you. Mind's what matters with these quacks, and if its mind over matter, it's their minds that matter." (He was drunk) "So they have their own opioids, but not what they prescribe. 10-year-old's a bit fidgety? Conk him out with Ritalin.

Four-year-old boy wears pink? Better get him all the hormones and estrogen he needs to chop his dick off. PTSD can't sleep? Well, solider on, or take the suicide pills like the rest. Rest like the best. And when that's done, what's what, yeah, they'll need a drink."

That was an odd rant, but I stayed on point.

"And Thane, I'm gathering, he's part of this club?"

"He's not just a member, he's on the board."

"Maybe he knows what they order."

"There's more."

"Yeah?"

"You have a short attention span, my friend. We were in the library. I told I went back to the cat spot. Then I ramble on about stars, and you forget all about it?"

"Oh yeah! What- what about the library? What...perspective?"

"Patterns, Trent. Symbols and signals. Reoccurrences. You have to notice the motifs."

"You lost me."

"Are you familiar with the phrase, 'Publish or Perish'?" That's right. Mike's academic background.

"Sure am, professor."

"Ha, well, Dr. Thane does publish, quite prolifically, as a matter of fact. Articles in the American Journal of Psychiatry, things like that. And his own books about the brain-meager attempts to understand the thinking of the beast that is man and mass market it. But of particular interest-and you'll love this-he's a novelist."

"I love it." I was sarcastic, but I had a dreadful feeling he was going somewhere dreadful.

"A mystery novelist."

"Oh." Getting deeper. My stomach sank.

"In fact, he's got so many, that you go to the library, one entire shelf is entirely Thane." He leaned in. "And do you know which shelf that is, Trent?"

"Of course, I do." I was bitter. His breath stank and so did the story- all the more so, I'm sure, because I believed each and every word. "Doesn't mean anything though. Could be just a coincidence."

"Coincidence-if it needs to be mentioned again-is for dumbasses and delusionals. Which one are you?"

"It seems a tenuous stretch though, Mike. Undead cat by the shelf of this guy's books, and he's on the board of one of five bars that stocks eyeball juice?"

"Sometimes tenuous is all we've got."

"If you're looking. If you *force* yourself to look. I mean, what would we even say to the man?"

"We'll cross that bridge when we come to it. And we will come to it."

I sighed. This was getting nowhere-perhaps. Or it was getting somewhere I didn't wish to go. Even so.

"Sure are a lot of stars out tonight," I repeated.

"*Starry, starry night*," he sung again, then stopped sharply. "That song is bullshit, by the way."

"Whoa. Wow. Language."

"Shut up."

"What do you mean?"

And then he sung-beautifully, I must admit, as if he did not despise the lyrics.

"*And when no hope was left in sight on that starry, starry night. You took your life as lovers often do.*" Was that a tear? "*But I could have told you Vincent, this world was never meant for one as beautiful as you.*"

We sat there in silence. Tragic. Beautiful. Poignant. Sometimes, when you're just trying to be profound, you are. Maybe profundity is in the eye of the beholder, in this moment a philosopher, now and then a drunkard, by and by a beast.

My friend. Mike Kripke. The conversation confused, confounded, even frustrated me, but at this moment, I couldn't think of anything else I would rather be doing than hearing him wax romantic about the mysteries of the universe, as above, so below.

And I could see his point.

"I guess...you mean it's glorifying suicide?"

"Fucking 'A it is. Nothing beautiful about it-I don't care how many lovers do it. And what's he talking about-Vincent's too beautiful for this world because he cuts his ear off and paints pretty pictures? What a load."

Devil's advocate time? (Not that I'm comparing Don McLean to the devil, mind, but how many times did we have to suffer through drunkenly botched attempts at *American Pie*?)

"Well, he was saying Vincent suffered for his sanity-"

"Sanity's nothing worth suffering for. It's the natural state. A billion people suffer worse off than him, never off themselves."

"I'm not saying it's right-or even sane" (*But it's all I have!* Finished Andrea Beaumont) "But if he saw no hope-"

"Hope is an illusion, young man. A figment."

"All the more reason, young interrupter."

"I didn't say it's not an illusion worth sticking around for."

"Even if you realize it?"

"Especially if you realize it. That's the thing, Trent. That's the entire thing, I suppose. Once you see the illusions, you can control them. Know what you're seeing, switch the channel."

I rubbed the bridge of my nose. I wonder if Mike was aware of his own illusions. He probably wasn't.

Hell, is anyone?

Chapter 10: The Death of Gaston

Lilith was-I know, surprising-a Disney fan. There was a live-action remake of *Beauty and the Beast* out, and she wanted to see it. And even though there's a $5 first run theater in Highland Park, I decided to be a fancy, impressive gentleman, and treat her to a fancy, impressive screening at the Disney Theater in Hollywood. You know the one. Or if you don't, it's across from The Chinese Theater, the screen is huge, and there are balconies and red curtains. It's like a night at the opera.

I wasn't particularly interested in the movie-but it was hard to beat the company. Also, there was a bit of a stir because this was the first Disney movie to include an explicitly gay character-supposedly. Some of the conservative mouthpieces I followed, most notably Matt Walsh, were outraged by the concept of a homosexual in a Disney film. It felt like 1996. Senator Bob Dole is whining about *Striptease,* and former President George H.W. Bush said that *Trainspotting* was a dumpster he didn't have to look into. Meanwhile, we got thirty million dead kids, but these Republican milquetoasts are spew-you-out-of-my-mouth lukewarm on abortion, and these are the issues they're focusing on.

Gimmie a break.

It was Le Fou, of course, Gaston's grubby little sycophant, telegraphed months in advance, played by Josh Gad, a chubby comic actor I had enjoyed in this or that. I was curious, how would they play it? Would it be nonchalant, a homo-washing of history, as if you could be out and proud in 16th Century France and everyone would be fine and dandy? Hey, crazier things have happened, right? If you can accept an anthropomorphic candelabra, then maybe a revisionist portrait of social tolerance in the late Renaissance is acceptable. I mean, who cares, really? I remember when Disney had this TV movie in the late 90s/early 2000s. Typical generic middle-aged non-specific

European Kingdom. Everybody made a big fuss over the fact that Cinderella was black. Also, the Queen was black, the King was white, and the Prince was Asian, so you figure it out. But it's so trivial. Yeah, maybe everybody in this fictional French village will be okay that the bully's sidekick is gay. It is a fairy tale, after all. (No homophobic pun intended. Good grief).

Would it even be explicit? How would they convey it? They weren't gonna show two dudes kissing, I'd wager.

Would it simply be implied? Unrequited and perhaps troubling to the closeted himself? Because now that I think of it, who else would be the target of the toadie's problematic affection?

No one inspires the love that dare not speak its name like Gaston!

That had to be it, wouldn't it? I mean, even in the cartoon, he's so fawning and servile that a homoerotic subtext wouldn't be the biggest stretch in the world. I'm sure FanFiction went nuts on this point years before the live-action remake was announced. They always do. Some people online have...imaginations. I read one story-actually fairly inspired, I'd say-where Hogwarts Castle gets it on with The Giant Squid.

Where was I?

Surely Gaston, predatory alpha male that he was, wouldn't reciprocate. His sights on Belle were singular and more than a little creepy. Man's got three buxom blondes sighing at his feet, but he only has eyes on the one girl in town who rejects him? Maybe he wants a challenge. Or maybe that's where the revisionism would come in. Plot twist! Gaston only pursued Belle because he knew she wouldn't have him, because he didn't actually want to get it on with a girl, and this deliberately unrequited public courting would serve as a smokescreen for-

Nah. It would all be Le Fou.

And how would that play out? I was picturing some delicious Highsmithian levels of idolatry and repression. Le Fou's Ripley to Gaston's Dickie Greenleaf. Needless to say, this would be the most interesting part of the movie.

Not that it'd be taken as the most progressive, necessarily. I mean, how could it, if the only gay character is a stooge who carries a pathetic torch for the foul villain? Hardly empowering for the gay community, is it? I'd be intrigued, but liberals are never satisfied.

I'm reminded of another swim into the waters of diversity. Disney patted themselves on the back a lot for finally having an African American Princess (in 2009!), but they changed the name from *The Frog Princess* to *The Princess and the Frog,* because the former sounded offensive. The reasoning being, it sounded like they're animalizing a black girl? Then they changed the eponymous princess's name from Maddy to Tiana because Maddy sounded too much like Mammy.

And it's like, you're not very good at this, are you?

•   •   •   •   •

Movies aren't ideal for first dates, I've always felt. Not a good time or place to talk, obviously. But this wasn't blind, and Lilith and I already had established a fair rapport. On top of that, it was her idea, so who am I to object?

Still, just showing up at the theater, exchanging a little small talk on the way to the concession stand, then sitting silently in the dark for two hours wouldn't do. So, I suggested we meet next door first. Disney has an absolutely incredible ice cream fountain - possibly in collaboration with Ghiradelli's-and the shakes and sundaes were yummy.

I entertained, briefly, the notion of showing up on time or even late (!), but I decided that would be uncharacteristically dickish. So yes, Trent Malloy delivered, as he always does. A good twenty-two minutes early. Walk around the block and hang out across the street with the giant Elmos and the competing Batmen. It wasn't as bad as the occasional coffee shop. There was, after all, plenty of stimulation. This was the set of D.W. Griffith's *Intolerance.* Look at those Elephants! We're in Babylon! Also, admonish yourself for leering at the sexy cop posing for photos, and semi-ironically tell someone who doesn't care that we're around where they filmed *Leprechaun 2.* (And that's true, by the way. During the tour of Hollywood sequences, the bland lead drives around a bus of tourists including Clint Howard and Kimmy Robertson.)

Enough of that. 15 minutes 'til our prearranged meeting. It was time to cross the street, take a seat in the fountain, peruse the menu awkwardly and play with my phone while uncomfortably waiting for the half hour before she shows up.

Except no. Because I walk in and there she was, 13 minutes early, waiting for me.

"Took you long enough," Lilith smirked, knowingly, as I pulled into the booth.

It really was extraordinary.

"I know, I know. I'm super early," she was somewhere between sardonic and apologetic-although with Lilith there was always a touch of irony. "Terrible, right?"

"I wouldn't say so. I'm an early bird myself."

She flicked her tongue in and out of her mouth. Like a sexy raptor.

"Does that mean I'm gonna get your worm?"

I sniggered nervously, the only proper response to such a brazen and unsophisticated come-on. Did she really say that?

Oh yeah? What was she wearing? Acid washed jeans, and of course, a lot of black. Leather jacket with a lot of patches, Misfit skulls, and Ramones motifs.

And her t-shirt. Oh boy.

It was a black sleeveless shirt that was cut across the center, making sort of a cleavage window. The shirt was held together by safety pins across the opening. Like the shirt Anna Tolputt (the British girl) wore in *Hellraiser: Hellworld*. Like a punk Power Girl. Very Disney-appropriate.

And yes, I did reference *Hellraiser 8*. Sometimes the allusion fits.

Not that her shirt did, necessarily. Fit, I mean. It was bursting at the seams, held together by safety pins. But that was the point, and it's impolite to stare.

"What's good here?" she asked, perusing the glossy menu. "Besides everything."

"Besides everything? I don't know. I haven't been."

"It'll have to be one of the sundaes, of course. We'll need two spoons." She glanced up. "Three if you want to join in."

"Might as well. Coming to ice cream shop- *shoppe* maybe- and not digging in is like going to the pool and not getting wet."

"I always get wet," she boasted nonchalantly, and my heart stopped. It was almost annoying how sexy she was. Someone once wrote that Jane March was so slutty in *Color of Night* (SPOILER ALERT) that she was almost unattractive. I don't know what movie that guy was watching, or what frequency his heterosexuality was tuned. Jane was adorable and attractively sexy in that movie. She does act very coquettish around Bruce Willis's Dr. Bill Capa, but you don't even find out how promiscuous she is until the end, and that's informed by other characters when she's not in the room (I don't think), and there are extenuating circumstances. I think it's an underrated movie.

Granted, the plot gets a little jumbled, and the tone can be over-the-top, but I think it's less "bad" so much as intentionally melodramatic in an early De Palmian sense. Roger Ebert once said that you can't fault someone for making a bad movie, only a boring one. For whatever else it may be, *Color of Night* is not boring, and I certainly found it memorable.

This is 1994, and Bruce Willis is making a departure from the smirking tough guy role he had always played up to that point. Dr. Bill Capa is more romantic and vulnerable, carrying the weight of the opening tragedy on his psyche, similar to the "sadness" Mr. Glass would later describe so eloquently in *Unbreakable*. I think the romance works too. When Bill whispers that Rose is "Quicksilver...light as air", it's dreamy and whimsical. That he narrates his own romantic musings strikes me as classical in the film noir sense. And counterintuitive to the whole murderous mess they get wrapped up in. I think the point is that these two troubled souls came into each other's lives at the right time, saving each other from darkness. For her part, Jane March is talented, beautiful and very versatile. She's capable of conveying seductiveness and innocence simultaneously, which is a challenge. And at the risk of plot spoilers, I'll just emphasize that she's really versatile. It's too bad she's not in more movies. And at the risk of sounding like a perv, the sex scenes are really hot, better than anything you might see on Skinemax. And the way they are filmed, I really don't know how Willis and March's genitals could not have come in contact in real life.

The supporting cast is excellent. Scott Bakula, Ruben Blades, Lance Henriksen, Leslie Ann Warren, Kevin J. O'Connor and Brad Dourif (also in a departure from his usual character type) are all great. There is some great direction with Capa's color blindness, particularly in the beginning and end-very vivid shots. And I really did not see the plot twist coming, even though it was right in front of my eyes the whole time.

But what really stays with me is the title and the character premise. *Color of Night* is a very evocative title, and I think color blindness is a striking metaphoric representation for the spark of life Capra loses and regains. That it happens as a direct result from a patient's suicide, his failure as a psychologist, makes it a literal manifestation of that celebrated sadness I keep talking up. Maybe I'm projecting-my idea of the movie is better than it actually is, but I don't know. I think it's a lot better than it's made out to be.

But I digress. I'm always digressing. Maybe that's why I'm not a novelist.

Where were we?

Ah yes.

"I always get wet."

"You're a saucy little minx, aren't you?" I don't know why I said that. But it worked.

"What?" she snickered, losing composure, but in a smiling way.

"Ah, see. You're not the only one who can casually throw out a disarmingly provocative remark."

"Is that what I'm doing? Trying to disarm you?"

"From where I'm sitting."

"Which is too far away. Stand up and get over here."

I needed no further encouragement.

"Scooch over."

"Nope."

So, I sat in the booth, and she didn't scooch. We were side by side, thigh to thigh. There were too many layers of clothing separating us, but I could feel the pressure of her leg against mine, which was nice.

Again, it was nothing to her. She blew it off as simply a way for us to both look at the menu at once.

"Cookie mudslide looks tasty." She ran her finger over the picture.

"I'm interested in the Caramel Cluster."

"I always say 'carmel'."

(That doesn't read in a transcript. I pronounce it carm-ul, she says care-a-mel)

"It's got sea salt!"

She rolled her eyes. "What's the big deal about sea salt, anyway? Is it better than table salt?"

"More expensive."

"White people."

"Hey, you think I'm bad, you should check out my parents. They go nuts for that gourmet designer sodium. They have black rock Hawaiian volcano salt, garlic Mediterranean, even some pink stuff from the Himalayans."

"You know, you never told me what you do."

"That's true."

"Man of mystery?"

"Man of mundanity, more like." I prepared for her groan. "I'm a writer."

No groan, no yawn, but full Enid Coleslaw.

"My. How LA of you."

"It's a living. You're a bartender."

"Bartender is a living. I'm guessing you're not paying the bills as a struggling screenwriter." She wasn't a cruel person. She was just calling it like she saw it.

"I never said struggling, and I never said screenwriter."

"It's implied."

"That it is. But I have paid…some bills."

Which was true. I optioned *Mermaid Squad* about two years ago, going rate for a pilot, and though that project went into turnaround and…not much had happened since, I did still feel light as air when I thought about it. And I had made real, substantial payments on certain monthly necessities.

"You seem hesitant, kid. You want some time to think about it?"

"Making ends meet, you want to know."

"I guess." She shrugged, then went back to the menu. "You're right. I bet whatever you do is boring anyway."

"I said mundane. Not boring."

"What's the difference?"

"I'm a detective."

"No, you're not."

"Well, I am. I'm not claiming to be Philip Marlowe or Harry D'Amour. But I do *do* film investigation services for The Angeleno Film Archive."

"Lol. Wut?"

"My title is archivist, but I'm basically a private investigator. Along with standard research for the programming, I track down rare prints."

"You search for lost movies?"

"Sometimes."

They weren't typically lost, just hard to find, and the people who had them had to be contacted and negotiated with, or I'd have to drive out to Santa Monica or Chino or the Victorville Film Archive to secure a copy of whatever.

There was one big mystery once. A real detective story. A cursed film! Only the curse wasn't real, but the heartbreak was, so enough of that.

"Well Trent," she said in a very calm *almost* patronizing voice, "It sounds to me like you're essentially just a researcher slash errand boy, and you call yourself a private investigator because you think it sounds cool."

"Yes. Even so."

(I like the Judge Holden response. It was a way to defer without surrendering.)

"Am I right?" she persisted.

I raised my hands, mea culpa.

"You have me."

"Well," she raised an eyebrow as she went back to study the menu, "not yet."

Am I sounding like a broken record when I say that everything she did was suggestive? But suggesting what?

And I mean that. In questioning the futile principle of evolution, wherein the entire point of living was being slightly better than the previous generation, so that you could pass your slightly better DNA onto the next slightly better generation and so and ad infinitum, GK Chesterton said that if you keep working on making a better hammer, you eventually question what that tool is for.

So, what was Lilith getting at, and what was I? Where were we going?

Sex?

Well...

The movie was fine by the way. Maybe that's not generous enough. Certainly, it was a spectacular achievement on a technical scale. The production design was magnificent. I'm sure thousands in the extended crew were proud of their incredible handiwork, as well they should be. And the performances were pretty good. I especially liked Ewan McGregor as Lumiere.

I don't know though. Shrug. Whole thing was not my cup of sentient teacup. Maybe it's because I could never get behind the moral of the story, such as it is. A snooty nobleman is mean to a beggar, so she dehumanizes his entire staff, children included? How is she NOT the villain?

And then, of course, Disney being what it is, I have my issues with*SPOILERS*

The Death of Gaston. The movie's moral view is how I'd put it.

Or maybe not. Maybe that is too harsh of a characterization. Perhaps I'm being harsh in declaring it to be the movie's moral view. But I feel that thing that happened presented in a positive/neutral light and actions taken by "the good guys" could be characterized as an endorsement.

For starters, I don't think that a bit of rudeness/lack of charity justifies turning a man into a beast and his servants into furniture. The Beast learns a valuable lesson through this experience, and the Witch never receives anything like a comeuppance, so I feel like the movie approves.

But what really has always rubbed me the wrong way is the death of Gaston. Maybe this isn't morality so much as what I've always found to be a cheap Disney storytelling cheat-which is the "kill off the villain while keeping the hero's hands clean" cheat. It's especially egregious in this case because we all just saw what a noble, merciful guy the Beast is when he spared Gaston. I think if the movie wants to celebrate that mercy, as it should, it has to let Gaston live.

Or contrarywise, Gaston is the real beast, a villain willing to burn down the castle and destroy anyone who gets in the way of his ego and desires. If he's attacking the Beast and the Beast kills him in self-defense, that's fine. Legally justifiable and morally acceptable. But own it.

But this way, showing the valor of the hero in not killing the villain, only to have the villain immediately die, it just feels like a cop-out. Having their cake and eating it too. I think it would be immensely more interesting if the mercy meant something, and Gaston got to live, exposed as the rogue he is. Or if in the heat of the moment, coming at him with a knife, yeah, The Beast kills him, justifiable so.

I know your works; I know that you are neither cold nor hot...So, because you are lukewarm, I will spit you out of my mouth.

Think about it Disney.

Oh, right, that gay stuff. Surprise, surprise, there was no gay sex in this Disney movie. Or any sex. Or any gayness, really. Le Fou and Gaston's relationship was pretty much what it was in the cartoon-until the third act. There were two moments that may have indicated this incarnation of an ancillary antagonist nobody really cared about until he was gay, and one to indicate he was not:

1. During the "Nobody *blanks* like Gaston" song, everybody is singing and dancing and rollicking, as they always were. In the heat of the partying moment, Le Fou jumps into Gaston's lap. This gets a disapproving stare, and Le Fou immediately backs up, asking "Too much"? Gaston agrees, yes, that was too much, and the celebratory ego-feeding song continues. (*What does this have to do with snakes and cages and The King of Wax?! Why are you wasting our mystery's time with Beauty and the Beast?!*). This would really be a throwaway moment if Disney hadn't made such a big deal over it months in advance. It'd be like "Silly, he's jumping all over the guy". Or at least, that'd what you could tell your kids.

2. At the very end, after Gaston has been defeated (Le Fou has become a good guy by this point), there's a big celebration at the castle, and everyone's dancing. Le Fou's dancing. With a woman. Then everybody changes partners, and suddenly a guy comes up and dances with Le Fou. Le Fou is shocked, eyes wide. No dialogue or development after it, and he certainly wasn't the one to initiate. Ducky had better chemistry with Kristy Swanson in *Pretty in Pink*, as long as we're on last-minute love interests.

Yeah, not completely convincing, but Disney is dipping its toe into the gay waters of diversity, so you wouldn't expect them to jump right in. Also, they included a bit to counterbalance:

1.   At one point, Gaston, in one of his nicer moments, expresses genuine warmth towards Le Fou, and wonders earnestly why some woman hasn't snatched him up yet. Le Fou says "I've been told that I'm clingy...but I don't see it."

Don't worry, we're going to stop talking about the sexuality of Le Fou soon enough, but just consider that. The only actual dialogue about the character's romantic orientation, and it's heterosexual. Of course, there's the closet and all that, but I dunno, he didn't sound like he knew he had a secret.

But maybe people with real secrets never do. I mean the secrets we keep from ourselves, something hidden, perhaps because it's frightening, or absurd, or any other reason it is unthinkable and must be hidden away. I wondered if I had any secrets like that. I liked to think I was an open book to myself, and I was an avid reader, but who knows. We tend to surprise ourselves.

"Some spectacle, huh?" Lilith was beaming, gleaming, as we exited the theater.

"Sure, very impressive."

"Yeah, you were impressed?"

"With the production design? Absolutely. They really brought the 17th Century French setting to life, and the special effects- I think they might have used motion capture for turning the servants into candles and all that."

"How about the LOVE STORY?" she teased, putting on a childish lovey-dovey voice.

"Sure. It was sweet. If you're into the Stockholm Syndrome."

"Ouch. But accurate."

"I call it like I see it."

"And you see a lot."

"More than my share, yes."

"And what is that? Or do you not share that, either?"

"Oh, I share, alright. In certain circumstances."

"What might those be?"

"Who wants to know?"

"Inquiring minds."

"They inquire a lot, don't they?"

"Yes, they do." She was smirking at our rapport. "Anyway Trent," she shrugged as she put her hands in her pockets. "I never thought of you as much of a romantic anyway."

"Which implies you've thought of me."

"Maybe," she was half-smiling, coyly.

Oh, I could weave her stories of crushes half-realized and unrequited love. Tell her the tale of the cobra woman and see if she didn't run away.

But no. Movie references aside, let each thing be its own, and that goes always for love stories.

"I was wondering," she said suddenly, "where are you from?"

So we're at that question.

"I'm from, here. I live in Glendale."

"I mean originally."

It's my accent. I moved around a lot as a child (Marine brat) and as such have developed a distinctive accent. I don't know why exactly or what. Some people say it sounds British, some people say New Jersey. Some say Australia, which is where Guy Pearce and Hugo Weaving are from.

I often get the question "Where are you from?", and in many contexts in regular conversations with people I've just met, where we're not talking about my background, I interpret this question to be code for "What's with your accent?"

I recently posted a video to Facebook asking my friends their opinions. I got two responses which were monumentally disappointing. One guy said I have an excess of skin under my tongue which made me sound different. He may have even mentioned the official medical definition. I was quite annoyed, as that is nowhere near as fun an explanation. Plus, the kid's Romanian and his brother laughs like Amadeus, so maybe he was just making that up because he wanted a monopoly on cool accents. I'd say the same thing about my former au pair, who is Swedish, who also responded with some stupid medical baloney. Neither are a doctor, and I hate their explanations, so I choose to ignore them completely.

I don't really know what to say, because no truthful answer to the first can satisfactorily answer the second. I grew up mostly in Virginia, but it's definitely not a Southern accent. Sometimes I just say I'm Irish, which is ethnically accurate but deliberately misleading. Lately, I've been outright lying and saying I'm Australian. I guess it depends what mood you catch me in.

Lilith caught me in an honest mood.

"I'm not *from* anywhere," I answered, apologetic. "I'm just American suburban white kid."

"There's more than one kind of white," she scoffed. "See what happens when you try to call me Honduran."

"I'm sure I could spit in a tube and mail it to The Illuminati, but I don't think you're asking about which European king which ancestor lived under."

"You're American."

"Raised in Virginia, went to school in Vermont."

"So why come you talk like that?"

"That's just my Rhotacism. Comes from ankyloglossia with unusually thick lingual frenulum, so it's figured."

"I have no idea what any of that means."

"Trouble with R's, that's all." I'm looking away from her now, down at my feet as we walk away from the theater. I want to get past this banality, never as interesting as it could be, "Just a little extra skin. I figure that's also why I eat so fast and kiss so bad." I chuckle self-effacingly, though I immediately regretted making a joke about kissing this early. Too late to not finish, though. "Too much tongue."

"Is that a real thing?"

It worked though. She smirked flirtatiously.

"Apparently. I mean, I didn't make it up. Ankyloglossia is-"

"No, dummy." She playfully punched my arm and left her hand there. Her hand squeezed with a meaningful pressure. Her eyes, usually so fearless, did not meet mine. Perhaps she knew my heart is racing as I anticipated what's next. "I meant is it possible to kiss with too much tongue?"

Not with Lilith.

Chapter 11: When You Have a Hammer...

...Everything looks like a nail.

So goes the old aphorism. It means exactly what it says. Metaphors are always are on the nose. Hammer on the nail, as it were (there I go). I was wondering if it applied to our current situation. When you have a hankering for a mystery, as I did with my detective stories and affectations for noir and Mike's Alex Jonesian paranoia did, you find one.

This was all reactionary, of course. The reason I was afraid to go nuts on this case, really surrender myself to the joy of being caught up in something fantastical and real was fear. Not fear of monsters or murderers or that erstwhile King of Wax. I was still entertaining the delusion that that would be cool. But I was trying to restrain it. Because right now, the real fear was disappointment. The real fear was that I was nearly 30 years old and wasting my time. Far too old to be chasing ghosts and goblins.

But there *was* something here, wasn't there? There was that cat, and that eyeball, and the mysterious bottle of Pin's Brew. Strange, eerie things were afoot, and though the decisions Mike made sometimes puzzled, sometimes infuriated me (Why leave Deakins Porthouse so easily?!), I couldn't deny some connection or at least some common theme that dared to be unveiled.

Well, I was all-in this time. And I wouldn't let Mike's Ding-Dong-Dash style of detective work sway me from finding what answers were there to be found. We both had curiosity, certainly, but perhaps I would have to have the discipline Mike didn't and hold a certain psychiatrist's feet to the fire. Demand he tell us why Schrodinger's ghoul was under his books while his club/bar had that mysterious and ever-changing drink.

He'd probably think we were nuts.

But then again, that's kinda what he does right? Someone's gotta be prescribing those expensive anti-psychotics, filling up those billable hours, and in extreme cases, justifying those institutions. A couple guys like us come in with a crazy story like that, he'd be thrilled.

Hammer, meet nail.

•   •   •   •   •

"I used to work over there." I glanced down the street at Warner Brothers Studio. It was true. Fleshscraper Productions, my alma mater as it were; my former unpaid employer was just a hop, skip, and a leap down memory lane away. I resented that internship at the time, while simultaneously cherishing it, but now, as with so many things, all I felt was nostalgia.

"Yeah, you told me," Mike grunted. We were in Burbank (duh), eating a belated brunch at Bob's Big Boy, which is a great restaurant, Austin Powers references aside. "You like that job?" He took a big soggy bite out of his au jus French dip. Never been a fan.

"It was alright, I guess. I didn't dig the salary, but I met some cool people, and it was a great experience."

"Your boss makes you blow him?"

"Classy."

"I call it like I see it. Don't tell me your Holly-WEIRD ain't full freaks and degenerates."

"I mean..."

"Trent."

"Well...No. No. First of all, no. Of course not. Nobody ever asked us to perform sexual favors. They were more respectful."

"Or maybe you just weren't their flavor."

I took a pointed sip of my chocolate malt. He continued.

"'Cause the way I hear it, a lot of those big shots are big-time pedos."

"Where do you hear that?"

"Corey Feldman was talking about it."

"Yeah. Okay. Of course. I'm not denying it-I never denied it. It's a problem. I just-at Fleshscraper, I didn't see any of that."

"Not even the casting couch?"

"Nope."

"Yeah, but I figure you'd say that." He smugly dipped a french fry into his brown broth. "A conspiracy of silence has many players, from the willfully blind to the blissfully ignorant."

"That's very easy to say, Mike. Very nice. But it seems to be based more on stereotypes, broad generalizations-just this simplistic garbage you hear one place and recycle out another. I have no time for it."

"Suit yourself."

"We have a plan of attack?" I asked, shifting gears. He wasn't too invested in the Hollywood Sex Scandal, so he had no problem moving on.

"Way I see it, you want an answer, you ask a question."

"No kidding. But who do we ask?"

"Dr. Victor-"

"I mean, obviously that's who we go talk to, but how? This is a private club."

"So, it is."

"I looked it up, Mike. It's not like The Magic Castle, where a guest can sponsor your visit-and we don't have a guest-I mean it is a *private* place. Shrinks only. Airtight."

"So, let's be shrinks."

I snorted.

"What, you got a lab coat in your bag of tricks? Can I be Dr. Nathaniel Essex? Can we play pirates next?"

Mike looked at me, shaking his head with a dismissive, patronizing manner.

"Oh, Trent of little faith."

"Fine, Mike." I was grumpy, but I still had an ace up my sleeve I was going to drop later today. "You win again. What is it? What's your angle?"

"Nothing to it, my friend. I just contacted the board, expressing my interest as a prospective psychology student."

"And?"

"My academic street cred opens doors."

"Right. *Professor*."

"He says with a bit of attitude."

"I'm just saying, Mike, I wouldn't stake much on your academic reputation."

"You're in a bitchy mood today."

Yeah, I could hardly believe I went there. But there I was.

"I'm just saying, look who's talking? You lecture me about these supposed indiscretions going on behind studio doors, but what about you, Mike? You tell me about the casting couch? How about the grading couch?"

Mike put his fork down. He furrowed his brow, wiped his chin. For a moment, I thought he was going to stand up and storm out. I thought he was going to hit me. I could see the cloud of fury cast over his visage.

Then pass. Mike shrugged like I had a good point or at least a good point in theory.

"That was different," he said simply. "Jean and I were amorously entangled in an intrigue the ruling faculty deemed inappropriate. Their penalty was a miscalculation based on a fundamental failure to understand the situation or a willingness to try. Our relations were mutually beneficial, but not mercenary. There was no exchange of favors for favoritism, coitus for credit."

"But you said it was mutually beneficial."

"Such is pleasure."

"Gross."

"I don't know what your sex life's like. Maybe it's not a mutual thing."

"But it's still inappropriate." Back to him, and now I as a prosecutor. "There's that power thing-a dynamic. It's not right."

"The institutions of power vis a vis a nonconsensual dynamic are mere artifice. Illusions cast by toxic feminism too cynical to appreciate the primal simplicity of the carnal act. From caveman to Casanova-the historic Casanova, mind-a guy could stick his dick in any welcome hole."

"Charming."

"And the holes were welcome. Two consenting adults, three, four, on the side of the highway, in a city bus. Wherever. Take your pleasure from any orifice. The only people who have a problem with it are the ones ain't getting laid themselves. Father Abstinence. Dr. Sigmund Freud. Ms. Feminist. Fornication is a sin, you love your mother, all sex is rape, priests, shrinks, or bull dykes, it's all the same. They deny their own pleasures, and don't want the rest of us to have any fun either."

"Regardless, what if they do a background check? And find said less-than-savory entanglement? I mean, the way it's reflected on your record, I'm sorry to tell you Mike, all the nuances of your mutually mature, uh, 'amorous intrigue' won't show up. Neither will your lovely history lesson. It's just gonna be a professor boffing his student. Which is frowned upon," I added, because I have a conscience, "as it should be."

"They won't do any background check," he scoffed dismissively at the idea. "It's a casual, informal meeting. And you really think these psychologists are so high and mighty? You think they don't have secrets of their own on the couch? A patient got a little too close? That never happens?"

"That's not the point."

(This was months before the Weinstein scandal broke, by the way. I wish I had something insightful or comforting to say about that, but I don't.)

"Anyway, these armchair emeriti are all too happy to lend an ear, help a bright young philosopher shift his focus to matters of the mind. Practically made their week, they're so glad for the attention. It's not brain surgery."

"Ba da bum."

"G-d damn," Mike said, not quietly, as we made our egress and he held the door open for two sunny buxom blondes entering. "Jim Morrison was right."

"How's that?" I asked when we were outside.

"LA Women, my friend," he grinned suggestively.

"Beach Boys too," I agreed. "Californian Girls."

"The women of Los Angeles," Mike began, as he stared into the restaurant at the girls taking their seats. "Are full of their own shit. They know they're hot. Walking along Hollywood Boulevard with their necks out. Fucking you with their eyes, with all that metal shit in their nose, their belly button, their clits. All that stupid ink." I took exception at that. "Then it starts to show."

"What?" I didn't like his tone. It was aggressively misogynistic in a pontificating way. "What shows?"

"The life of a whore." I had been fixated on his words, I hadn't noticed he had started to smoke. "It brings sores on their lips and AIDS till their hair falls off."

"Gross."

"When that happens," he continued. "Their snatch loses its finery. All those tongue studs and kitty rings fall off, their ink fades, and a trophy bimbo who's not good for anything but looking good, what does she lose? The bangles and headbands and magic crystal necklaces, the opal earrings and puka shell bracelets. The Victoria Secret thongs and Kardashian perfume and little toy Chihuahuas. All gone. They can't ride in a Ferrari when there's no guy to blow."

"Mike. Stop."

He didn't. He was on a rant.

"They used to smell like lavender and dreams, now they stink like blue waffles and regret. Hair used to glitter, now it's dry and flaky, shampooed with dishwasher soap. They were beautiful. Now they're branded. Used to dress in designer silk, now they're fighting over used sweatpants at the Salvation Army. Their studs are gone." He shook his head in disdain at these hypothetical dudes. "Fell on their own dicks. 'Warriors in battle', right? The hills of Hollywood gonna lament and mourn; destitute. They'll just have to sit on the ground." He pointed at me, urging me to take notice. "And on that day, six, seven whores will go up to one guy. Some poor rich nerd they didn't even spit at before. They'll say 'I'll suck your dick, I'll eat your ass. Just, please. Save me from my own fuck-up.'"

"Mike," I wasn't sure how to start to rebuke him, so I used a term I wasn't sure he would even understand, "you sound like a Nice Guy."

• • • • •

The Pick and Hammer was a large white building in a particularly sunny part of Burbank. Green grass galore. This was Tim Burton country, for sure.

"Hey Mike," I said off-handedly as we got out of his car. "There's something I remembered-I mean I neglected to tell you."

He stared at me cock-eyed, not losing a step in his gait as we walked across the smooth, clean sidewalk to the entrance. It was kinda cool, kinda unnerving, kinda irritating.

"Yes? And what might that be?"

"Well-and it's probably nothing, mind-but coincidentally it turns out that another gentleman showed up at one of the bars - La Cuevita, in fact - and actually asked for Pin's Brew by name."

Mike stopped in front of the door to the establishment, so close, yet so sealed off, and tried to think about that.

"Well...hmm." He was thrown for a loop, which I was secretly enjoying. Also, it was clear he was trying to play it off as inconsequential, which he wasn't very good at. "Pin's Brew. That's no big thing, is it?"

"No big thing-Mike, that is THE thing!"

"Well, how'd you find out about this?"

"I went back to La Cuevita, started talking to the bartender about that drink, and she mentioned that some guy showed up-perhaps the very day after us-specifically asking about that drink!"

Mike rested his head against the door. This was not part of his plan. I should have been a friend and sympathized with his agony, but I was relishing this. Sick, right?

"And at no point did you think this was worth mentioning to me?"

"No. I did think it was worth mentioning to you. That's why I mentioned it to you."

"You know what I mean."

"Look Mike, the point isn't at what point I told you about this. The point is that..." (What?) "Well, someone is in the know about Pin's Brew."

He stewed on that for a good long while. He was uneasy but unsure about how to proceed.

"Well that doesn't mean nothing necessarily, does it? It is a drink. We saw the brewery for crying out loud. It's just a..."

"Coincidence, Mike? For serious, you're trying to sell me on a coincidence? You've been throwing all these conspiracy theories at me and-"

"Alright, alright, dammit! So, who was the guy?"

I shrugged.

"Truman Capote meets The Undertaker."

Mike stared at me blankly.

"I have no idea what that means."

"Me neither. But he said that Pin's Brew- which they didn't have, by the way, at least not by name-he said it tasted like Elderberry, jade, and *sadness*."

Mike spit on the ground.

"Sadness? Pretentious douche, ain't he?"

"If that's your target, sure." I did think that attacking this figure's style was a tiresome gambit and hardly the most pertinent point, but we were already at the destination of our next query.

"Well Pin's Brew is not unheard of..." he trailed on unconvincingly. "There's no inherent connection necessarily..." A big sigh. "We're here. Let's get to it."

I nodded. I did my bit. Now Mike had the reins, as always.

•   •   •   •   •   •   •

At the front, a nice-looking young man with slicked-back hair and epaulets asked us for our credentials. Mike explained that we were guests of one of the club's esteemed members.

"Dr. Eugenia Price," Mike said confidently. "She'll be expecting me."

The host (I guess) looked at his book. "Expecting *you*, yes. Mike Kripke. One guest." I swallowed and felt that tingle in my nose. This may be awkward. "I'm not seeing two- I don't see a plus one, is the only thing."

I looked down, too ashamed to even meet this nice guy's eyes. What was I even doing here?

The Host closed his book and smiled broadly. "But I'm sure it's alright. Go right in!"

"Much appreciated." Mike would have tipped his hat if he wore one.

"Thanks," I mumbled as I past, feeling exceptionally small.

The club was fairly low-key. It was like a classy hotel lobby, with a lounge and library. All about, at the bar, in the chair, walking through the hall were...I guess they were probably psychologists. No lab coats, certainly, but then you'd expect that. Nor were there raving mental patients. Unless the inmates were running the asylum.

"Nice place," I muttered to Mike, my spirits lifting now that we were in.

"Yes sir. Now the perfunctory matters, then the real deal."

"Perfunctory?"

My question was answered not by Mike, but a physical embodiment of what was perfunctory.

"Professor Michael Kripke!" A genial woman, well-dressed in a conservative pantsuit, was strolling towards us from across the study (it was a room filled with Ottomans, and I'm not talking about the Turks). She was about mid-fifties with a calm demeanor and a pleasant smile. She reminded me of Dr. Quinn, Medicine Woman.

"Or do you prefer Lieutenant?" she asked as Mike shook her hand and turned on the charm.

"Mike, please, Dr. Price. We're all students in the same school of thought."

"School of thought." She couldn't contain her smile. "I like that. And it's Gina, of course."

"Of course, it is," he said with a grin.

She giggled. Mike nudged me.

"This here is Trent Malloy."

"Hi." Mike was between us, and "Gina" was not making a move towards me, so I didn't go for a handshake. I just raised my palm weakly.

"Oh hello!" She was so warm. "Are you a former student of Mike's?"

Mike sniggered. I was offended at the very concept, yet I didn't know who else I could be in these circumstances in this place. "No. I'm..." Help me out Mike, please. "Well, I'm with Mike."

Mike looked at me sharply, as if disappointed I couldn't come up with a better lie to more legitimately ensconce myself.

It didn't matter. Gina brightened.

"The more, the merrier! But I'm afraid I can't invite you to my office while Mike and I discuss his proposal. Feel free to explore the grounds. We have a very exclusive library. Some first edition Freuds."

"Any Jung?" I perked up. I always preferred Jung.

"Of course!"

Mike slapped me on the back, a little too hard to be affable. "Trent, dear, go have a drink or several. This won't take long."

"It was nice to meet you." Gina nodded.

"Yes, I – you too." But they were already off, leaving me standing in the middle of a richly carpeted room, trying to gather my bearings. Again, what was I doing here? I was no psychiatrist or potential psychiatrist. I was no detective. I felt like a fraud.

Which I was.

I wandered into the library, which smelt of many leather-bound books. I've always loved the smell of books. Library books especially. And thank God, there was nary a wailing cat in these premises.

"Can I help you?" The Librarian, an orange-haired gentleman in his late 30s, sat behind the podium.

"Just browsing."

"Well, you have to be a member to check items out."

"Understandable." I bowed slightly and started to exit, but he piped up. "Sir."

"Ah?"

"You're free to browse. You can even take one book out- so long as it's on the premises. Read it in the garden if you like, or the restaurant."

"In that case, Got Jung?"

He did, and after perusing some first and second editions, I choose *Mysterium Coniunctionis: An Inquiry into the Separation and Synthesis of Psychic Opposites in Alchemy*, a late work filled with some of that mystic pseudo-scientific jumbo I'm into. I didn't understand the title, let alone the text, but I felt smart reading it, and perhaps it connected to the occult arena we were circling.

I wandered over to the bar, which, if you'll remember, was our original destination after all. It looked well-stocked, with plenty of vintage liquor, but I was nervous about ordering alcohol at a den of psychiatrists. Wouldn't they judge me?

"Can I have a ginger ale?"

Sue (for so she was), the short-haired bartender in a ridiculous red vest, shook her head. "We have Sprite."

I frowned, but only for an instant. I didn't want to be a bad sport, but that did annoy me. If I had asked for 7UP, sure Sprite would be an acceptable alternative, the Pepsi to its Coke, the Pibb to its Pepper,

The Pin's to its Pimm's?!

Ooh, right. Priorities. But how to ask?

"Yes, that's fine."

Out with the hose gun, that most appealing of dispensers.

"Not a giant drinker, I discern." It was a golden-throated voice with a thick Western European accent. Dutch or Belgian, I'd wager. I turned.

He sat at the other end of the bar. Wispy blonde hair and a craggy countenance. *At 50, everyone has the face he deserves.* So said George Orwell. I wondered about my new friend, what sins he had committed to earn that discrepancy, angel hair and rocky visage.

"To be honest," I raised my lemon-lime glass and let the self-effacement begin, "I was worried about how I would be perceived, you know, drinking in a place like this."

He chuckled affably. "A bar, you mean."

"*This* bar. At this place. You know surrounded by..."

"Shrinks." He licked his lips. "Don't want to be diagnosed as a morbid drunk, I understand."

"Exactly."

"It's a Catch-22, of course. Because if you come to this bar and don't drink, you must be a lunatic."

I liked our rapport already. And he was a Rutger Hauer type, which was cool.

"And here I thought tee-totaling was the correct option."

"No son, teetotaling went out with phrenology." He stood up and crossed over to sit beside me. "In fact, this establishment prides itself on several unique cocktails." He tapped the lacquered surface of the bar. "The Frontal Lobotomy is especially...effective."

"That can't be in good taste."

A wry half-smile. "Nothing that tastes good ever is. If that's not to your liking, try a shot of Shock Treatment."

"Sick!"

"That's the idea."

"Well then perhaps my initial instinct about the name of this...place wasn't so far off."

"I'm sure it wasn't." His voice was loaded like he was amused but challenging. I elaborated.

"See, I had thought that your bar-and this is a bar-"

"Astute."

"That it was operating in the British pub tradition. The Blank and Blank.

The Nag and Weasel. The Fox and Hunter. The Whathave and You."

"And it is."

"Yes, The Pick and Hammer. So it is that, but what is it? Precisely, what are The Pick and Hammer referring to, besides simply fulfilling the role of the titular necessity?"

"You figured it out, I wager."

"It's not hard, but it is perverse."

"Always," he agreed.

"Your club, you glibly, flippantly, *in the title*, are referring to, to barbaric methods. Ice pick through the eye-I guess that treated schizophrenics?"

"And homosexuals, yes," he added, "back in the day", almost as an afterthought.

"So, isn't that outrageous? Doesn't that piss people off?"

"Sir," he drew it out and narrowed his eyes tiredly while crinkling his smile. "Who cares?"

I had to give him that. I wasn't that sensitive about it. I was just worried about how it would be perceived. But really, it wasn't my problem.

Nor was it a problem, actually. So I should probably just shut up. Nobody was even claiming offense over that crack about homosexuals (which, to be fair, was more of a fact than a slight), so I guess we were all good.

"What's this you're reading?" he leaned over my shoulder to take a look.

"Jung. I was just...browsing. He arouses my curiosity."

"Jung, yes, of course." He nodded. "One of the great psycho-mystics of the 20th century, not yet entirely debunked."

"Yet?"

"There's always time, my boy. But I think Jung's got a few decades left. His...mythology does so draw the interest of minds such as yours."

"I must admit, as fascinating as I find it, I don't understand much."

"That's not a paradox at all. Curiosity, in fact, is bred by confusion."

"But what does that lead to?" I implored. "What does that mean? What does *this*" and I picked up the book. "Symbolize? Alchemy?"

"Symbolize. Yes. That's good. That's exactly right. It isn't *is*. It is something else. A symbol. A stand-in. An allegory in the Platonic sense. Jung saw what many men forget. Many men in my field, yes." He took a pensive sip of the brown liquid in his tumbler. Some refined brandy, no doubt. "The doctor appreciated the value of archetypes. Why throw out the arcane figures and reoccurrences that have been with man since time immemorial? If we crawl into the abyss, we find the beast."

"The beast?"

"The beast, yes. And if we prod the sleeping beast..."

"Dangerous."

"All discovery is. We prod the beast, and find, in these ancient ghosts and bogeys, that what once was fearsome and monstrous-the ghoul in the graveyard, the specter in the shadows, is at once natural and familiar. And therein is the value."

"Because..." I begin slowly, attempting to appear thoughtful rather than out of my element. Because I didn't know what I was talking about. "One can utilize what we learn once the monsters are brought into light."

"Yes." He pursed his lips. "That's what we must do. Because those monsters are far more familiar than one might wish. And if they are not friend, they must be fiend, and one dreads to imagine."

"The ubiquity of evil." I stared into my drink solemnly.

"'Evil'" he repeated and chuckled dismissively. "Tell me, are you familiar with The Erl-King?"

A chill went down my spine. Why that old tale?

"I am. I heard it in grade school." I didn't like to think about it, but there we were. "Sixth grade." Same week as the colonial incident, in fact. I prayed that was a coincidence. "A father and son are riding through some dark old German wood.

"Yes. They were."

"The son, he's afraid."

"Of?"

"He's not sure. It's a creeping feeling. He knows something's wrong. Something's watching. Something-someone is hunting him."

"Go on." His voice was calm. Cold. Clinical. Urging me to continue, though I wanted to stop.

"He tells his father he's scared. His father reassures him. There's nothing wrong. The son pleads. The father rides faster. And then...it goes on. Faster and faster. The horse rides. The wind blows. The boy screams. The father can't ride away. He can't escape The Erl-King. And even..." I closed my eyes. This story made me so sad as a kid. "Even when they're out of the woods..."

His piercing blue eyes had a terrible knowingness. He spoke with a loftiness that conveys the operatic nature of the Goethe he quoted.

"Dear father, oh father, he seizes my arm! The Erl-King, father, has done me harm!"

I tried not to shudder. It's not that I'm scared. Duh, Erl-King's aren't real.

I'm not frightened, or even disturbed, really. Like I said, I was saddened.

"The ride is over. The boy is dead."

He sat back.

"And what do we glean from that?"

"I don't know," I said resignedly. "What was it all for? Is it just that he should have listened?" I felt a pain in my stomach, an aching sympathy for the boy. "Parents never listen. Not about monsters."

He cocked his head as if he hadn't considered that angle.

"Ah, but what is the monster?"

"The monster. It's-" The question confused and perturbed me. "It's the Erl-King. That's what he is. I guess he's the Elf-King, king of elves, that is, or like a ghost or a goblin? He's his own thing."

"Symbolism." His words were loaded. "Is it not possible he is the father himself?"

"No!" That was louder than I intended.

"Very well. We shan't dwell there. But there are others it could be or could be it. Jung himself came to The Erl-King by way of Jack Frost."

"Jack Frost?" I repeated, incredulously.

"*Jack Frost nipping at your nose!*" The words sounded uncanny in his Belgian inflection. "Of course, the child-snatcher is also Jack Frost."

I didn't give him the satisfaction of the disturbing realization that came to me just then, yet another one of my precious movie references. That Jack Frost was *also* the Father. Just ask Michael Keaton. Good grief! The father who dies and returns to his son as the living snowman. Supposed to be heartwarming, but actually a little creepy.

Around the same time, there was another movie called *Jack Frost*. Another man dies and returns as a snowman. Only this time he's a serial killer. My uncle had the videotape, and when we visited, I would take it off the shelf and look at the box with unease and fascination. It smelled weird. There was a picture on the back, both enchanting and repelling, of a young naked Shannon Elizabeth being attacked by the snowman in the shower. In future years, out of lust for Shannon rather than any disturbing draw of the snowman, I would come across screen-caps of that scene online. How to reconcile the prurient arousal her naked body elicited with the ridiculous and horrifying fate she encounters? When I actually watched the clip, it appears (though the YouTube comments were not in complete agreement) that Jack Frost, that foul, demented snow monster, is actually *raping* the character. There was some mild disagreement about whether it was violent assault or actual sexual violation.

How, after all, could a snowman rape? But the thrusting motions of his frosty pelvis onto the poor naked woman, and the suddenly southward placement of his erstwhile nose, his phallic carrot...

And it saddened me. Again, I was not scared. Snowmen never frightened me, even psychotic killers cosmically reincarnated in snowy form. It was too ridiculous. But it was because it was ridiculous that it was sad. What a grotesque fate, and who could take it seriously? She was still raped. Still murdered. Still violated by a preposterous abomination, but you gotta figure that more than half the audience watching that goofy creature slam her with cheesy late 90's effects are going to be laughing or rolling their eyes. But that pitiful 22-year-old virgin who didn't even have the appetite for real porn would see how that scene ends, the lingering shot of her dead eyes, the blood dripping from her mouth, and feel more melancholy than arousal.

And then I remembered a *Goosebumps* book with a walking, talking snowman. *SPOILER*!

He claims to be the heroine's father! I think it may have been a ruse, but still, the connection is there.

So.

A man dies. Is transformed. Comes back as that snowman. That "Jack Frost". Father or killer? Which Jack Frost was more real?

"One surmises a contradiction," I said flatly, "for how can Jack Frost, the icy imp, be the horse-chasing king of the woods as well? They are two different figures."

"And yet did Jung not also say, 'Seek the coldness of the moon, and ye shall find the heat of the sun'?"

"Duality."

"Precisely, my boy. So Jack Frost may also be the father as he is the watcher in the woods, as he is the whisperer in the wind, and so much more. He may be an angel of ice and a demon king, burning..." He trailed off and chuckled, aware he was getting carried away. "Ah, but listen to me, waxing poetic. You're not really this interested in alchemy, are you?"

"Alchemy?"

He nodded. Most natural thing in the world.

"How one archetype is transubstantiated into another."

"I had always thought of alchemy in the medieval sense. You know, turning iron into gold."

"It's that too. Or straw into gold!" he raised his arm with shocking rapidity. He was signaling the bartender-ess. She put a shot glass on the table.

"Rumpelstiltskin." He chuckled. I could hear the liquid pour into his glass. "Who is also, of course…"

"The Erl-King," I finished for him wearily.

"You've got it," he raised the shot glass, red liqueur sloshing.

I looked into my pathetic Sprite. No, I had nothing to raise back.

"Father Devil becomes Erl-King, Jack Frost, Rumpelstiltskin. Alchemy. Straw into gold." He winked at me. "Pimm's into Pin's." And down went the green drink down his hatch.

"That's-that's…" I was speechless and incoherent. This wasn't fair. Life shouldn't work like this.

He stood up and slapped me on the back, hard, as if trying to make me cough up whatever it was I was choking on.

(The truth, perhaps, terrifying and inedible)

"You're an excitable sort, aren't you?" He leaned in, whispered in my ear, "what monsters are you fighting?"

I closed my eyes and shook my head repeatedly.

"Perhaps you come to my office," he mused casually, briefly slipping into the foreigner's diction, "I give you free consultation."

"A routine exorcism." I didn't open my eyes as I said this, but I heard his waning chuckle.

Maybe there was something funny about that. Maybe this was all just one big joke.

But not ha, ha funny.

When I opened my eyes, he was gone. I tried to see the bottle of Pin's, that blasted enigma, but there were so many bottles of liquor up there, and I didn't really want to find it anyway.

But I saw something else, which was quite noteworthy. Maybe Mike would approve, assuming he was still in the land of the living.

There it was, right on the bar.

Dr. Victor Thane
BOARD CERTIFIED PSYCHIATRIST
p: (310)123-4567   f: (310)123-4567
drthane@thanepsyd.com
10438 Santa Monica Blvd #3008, Los Angeles, CA 90025

Chapter 12: Heavenly Creatures

Third date being what it is and modern adults in a modern fallen world being who we are-that's a cop-out, of course. Can't blame society's loosening sexual morals for my own depravity. It didn't matter how mainstream or commonly acceptable said depravity is. Sin is sin. Even if one enjoys...

The joy of the thing called sin.

But I get ahead of myself.

•　　•　　•　　•　　•

Technically this would only be our second pre-arranged outing, the first since she left me in lingering ecstasy on Hollywood Blvd before she went for the train. Storm Trooper on one side, Goofy on another, I saw her off, descend into the sub-terrain. There was no guarantee of a follow-up, of course, (there never is), but I was hopeful. We got along more than well. That was a lot of tongue, at any rate.

But since it would be the fourth time we saw each other, and the second occasion was a second occasion (when I came to the bar for her, and she welcomed me), I'd be so forward in my Lloyd Dobler mental gymnastics to consider this that monumental event.

And now, as THE THIRD DATE approached, we all knew what that meant, cultural cliché well established, it seemed that the time to do the thing that adults do was coming, or a decision had to be made soon anyway. As usual, with the approach of sex, I was enchanted and repelled. Driven by my libido and tortured by my conscience. I really did like Lilith. She was fun. She was funny. She was clever, and we got along. Her wit was like a hot knife-by which I mean she had a biting rapport but a subtle wit. I'm sure she had to develop a tough skin working in that bar with all those weirdos perving on her. Weirdos like me. Yet she liked me-or seemed to anyway, which, let's be honest, was all the same to me.

And of course, I was immensely attracted to her. It was like high school lust, the kind you don't know how to properly contain yourself or behave in polite society. Jeepers Cripes was she sexy! And if that tension was there and not just in my lurid imagination, then something was probably going to be done sooner or later. Probably Lilith.

The fact that the middle of our date was to be at her house was also a good indication.

It happened like this. We were texting, something that had become routine over the past week or so, and the rapport was now written as well as spoken. Which was fine by me, given that I'm better with the pen (the keyboard or finger, as it were) than the tongue.

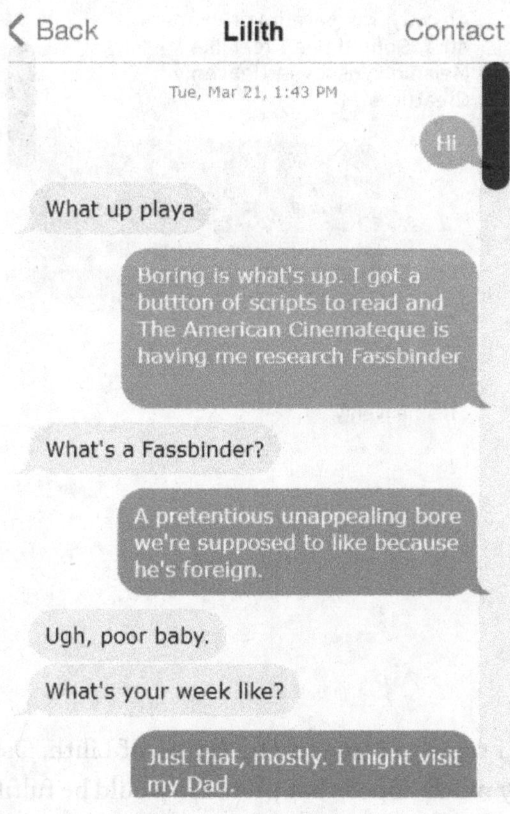

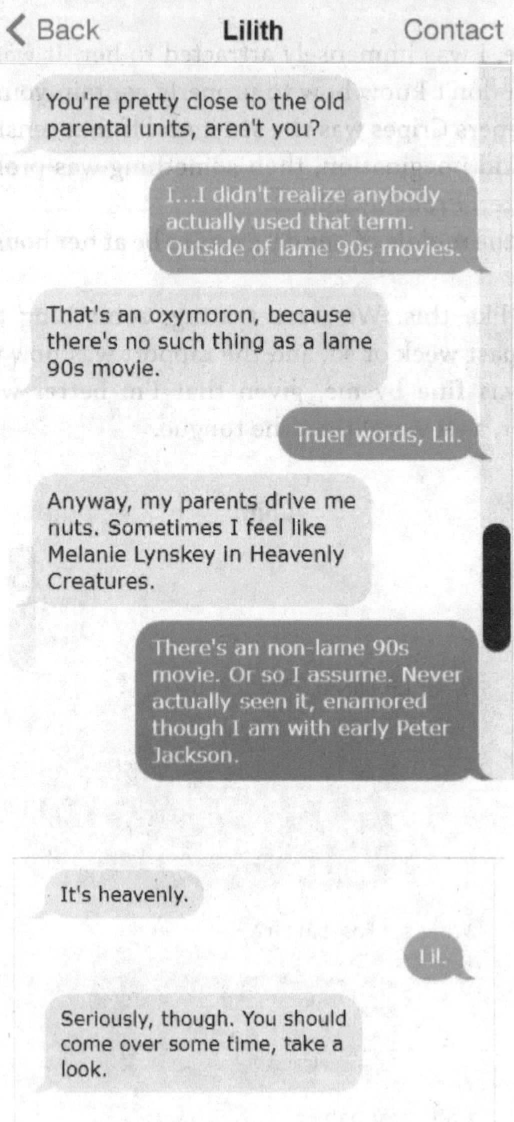

So that's how I came to come to The House of Lilith. Ostensibly to watch a movie, and I very much hoped that pretense would be fulfilled. But we knew it was a pretense. "Netflix and Chill" had become the millennials' answer "Would you like to come up? For coffee?" and I was coping with a response. Mostly internally.

Because when we met for Dr. Death's Suicide Pie (a particularly hot and rancid-in-an-oddly-appealing-way pizza), she suggested we take the night back to her place, I raised no objections.

• • • • •

We took her car, and I was getting into the passenger side-

"Just take all that off."

There were some crumbs, an uncharacteristic pink blouse, and a certain red hat that would prove quite revealing.

I placed the clothing in the back without comment, though perhaps I looked at it for a fraction too long, and she noticed.

"It's not ironic, by the way." She grabbed the cap from me and tossed it in the back.

"I didn't say anything."

She looked at me suspiciously.

"You're probably thinking how fucked up it is for a 'Mexican' to want to MAKE AMERICA GREAT AGAIN."

"I know you're not Honduran."

"My parents were Cuban. I'm American," She started the car. "And I mean it."

Wanting to avoid politics, I addressed the racial implications.

"You know people always get mad at white people for our lack of finesse. Like we're racist because we can't immediately tell a Colombian from a Nicaraguan, or a Japanese from a Korean. But there's a double standard there. I mean, just by looking at me, could you tell if I'm of Polish or French descent?"

She smiled and took one hand off the wheel.

"Nah," she said, tousling my hair. "You're Irish."

Lilith's house was an inglorious little cozy in Highland Park, no surprise there.

"You live alone?" I asked innocuously as she wrestled with a mess of keys like a jailer, trying to find access.

"Why? You looking for a place?"

"Just curious."

She finally found the right one and let us in. The living room was cluttered with boxes and video games.

"Curiosity killed the…CAT!" she started the sentence, alluring, locking me with her smoky, "F Me" eyes (sorry, it's accurate), but finished it with a shriek designed to bring out the feline, I suppose.

And here he was, a little black cat scurried out from under the couch, it seemed, and Lilith scooped her up into her arms.

Lilith was cooing and stroking the adorable kitty. It was odd and endearing to see in her this affection, removed of cynicism and affected adultivity.

Alas (?), it was not to last.

"Would you like to pet my pussy?"

"You can do better than that," I said, mock disappointed in her lack of subtlety as I reached out to pet.

The cat responded favorably, opening and closing its mouth in a darling meow and, to my surprise, Lilith dumped him into my arms.

I tried -and succeeded (barely)-at not dropping the cat as Lilith strolled further into her domicile. She threw me for a loop with that sudden gesture, but I caught it and kept my cool. Assuming, of course, I ever had any cool to speak of.

"What's its name?"

"Cat," her voice came from the kitchen.

"Yes, what's your cat's name?"

"It's Paula's cat." I heard the fridge open and hum.

"What's Paula's cat named?"

"Cat." She appeared in the kitchen doorway, holding two Coronas. "Its name is Cat."

"*Breakfast at Tiffany's* or that old joke via Lyman from *Garfield*?"

She slumped down on the couch and held one of the beers up. "Explain your references, son."

I sat down next to her, "Cat" still in hand, now in my lap, and took the beer.

"Well in *Breakfast at Tiffany's* Holly has a cat she doesn't name because…" What was it? The book and the movie may have had different reasons. "I don't know, she says it doesn't belong to her."

"That's right," Lilith purred, tousling Cat affectionately. "You don't belong to anyone."

"Lyman," I went on, "Jon Arbuckle's erstwhile roommate, said he used to have a cat, but didn't name it because why bother naming something that won't come when called?"

"Lame. That's a lame joke."

"I agree whole-heartedly," I concurred, "what's more, it's problematic for what it implies about the nature of names, of pets, of identity itself."

"What do you mean?"

"Well, it's like you only name something because of what it means to you? That the cat has no value of its own?"

"Hmm. Maybe it's saying that if the cat won't respond to that name, that if it won't even acknowledge it, then to what degree can it even be said to be its name?"

I thought on that.

"Nah, like you said, it's just a lame joke."

"Know any good ones?"

"Do I...Yes!" I thought, inspired. "I made one up."

"Okay."

"Now it's not very funny, but it IS a joke. It has all the parts required, set-up, twist, punchline."

"Well, now I have to hear it."

"300 rhinos walk into a bar," I began, with the anecdote that had annoyed my family ad infinitum, "The alpha male is feeling a bit queasy and excuses himself to use the facilities." I had perfected -or memorized through repetition-every beat, every cadence, every micro-expression of the performance. I told it the same way every time, and there were many, many times. Now I had a new listener, and she was listening. Perhaps cynical, perhaps indulgent. "The second in command orders 299 banana daiquiris."

"Math checks out," Lilith quipped.

"Indeed. The bartender takes a look and says, 'You know, you rhinos are the second oddest bunch I've seen in here all day.' The rhino says, 'Really, what's the oddest bunch?' Bartender says, 'Everyone who stayed in the bar when they saw 300 rhinos coming!'"

And I smiled sincerely like a little kid who just did a neat trick to please his folks.

And it worked. After a second, her cold demeanor cracked. She giggled silly.

"Stupid," she chuckled. "That's stupid." After a brief and gentle facepalm, her hand was on mine, and I relished it.

"Of course, it is, my dear. But it's mine. It's a joke, and I wrote it. I have it. That's mine now."

"Oh Trent. You're too much. Or not enough. I don't know."

She leaned back with a blasé shrug I found sexy. But then everything about her was.

"Why do they call you Lilith then?"

"Because I am Lilith."

For so she was. But my brain was conjuring demonic, Biblical imagery now, perhaps appropriate for the sinful thoughts she inspired, and I dared to press the issue.

"You mean it's your name, or you literally are?"

"I know what you're getting at. It's not funny, dude."

"Didn't mean it to be. It's an odd name though."

"I'm an odd girl."

"I'm learning."

"I'm teaching."

"I'll have to study an advanced course then."

"Anyway, you can ask my parents."

"Can I ask your parents?"

Her expression soured. Like, more than normal even.

"No. They're assholes."

"Ohhhhh kay. Sorry."

(I wasn't sure how to react to that. My folks were fine.)

"It's okay, dude. Whatever. You know, I'm on my own now. Like, completely." She glanced down at Cat briefly, as if expecting objection, but finding none, she went on. "And it's strange because when you're little...they're gods, right? Mommy and Daddy."

"'Mother is the word for God on the lips of every child,'" I quoted *The Crow*, and she didn't notice.

"Exactly. Exactly. And they can be good gods or evil. But they're your whole world. Then you grow up, and it's like, Jesus, is that all they are? I can do better than that."

"I think we all think that. It's like how nobody thinks they're a bad person. Or the Butler's Fallacy."

"The butler did it?"

"No, it's not *Clue*."

"There's no butler in *Clue*."

"Doubly irrelevant then. No, the Butler's Fallacy- or maybe just Butler's Fallacy, like Butler was the guy's name. Something like that. I read about it in *Nearer My God* by William F. Buckley. It's the idea that just about everybody has, whether they admit it or not, that if they were God, they would have made the world better than it is."

"I get that. I mean, it wouldn't be too hard. Look at this place."

She gestured around, ostensibly to this imperfect world we call creation, but more immediately (and perhaps unintentionally) to her own shabby, unkempt domain. I think there might be something significant to that. God created everything, but Lilith was in charge of what was right here.

"But the thing is," I went on, "Nobody really knows that. It's absurd, isn't it? That you could do better with omnipotence *without* omniscience. That you know how to make a better world than all-knowing God."

"That's assuming God is all-knowing," she retorted dryly.

"Do you believe in God?" I was going to have to ask her eventually.

"Which one?"

She didn't say it in an obnoxious, Neil Tyson Degrassi/"One fewer god"smug atheist way. It was more playful and detached. She was sipping a beer, not about to take out Russell's Teacup.

"I dig Odin," I went along because I was really in no mood for the theological discussion I started. "Dude had a real commitment to wisdom. Gave up his eye!"

"I like the Norse. Freya's my favorite."

"Goddess of Love, right?"

"Beauty too. A real party girl."

"TGIF."

"Yeah, 'cause of Friday. And Freya was my daughter's name."

(Needless to say, I didn't know that.)

"Where's your daughter now?"

"Deceased," she said this with a nervous little laugh and a strange, almost apologetic smile, as if she was sorry for embarrassing me with this admission.

"Oh." I was mortified. Ashamed of myself for asking such a brazen question, even if I didn't know the answer was going to be so horrifying and sad. I was nonplussed at her nonchalant manner, and woefully aware of how inadequate anything I could say to console or apologize for my lack of tact would be. "I'm sorry." I stammered, hoping that would suffice, in the moment at least, to offer my condolences as well mea culpa for asking the question in the first place.

"It's ok. I'm over it." She shook her head casually, shrugging even, with that weird forced smile. "I'm so over it."

What strange creature was this? Whither Lilith? What immortal hand or eye, did craft her fearful cynicism, her dry sardonic wit, her inescapable sexiness, and her inscrutable detachment from normal human reservation?

She grunted, perhaps a nonverbal acknowledgement of a perhaps now mutual discomfiture and got up.

Strolling over to the plasma screen, she prepared tonight's entertainment.

"Anyway, Mr. Malloy, much as I'd like to play doctor, you're not my shrink, so let's start the flick."

It would have been better to have kept my mouth shut, of course. That would have been a response, eliciting neither information nor reaction. Prudent, but wise? I was internally telling myself, frantically and repeatedly "*None of my business. None of my business. Why did you say anything?!*"

But...wasn't it now my business, to some extent? If you're dating somebody, don't you want to get to know them? Isn't that the point? And what of love?

Certainly, there was mutual lust, clearly established by this point (though I still had trouble understanding it on her end), and friendship, and perhaps affection. Warm affection I felt towards Lilith despite, or perhaps even because of her curiously appealing chilly disposition. If it were ever to go further, and I had my hopes, it would not be all out of line to find out such important biographic information.

But all in due time. Even lacking foreknowledge of such tragic biographic revelations as I did, I immediately knew there were more tactful ways to gently ask about her child.

"*Aww, how old is she?*"
"*She's dead. Thanks for asking*"
OR
"*What is her name?*"
"*You mean what WAS her name?*"
Maybe simply:
"*I didn't know you had a daughter.*"

Because after all, what happy answer could there be to "Where is your daughter now"? She clearly wasn't here, now, and Lilith's dry response to "Do you live alone?" did nothing to indicate she had a young, biologically connected dependent for a roommate. So, what could the answer be?

"*She lives with her father. I hate him.*"
"*I don't know, she ran away.*"
"*Don't ask!*"
Yikes.

"*Upstairs, asleep*" seemed unlikely, as did any iteration of slumber parties or spending the night at grandmother's, so I came back to the fact that there really was no upside to me asking the question in the first place. I felt embarrassed and small, for so little comfort I could give, and the sad truth was, I wish I had avoided the necessity in the first place.

And then the DVD was loaded, and she was by my side once more. Her thigh again pressed against mine, and neither her denim nor my own could hold back the warmth and unmistakable pressure. And she leaned into me, indicating it was appropriate for me to lift my arm and place it up on the sofa, giving her entrance to intimacy. My arm around her, her soft head leaning against me, I soon forgot the sad subject, and the flickering images on the screen and the nearness of her body soothed me into a placid waking dream.

•   •   •   •   •

Heavenly Creatures was an interesting movie. Simple premise, VERY well acted and directed in a unique way that the forensic cinephile could identify as unmistakably Peter Jackson.

(Whether that is a good thing or not is a matter or subjective opinion. As this is mine, I'll only state it's a *The Lovely Bones* situation, where the inherent drama of simple tragedies may be distracted more than I was, and the critics minded more than I did.)

You know the basic plot. Or maybe you don't. There are these two teenage girls in 1950s New Zealand. 13 or 14 years old. One, of course, is the celebrated Kate Winslet, who would later gain fame as the starlet of the highest grossing movie of all time (for its time). The girls befriend each other, find a number of common interests, including the Italian crooner Mario Lanza, a man I had never heard of, but whose voice and cultural legacy I instantly recognized and acknowledged as real.

"No one else can end this yearning."

Was one of his lyrics.

What really gained my interest, on a thematic as well as a visceral level was THE FOURTH WORLD.

This was a concept, a place, an imagination that Kate Winslet's Juliet described. She told the Catholic Pauline that when she died, she would not go to Heaven or Hell, but rather this strange magical kingdom where all was right and good and in keeping with her own private fantasy. A fantasy, now, for two. If Pauline would accept, and naturally she did.

Their own little world, full of make-believe, mutual crushes on 1950s heartthrobs ("The Saints"), and a growing resentment of the parents and authority figures who conspire to keep them apart.

And yes, latent and eventually explicit lesbianism. Because let's be honest, that's what a lot of guys were watching for. Not me. Oh, I have my fair share of prurient interests, to be sure, and (older!) Kate Winslet has certainly figured with her figure, but Sapphism has never been a turn-on. Can't place myself in the fantasy. Also, I'm intimidated by lesbians. Emasculated even. The whole don't need a man thing. Makes me feel inadequate. And politically irksome. Fish without bicycles. Whatever. No sweat off my sack.

And one shouldn't be attracted to these girls anyway, being that they were in their younger teens. I'm sure Winslet and Melanie Lynskey were much older, perhaps even 18+ when the film was filmed, but they still looked like children.

That wasn't enough for Lilith, however, who nudged me when the sex scene finally came.

"Is this turning you on?" she joshed suggestively.

I mean, I guess I should have said yes? I'm not a dummy. I know we were technically supposed to be doing it right now, but I didn't want to, and I was caught up in the movie.

And no, it wasn't. Even if the girls were women and I was into two women, the actual lesbian sex was interspliced with grotesque invasions of fantasy caricatures of Orson Welles and the sorts. Like right now Pauline is on top of Juliet. One second later, she's replaced by Harry Lime. In the narration, Pauline says they were imagining how The Saints would make love. So, these girls are thinking about men while they have sex with each other. For lesbians, their homosexuality had an unmistakable heterosexual undertone.

And then came the murder, and I didn't know what to make of it all.

"Tis indeed a miracle, one must feel, that two such Heavenly Creatures are real."

So, she said. But was the miracle from God, or was it something else from the Other Fellow?

And then the movie ended, and we sat there in silence. I was still processing the narrative feature, but I could sense an air of disappointment in Lilith. Which didn't make sense, because it was her movie. But she articulated.

"You're a slow study, Mr. Malloy."

"How's that?"

She turned to me with an exaggerated frown. "You know I don't remember the last time I made it through a whole movie with a guy without making out-"

I planted one on her. Right on her soft, luscious lips. Not just to shut her up in the Nelson Muntz sense, but to prove myself, and to drink. We drank deeply of each other, tongues caressing, sloppy, mammalistic, stupid ecstasy.

"It was a pretty weird movie," I broke it off. "I liked it."

"Mood killer."

"Mother killer," I corrected.

"We should all be so lucky," she drolled.

"Careful, Lilith, that's matricide."

"I wish."

"God, you're dark."

"I know." She smiled brightly, then kissed me affectionately on the cheek, a move more endearing and intimate than any of our necking thus far. "That's why you love me, baby."

She stood up.

"Let's continue this conversation in more comfortable quarters."

I followed obediently as her swaying hips led me across the cluttered apartment, into her boudoir.

Imagine my shock when I saw a guy already on the bed.

"Don't mind Piebald," Lilith said, crossing the room and picking up the floppy doll. Ragstitch looked like a medieval jester. Red and yellow, like...

"He's not the jealous type," she said on the bed, clutching the strange little fellow. I was trying to place him. I was no longer afraid of dolls, but I was curious, allured and yes, a little unsettled by a vague familiarity I couldn't place.

"What...is he?" I asked, cautiously approaching "A clown?" I reached my hand out.

"No!" she pulled the doll away, hugging him to her chest. "Clowns are creepy. Piebald's what I call The Piper."

For so he was, for attached to the little doll's hand was a felt flute.

"He's the Pied Piper!" I realized, sitting on the bed, scooching next to her.

"Yeah, Pied means piebald, which is this design, so that's what I call him." She scooched back, closed the gap, and we were touching at last.

"Does he keep away the rats?"

She smirked, "well I haven't seen any."

"You like that story?" I asked casually, staring at the doll, ostensibly, but really at her breasts. Not too tricky, being that she was holding Piebald by her chest.

"It's fun. In a creepy sort of way."

"Lilith, that describes you exactly."

She patted my hand, smiling affectionately.

"I work at it. But Piebald...it comes naturally."

"He's naturally creepy?"

"His story is. You familiar?"

"The Pied Piper of Hamelin? Sure."

"Most people think it's a tragedy. Three parts you know. The rats pillage the town, the Piper drives them out, the elders refuse to pay, so he plays the children out."

She lay back on the bed, holding Piebald above her, making him dance across her stomach.

"Where did he take them?" I asked.

"Somewhere far away," she replied so dreamily I thought she was going to fall asleep, which would put a prompt end to the possibility of a night of carnal pleasures and vice. My libido lamented, and my conscience rejoiced. But I? Again, enchanted and repelled, I didn't know, and I couldn't tell you now, if I wanted her to fall asleep so I could leave, or if I really did want her awake and mine.

"Far away," she repeated, "To some…No." She sat up. "It was the mountain. He played his pipe, and then he led them right into the mountain. A door opened up in the mountainside. And they all walked in."

"What was there?"

She was looking at me with an enchanting gaze. F-me eyes, the vulgarian would say, and I would think, but right now there was something innocent about her. Perhaps it was the fairy tale she so elegantly recited.

"*A joyous land, joining the town and just at hand.*" She took my hand and intertwined our fingers. She did not break eye contact. "*Where waters gushed, and fruit-trees grew.*" She was looking at me, looking at me with desire, with lust. Imagine that. Being wanted by someone so wanted. "*And flowers put forth a fairer hue.*"

And the mention of flowers she closed her eyes and leaned in, head against my chest. Perhaps she was listening to my rapidly beating heart, but then she breathed of my essence as if there was any scent I had worth her attention.

She looked up at me. She had her hand on my face. She was feeling me like a blind woman trying to get an impression of the one who lay in front of her.

"*And everything was strange and new.*"

I closed my eyes, wanting to hold onto this immortal moment, for I knew I would cherish it, just as I knew that once it passed, it would never come again. I was treasuring this present just as I was mourning its passing. I knew my moral misgivings were valid, but as she lay on me, all thoughts and hesitations faded away, into the mist of a sublime blank I can't describe and don't really want to. It was the shear ecstasy of experience, warm and electrifying, infinite and transient, comforting and frightening. And then, just then, I was content.

And then we sinned.

Chapter 12-A: A Serious Question

Will this keep me out of Heaven?

The straight forward answer is simple enough. Yes, Trent, premarital sex is a mortal sin. You are a fornicator. Repent now or suffer forever. You've got to change your evil ways, baby.

And yet-and here the smooth talker tries to rationalize his own misdeeds, so I'll check myself before I wreck myself. Yes, it was a sin, a terrible one that God and his Church cared about even if society didn't. Perversion of love and the procreative act, yes, I agreed.

But I felt more than shame. Pleasure in the moment, remorse afterward, but my feelings were complicated. I doubt it was a dulling of my conscience. If anything, I'm more morally refined than I was in my youth, in my greener, innocent days where I had not yet articulated such a keen sense of sin and virtue in an unvirtuous world. Today I read Chesterton. So, I think I'm a good Catholic in the sense that I know I'm not.

At any rate, my feelings towards my partner in crime were affectionate. Tender curiosity, as Carraway said, though perhaps I did already, in fact, love her. I didn't know what lay ahead. I was hopeful yet cautious.

Because really, how long could this go on?

How do they do it? Really, how do so many young, unmarried Catholics exist as premaritally sexual beings? If they live with their girlfriends and boyfriends, how do they live with themselves?

Two possibilities:

1.   They don't care, they literally don't care about God and the Church, morality, and sin, and all that. They have their sex, keep their nominal allegiance, lapse away.

2.   Or, perhaps even more perniciously, they do have a conscience, but

they have perverted it to suit their perversions. A fellow does consider himself a good Christian, buuuuuut, he really likes his girlfriend, and he wants to, you know, "do it". So, he rationalizes. Surrenders to modernity. Lies to himself. "Well, the whole no premarital sex thing is a medieval remnant…" "It's not one of the 10 Commandments…" "God wants you to be happy…"

God doesn't want you to be happy. Not in that way. If it makes you happy, can it really be so bad? Yes, Sheryl, it can, if it is a sin. Maybe that isn't even true happiness anyway. No real pleasure in it.

Was there a third option for the fornicating Catholic? Well, there had to be because I exist. I just wondered if there wasn't anybody else like me in this too-big world. 1 billion believers in my church, but were there any with my predicament and my exact response? Were there other guys who bedded their girlfriends, confessed that sin, went back to her, and repeat? Are there women who don't tell their lovers what they tell their priests? What kind of life is that to lead? How to justify that? What a moral cheat! What cowardice!

Again, I quote:

I know your deeds that you are neither cold nor hot. I wish you were either one or the other! So, because you are lukewarm—neither hot nor cold—I am about to spit you out of my mouth

You can't keep that up. Get hit by a bus halfway between her bed and the confessional and see how your clever little scheme pays off.

How unfair it was too, to the other involved! To enjoy her body at night and then run off to feel sorry for it. What kind of absolution could you get if you intended to do it again, and again, and again? How would she feel if you told her that you love her, but what you do together is putting your soul in mortal danger?

"Why do you like me?" I asked afterward, running my fingers through her cool, ebony black hair.

"You're…interesting," she purred, almost like an afterthought to follow all the things that were remained unsaid.

I took it.

I love to let down the atheist, but I could imagine his reaction of disappointment, frustration, and derision at my stupid little moral panic. In this great big empty universe, what did it matter what two consenting adults did in the dark? Ease up, Trent. Life's too short…

But Hell's too hot and eternity's too long.

I thought back to that hypothetical heretic, and what he would think of Heaven. It seemed so far away, it's not hard to believe there are people who don't. Such a perfect, unreachable place, and sometimes it felt like the better I felt here on Earth, the less I'd get afterward.

He would call it a pipe dream, wouldn't he? A fairy tale, like Juliet's Fourth World, Paradise, Terabithia, Big Rock Candy Mountain, or that magical place children only got to when the piper played his special tune, and the mountainside opened. Perfect places, the likes of which we can only dream of here.

Well, to Hell with him. I'll keep my dreams, as well as my prayers, and, for now, it seemed, my sins. God help me.

It was only after I left Lilith's that I realized what the astute reader would no doubt have already put together. I had walked out of her little house, down the steps and to the street, when it struck.

The reason why that doll on her bed was so strikingly familiar. Because I had certainly seen his likeness before, and it was not something I relished reliving.

The Pied Piper.

Piebald.

Red and yellow jester.

The mascot for Pin's Brew.

Chapter 13: That Whole Ball of Wax

Oh yes. My appointment. And not the dreaded but ultimately harmless optometrist!

Mike's reaction to missing the whole show was, naturally, mixed. Personally, I was irritated that he spent nearly the entirety of our time at the psychiatrist's club sweet-talking Dr. Price, pretending to be interested in taking up a study, continuing whatever bullcrap he had to use to get in here in the first place. I mean, it was all ostensible, nominal, an excuse, right? How much time did he have to put into it?

And it was a coincidence, a pure *preternatural* coincidence that I just so happened to be sitting next to (well okay, he was at the other end of the bar, but he came over) the man we were there to see in the first place. But Thane's Ahab was Mike, not I, and I didn't get the chance to confront him (as we were there to do) with the fact that there was a dead cat under his books at the library and an eyeball in the alchemic drink he was so fond of, that surely he was the one responsible for its placement here, one of only 5 bars in Los Angeles.

Tenuous, in fact. The desperate, pitiful threads of two madmen, Mike and I, clutching at straws in search of some connection and meaning.

But Thane was like that himself, no? This was a guy who connected the Erl-King to Jack Frost to Rumpelstiltskin to Dad. And Pimm's changed to Pin's in his glass, in his hand, which I'm pretty sure was deliberate. In which case, he should have an open mind to whatever dark madness we threw his way, and what I feared to God was he could give as well as he could take.

So, the second coincidence was Mike's timing in casually missing the point. Missing the "good" doctor at any rate, as just as soon as Thane shuffled off, Mike came in.

(Hadn't seen them in the same room yet, I'm just saying).

I saw him walk to the front of the room, Gina leaning into him. She looked giddy, like she was still laughing at a hilarious joke, and calm.

"Celine peaked with *Journey to The End of the Night*." I heard him before I saw him. He was saying it in a casual, matter-of-fact tone. "Nowhere else is he so triumphant and assured of his pessimism."

"Nor is anyone else," she agreed.

They had stopped walking and were just standing around awkwardly, like a couple in the end of a date. In earshot and my peripheral vision. It was like I was next in line at Confession and was trying not to overhear.

"'I cannot refrain from doubting that there that there exist any genuine realizations of our deepest character except war and illness, those two infinites of nightmare,'" he recited. "Take it from a soldier, the man had a point."

They were framed in the doorway now, and I wondered how long they would continue this display before she asked:

"Is that your friend?"

"There's my boy." I had been made, and I felt insanely self-conscious as if I was an outsider intruding on their intimate moment. "Hey Trent!"

I shifted in my seat and gave a weak little wave.

"Oh. Hey Mike. Dr.- or, Gina."

He swung around and turned to her, holding both her hands and looking her in the eyes.

"To be continued."

"I would love to keep picking your brain...Lieutenant," she added playfully.

"Any time, doctor." He kissed her hand, and she was practically blushing. "Anytime."

Then she gave a wave more girly than weak and strolled off.

"And that's that." Striding up behind me. His skin was flush, his tone was laid back, and he kept on grinning. He was even making a show of clapping his hands together, dusting them off, job well-done like.

I spun around on my chair. I was still shaken by my strange talk with Thane (bad rhyme, not a typo), but Mike was pulling me back to a level of reality I could identify and cope with.

"What's what?"

Mike copped a squat next to me, a stupid grin on his face. He was seemingly very pleased with himself, which was odd in these circumstances.

"Dr. Price- excuse me, Gina, we had ourselves quite a little chat. Aaaaand, she's gonna be writing me a letter of recommendation!" He chuckled, and I wondered if he had slept with her. Then I felt bad for wondering that.

"For what?"

Mike shrugged pleasantly.

"For whenever I decide to apply to whatever psychology program."

"What can I get you?" That was Sue.

"Let's see, gorgeous." Mike looked up at the well-stocked rack above the bar.

Then he looked down at the bar itself, and there went his uncomplicated good mood. He frowned.

"Come back later."

"I'll give you a minute," Sue said, shrugging and slugging off to the other side of the bar, where approximately no one waited.

Mike was slowly nodding, focused intently at the little white square of destiny in front of him, contemplating its meaning and mulling over what was next.

"Trent," he began slowly. "What is this?"

Dr. Victor Thane
BOARD CERTIFIED PSYCHIATRIST

p: (310)123-4567   f: (310)123-4567
drthane@thanepsyd.com
10438 Santa Monica Blvd #3008, Los Angeles, CA 90025

"Providence."

Providence, I mouthed to myself one week later, sitting in the booth at the Pink Taco in Century City. Enveloped by cushioned leather, a plate of cheap corn chips and mild salsa on the table before me, crumbled chips surrounding a margarita.

I say Providence, and I mean it in the big P, William Jennings Bryan/Nathaniel Hawthorne/Moby Dick sense. I say Providence because I am a Christian, and I have to believe that His Divine Hand is at work, rather than the infernal claw of the devilish one, or the stupid coincidences of a thoughtless universe. Serendipity was a useless New Age concept, "I'm not religious, but I'm spiritual", put your thoughts out to "The Universe" bunk. I wonder if there was a scene of John Cusack in the rain.

"You know why this place is called this?" Wiping the salsa from his upper lip, Mike grinned like a frat boy. "Why it's called Pink Taco?"

"No," I chuckled. "And neither do you."

Mike was too far gone on his clever and not at all sophomoric joke brewing to catch that I was doubting him.

"Come on, man. *Pink Taco?* Don't you get it." He leaned in conspiratorially and dropped his voice. "It's *pussy*."

He let the word stand in the air a moment, cool and naughty. He cocked his head back, challenging me to let him know what I thought.

So, I did.

"Actually, the founder of Pink Taco-I forget his name-he said that the title doesn't refer, you know, to that...It was actually a matter of controversy. He wanted to open a new one somewhere. Santa Monica, Orange County, I don't know. There were protests in the community by those voicing your exact same concern."

"Hey, I'm not concerned." Mike took a sip and leaned back, eyeing the wait staff. "I think it's beautiful."

"But it's not. I mean it wouldn't be beautiful even if it was true, it'd be gross and immature, but the guy, the founder, they make this uproar, saying 'How can we have a restaurant in our town that's a euphemism?!' And he denies it. He says that if he wanted to reference that, he would have just called it that."

"Called it what?" Mike was smiling playfully while he chided me, knowing my distaste for naughty language.

"He would have just called it, you know, Pink Pussy, or whatever if that's what he really meant."

"And you believe him?" Mike was skeptical.

"Not at all."

We both laughed. Did he really expect anybody to buy that his restaurant's title was only provocative accidentally? I didn't know the guy at all, couldn't even remember his name and am not bothering to look it up now, but I imagined a Joe Francis type or that pervert from American Apparel. A guy who made it rich young with an obnoxious, hypersexualized business and that translates to big bucks to fuel his loud libido and genuine douchiness. Frat boy entrepreneurs make it big.

"I must admit," Mike began, dipping a chip. "I am a little disappointed that the place doesn't live up to its name. A titty bar that served tacos, THAT would be worth coming out for."

"I am also disappointed, but for less sinful reasons. When I first heard about this place, I imagined that they would have actual pink taco shells. You know, hot pink hard corn. I think that'd look pretty cool."

"Yeah, it would." Mike got out of the gutter for a moment to acknowledge the simple aesthetic deliciousness of the concept. "Like, pink pink, right? Dyed pink?"

"Exactly. It would have been awesome. But then you get here and no pink tacos! They're not on the menu! What's up with that?"

Mike was shaking his head, agreeing with me. "Fucking 'A man. Let's see some multi-colored tacos."

"Right?! It's what the consumer at your restaurant is led to believe, quite naturally, by the sign outside telling us what you're selling! And I'll tell you the other thing, it'd grant them plausible deniability as well."

"Damn. You're right."

I was pleased he understood.

"Because right now, the obvious question is, the elephant in the room-"

"- Why are you dirty dogs calling yourselves Pink Taco if it's NOT about pussy? I see what you mean, Trent."

"But if they had actual pink tacos, it doesn't matter who isn't fooled, because at least you have something to point to and say, no, THIS is what we're talking about. I don't care if you think it refers to vaginas, we're called Pink Taco because, guess what, we sell pink tacos!"

I didn't tell him the other reason I was disappointed, the sad, shameful reason. I've never claimed to not be a sinner, and I would be lying if I said some part of me wasn't hoping for an establishment centered around sexy waitresses. Something like Hooters but wearing pink. Exactly like the movie *Still Waiting...*, if that wasn't too obscure.

But my thoughts on my own less than admirable nature were interrupted by Mike going back into pretentious mode. He does that.

"Still, one must admit an appeal, publicly acknowledged or otherwise, in the yonic evocation, so brazen and yet untoward. An appeal to some subconscious desire, right there in our faces, middle of Beverly Hills, to see the naked removed from its hidden state. To see the nude unclothed. Right in front of our food? The pleasures of the flesh."

"That's all nonsense, Mike. And we're in Century City."

"None the less," he grunted.

"ALL the less," I corrected. "What are we even talking about?"

"Strategy," he said, licking the sauce off his fingers. "Drink your margarita."

"I probably shouldn't." I eyed the half-empty glass. Those ones always had a habit of sneaking up on me. "It'd be best to keep a clear mind ahead about me in these circumstances. We don't know what we're up against."

I realized how silly that sounded, but Mike agreed.

"Most definitely. Which is why I'm packing."

It took me a moment.

"What, heat?" I sat up, alert. "You got a gun Mike?!"

"Why don't you announce it, Trent? Call on the LAPD while you're at it."

"I'm sorry." I calmed down, embarrassed. Luckily no one had heard.

"Hey, I'm white. I might survive the encounter."

"That's in poor taste," I mumbled.

"The truth usually is."

"But what are you gonna do, man?" I leaned in. "A gun? That's insane. Who do you think is going to be there?"

"Dr. Victor Thane. Our man."

"Our man," I repeated. "I don't know what you think that means. And I don't know how you think we're going to confront him."

"Easy." Mike stood up, ready for us to take our leave. "With the facts."

"And what would those be?"

"I haven't decided yet."

• • • • • •

Dr. Thane's office was on the third floor of a skyscraper in Century City. Nestled away there, one could imagine any sort of heinous malfeasance hidden from the willfully ignorant Los Angeleans.

We were walking across the wide empty lobby when the elevator doors opened, and a lithe blonde sprite ran out and embraced me.

"TRENT!" Chip had me in a bear hug, for so she was Chip, from the metro transit authority. She was still in uniform, but she was now liberally perfumed, and her lipstick was smeared. "It's good to see you!"

I pulled away, taken aback, and stared into her ice blue eyes, two cold pinpoints above that preternaturally wide smile.

"We met a couple weeks ago." She laughed awkwardly, which I suppose would be a humanizing trait in others, but here sounded as unnatural as anything about her. "At Union-"

"I know exactly who you are," I cut her off curtly, which wasn't true at all, actually. I really had no idea who she was, really, except that her name was supposedly Chip, she ostensibly worked for the Metro, and we had one brief, odd encounter earlier. I certainly didn't know what was going on with her, if I had ever actually told her my name, and what she was doing here.

"Hi." Chip turned to Mike, who was both curious and dismissive, trying to keep his distance. "I'm Chip. I work for the MTA."

"How do you know Trent?" he grunted, trying to gruffly pretend he wasn't curious by this strange and bubbly intruder.

She laughed again, high and unsettling.

"Oh, you know," she brushed her nails along my arm. I had goosebumps, and I'm not entirely sure if they were bad ones. "This and that."

"The train station," I mumbled honestly. "You were telling me about the fish."

Her eyes lit up, big as anime lollipops made in the third circle of Wonka's inferno.

"That's right! The fishies..." she drifted off as if envisioning an aquatic spectacle, the likes of which lesser minds could only dream.

"What are you doing here? Chip?"

"That's so good of you to ask, Trent!" Mike grabbed me by my arm and gestured toward the door while she gushed. "I'm so super in so many ways. We've been laying track up at the Miracle Mile-"

"Sorry, we have an appointment to get to." Now Mike was literally pulling me away from Chip and into the elevator.

Which is why I felt myself in the automatic position of apologizing to an ambivalent pixie whose makeup and intentions had yet to be ascertained.

"Yeah, we're going up now. I'm sorry," I said apologetically, as I walked with Mike towards the closing doors, my attention divided between him and Chip, who I tried to face. "We'll...excuse."

"Yeah, no problem. We'll talk soon!"

She was still standing there, still smiling, when the doors closed, and the elevator took us up.

"Perhaps there's some...connection," I mused half-heartedly, and Mike barely even favored this with a glance. Yes, there probably was, certainly. She was weird enough, after all. Yet so inarticulate and flighty that we had little time for her. A cheery young woman greeting the unsolicited with banal pleasantries was less sexy than a mysterious psychologist waxing melodramatic on Erl-Kings and madness, even if she was, on an aesthetic level, technically sexier. I tried to file away this Chip in a less busy part of my preoccupations, throw her file in the dustier corner of my library, and hopefully one without any cats, living or dead. I did privately admit that it seemed she would likely end up being more important than would vocally be acknowledged by Mike or me. Or Chip, really. I did intend to treat her like a real person, whatever she was. She didn't seem too eager to straight up volunteer her own purpose, so we left it as a mystery for the moment.

Dr. Thane's office on the third floor was cramped and unextraordinary. The waiting room had only four chairs, one of which was occupied by grotesquely fat man engrossed in the Highlights magazine. A diminutive woman in spectacles was talking to the receptionist, a professional, thirty-something brunette.

"I'm sorry, it's just not on your policy," the receptionist explained. "You'd have to go out of pocket."

The woman's lips stretched thin like they were sucking a lemon. "My employers don't approve of psychoanalysis. And we're a family company."

Mike tapped on the leap of the ficus on the corner.

"Fake," he nudged me.

"You should pee in it," I whispered back.

We chuckled, but then he pointed out, "careful who hears you say that in here, Malloy. Guy might think you have some sort of a fetish."

The woman at the front was fidgeting a lot as she tried to gather her bearings. "I was wondering if we could work out-with indiscretion of course-"

"Of course."

The gentle swing of the office door, and Thane himself, well-fed and perfectly at ease in his environment, stepped into the cramped room to survey his little kingdom.

"So, who now then?" he asked the room in a genteel yet authoritative command.

He glanced over us. The Goofus in the corner did not stir. I sat up and saw Thane, and I knew contact had been established.

"Dr. Thane, Mrs. Winslow was inquiring about a payment plan" his assistant prodded, but his attention was clearly elsewhere.

"Uh huh," Thane patted Winslow on her shoulder while keeping his gaze on me. I stood up but wasn't sure if I should say something. "We can set you up with a deferred...Dinah, do whichever."

Mrs. Winslow may have been offended by this brush off, but Thane didn't care. He glided across the room (soft carpet with one of those abstract Kandinsky/pizza parlor designs. If you've ever stared at the floor of a Chuck-E-Cheese, you know what I'm talking about) toward my presence.

I stuck out my hand out of obligation. It seemed like the thing to do. In truth, I was mortified at my very presence here. Chip's interruption hadn't helped.

"Hi, Dr. Thane. I'm Trent Malloy. We met at The Pick and Hammer."

"Of course, of course." He was shaking warmly, vigorously, with two hands even. He had less problem than I accepting our meeting as if a casual conversation about snowmen and alchemy would only naturally lead to an actual follow-up exam. "I'm glad you came."

"You mentioned a free consultation..." I trailed off because it was embarrassing and by this point unnecessary.

"Yes, I remember. Let us go."

I followed the good (?) doctor's swagger through his antechamber. Mike stalked after.

"We didn't check in," I said apologetically, to no one in particular. Thane waved his hand and Dinah frowned, but nothing more came of it.

· · · · ·

"Clear psychosis," Thane remarked as he took his seat. "Dissociative identity disorder." He was joking affably as he gestured to Mike, the uninvited.

I was awkwardly sitting down across from Thane, because what else could I do, and Mike was slouching against the door, making sure it was closed.

Sensing his joke was not appreciated, Thane did what all Dads did in that case, and doubled down.

"It appears that the singular patient I set an appointment with has split in two - and in fact is including me in his delusion. A projected-"

"We get the joke, doc," Mike brusquely interrupted. "It's not very funny, and it's beside the point."

"And what is the point, Lieutenant Kripke?" Thane let the honorific sit as if challenging us to question.

Mike tried not to let it faze him, but he wouldn't let that slide.

"You know me, Doc?"

Thane shrugged.

"It's nothing supernatural. You were a guest at my club-"

"*Your* club?"

"The club," he relented. "Our records are meticulous."

"Fair enough." Mike swaggered around the office, pecking at the bookcase. "Maybe now you can answer some of our questions."

"Would these be the same questions you were going to ask me had you not been waylaid schtupping Dr. Price."

I coughed up, that is, I ended up choking on the inappropriate laugh.

Dr. Thane turned to me.

"Can I get you something to drink? Some coffee? A glass of water?"

"How about a shot of Pin's Brew?" Mike had stopped across the room and was looming over Thane's desk. His face was a bit red. It would be uncharacteristic of Mike to take embarrassment over the mention of an intrigue with the lady psychiatrist, real or imagined, but there it was.

"Pin's Brew," Thane repeated, rolling his tongue over the words.

"You know what I'm talking about."

"Of course, I do. The liqueur. It's tremendous. I ordered it for the club. Only it's a bit early for a nip."

Mike shook his head. "Trent told me all about your alchemy."

"I said..." I was apologetic, on the spot. "I mean, Victor and I were talking..."

"You saw him change the Pimm's to Pin's!" Mike snapped.

"I don't know what I saw," I admitted, much to Mike's aggravation.

Thane chuckled.

"Yes, you do. Certainly, what once was Pimm's was Pin's instead. Of course, that happened."

Mike looked from me to Thane, plotting his next move. The psychiatrist went on, maddeningly genial.

"And of course, I'll answer whatever questions you have in mind. I'm sure that I could clear a great deal up. This needn't be an adversarial atmosphere at all." Thane gestured to the seat next to mine. "There are two chairs."

Mike walked over to the empty chair and did not sit down. Perhaps he thought he was exercising his power, but it just made me uncomfortable.

"Start with the dead cat in the room," he sneered.

"Dead...cat?" Thane appeared genuinely confused. "I'm not familiar with that expression. Would you please to elaborate?"

"Oh, come off it, Thane!" Mike had no patience. "You said you'd help!"

"I will!" he responded defensively. He seemed more normal and innocent by the second. "But this dead cat you speak of?"

"It started a couple of weeks ago," I explained, hoping to take a diplomatic position. "Mike and I were in the library, and we heard a cat meowing. Whinging bloody murder. We follow the sound-"

"-Into the mystery section," Mike added pointedly, and Thane got the point.

"And there was a cat. A dead cat!"

"I'm sorry," he offered his flat condolences.

"It had been ripped open. It was sick. Ripped right open, but we had just heard meowing!"

"Fascinating!"

"It happened!" Mike thundered.

"I believe you," Thane responded. "I believe you both. In fact, I'm quite sure that happened."

"You-you are?" I asked uncertainly, as I wasn't sure I believed it myself.

"Oh yes. For why else would you make it up? For fun? For laughs?"

"This isn't fun," Mike said with steely resolve.

"No. But it did happen. It sounds like a, what's the term, an Infernal Phenomenon?'

"You say that like it's supposed to mean something." Mike was impatient but curious.

"No, it wouldn't," he conceded. "So, I'll explain. It's not a technical term, of course, and likely he would not approve of even having a term at all, the nature of these incidents being intrinsically irrational, inexplicable, and maddening by nature."

"Incidents?" Mike asked.

"*He*?" I asked.

"But what are we really talking about here? In 1284, Hamelin, Germany, there is a mass, and as yet unexplained disappearance of children. In the early 20th Century, Charles Fort records raining frogs. San Francisco, 1981, 18 Laotian immigrants die in their sleep, frightened to death."

"The inspiration for *Nightmare on Elm Street*," I pointed out.

"I'm sure."

"But what does it all *mean*?" Mike groaned.

"The point is there is no point. And I can understand one finds this intellectually disingenuous, the subversion of reason, indeed. But your perplexion is the intention." He grinned mischievously, which reminded me that he was perhaps an agent of this chaos and not simply an explainer. "So, the reaction you have when you read of these occurrences-"

"We didn't just *read* about these things," Mike said sharply.

"Though we were in the library," I added, and Mike favored me with a smirk, showing that we could have some fun with this, even all things considered.

"You said," Thane responded dryly, "you found a dead cat."

"Under your books!" I snapped, tired of Mike's prevarications. "You've written so many mystery novels, you got an entire shelf at the library."

"I'm proud!"

"But the dead cat was right there! Right at your shelf!"

"Oh?" Again, he registered genuine surprise, and I could tell he was not holding anything back. It was fascinating to discover how much he knew and how much he was willing to tell-Everything, it seemed. He reviled in revelation but was surprised at some of our details.

"Tell him what happened next, Trent."

"Yeah, well…" I chuckled nervously. "You know, I think I will take that drink."

I don't know why I said that.

"Thirsty, Mr. Malloy?"

"Skip it." Mike wanted me to get to the point, but…how?

"Well, Mike and I were at a bar called The Misfit, in Santa Monica."

"One of only five bars in Los Angeles that stocks Pin's Brew," Mike pointed out.

"And mine is another." Thane was curious, but he didn't see where this was going.

"Well yeah, but we didn't know that at the time," I went on. "We didn't know that at all, because we didn't even know what Pin's Brew was. We were drinking Pimm's Cup."

"A light cocktail." Thane licked his lips. "Fruity." He held out his hand and waved it a bit, perhaps in a "swishy" gesture, to indicate Mike, and I were fruity for drinking it together. "Made from Pimm's No. 1. Herbal Liqueur. I'm familiar, but not a fan."

"You were drinking it though, that day at The Pick and Hammer."

"Hmm."

"We liked it anyway. So Mike suggested we order the entire bottle."

"What do you think, Doc? I make a mistake?"

Thane shrugged at Mike's challenge.

"It's nothing to me if you order an entire bottle. Thirsty boys."

"We ordered a bottle of Pimm's," I continued, "The waiter brought out a bottle of Pin's Brew."

"WITH A FUCKING EYEBALL IN IT!"

The air went out of the room. Mike was still fuming. I had to tell myself not to be apologetic, though my nature being what it was, I was.

After a moment of quiet introspection, God knows what he thought of us…

"An eyeball you say."

"A severed human eyeball, just floating right in the drink. Looking right at us." Mike was angry, and who could blame him?

"How did you know it was human?"

Mike grit his teeth. It was a fair question.

"That's not the point!"

"Oh dear."

"So, you see, Dr. Thane." I tried to be civil, neither furiously unbalanced nor cryptically taunting because somebody had to be a straight man and an adult. "We really did this…this investigation, put two and two together. I know it sounds crazy."

"It doesn't."

"But there's an unexplained dead cat right by your books, and then this super-rare drink- which does seem to change properties, it's hard to explain, we went to this bar in Highland Park…" I shut my mouth there and changed course, not wanting to involve Lilith. Thane smiled, which unnerved me. "So, if we're grasping at straws here, I'm sorry-"

"I'm not," snapped Mike, who never apologized for anything in his life.

"You're one of the rare people who knows about Pin's and ordered the drink-in fact, I saw it change in your glass. Pimm's to Pin, exactly like us." I finished, exhausted.

The doctor took all that in. He seemed strangely impressed.

"So. You followed the bread crumbs, like a good Hansel and Gretel. Well done, boys."

"You have anything to say?" Mike leaned forward. PISSED.

"Not really. I should like a moment to process."

"Take your time, buddy."

"It is a fascinating story. I believe every word, as I've said. And it does make sense you come to me-as much sense as anything can in these affairs, and I assure you that is the intention. The idea is to madden and infuriate. He doesn't want you to understand. He wants you to be scared, disturbed, shaken-"

"HE?!" Mike again demanded.

"God?" I volunteered, though hopefully not, from the sound of it.

Thane had a good long laugh at that.

"I'm glad you're so amused." I was offended and hurt. Why should my Lord be laughed at?

"No, no, forgive me," Thane held up his hand apologetically. "But no, not that King."

Something burned inside.

"What King?" Mike demanded.

Thane thought about it and then decided to go all in.

"A demonstration."

He reached over and opened one of his desk drawers. In an instant, Mike was at his side, revealing his gun in its holster. He had his gloved hand on Thane's shoulder and was daring him to make a move.

"Think again."

Thane froze, not out of fear. He was nonchalant. He gestured to the open drawer.

"But it's only a candle." Mike instinctively stepped back, almost jerked. Thane's eyes twinkled, and he smiled. "Nothing to ever be frightened of, no?"

Thane put the candle on the table. Organic looking, about the size of a small jar, wax colored.

(By which I mean it was that pale, sickly yellow. I doubted it had an artificial scent as well.)

"You'll indulge me three more accessories as well. This really is a helpful demonstration."

Mike didn't object. Didn't say anything. Didn't move either.

Thane gave a pleasant shrug.

"Silence is consent."

I winced.

"Please don't say that."

Thane reached into the cabinet and took out a little mat. Black velvet, like a jeweler's. It was covered in wax stains. He placed the mat on the desk and placed the candle atop the mat.

"For the wax," he explained helpfully. "So it doesn't get on my desk."

Back in and he took out a box of matches.

"I'm going to light it, you see. But first."

He reached into his desk and took out a chunk of honeycomb. Just a brick of it. He snapped off perhaps an ounce.

"Only need a little."

He then used his hands to roll the wax into a ball, the way we did with Play-Dough when we were kids.

"Keep your eyes on the ball, as they say. The Ball of Wax."

"The...whole ball of wax?" Mike volunteered.

"That's it."

Thane struck a match off the box and held it up, observing the flame. The spark glittered in his eyes.

He lit the candle and then presented the match, holding it right in front of me.

"Make a wish," he challenged.

I had another idea. Throw this guy off base for once, because he's the one who deserves it.

So I reached out with my thumb and forefinger and squeezed the flame out. I made no effort to take the match from him, so it was all the demented doctor with all his mind games could do to remain subservient while I had my fun.

And I didn't flinch.

"The trick, Potter," I affected an English accent, "Is not minding that it hurts."

Mike smirked out of the side of his mouth, proud of me. I glanced at him and smiled back, before I returned my gaze to Thane, challenging him to respond.

He frowned but quickly recovered. He dropped the match and smiled. Now for his big show.

"Descartes," he said simply.

"I think therefore I am?" I volunteered a moment before regretting I didn't use the Latin *Cogito ergo sum* to sound more intelligent.

"So, what?" Mike sneered, looking at the burning candle.

"Watch, my sons, and listen."

He recited, I later found out, a bit of the famed philosopher's treatise from memory, with graphic illustration and improvisation, allowing for the interruptions of Mike and myself. Quite impressive, especially considering what happened next.

"Let us begin by considering the commonest matters, those which we believe to be the most distinctly comprehended."

"The things we understand the most?" I asked.

"Or that we think we do." Mike was more on the spot. Cynical?

"To wit," The Doctor went on, "The bodies we touch and see." Mike and I looked at the ball of wax. What kind of body was it? "Not indeed bodies in general, for these...generally ideas are usually a little 'confused'." He waved his hand and gave a little apologetic smile by way of acknowledging the confusion. "But let us consider one body in particular. Let us take for, example, this piece of wax." We considered it. "It has been taken quite freshly from the hive, and it has not yet lost the sweetness of the honey which it contains."

I observed the neat little ball in his hand. He was not disturbed, evidently, by the dripping of the honey, which was still so sweet and sticky. My mouth watered.

"It still retains somewhat of the odor of the flowers from which it has been culled."

He raised the ball to his nose, closed his eyes and took a whiff. He then granted me the same flavor. I leaned forward, eyes closed, and inhaled. Flowers. Bees. Sunny days. Honeysuckle. As I've said, the olfactory is indeed, and always has been the most evocative sense.

Mike declined.

Thane twirled the ball around, master prestidigitator, to show us there was nothing up his sleeve, this ball of wax was nothing more than that.

"Its colour, its figure, its size are apparent. It is hard, cold. Easily handled."

He handed me the ball. Wary though I was of the stickiness, I was intensely, insanely, inexplicably curious. I wanted to hold the wax in my hand, though I was also afraid. Enchanted and repelled, as Nick Carraway. Horrified and comforted, as the children of Slender Man. But over what? Frightened by false fire? Surely it was just a little beeswax, and nothing else.

"And if you strike it with your finger." He reached out and gave the ball a little tap. "It will emit a sound." An unsettling little ring went out, and not even Mike was immune from wincing.

But my hand did not shake, and Thane took the ball back.

"Finally, all the things which are requisite to cause us distinctly to recognize a body, are met within it."

"Noted," I took on a dry legal tone. "Things have traits."

"What's the point?" Mike grumbled.

"But notice!" Thane snapped, as this was tremendously important, no trifle, and we must pay close attention. "That while I speak and approach the fire…"

He held the ball of wax out near the flame. The wax started to melt.

"But notice that while I speak and approach the fire what remained of the taste is exhaled, the smell evaporates."

It was almost tangible, the flavor fleeing the wax like a ghost.

"The colour alters, the figure is destroyed, the size increases." It was being mutilated as it melted, transforming into something unrecognizable, which was, of course, his point. "It becomes liquid." Dripping onto the mat. "It heats, scarcely can one handle it."

Thane's hand shook as the wax heated in his hand, but he did not let go. I noticed Mike's gloved hand twitching. He kept his eyes on the flame, but I wondered if he could feel the wax.

"And when one strikes it, no sound is emitted."

He dropped the wax silently onto his desk. Then he looked at us, challenging us to consider the riddle of the wax after we had observed its outwardly physical traits.

"Does the same wax remain after this change?"

Mike looked at the puddle on the cloth, so different from the initial chunk. I made an attempt.

"You mean to ask…is it the same wax?"

Thane nodded.

"We must confess that it remains," he stated obviously, "none would judge otherwise."

"But you're right though," I tried to concede, though it was not perhaps a concession he wanted. "It had changed."

"So it has, Mr. Malloy. Then I ask myself. What then did I know so distinctly in this piece of wax?"

"Well, it's…wax." I volunteered lamely, and he grinned.

"And what is wax?"

I had no answer.

"What then did I know so distinctly in this piece of wax? It could certainly be nothing of all that the senses brought to my notice, since all these things which fall under taste, smell, sight, touch, and hearing, are found to be changed, and yet the same wax remains. Perhaps it was what I now think, viz. that this wax was not that sweetness of honey, nor that agreeable scent of flowers, nor that particular whiteness, nor that figure, nor that sound, but simply a body which a little while before appeared to me as perceptible under these forms, and which is now perceptible under others."

"Wax is a body, a form," I struggled. "In the Platonic sense."

"We are doing Descartes' thought experiment, but he and Plato were on the same page, certainly. And what, precisely, is it that I imagine when I form such conceptions? Let us attentively consider this, and, abstracting from all that does not belong to the wax, let us see what remains."

Mike and I looked at what remained, that silent, stenchless little puzzle, and the doctor waxed on.

"Certainly nothing remains excepting a certain extended thing which is flexible and movable."

"That thing is not flexible and movable now." I pointed to the puddle, which was drying on the cloth.

"Not now in this state," he countered, "but it is a state it has reached after being acted upon by external factors. And the fact that it was there as that, is now here as this, demonstrates, in fact, that it has been flexible and movable and may be again."

Mike stewed. He didn't like this. Any of it.

"When I distinguish the wax from its external forms, as if stripping it of its clothing, and look at it in its nakedness, then even though there may be an error in my judgment, I cannot perceive it thusly without a human mind."

"Ah," I said, getting it (or pretending to) "The senses can be deceived, or misled, rather by sensory perceptions which are by nature transitory and malleable."

"Precisely!" Thane smiled warmly, glad that his student had learned the lesson. "We must then grant that I could not even understand through the senses what this piece of wax is and that it is my mind alone which perceives it."

"You're talking about the soul of wax," Mike grunted dismissively.

"As elegant a way as any to put it, Lieutenant. But it is not so much my point that wax has a soul, but rather that it, like all things, may be shaped and shifted, and must be perceived in a greater sense."

"What other things?" Mike was suspicious, and rightly so.

"Reality itself, my dear boy! Reality and horror."

"Horror is more of a state of mind," I argued.

"But like the wax, my son, we ask what it is. Because what horrifies can also madden and enlighten-supposing that's not all the same. The Great Shifter, that is his purpose, with this aforementioned phenomenon. To take one thing, turn it into another, and leave the observer in a changed state himself for standing witness."

At this, Dr. Victor Thane stood up, begin to pace the room and bloviate.

"So, the city fathers find their exterminator melt into a child snatcher. Rain comes down as frogs. Sleeping Laotians wake up in death. In your case," he extended a finger accusingly, "The mewling of a cat, once a sign of life, is now a ghastly harbinger of death, as if in grotesque mockery. To say nothing of the simple transmutation of one liqueur into another! Jack Frost is the Erl-King! And why?"

"Why?!" Mike stepped forward, demanding an answer.

Thane's smile was so cruel in that moment when he said it. He didn't shout. He didn't need to. He didn't whisper to underline the menace. He didn't need to do that either. He just said it simply, knowing full well the meaning. We all did.

"Wax."

Mike stepped back, frozen. But he could still hear the eerie creak of the door opening behind him.

How do I say this?

How do I ever bring it up?

I'd say I don't even believe it myself, but after everything I've witnessed, would you believe that?

Still a nasty shock though.

For Mike especially.

•   •   •   •   •

The door opened, and a grotesquely fat man stood in the archway. His left hand, hung down by his side, still clutched the wrinkled Highlights magazine.

He was fatter than the last time we saw him. Sweatier. And his hair was patchy and starting to gray. But the eyes, those little black beetles scuttering in a pool of pink flesh, were exactly the same.

"And here," Dr. Thane announced, "a personal phenomenon you may both find intimately unsettling."

"Do you like the candle?" The phenomenon's voice was low and guttural with an air of mocking.

Mike was backed up against the wall. He opened his mouth, but no words were coming out. I could hear his short, frightened breathes.

Dr. Thane stood up, smiled smugly. "**John Henry Bowers, I know you've** already met."

I looked from the monstrous Chandler in the doorway to Mike, frozen in fear and pressing against the bookcase.

"He was a patient of mine," Thane explained, "when I was a consultant for a state hospital back east. You know the kind I mean."

The Chandler (as I will always know him) took a heavy step forward, and Mike pressed his back further against the books. He finally croaked out.

"*No.*"

The Chandler didn't care. He spread his thick lips in a grotesque grin.

"Light the candle?" he taunted.

I was freaked out, believe me, like I hadn't been...ever. But I wasn't paralyzed like Mike. I was still sitting down. The only one in the room, which is an awkward position to be in during the best of circumstances, to say nothing of this singular scenario where a demented doctor beckons in the monster of your youth to torment once more your best friend, torn to shreds by fear and decades of doubt.

I made a bold gambit. Perhaps I was so afraid that it went back around and got brave if that's the way it works. Maybe I was scared stupid, and therefore too stupid to realize what I was doing was insane. Or maybe because I knew the situation was helpless, I was thinking, to Hell with it, have some fun.

So rather than stand up and apologize, I sat my ground and put on a shtick.

"Excuse me," I interrupted, and indeed it stopped the Chandler in his tracks, paused his advance on Mike. "Are you saying, 'Do you like the candle' or 'Did you light the candle'?"

He turned his beastly head toward me and sneered. "The candle," he grunted.

I kept my voice from shaking, but I had that embarrassed burning in my nose. The act I was playing was downplaying the horror, which to be honest was all I could do.

"Yes, I heard, you were talking about the candle. I mean, that makes sense, because you always were obsessed with candles." I was talking fast and nearly running my words together, but it didn't matter now. "But either way, the answer's no. We didn't light the candle. We didn't start the fire." I laughed a little. "No, HE is your man." My finger snapping out like a spear, I pointed at Thane, who frowned.

"Stop pointing at me."

"He lit the candle!" I continued as if the Chandler was simply here on a quest for that culprit. "You want him." I shrugged. "And if you're asking if we *like* the candle-it's hard to tell because you slur your words-then obviously no. Do we, Mike?"

Mike swallowed, avoided looking at the beast in front of him. He breathed out, composed himself, and answered, "no."

"So clearly, whatever's going on here is between y'all, and I think Mike and I are just gonna split."

"Where do you think you're going?" Thane rose, his question filled with scorn and dismissal.

"Well that's not really any of your business, is it?"

"*Trent*," Mike hissed through clenched teeth. "You're making it worse."

"Oh, I am not," I rolled my eyes, but I was shaking inside. Truthfully, I did believe my words, as I was soon to articulate, but it didn't help me feel any better.

Thane stepped forward and gripped my shoulder. "Your friend is right," he squeezed.

"The Hell he is!" I shook his hand off. "Everyone in this room knows that whatever you and that fat Colonial maniac-who can't even dip a candle to save his life, by the way-whatever you're going to do, you were always going to do it, and it has nothing to do with what I'm saying now."

"You can't think you're helping your chances." Thane put on a cruel sneer, but I could tell he was more infuriated than amused.

"That's because we HAVE no chances. Duh! You guys want to kill us, that's on you, but-"

"Should I now?" The Chandler asked, his voice for the first time a little uncertain. Human, even.

"You're not talking your way out of this, boy!" Thane snapped.

"Then you concede I didn't talk myself into it," I pointed out. "We may be dead, but we don't have to feel guilty about it."

"How do you feel?" The Chandler asked as he looked into Mike's eyes.

Thane seethed. "You have no one to blame for what's coming next but yourselves."

"That's victim blaming!" I tried to smirk at Mike, but who was I fooling? "You gonna slut shame us next?"

"This is as inane as it is futile." Thane turned away from me disgusted. "Do it now."

The Chandler looked from Mike to me and back again. He shifted uneasily, as if uncomfortable in his own skin.

"Now," he repeated, chewing over the world like a gritty piece of tallow.

Dr. Thane nodded, and he turned to me, more angry than jovial now.

"Your path is at an end, my friend."

"Well, if it means I won't have to hear any more of your waxing about Jack Frost and Descartes, bring it on."

Thane looked at Chandler and waved his hand, impatient.

But Chandler bit his lip nervously. "They're not...disturbed," he stated weakly.

"That doesn't matter in the slightest," Thane sighed wearily, turning away from me and heading back to his desk. "Get this over immediately."

After a loaded moment.

"No," The Chandler mumbled, but it was clear to all in the room.

Thane faced him, annoyed.

"What do you mean 'no'?"

"No means no, doctor," I smirked nervously.

"Shut up. Bowers, you have one thing to do. It's very simple."

"I don't think..." he whined.

The idea of independent thought upset Thane even more than the first refusal.

"Of course, you don't! Nobody's asking you to think!"

"**HE**..." The Chandler threw some of his not inconsiderable weight in this preface, "wouldn't like us to. If the time's not right. If their reactions are not disturbed."

"'He.'" Thane could barely stay contained, "Now I have to hear you tell me about what 'He' would decree? As if you could even tell the difference between the voice of God and the voices in your own middling head! Ha!"

"Lover's spat." I stood up at last. "Mike, we're leaving."

"You're not going anywhere!" Thane roared.

"Watch me." I then slipped between Mike and the hulking monster in front of him, turned to my old friend, and gestured to the door. "Let's go."

The Chandler did not stand in our way. He actually shifted in his sides and turned to The Doctor. "What do we do?"

"I told you what to do!" Thane stepped up to him and roared in his face. "It's still beyond me why I had to pluck your medieval mind out of that pisshole, but I'm regretting it more and more."

Mike finally sprang into action-by which I mean he stepped past The Chandler, and we were on our way, without resistance.

"You mongoloid!" Thane was poking The Chandler in the chest repeatedly.

"Don't think that you're not next! When I'm through–"

The Chandler backhanded Thane, hard. Thane stumbled back, eyes wide in shock at the physical violation, and he hit his head on the edge of his desk. It was a nasty gash, I could tell from across the room. The kind of impact that caused major brain damage.

The shake of the impact knocked over that blasted candle, and the wax and Thane's desk being made of suspiciously combustible materials, his workplace was immediately, preternaturally, covered in flames.

"Mike, let's leave now!"

The Chandler stood his ground, mesmerized by the growing conflagration, which has spread like a speedy demon to the floor and the drapes.

Mike needed no further prodding. He ran with me, with all our strength and our speed. Whatever gifts God had given us to aid our escape, we put to use.

Leaving the fire and the beasts behind us, for so then we thought.

Chapter 19: Agent Toastman

I needn't go into the details from Mike and I fleeing the fire, calling 911, and the curious chain of events that led to our stay at the Los Angeles branch of the Federal Bureau of Investigation. Or maybe I should, in the interest of a more complete story, but I won't. Such details are trivial and meaningless to me now. Suffice to say that I called 911 like a good citizen, over Mike's objections, and convinced him to stay outside the building with me while help arrived.

Perhaps he was right, that it wasn't necessary for us to stay. We bolted out of the office and down the stairs as quickly as we could, but with the entire floor on fire, it was arguably unnecessary for us to make the call ourselves, therefore placing me and Mike in a position hard to explain to the authorities.

But I'm just not that guy. I'm not a flee-er.

(*Unless you're leaving Mike behind…*)

Anyway, we did our bit. Waited for the fire department, stood by the gathering, horrified crowd watching the smoking corner window (The Chandler never came charging out), and carefully explained we had seen an arsonist. We agreed to come to the police station, tell them the same thing. All we said was that we were meeting Dr. Thane when a man came in and assaulted him before setting the office on fire.

Which was true.

We hadn't been in the office 26 minutes before we were asked to take a little ride, over to the FBI. It was so quick. It was like they were waiting for us.

· · · · ·

It wasn't an interrogation room like you see in the movies, nor was it a private office. It was actually a conference room, and I sat at one end of a long table like I was chairman of the board. I did think it odd and unnecessary that I would be "talked to" (Not interrogated! Not under suspicion!) separately from Mike, but I didn't say anything, because, hey, no resistance.

"You'll just wait here," Candace, the businesslike but subtly comforting agent explained to me as she led me in. "Do you want some coffee or something."

"Maybe a water?"

"Sure."

Then she left, and I was sitting alone in this great big room, alone with my stupid little thoughts.

"Well Trent," I sighed dramatically. "You've really got yourself into a fine mess this time!"

I was trying to quote Laurel and/or Hardy, whose movies I had never actually seen, but I botched it.

There was a binder on the counter, and I was curious. Well, bored, and the tedious contents of said top-secret FBI files, in reality simply the notes of the last meeting concerning reassignments of local assistant directors and a schedule of upcoming bureau luncheons, only exasperated that boredom. Even in the upper echelons of power, it seemed, was there the tedious and the logistical.

I was looking at a list of names on a hot pink sheet of paper in laminate casing when the door open.

"Sorry!" I dropped the binder on the counter and immediately begin to think of ways to apologize for myself.

"A telling personality trait, that you should apologize as soon as I walk in the door. What for?" His voice was clear and mellifluous. Curious and probing, but without demand. Authoritative, but not aggressive.

He was tall and smooth-skinned. His suit was clean pressed, the whole ensemble sparkled, in fact, from his squeaky black shoes to the ash-gray tie residing near his polished American flag pin.

His eyes were incredibly blue, striking in fact, and his well-combed sandy blonde hair was a little longer than I'd expect for an agent. Especially with the sideburns. Sheesh.

I was fantasizing about the FBI Agent in my story being a hard Michael Shannon type, but instead, I got a guy who I'd say was more like a young Keir Dullea, except nobody would know what I meant.

"I didn't mean to-" he handed me the bottle of water that was in his left hand and held onto the right. "I mean, it was just sitting there."

"Let me." I slid the binder across to him. He was standing right next to me, almost reading over my shoulder, and perhaps I should have felt uncomfortable, but there was something about him that put me at ease.

He flipped through the binder, glancing down at a few pages, up to meet my eyes briefly, then back to these precious three-punched files before closing the whole thing.

"Nothing to it." He smiled. "It is a roster sheet, describing new faculty assignments. Hardly top secret, though someone should not have left it out." He gestured to the table, and I sat down. "I do not say this as a matter of propriety-as I have indicated, appointments of that stature are public knowledge. It is just not proper meeting conduct." He shrugged. "A poor way to run things."

I was relaxed enough in his presence that I felt I could crack a little joke.

"And here I thought I had stumbled across the X-Files."

He smiled warmly and actually started to whistle the tune.

"The connection you make is natural. And welcome. The Bureau gets a better rap in fiction than the news."

"Liberal media," I said, and my nose burnt because I didn't want to get political. "I always wanted to be an agent myself. I always wanted to whistle too, but I couldn't pull either off."

"Ah, but a man's reach should exceed his grasp. Or what is heaven for?" He said this with a manual flourish, waving his hand with some significance.

The same hand with which he then extended me with a curiously fluid motion, pointing to the heavens with one finger as he quoted Browning, then full handshake business, within the blink of the eye.

"Special Agent Ted Toastman. Criminal Branch, violent crime."

"Uh, Trent Malloy...The Angeleno Film Archive."

He had a firm, warm grip. Something was reassuring about it. Hank Hill would vote for this man.

"The Angeleno Film Archive. That is your film school?"

"No, I'm out of school. It's an organization that does film screenings."

"A movie theater." I frowned, which he picked up on. "I do not say this dismissively. I am just trying to make an assertion based on available evidence. Please, correct me."

"No, it's fine. We just put on special screenings at various theaters. The Egyptian in Hollywood and The Aero in Santa Monica."

"And what do you do for this cinema?"

"I'm a detect-an archivist, I mean." I decided that when you're talking to the FBI, complete honesty was the way to go, and even hyperbole should be downplayed to be on the safe side. "I look for lost films, track down rare prints, my little detective work." I smiled slightly, almost by way of apology for my almost-boast.

"Sounds like a fun job."

"It has its ups and downs. Pay's nothing to write home about."

"I hear that." He cleared his throat and reached to the file he was carrying under his arm. Placed it on the table and went through its contents. Its content, rather, as there was but a single paper there, which he promptly held up for me to see.

"Your statement to the police. Succinct but illuminating." He glanced at it. "Says that you and your pal were visiting Dr. Victor Thane when an intruder burst into his office, assaulted the doctor, and started the fire."

"Yes." I was nervous. I didn't know just how much was going to be covered here. I started to stammer, to correct and clarify, "By start the fire, I mean that was accidental. Dr. Thane had a candle lit on his desk. When he, the-the intruder-" I stumbled over that, but Toastman didn't react, audibly or otherwise, "pushed Dr. Thane, the candle knocked over, and that's what started it."

"That is still criminal liability on his part. If and when we find this perpetrator, he has a lot to answer for."

"You didn't-" A cold panic went down my spine. "We ran out of the office, the whole place was ablaze. It was so...flammable." My voice was shaking, frightened.

"Everything is alright." His voice was steady, calm. He knew what he was doing.

"Just...you didn't find him."

"I understand your fearful incredulity. Thane's office was an inferno when the first response got to it-and thank God they arrived when they did. And thank you for your warning. Dinah Braxton, Dr. Thane's receptionist, and Saul Nussbaum, his next patient, are grateful you got them out of there."

"We had to. The place was lit up."

"In the hours since your initial report, a team has examined the-I am sorry to say-'ruins' of Thane's office. And taken away the body of the deceased man himself. Certainly not an appealing sight," I shivered. "But of the assailant, no, I am afraid he is still unaccounted for."

That was distressing on multiple levels for multiple reasons. One, Chandler was still out there. Who knew what he was up to next. What horrors!

Second, there was a crime without a culprit, but Mike and I were in custody, so would we do? Imagine that, becoming the suspect after all that.

"Now we have got teams perusing the security footage of The Lacombe Building. If our man passed through the lobby or one of the stairwells, took a ride in the elevator, he will be there."

"He'd have to be then. I mean, it's not like he just apparated in Thane's office."

(Or so I was trying to convince myself.)

"Of course. But we would like to know just who we are looking for. You said in your statement that he was a large man, approaching 6'5, and corpulent."

"Yes, and balding with pasty, sweaty, skin," I closed my eyes, so painful was the recollection but in doing so could only see that monster again. So, I unshut my eyes and welcomed back the warm light of the conference room and the clean-shaven, handsome face of the agent in front of me. "Can I be honest with you?"

"The best policy."

"I..." I started breathing in and out, trying to steady my nerves. This was difficult. It was more of a horrifying ordeal to describe The Chandler to a friendly officer of the law than it was to actually be confronted by him in Thane's office. My chill and swagger had been burnt up, and I was afraid again.

"Trent, are you alright?" He sounded genuinely concerned. "Are you undergoing a panic attack?" He put his hand on my back, comforting.

"No, I don't have panic attacks," I sighed, somewhat calm now that I had resigned myself to confessing. "It's just...I can't give you just a description. I know exactly who he was."

"Interesting," he responded with a loaded, ambiguous intonation that could indicate it was interesting in a multitude of ways. "Tell me more."

"It's hard to believe. You won't believe me. I mean, I can hardly believe it myself."

"Trent," he said simply. "All we can do is try."

"Okay, well, we grew up together, Mike and I-that's Lieutenant Michael Kripke."

"No, it is not."

"What?" I didn't know what he meant by this interruption, but he rolled his hand with the "continue" gesture. "Back east. We went to elementary school. And we were buddies."

"I would say you still are. So it seems."

"I meant we used The Buddy System. On field trips."

He smiled with a sense of familiarity. "We did the same thing when I was in school," he chuckled, "and in The Bureau, as it is. Field trips, field assignments. All the same."

"The former is usually safer than the later," I responded, "But that day…"

"Which?"

"Colonial Williamsburg." Was that glint of recognition in his eyes? "Back in Virginia. It's sort of this, living museum. Like a Renaissance faire but in colonial times. Everyone is-"

"I knew exactly what you were talking about immediately after you said it. We had a similar institution in my hometown. Pioneer Days. A different time and place, but the same conceit."

"Right. Right," I nodded. I guess those sorts of living history play act parks were common enough that no further elucidation was required.

"We were walking around the village. And we came to…the candle hut, I guess. I don't know. That sounds more like a place at an upper-class strip mall like the type they have in North County. Like Pottery Barn. Maybe it's called The Chandler, named after the craftsman who resides there. Anyway, the candlemaker, he's called The Chandler. He was a weird guy. He made a candle in front of us, and it…sucked. I didn't say anything, but Mike did. He called it a crappy candle to the guy's face. And he didn't like it. He grabbed Mike's hand and shoved it into the burning hot wax. Held it there. The skin scaled off his bones. That's why he wears a glove." I took a tasteless sip of water. "I ran away."

"And the Candlemaker?" he pressed gently.

"He was arrested. It turns out he had applied to work at the park a couple times. Couldn't get hired. He snuck into the park and just stayed there. I guess he had some mental problems. They didn't tell us much about what happened to him. Like I said, we were 12."

"Did they tell you his name?"

I swallowed.

"John Henry Bowers."

"His middle name," Toastman noted.

"Like a serial killer or a presidential assassin," I agreed.

"But this is when you were 12."

"Yes, and I know it sounds like a non-sequitur. But…" I leaned in, and he joined me for the improbable part. "It was him. Here in Los Angeles, over a decade later-closer to two even! The Chandler. He was the attacker. It was him!"

I felt one weight lifted from my chest now that that secret was out, but a new one now that I had to live with the consequences of telling someone else.

Toastman did not respond with incredulity or doubt, however. Instead, his face lit up. Broad smile, bright eyes. He slapped me on the back gregariously, which I appreciated even if it was not protocol and this point in the investigation.

"Well done, Trent! Well done! And kudos for coming forward with that information. I am sure the personal doubt alone was considerable, let alone your trepidation with imparting that crucial revelation to an authority figure."

"Kudos?" This was unexpected. And surreally positive.

"We know quite a bit more about Dr. Victor Thane than you, and your friend do." He paused, reconsidered. "That was our assumption anyway, as I really do not know exactly what you knew about Thane-or your business with him for that matter."

I had told myself and God that I would tell the truth and nothing but the truth. But I did not have to tell the whole truth-even though this young, reassuring agent was impelling it from me.

"What was your business with the deceased?" he asked without pressure. "Doctor-patient confidentiality notwithstanding, it is a minor issue I would not mind cleared up."

"Oh yes." How to explain our presence in that office of horrors without mentioning undead cats or stray eyeballs? "Mike and I, about a week ago, we were visiting The Pick and Hammer."

He knew the place already.

"That would be the private psychiatrist's club in Burbank?"

"That's right." His familiarity would save us a bit of time, but was it a good thing?

"Thane is on the board of directors, and he is a co-founder."

"Yeah-I mean, sure-I mean okay." Was I supposed to know that? "But we weren't there to find-" I was about to finish saying "We weren't there to find Dr. Thane", but that would be a lie. So, I told a truth that did not reveal so much. "There's this rare liqueur..."

"A liqueur?" Agent Toastman was not expecting this.

"Yeah. I guess it's made with herbs or something. Pin's Brew, it's called."

"Should I be writing this down?" He had his eyebrows raised, semi-amused as if we could both acknowledge that this was a trivial detail.

"Heh, no. But that's sort of how we got there. Mike had gotten a taste for

Pin's Brew." Which was true, in a matter of speaking, if "taste" can be manipulated into "interest", though it did unfairly shift the blame. "And we looked up where to find it. Turns out there are only five bars in LA that even serve the stuff."

"Is that a fact?" He did not sound impatient with these details, which I thought was actually a bad thing. I didn't want him pulling on that thread.

"Yeah. And Mike's got this interest in psychology. He may go into it next, as his field of study-I don't know if he's mentioned that?"

"To me?"

"To anyone." I hadn't considered who Mike may have been talking to. "Mike makes contact, or maybe he already knew her, with a member of the club. Oh...I'm sorry, but I forget her name." Which was true, not an obfuscating tactic to sound more genuine and unprepared. I honestly didn't remember. "Dr. Price maybe? Anyway, long story short, Mike gets us into the club, and while he's talking with her, I go to the bar. And there I bump into the late doctor, the deceased that is, Dr. Thane." I then emphasized, "meeting him for the first time. I didn't even know who he was. And we talked."

"What did you talk about?"

"Oh, you know, this and that." I waved my hand dismissively. What on Earth could be gained by inviting Jack Frost to the FBI? "It was a friendly and, uh, informative chat. He invites me to his office for a free evaluation."

"To which you take Mike." I opened my mouth, but he was already shaking his head as if he had made a misstep myself. "Forgive me, that is irrelevant. You were in Dr. Thane's office, and that's enough. So, you and Mike are talking to Thane when Bowers comes in and attacks."

"That's correct."

"Did he say anything to the doctor? Did they have an exchange?"

"Yes, yes, they did. They had an argument." I was straining, because I was talking moment to moment, and constantly regretting my last sentence. I said nothing more, and Toastman began a new inquiry.

"How much do you know about Victor Thane? Really?" Thank God he didn't wait for an answer. "Your stated purview being what it is, you may only see the deceased as a private therapist and member of an exclusive social club. And yet..." He spread his arms, inviting me to take in his presence. "Here I am."

"Y-yes. I see that."

"Did it occur to you to question, Trent, the nature of The Bureau's interest in this particular affair?"

It had, but I held my tongue. Sometimes in seeking a question, you give away an answer.

He continued.

"We are not in the habit of taking an active role in the matter of every battery and arson, as I am sure you must be aware."

"Yeah. Yeah, I figured."

"As it so happens, Dr. Thane was already under investigation. By yours truly. Would you like to know why?"

"Because your superiors assigned you?" I felt like lightening the mood a little, and it worked. Toastman smiled slightly. Benevolent. Indulging me.

"Sure. At the time of my initial inquiry, the man in question had recently left his post at a state-run mental facility back east. Virginia, in fact. His departure was cloaked in scandal. One of his patients, one John Henry Bowers, had recently escaped custody. There were other patients of his, some of a violent or aberrant nature, who had also broken the confines or otherwise been questionably discharged by the doctor himself."

"What other patients?" I dared to ask, imagining a preternaturally chipper young blonde who might have an origin story after all.

"Never you mind that. The point is that Thane was under suspicion of malignant incompetence. The bulk of the official consequences for Bowers' escape came down on the security personnel. And yet still, I found it bore noting that Bowers was only transferred to a lower security wing on Dr. Thane's recommendation. The ill-advised releases of several other high-risk patients under protest of his peers-as the residing director, Thane had final authority-raised my eyebrows considerably. Especially given that the hereto mentioned had failed the terms of their probation by neglecting to check in with court-ordered parole officers and psychiatrists. They remained-and remain-unaccounted for."

This was a whole new batch of information to take in. I was trying to make sense of it, and I hoped he wouldn't give me a hard (er) time.

"So, to be clear, you're talking about-what are you talking about?" I knew my Stan Grossman impression would go over his head. "What exactly do you think Thane was up to, besides dangerous incompetence?"

Toastman tilted his head and begin to explain himself.

"I differ from other agents, Trent, in that my approach to investigation does not begin with speculation as to motives. I see 'why' as a highly overrated question. It is my preference to stick to the facts as they occur, and not encourage the mind of the detective to run wild in an attempt to craft a narrative before sufficient information has been revealed." He shrugged, acknowledging the unconventionality. "Conventional wisdom holds that one can and should forge a hypothesis based on available data as soon as possible, but I defer. Confirmation bias is a pernicious fallacy. Evidence is manipulated to reach a foregone conclusion, either consciously by some manifested prejudice or simply through the unintended consequence of operating under a theory in the first place. It is a risk I hesitate to take. My friends and colleagues dismiss my perspective as unimaginative, but I'd call myself deliberate, cautious, and pragmatic." He smiled, indicating that he did take delight in his worldview. "I like to think of a criminal case-or any mystery or question, in fact, as something akin to a jigsaw puzzle with no picture on the box. You put the pieces together as they match, and only as the picture emerges do you realize what you're looking at."

"A puzzle without a picture. I like that. They should make those."

"My cousin has some. She has won several tournaments."

"Of jigsaw puzzle completion?"

"Yes."

I rubbed my forehead. I was thinking about Toastman's cousin now, but this was off-topic, surely.

"What are we talking about?"

"The current subject, Trent, which is whatever subject we currently are conversing about. Therefore, it is our choice. To your immediate and preceding question, I had not ascertained the nature of Thane's entanglement, and I was remiss to wager a guess-an appropriate aphorism, for all guessing is a manner of gambling, and I was raised Mormon. There were multiple possibilities being considered. Collusion, coercion-either by the inmates themselves or a sinister third party, or..."

"Coincidence?"

His look at me grew more pointed.

"Was it coincidence? Coincidence that the man you bump into at a bar should be the former doctor of the man who terrorized you as a child? A following coincidence that as you visit the doctor's office, that same childhood terror should attack? In your estimation, is this just happenstance?" He put an emphasis on the *is*. He really was curious, and true to his word, he didn't pretend to know the answer.

"I don't...Ahhhh," I sighed. "That's one Hell of a question, dude." Which was perfectly true.

"Fine, fine," he raised his hand, conceding. "That is fair. But perhaps you may articulate some of the particulars of the dialogue between Thane and Bowers. Assuming it was not a completely wordless altercation and you remember what was said."

"I do." I gritted my teeth and lowered my head.

I was looking down, and I noticed how immaculately pressed Toastman's pants were. It brought to mind *The Doors of Perception*, when Aldous Huxley takes mescaline and spends eight hours staring at the crease in his trousers. He saw something profound in it, but he was really, really, high.

What a weird thing to think about.

Maybe it was just my brain trying to find something else to occupy itself with, away from the unpleasantness I now had to confront head-on.

"I want to help you Agent Toastman. But there's something...big here. Something sinister, I don't quite understand, and I have no idea how to begin telling you."

I looked up. He was nodding, with no ill will, and he patted me on the back compassionately.

"So then let us begin with the truth, no matter how dubious or frightening, and go from there."

"The truth?"

"It is as good a place to start as any."

I nodded. Here goes everything.

"I have come to believe that there is a man...and perhaps that's the wrong word, though I can't very well think of any other. Force of nature perhaps, a malevolent entity? I don't want to say 'demigod', though God only knows what kind of designation would be appropriate. A King, simply enough. Succinct and fitting, and that is how this presence has been referred to. THE KING OF WAX. I believe he had surreptitious agents of unknown numbers and a sinister agenda of unthinkable evil. Of course, I can't prove this, I don't know it, and I certainly don't understand. But I do fear. It seems clear to me that Dr. Victor Thane was aligned with this figure. He said as much to me. He and Bowers, it would appear, were in strange league. I don't know the nature of this wicked cult. Bowers said that "He" wanted us to be...disturbed. He acted like this was a prerequisite to killing us. Thane wanted him to get it over with. When Bowers refused to comply, deferring to his belief that his dark god would not wish it *yet*, they argued. The Chandler struck the Doctor, knocking his candle over and starting the fire. Mike and I ran, and here we are."

"Here you are." Toastman was clicking his pen over and over. I hadn't noticed he had taken out a little notebook and was scrawling the best bits of my madness down. "Trent, I am sure you cannot expect me to believe this."

"No," I sighed, "I didn't think so."

"This is not to say I dismiss your entire account offhand. I simply mean to acknowledge your self-skepticism and reticence in coming forward with such an account. That attitude is what gives me the most pause."

"What do you mean?"

"All you have told me is that Thane and Bowers were affiliated, which is probable, even demonstrably likely. And that they shared a belief in this figure you speak of so ominously. This all fine and plausible enough, but it is your reluctance to mention it that puzzles me. Surely you are aware that the existence of militant cults is not unheard of and may be in The Bureau's purview."

"Yes." I was nodding, now aware I had tipped my hand. If I had just called Thane and Bowers two nuts who worshipped the devil, okay, that comments on them. But now I had brought attention to The King.

"So, the panic in your timbre and your hesitancy makes me wonder if you are in fact ascribing supernatural characteristics to a being you actually believe in yourself."

I laughed nervously.

"That'd be absurd."

"Would it?" he prodded, though I couldn't tell how open his mind was. "Evidently, Thane held an association with Bowers, and quite likely, several of his other former patients. That there was some sort of occult sect is as plausible as any explanation at this point. Surmise that the cult still has a ringleader higher than Thane, why is it impossible that he calls himself The King of Wax?"

"I guess that's not...impossible." I was treading thin ice here. Whatever he was, he wasn't some simple human cult leader. I knew that much.

"If he is said to a wholly supernatural figure, however, then we run into trouble." Toastman leaned in. "Trent, is there anything else you want to tell me?"

I swallowed.

"No. No. I mean, yeah, they were talking about this...guy, sounded pretty weird, creepy. So, I guess I didn't think it was right to mention their 'god', cause he's not real, not it doesn't matter? Sorry, I guess it is relevant. Anyway, I told you what I saw." I bit my lip, desperately praying this ordeal was reaching its end. "Can I leave now?"

Toastman stood up. He gestured towards the door.

"Be my guest. You have been very helpful, Trent."

"Thank you," I kept my eye on him while edging to the door.

"We have each other's contact information. Let me know if there is anything else you can think of, and likewise, I will keep you in the loop as pertinent details arrive I deem fit to share with you."

"Thank you."

I was almost out, almost ready to reunite with Mike and leave this unhappy chapter behind, move to the next mystery when I heard Agent Toastman wish me farewell.

"Enjoy the night."

• • • • •

I got to the lobby. Mike wasn't there. I turned to Candace, the receptionist (if that's accurate).

"Do you know if Mike Kripke is still in debriefing? Can you say?"

I was wondering if I would have to wait a spell or even explain myself to Candace. She invited little conversation with her reply.

"He left twenty minutes ago."

Huh.

"Oh. Okay. I guess he didn't have as much to say."

"He didn't say much. He said they had to either charge him or release him."

Nice, Mike.

"So, where is he?"

"They released him."

I looked around. He truly was gone.

I turned to Candace, busy computing what she was and disinterested this night in the further plights of one T. Marshall Malloy.

Naturally, I called him, still standing in the lobby at an awkward pose.

The phone rang.

And rang.

Finally:

"*This is Kripke: If you have something important to say, you don't need my invitation. If it's not worthwhile, save my time and your voice.*"

This "greeting" of "Kripke's" was as hostile as it was pretentious.

"Mike, where are you. I just got out, and I'm in the front lobby, so, call me back."

Had he left? Like, left *left*? Just bolted? Did he not think we had a lot to talk about? Perhaps that was the thing. He was processing this mania in his own way, the soldier's way, and didn't want to discuss it. Take some time alone with his thoughts.

Fair enough, but he was my ride. My car was in Glendale. I could have ordered a mensch or found a bus, but unlike Mike, I did desire human company in this time of worry.

Chapter 15: Cancer Pizza Party

"I was in 8th grade," I told Lilith. "We had done something special."

"We?" she ran her finger along my arm, casually making circles and raising goosebumps.

We were sitting on a bench on the UCLA campus, looking out at the placid green campus, enjoying the cool dusk of what we filmmakers call "the magic hour." The campus was walking distance (if you had the time), surprisingly, from the FBI building. Lilith had consented to meet me there. I hadn't told her where I was coming from or shared the shivers of that walk.

"I'm hungry." I stood up, looking out at the school with such eager young minds yet untainted by the cold ugliness of a reality that...

Skip it.

"Let's get something to eat, and I can tell you all about the pizza party that never was."

She was game. Very patient, all things considered. Lilith stood up.

"Can we get pizza then?"

•   •   •   •   •

"Do you believe in evil?"

I couldn't really open up to Lilith on the UCLA campus, scenic stop-over that it was, and perhaps opening up to her about all this wasn't an option. But pizza was. We found a nifty little pizza place in Westwood.

"You're looking at her!" she grinned, strings of cheese still hanging from her mouth. The juxtaposition with her grave black lipstick was odd and upsetting.

Also, cute. Irresistibly so.

But I wanted some serious conversation. Honestly, as drawn as I was to her, this Goth act was wearing thin, especially when juxtaposed with the real primal horror I was facing down.

"I don't mean your brand of Nightmare Before Christmas trick-or-treat makeup. I'm talking something real." That sounded crueler than I intended, and Lilith knew her.

"I'm real!" She scowled. "Fuck you, Trent. What do you think I am, a walking Hot Topic?"

"I'm just saying, I feel like you're a bit…affected. Like me. We all are." I put my hands atop hers to assure her this wasn't a judgment on her alone. "God knows I exaggerate my more endearing personality traits to try to craft a character."

"Yeah?" She pulled her hands away from mine, thus breaking my heart, and asked scornfully, "so what's your character?"

"Sort of this…esoteric, erudite but innocent Catholic cinephile detective. A deadpan snarker who communicates in far too many references. A nerd with a heart of gold and a lot of internal rules that act as breaks on my desires, to quote The Great Carraway."

"And there's one of your references, alright." A smile cracked that cold stony visage, to my heart's great relief. "You really think of yourself like that?"

"How do you think of me?"

"Who says I do?" But she was smiling playfully, and she reached out and bopped my nose.

"I didn't mean anything by it, Lilith. I've just had a real weird day. I've seen some horror, and I want to talk about it. I didn't mean to insult you."

"It's fine." She shrugged, and her tone took that same casual note of detachment as when she mentioned "I just think you should know I have had a dark life, for real. I was a crack baby, and I used to live in motels."

"I'm sorry. I didn't know that."

"You didn't ask. You didn't bother to find out." She blocked my objection. "I don't think it's because you don't care-because I know you do-but this misplaced sense of discretion isn't an attractive quality. You think you're being a gentleman, but you're just being distant. Ask me questions. Ask me if I fucked my father, even."

I drew a blank, swallowed, and lowered my voice.

"Did that happen to you?"

She sighed and rolled her eyes.

"Just my point is, get personal."

"Okay. Okay, I'll keep that in mind."

"Thank you." She sipped her Mountain Dew, and I started.

"What happened to..." But I wasn't there yet. "What happened to me today, is, I was actually at the FBI..."

"What? What are you talking about?"

"Cliff notes version. I was visiting this...doctor's office and this...this guy bursts in. A psychopath. He attacked the doctor, he KILLED HIM!"

"Holy shit."

"He set the office on fire."

"You're making this up?"

"No, I'm not making this up!" But I calmed because I could not blame her for incredulity. "It was scary. I can't believe it."

"Hey. Trent." She leaned forward and held my hands. Intertwined our fingers and rubbed them, a dance of digits as she looked into my eyes. Her own were uncommonly wide opened, lending her a refreshingly sincere look. When you're not looking at her smoky eyeliner and Egyptian Goth mascara conveying sexiness or sarcasm, she was capable of comfort. "I believe you, man."

"Thanks, Lil." And her earnestness now made me sad, because I knew my brief line about a maniac at the doctor's office was tragically, criminally insufficient an explanation. It was completely true, but it was not the complete truth. And she deserved it. "I'm sorry. But there's more. Oh God, there's so much more, and I don't know how to...what to..."

She ducked down and kissed my thumbs and then twiddled them back and forth. "And you can tell me whatever you want. When you want to. Or not. It's okay."

"Thank you. I really appreciate that." I laughed nervously. "I really wouldn't know where to begin. Grade school, I guess."

"To your pizza party?"

"No, that was 8th grade. Junior high. Or middle school. But that's an excellent digression, affording me to change the subject."

"I'll give it."

"It was a class effort. I think it was a reading assignment or something? It was a yearlong project anyway, maybe raising money or consistently scoring the highest. Part of a nationwide competition. I don't know."

"Well, you don't have to go into so much detail."

"Yeah, I know. The point is that we, the class, earned a pizza party. Not won it through the luck of the draw or anything. We earned it...because we scored high or put in community service? Dammit, I wish I could remember more."

"But that isn't the point."

"No, it isn't. So, we've got this pizza party coming to us. And we're jacked, because we're kids, and it's pizza."

"Everybody gets jacked over pizza. It's like sex."

"Thank you, Sharon Stone. Or was that Woody Allen?"

"That's just like an old joke."

"Our teacher is Mrs. Laughlin. Our part-time assistant teacher is Mr. Skaar."

"Mr. Scar?"

"He was Scandinavian. He actually pronounced it Skoor. Like that candy bar. This was near the end of the year, and one of his away days, Mrs. Laughlin gives us a choice. Mrs. Skaar has cancer."

"What kind did you choose?"

"No, we didn't choose the type of cancer. But Mrs. Laughlin tells us his wife is in the hospital, and she suggests we cancel the pizza party."

"What a bitch."

"No!" I laughed. "Wow. I don't mean-she didn't want to cancel just for the heck of it. She said we could instead use the money we would have spent on the pizza party on Mrs. Skaar."

"I got that. It's lame."

"You're two steps ahead of me. Because it sure sounds noble, and there was only brief discussion where we all agreed how nice it would be to sacrifice our fun for the greater good. I just didn't understand the logistics. I didn't immediately understand how giving up our pizza party would help a woman with cancer. I asked my friend Ashley, 'How much does the chemotherapy cost?' She just looked at me weird and said 'We're not paying for the chemo!' Like it was obvious."

"It was, dude! A pizza party is what, $50? Chemo costs thousands!"

"Well I didn't know that! I was in 8th grade!"

"Yeah, and Doogie Hauser was 10."

"And fictional."

"You were seriously thinking you were going to pay her medical bills with pizza money? That's one Hell of a tip, dude."

"No, see, I didn't. I immediately questioned what was being asked. It came out that the money we were going to spend on pizza would go to flowers, cards, Beanie Babies, various sundries to cheer her up in the hospital."

"Duh. And gay."

"We all voted to give it to her, of course. Come on, you're gonna lay that trip on a bunch of 8th graders? Like they're any chance we're not going to succumb to the guilt and pressure to be magnanimous? Tell us there's a woman dying in the hospital who wants our pizza party and we're going to brat out? Kids are generous and easily swayed by guilt," I said of myself. "People always forget that," I said of others.

"She didn't though, did she? Did she even want your pizza party money?"

"That's my point! She didn't ask for it. It wasn't her idea or her husband's, and I've always wondered what her reaction was."

"Didn't you know when that still living and now healthy woman visited your class to thank you for your pizza money curing her cancer?"

"Never heard from her. It was near the end of the year, and Mr. Skaar only came in a couple more times, didn't talk about his wife. Mrs. Laughlin never even told us that she really appreciated our kind gesture. And that's 8th grade, so we weren't back in the fall. I never found out."

"That's a bummer, I guess. Maybe she died."

"She could have. But I still have to wonder, and I ask myself this, and I'd ask you if you were in that position-"

"I'd take the pizza. You kidding?"

"No, I mean if you were Mrs. Skaar."

"It'd depend on what kind of Scandinavian he was. If your 8th grade TA was a Varg Vikernes death punk Viking sex god, then sure, I'd hop on his. But if he's some pansy socialist Swedistan hide-your-crosses-to-please-the-rapeugees sap, then forget it."

"Um." (Yes, her Norse commentary was appalling, but moving on) "I don't mean literally you marry him. I mean, if you were in his wife's position. Would you even want to deprive a bunch of middle-schoolers of their pizza party for some creature comforts in the hospital? I'd feel awkward. Center of attention like that and taking something from them. I'd say let them eat pizza."

"I get where you're coming from," she mused, serious now. "Maybe she would want them to know their generosity was appreciated, and then everybody wins because the kids feel like they did something good, and she accepted it. That's like an inner joy that lasts longer than pizza, and it means more than a little hospital teddy bear. Don't think of it as her taking your pizza. Think of it like she accepted your gifts, and that's a gift she gave all of you."

"Wow. That's a really good point."

She gently kicked me under the table.

"Told you I was smart."

"Was there ever any doubt?"

"I'm sorry you didn't *get any* in 8th grade though." She raised her eyebrow provocatively and smirked, evoking the early juxtaposition of sex and pizza, and now I also took the opportunity to accept her invitation to ask an invasive personal question.

"Well no, I was a kid. Did you?"

"Junior high was a very boring time for me. Mom and Dad sent me to Immaculate Heart." She scrunched up her face. "No boys allowed."

"Did that really hold you back?"

She shook her head and took on an affected, soap-operatic tone, raising one hand to her brow in a dainty flourish.

"T'was too late. I was already a fallen woman."

"We're all sinners." I tried to sound magnanimous, but she insisted on upping the ante.

"Boy, I gave my first blow job in the sixth grade." I managed not to choke down my Mountain Dew, and she went on, "Anyway, how'd we get here? Cancer pizza party?"

"Small comforts, is my point. I was sitting on the bench at UCLA, waiting for you, and I just wanted something to take my mind off the horror. And it's like, what can we do? If you're in the hospital, you're being eaten alive by your own body. That sickness inside and the kids won't eat pizza, they gave that up. It's for you. But that money's not going to pay your medical bills. Not even close. It'll get you some sweet candy or nice smelling flowers, but how does that help?"

"It's a distraction, maybe?"

"Like the Chimpanzee's Tea Party."

"Now there were chimps there?"

"Not there, not at our pizza party- which we didn't have, anyway. This was when I visited Europe. Amsterdam."

"At the Red Light District?! Damn, son, you're into some freaky shit!"

"No, ha." I didn't tell her about the pallid, desultory hand job I actually got there, still a source of shame. "This was the Anne Frank house. It was a postcard she had on her wall. Along with pin-ups of movie stars like Lionel Barrymore and Clara Bow. She was really into Hollywood. And she had this card, a photo. It'd be a meme these days, but I guess back then people actually used to buy them in shops. A photo of chimps at a table, monkeying around, holding teacups."

"Aww," Lilith cooed.

"Yeah, I know. But I can't imagine. That kind of life. Having to be kept away in a dark attic all day, afraid of the men outside who want to kill you and your family and all your people. That's no kind of existence. And she was just a little girl. I just hope, maybe when she looked at this silly little picture, Anne Frank smiled."

"Excellent," Lilith said it like she really responded to what I was saying, that she found it touching.

"But at the end of the day..." It was the end of the day and a long, dark one at that. It felt like I had woken up in another century, another country than the place I was now. "The Holocaust. Cancer. A psycho from the past murdering someone in front of your eyes. It all happened. It's all set in stone. There's no changing that, especially when it's ongoing. So, these...little comforts? Distractions? What can they-"

"Shhhh," she was hushing me as she closed the distance between us and gave me a kiss. Slow and sensual. I closed my eyes and surrendered to it.

"So?" she asked in a beckoning voice, "Did I take your mind off it?"

I smiled.

"Lilith, are you a night creature?"

Eyes sparkling, alluring and dangerous.

"No," she purred, "I am **the** night creature."

We then went to my place in Glendale. There did Lilith repose, and find herself a place to rest.

Chapter 16: Lilith

That last line, was, of course, Biblical in nature (in case it wasn't on the nose enough already).

I'd been thinking a lot about that lately. Lilith. Both in the sense of my girlfriend and her of the apocryphal variety.

It may be, I thought unfortunately as I lay on my bed, my hands under my head in a contemplative pose, staring up at my *Rocketeer* poster, a masterpiece of art deco promise, that neither of those designations was accurate.

Firstly, Lilith and I, though we had been seeing each other for weeks now and had, you know, on multiple occasions, had not actually articulated the nature of our relationship. It's such an awkward, obligatory, and unromantic conversation to have. How does one even go about it in a suave way? How do you ask, "So are we like boyfriend and girlfriend now" without sounding like you're in high school? Like I mentioned earlier, Darcy always said it was best to DTR after about a week. Her acronym spelled "Define the Relationship", but I shunned that term for its obvious and perhaps intentional similarity to the *Jersey Shore*/Tinder generation of degenerates' call of Down to Fornicate. I had changed my Facebook status to "In a Relationship" to the cyber applause of over a dozen "Likes" and "Loves". Eddie Deezen, voice of Mandark, wrote "CONGRATULATIONS!" on that status. But Lilith wasn't my Facebook friend, so there was no way to see if she reciprocated said update in question.

And it was in question. The intricacies, of the fairer sex in general and dating in specific, have long been lost on me. Even Agent Dale Cooper said it was a mystery there was no sense in trying to figure out. I mean, how could we? That may be a sexist sentiment as well as a naked admission of my own romantic incompetence, but hey, who's writing this novel? I suppose I could bide my time, attempt to figure out where she stood without tipping my hand, hint I wanted something more without scaring her off, and gradually discern a complete picture and even ease it towards a position in my favor.

Or, you know, I could just be a man and ask her.

As for the latter, it turns out that her antediluvian namesake was not necessarily the subject of Biblical apocrypha strictly. I had heard of Lilith as a Judeo-Christian mythological figure, of course, but not paid her much attention because (I assumed) she was non-canonical. I had heard about the legend of Adam's first wife who refused to submit and was banished from Eden for her insolence. That she subsequently became a female demon, a succubus, the first vampire, or some combination of all three. I probably also thought Lilith may have played more of a role in Islam. I thought it was an interesting story. She was a memorable and sexy figure. I mean, one of my favorite movies was Vincent Gant's *Cobalt Requiem*, that criminally underrated supernatural noir where Val Kilmer's irascible yet endearing detective Jack Hardy gets entwined with Madonna's succubus, who turns out to be (SPOILER ALERT!) Lilith herself. Interesting in fiction, but I didn't believe in her. It was not out of my scope of beliefs there could be a fallen angel named Lilith, but the Genesis of His Roman Catholic Church did not include such a story. God did see that it is not good for man to be alone, so then he creates Eve from his rib. Nothing about any subordinate first attempt. Rome didn't acknowledge this account, and thus neither did I.

Well, imagine my shock when I found out, upon further research inspired by my dating a girl with that name, that Lilith was not confined solely to old wives tales and apocrypha like the Book of Enoch, but actually was mentioned, BY NAME, in The Bible. THE Bible. The CATHOLIC Bible. MY Catholic Bible.

I came across this fact in my research (read: Google search). Online resources give you a rich history of comparative religion, alternate interpretations (a common and boring explanation was that this text referred to some manner of owl), and feminist grievances. But even a wonderful resource like biblegateway.com, which offered the full text from multiple translations, there was nothing so pure and satisfying and tangible as reading it in my own Bible. Solid, in print, away from any other commentary. So, after the internet told me where to look, I took out my Good Book and looked for myself.

The relevant passage was Isaiah 34:14.

"Desert creatures will meet with hyenas, and wild goats will bleat to each other; there the night creatures will also repose and find for themselves a place of rest." (Isaiah 34:14, *The New Adventure Bible*.)

So that's pretty interesting. "Night creatures". I liked that. You'll have noticed I borrowed that phrase to refer to my Lilith. Ambiguous. Mysterious.

Could be anything.

It's not Lilith though.

Until I visited my parents next, stayed in my old bedroom, and thought to crack open the large leather-bound Bible I had from years past. Both this and the one I kept with me in Los Angeles were legitimate Catholic Bibles, and now I was in, at last, for the Earth-shattering reveal:

"There shall the lilith repose, and find for herself a place to rest."* (Isaiah 34: 14, The New American Bible, Saint Joseph Edition)

There was, of course, a footnote:

**Lilith*: A female demon thought to roam about the desert.

So, there it is. In MY CATHOLIC BIBLE (one of them, anyway), Lilith herself, or the lilith, described by name and not some vague "night creature", with a footnote identifying her as not any kind of owl, but an actual demon.

Now from a certain point of view, this should not really be so shocking. It was The Bible, after all, a religious text that if you looked really closely was filled with all sorts of supernatural spectacle, some of which, angelic and demonic alike, were quite elaborate and the stuff of legends. The origin of the Nephilim, the bizarre description of Cherubim, the Beast from the Sea (or half of Revelations, to be honest). A female demon in the desert wasn't really the oddest thing on Heaven or Earth or other places, was she? But there was the culture shock, the surprise that something I had previously dismissed as non-Bible, apocrypha, non-canonical mythos with little bearing on my actual religion despite its place in the common consciousness, did in fact, make an explicit appearance in the text itself.

Then, of course, there was the personal interest, which I shall get to now.

The juxtaposition of a woman with the same name as an infamous demon entering my life with the series of increasingly, I'll say it, *devilish* events (one of which occurred at the very establishment at which she was employed), did beg the obvious question I had been turning over in my head for some time:

Was Lilith...*Lilith*?

Absurd, of course, but then so were so many of the things that had happened lately. A dead cat. A stray eyeball. The inexplicable transformation of one liqueur to another and the creepy coincidence that brought a monster back from the past and into our lives. So, I may be excused if a supernatural question such as thus did arise. Granted, it certainly wasn't doing any favors to the woman herself (assuming she was), but a guy in my position couldn't be too careful. I know that if you love someone you have to trust them, trust them completely, trust them with your life and your heart. But this was no ordinary situation, surely. If she really loved me back, she would understand.

If The Great Shifter (the keen reader would have noted that term) had, in fact, placed an infernal creature in my path, he could scarcely have chosen a more pleasing form. I was in a completely unique and impossible situation. I was difficult for me to imagine a greater polarity even in theory than the one I faced now. Either Lilith was the human woman I loved, or she was an actual demon sent to distract and perhaps destroy me. A middle ground was hard to discern and making a misstep would be disastrous.

Was there anything other than her name to suggest that she was anything other than what she seemed?

The serpent was said to be the most subtle of God's creatures, but ink on her back was not. Still, an uroboros tramp stamp could just be bad-girl pretense. Didn't prove anything. What else?

I was alive in 2008. I read Grant Morrison's cerebral epic *Batman R.I.P.* In that storyline, Batman faces one of his most vexing foes yet, the brilliant and mysterious Dr. Simon Hurt, who challenges the Caped Crusader's very sanity and identity. There were months of speculation as to the true identity of this villain who had seemingly appeared out of nowhere. At one point Hurt would claim to be Dr. Thomas Wayne, but we all correctly predicted this was simply a deception to further vex The Dark Knight. No, the most interesting theory, in my opinion, was that Dr. Hurt was The Devil himself. There was a pertinent blog that made a strong case. The Joker (currently The Thin White Duke of Death) told the man in question "Pleased to meet you. Big fan of your work. But don't ever call me your servant." A random henchman, talking about Hurt when Hurt was the demented head of Arkham Aslyum, conducting needless experiments on the criminally insane, said "Dr. Hurt is the devil" (the blog-I wish I could remember-described this line as "astonishingly frank", which is true), and the World's Greatest Detective, in the closing narration of the final issue in this storyline, ponders *Did I find the devil waiting? And was that fear in his eyes?*

I bring this up not only as a nerdy tangent but because I see certain parallels. Hadn't there been astonishingly frank lines vis a vis Lilith? Hadn't she said, and I quote "I am Lilith" when I asked her why they called her Lilith? Confronted with another translation from that same Bible verse, hadn't she declared herself to be THE night creature? Was her dark, seductive nature at this time mere coincidence?

But surely, she was human. I mean, that's the only conclusion a sane man could come to. She had a last name. Vasquez. And she had made reference not only to a mother and father but the fact that said parents had sent her to a private middle school, where she was disappointed by the lack of members of the opposite sex. She had Goth sensibilities, obviously, and there was no doubt she was at least as much of a sinner as I, but human all the same.

My imagination had run wild, naturally, and I wondered now if this wasn't simply further self-sabotage. The depressing fact of life was that I was still waiting for…something. Someone, rather. That I was still, conscious of the fact that it was subconscious, waiting for the love of my life. Like Sonny Burns (*Going All The Way*, Jeremy Davies in the adaptation), I guess I was waiting for my life to begin, fourth decade beginning though it was. I was settled well and good enough as a single man. A decent job, my own place, etc. But I was single, and I was feeling my age, as far as settling down and expanding the Malloy family line went (and my parents contributed to this, as far as nagging went). Ever the procrastinator, I had spent my twenties dating one woman after another with varying levels of seriousness, but no real feelings of marriage or kids in mind. That would all come "eventually". But how much eventually did I have left? Wasn't it well past time to meet a nice Catholic girl? Yes, that was the thing. I could only marry within the Christian faith and marrying within the denomination would be the most convenient. I didn't have the energy to convert someone.

Not the easiest though. I had gone to one embarrassingly awkward singles event at my church, and I had joined a Catholic dating site with scant results. I hadn't been able to get Lilith's religious beliefs, if any, out of her–though that was, admittedly, through a lack of trying and pushing the question. Was it racist to assume she was raised Catholic? If you use ethnic shorthand, sure, that's probably not the best, but she had mentioned going to a private girl's school called "Immaculate Heart", which didn't exactly sound Presbyterian. Of course, M. Night Shyamalan went to Catholic school too, so that doesn't necessarily mean anything.

I sighed to myself and sat on my bed, rubbing my forehead. This was a lot. Contemplative and nostalgic (but no, not drunk), I gave Freddy a call.

"Trent?" my ex-girlfriend was surprised, but not unwelcoming.

"Yeah. Hi Freddy."

"What…What happened?" The assumption being, reasonably enough, that a call this out of the blue must be related to something catastrophic. It had to be a bad thing.

"Oh hey, nothing. I was just…" What? "Thinking." Brilliant. "Wondering.

What have you been-it's been a while, I mean."

"Yeah. Yeah. It's...it has."

"So, I just wanted to, you know, catch up?"

"Oh. Cool."

"Yeah." I was rubbing the back of my neck self-consciously. "So, what have you been up to?"

"This and that. You know, I'm really busy these days with work and everything."

"Yeah. I saw you were on *The Walking Dead*!"

"Did you see it?!" I could tell she was lit up, but I couldn't lie to her.

"No, I didn't unfortunately. I don't watch much TV these days. I don't have a TV, you know, so just Netflix and Hulu and the like."

"Oh." The disappointment in her voice was palpable. "It's on Netflix."

"Right. Yeah. I should check that out."

"Have you ever watched the show?"

"I watched some of the first episode." Shrug. "Wasn't really my thing-" But I shifted gears quickly. "But that's super-cool you landed that part. You were Michael Rooker's daughter?"

"Yeah, he's so sweet."

"I bet. I loved him in *Guardians of The Galaxy*."

"Yeah, he was great...So what are you doing these days?"

"You know, I'm still writing. Still with The Angeleno Film Archive."

"Working any major cases?" I could hear her playful smile. She does not take me seriously as a detective. Nor should she.

"One thing." I was cagey. "A lot of weird stuff."

"You mean weirder than The Cobra Woman? Or Andrew Lawrence?"

Note to the reader: Now The Cobra Woman, despite the supernatural implications of the story I'm telling now, was not some serpentine goddess. She was just Elena Diaz, a seductive femme fatale who murdered a couple people to hold onto a lost film I was tracking down. "Andrew Lawrence" (for so he called himself) was a creepy, charismatic pervert who caused some trouble for Freddy and me.

"It's...I don't want to go into it." Good strategy. The more she knew, the more danger she was in.

"Whatever."

"So yeah. I was wondering if, I don't know, maybe you'd like to get lunch someday, catch up when you can and what not. Or whatnot."

"Sure. I mean, I'm really busy these days, my schedule's kinda all over the place, but that'd be nice."

Then we made our niceties with no specific plans and hung up. A thoroughly unsubstantial call and that itself was telling.

I had at one-point thought that Freddy was the one. Certainly, I loved her, and some say that's all that counts. She was hardly my parents' ideal, wasn't even a Christian (she was a Scientologist), so she wouldn't conform to that mythical nice Catholic girl ideal. But then again, who does?

It is odd also, to think that you could be in love with someone, and then not anymore. But it's a slope, not a light switch. When you're both in love, you're at the top of a glorious peak. You can't breathe, but she's in your arms, you're in her eyes, and that's the only thing in the world that matters. But then one thing happens after another, and you come down. Sometimes a great big fall, the shock of infidelity or the thunder of an irrevocably unkind world, sometimes a slow, gradual stroll down the hillside, owing to complacently or boredom. Curiosity for that ineffable "something else". However it happened, once you were there, and now you're here, and it's little use looking back to see how you fell, though we always do. They say tis better to have loved and lost, but I find no solace in that trite cliché. Instead, I turn to the magnanimous words of the great President Richard Nixon:

Only if you have been in the deepest valley can you ever know how magnificent it is to be on the highest mountain.

I sat back on the bed, my energy drained by that brief but saddening call with my ex, when suddenly the phone buzzed again to knock me out of it.

I lethargically reached over to grab the phone, and then I bolted up when I saw who it was. After my unanswered calls, voice messages, and texts, finally.

"Mike! Geez!" I was both relived and annoyed. "Where have you been?! I called you like, 8 times!"

There was silence on the other end of the phone. It was unsettling as it was irritating. Usuall, when I pick up the phone, I don't say a word, I wait for the caller to initiate the conversation. *They* called *me*. The onus is on them to say something, right.

But I was so eager to hear his voice I was ready to pull it out. I wouldn't accept a bad line or a broken connection. Mike, talk to me please. So, I repeated.

"Mike?"

Now at this point, I noticed the phone was very hot against my ear. This happens sometime, but not like this. I worried for a moment about all those exploding smartphones from the previous year, but I dismissed that concern as irrational. Those were exceptionally rare, and it wasn't even my brand.

Still, disconcerting.

Next was the noise. It wasn't static-that I was sure of. It wasn't electrical at all. It was a buzzing, fast and frantic and insectile. Like bees.

Burning and buzzing. What did that add up to?

"Not Mike."

I stood up, as did the hairs on the back of my neck. Bumps along my arms, and there was nothing I could do but listen. The voice was low, yet strangely effeminate. Playful but commanding. It was so eerie, so otherworldly, I could not be sure it was a sound emitting from the mouth of man, rather than a random buzzing from the apiary that sounded, by chance, like English tones. And still, as a honey coated tongue wove and waxed words of discomfort, I was enraptured, an in my fear and trance, stood silent as the grave, still as the dead.

"Terror, pit, and trap are upon you, inhabitant of the Earth." Whatever that meant, it was true. I felt myself nodding. "You've been loooooking for me," he drew the words out, teasing me excruciatingly.

"N-No I haven't." I heard those words, felt my lips move, but it was like choking up an ice cube.

"Maybe you didn't know it. Maybe you don't know what's going on. Maybe you're LYING!" he snapped so vehemently I almost dropped the phone, and then that alien voice mellifluously cooled to almost a lullaby. "It doesn't really matter, does it?

"How did you get Mike's phone?"

Then the creepiest laugh I ever heard, fork on the chalkboard, sand in your teeth.

"Why would you ask such a boring question? Isn't there anything else on your mind?"

"Don't you-" I swallowed, because I was going to ask a question I didn't want the answer to. "Do you know already? Can you read my mind?"

"I don't need to read minds to read you, Trent. You're an open book. A light, insubstantial tome that doesn't even belong in the mystery section because nobody cares."

"I didn't go into that section." I felt compelled to defend myself. "I mean, I did. But not on purpose. It wasn't my intention."

"Intention so rarely matters. It's intangible, effervescent, and at last, disappears, like the morning frost on first dawn. All that matters is all that is done."

"But I was only there because of the cat!" I heard its undead mewling in my mind's ear.

"And meow you're here, talking to me." Perhaps he did say "now", but he knew what he was doing. "Nobody made you, Trent. You always had a choice."

"Mike didn't." I was a little bolder but regretting it. "When you shoved his hand-"

"I'll stop you now because that wasn't me and you know it, and that's really neither here there."

"But he's on your side, isn't he?"

"Sides. Sides. Siiiiides," he sighed into a "sides" and I could imagine a wicked smile melting across an unimaginable visage. "Are you under the impression that we're playing a game?"

"If we are, it isn't very fun." I felt like crying, but I knew my cold tears would go unseen, or worse, elicit a cruel laugh from the other end of the line.

"I never BEG," the voice dripped maliciously, "It's neither couth nor does it fit my suit. But I do differ."

I held the phone away from me for a moment so that I could escape the heat, if not the flame.

"What do you want?" I asked flatly.

"10 acres of vineyard shall yield but one liquid measure."

I shook my head.

"But what's the point of teasing? You know I don't know what you mean. This is pointless. I'm going to hang up!" I shouted, but as I did, I felt small and insubstantial, like a flea on the floor in a big empty room.

"You won't," he said with quiet authority. "Are you watching the news?"

"I don't own a TV."

"Stick your finger in the air. Look in the entrails of an owl if you must. I'll wait."

On glass eggshells, I walked across the room. Opened my laptop as quietly as I could, pulled up CNN.com

Politics. President Trump was exchanging harsh words with North Korea.

International. An attack in Pakistan killed 20.

Sports. South Carolina had won a national title in the Women's NCAA.

Entertainment. Kim Kardashian had posted a racy photo.

California-

Oh yes. There it was.

BRUSH FIRES IN NORTH CALIFORNIA CLAIM 18

6 dead at Deakins Porthouse, including Anthony La Cire, steward of the winery.

A photo of La Cire's genteel smiling face graced the screen. He was 49.

"Oh, those Santa Ana winds." I was being taunted. "They don't usually get up that far north. But one supposes certain accidents of climate cannot be predicted."

"Why..." I was rubbing my face, already dreading the wave of guilt that would haunt me when (and if) the shock wore off. "Why would you do that?" I started to mumble, trailing into oblivion. "Doesn't seem necessary..."

"'Do', Trent? And when did I say I did anything?"

"Is it...my fault?" My voice was shaking. It was unbearable.

"You've had your last drop of Pin's Brew," That should have been an irrelevant non sequitur, but the devil is in the details.

"Where's Mike?!" I suddenly asked. It was such an important question.

"No more of that delicate liqueur. What's Piebald to do?"

That sly reference struck me like a lightning bolt.

"You don't!" I roared against all rationale. "Just! Leave her out!" I cried, desperat because I couldn't force, and it seems that begging is my natural state. "Please! Please, please, please. I'm sorry. I'm so sorry. But you know she hasn't anything to do with this?"

"Hasn't she?" Haunting. "Do you even know what 'this' is?"

"Of course not!" I snapped. I had given up my dignity for nothing. "I don't know anything about this! Your wicked game is as rude and spiteful as it is wicked. The more I see, the less I understand. It's madness!" I continued past the laughter. "I don't know if you're a cult leader or a witch doctor, or...I don't know what!"

"A monsterrrrr," I couldn't discern the tone, if ever I could, or even if it was a question or statement.

I slumped down. Defeated.

"Well, you're something."

"You know me by my works. I burn, and I burn, but I never melt. You know this."

"Do you ever wonder why you're this way?" I asked idly, with no expectation or real desire of a real answer.

"A secret: You think they drink blood because they're vampires. They're vampires because they drink blood."

Then that infernal buzzing again. The heat against my ear again was unacceptable. I set the phone down, resisting an urge to throw it across the room.

My ear was still hot. Burning in fact. It stung! I swatted at my lobe in reaction to the sudden, concentrated pain.

And there was a bee! Oh dear God, a bee buzzing around my room, as if it apparated out of the phone itself!

No time to panic, I promptly opened the window and scarcely had to shoo it out before it was gone. Not burst into flames, nor sunk into the abyss. Simply flew out, like an ordinary bee.

I then noticed a peculiar wetness on my cheek. Very similar to the feeling of a fresh shaving wound. Identical, in fact, for it was blood running down from right under my lobe. It'd be funny if it weren't so horrifying. A bee sting is a minor annoyance. I had never known it to break the skin, to draw blood.

It wasn't much. I drew my hand away and looked at the blood on my fingers. It was looked so bright, so red, so vivid. I daresay I was tempted to taste it.

But no. I frowned with scorn at an unseen foe as I rubbed my bloody digits off on my rough jeans. The time for being bullied was over. I had no use for fear or playing the little games set before me by frightful fiends who hadn't even shown their face. I would not be a vampire.

I would be a hero.

Chapter 17: Hello, Ms. Chip

My plan was brilliant in its stupidity. It was also creepy, of course, but so is everything in this story, myself unfortunately included.

I was going to STALK Chip.

Now I know how that sounds. Creepy, right? But give me a break. We were at the threshold of Hell here, and maybe the only way to get out was to go all the way in.

Besides, it's not like this was going to work anyway, right? What exactly was my plan? Dr. Thane, at least, was polite enough to give me a card with the address of the tangible office where he kept regular hours. He may have been affiliated with infernal agendas, but he was of this world, was flesh and blood and visibly human. Easy enough to track down, especially when he gave you an invitation.

Thane was gone, however, and I had little obvious recourse in finding other agents of interest. I would very much have liked to leave well enough alone, but well enough wasn't well enough. Bowers was still out there, and he wasn't all. That phone call was haunting in the moment and infuriating in retrospect. What had I done to be bullied by such a powerful and incomprehensible force? Was I consigned to be badgered and chilled for the rest of my life, and the ones closest to me thrown in Hell's danger as well? I didn't think that was fair, and it certainly wasn't acceptable. But what was I to do?

The way I saw it, I had two avenues to explore, two people I could turn to, resources to explore.

A. Agent Toastman

B. Chip

This may certainly be my fervent imagination, projection of internal delusions. I want to believe the X-Files are real. In our lengthy and personable conversation, Toastman had taken more than he had given away, but I couldn't help indulging my fantasy that he had been "on" this case for a while. Perhaps The King of Wax was his white whale. I liked Toastman innately. He seemed a friendly, principled sort, and I enjoyed embellishing him as a Mormon Mulder who could come through in the end. Perhaps he had a file on...all this. But not likely, and I certainly wouldn't be privy to it. I couldn't think of a way to approach him.

Which brought us to Chip. I knew where she worked. Allegedly, anyway. Not that it was beyond these people to lie, of course, but she was wearing the same uniform on both occasions I saw her, and it was as much a lead as anything. She very well could have been posing, and this did seem likely, given her nature and the general befuddlement encouraged by her group. I had to try though. The Los Angeles Metro Transit Authority had thousands of employees, I imagine, and how could you find one from the pack? I didn't even know her last name.

She had told me where she was working, however. A quick perusal of the Metro's website and Twitter feed confirmed that they were indeed laying track out by the Miracle Mile. Expanding the Purple Line, in fact, planning to take it all the way through Beverly Hills, past Century City, and into Westwood. I was struck by the ambition and the implications. It was hard to imagine a train, even a subway in Beverly Hills. That would make that whole island of luxury and decadence just a little less insulated. And how would the Brentwood brigade react to the barbarian invasion?

I drove out to Wilshire and La Brea, and sure enough, construction was underway. Beautiful area, the Miracle Mile. The LACMA was an excellent museum. I loved their symposiums on certain filmmakers, like Tim Burton. I'll also never forget my fondness for The La Brea Tar Pits and the date I had there.

I finally managed to find a parking spot and made my way over to the construction site. A lot of drilling going on and fractured concrete. The area was sealed off with that weird orange plastic sheeting. Uh, what's it called? Looks like a grid of roundish squares. Yeah, a grid. That should suffice.

I got out of my call, still across the street, and looked. I felt foolish and insufficient. Like I was really going to see Chip there. That assumed a lot. For one, that she wasn't lying, that this perky fanatic really did work for the Los Angeles County Metropolitan and Transportation Authority. And that her particular occupation would take her here, rather than in the office or a hundred other sites. And that she would be working right here right now. I shook my head at my own idiocy. What a waste of time.

And yet…there she was. I saw her from behind at first, saw her behind, noticed how tight her pants were. Still had that impeccable blue vest, and now she was wearing a yellow hardhat and wielding a clipboard. God, it appeared, had smiled on my mission that day.

Or was it God?

• • • • • •

I waited for the walk sign to come on, and I hurried over. Chip was talking to a couple of the workers, burly men in orange vests.

"Now I don't want you to be upset with yourselves," she chided. "But we would like this to be done sometime sooner than 2023."

I stood by the fence, awaiting the opportunity to announce myself. I still didn't know what I was going to say.

"I'd really like to hear back from Ladwhip," a guy with a scruffy mustache was saying. "We drill into the wrong wire here, we take out half the grid."

NOTE: I realize now that he was saying LADWP (Los Angeles Department of Water and Power), but approximating a pronunciation rather than saying each letter. Ladwhip sounded like the name of a medieval pageboy.

"Oh, Hugo." Chip scribbled something down.

"My name is Hector," he protested.

"I wasn't talking to you," she explained calmly. This confused him.

"There's no Hugo here."

"Anyway," she sighed and shook her head in a flighty, girlish manner. "It's not my business to distinguish Hugo from Hector. If there's no Hugo here, he must be elsewhere."

He persisted.

"There's no Hugo on this crew."

"You can't be saying there's no Hugo, anywhere. Everyone's somewhere, and if they're not, then they're not someone we're talking about. Ergo, Hugo is real," she shook her head. "I certainly don't think we'll be taking any grids out. You have to be in before you can be out, and as we're all above ground right now, there's not much that can be done for the subterranean."

She reminded me of Alice there. And her crew was nonplussed.

"Sir." I turned around. A stocky foreman was standing next to me. "You can't be here." He was shorter than me, which I found odd.

"I'm not here," I clarified. "I mean, I am, but I just want to talk to your boss for a minute."

He frowned.

"Phil Washington works downtown. You're not talking to him."

I looked over to Chip, then back to my accuser.

"Of course. But in this moment, uh, at this site-"

"I'm the boss here, junior. Let's move it."

I turned to the grid.

"Chip!" I shouted stupidly. The man beside me did not approve, but there was little he could do before she heard me, turned her head around at an impossible angle, like some sort of owl, and that Jack O'Lantern grin was peeling up her face.

"Trent! Wowsers!" She turned to the workers. "Take five, boys. I've got to talk to Mr. Malloy!"

And she strolled up, right to the fence, and for one moment that smile seemed so sincere and her countenance so pleasant that I couldn't help but indulge the whimsy of a fantasy, something more wholesome and less sinister. Receiving a smile like that from a girl with a pure agenda. I thought of high school suddenly. Even though I didn't date back then, I started to wonder what if I had. What if Chip and I had gone together? Maybe I could have saved her from this path, and her smile really would be so sweet.

But this is not that kind of story, and Chip, alas, was not that kind of girl.

"What are you doing here, nosey?" She had her hands in the grid and was hanging onto the plastic, pulling it back and forth playfully.

"I suppose I am nosey," I relented, "I have been doing some investigation."

"Really?" She beamed, curious. "Like a detective?"

"Well, that's what I do, honey." I put my fingers up to the grid, right above hers. "I'm an archivist for The Angeleno Film Archive."

"What does that mean?" She screwed up her face, exaggerated befuddlement. Chip could be on Sesame Street.

"I research films and track them down sometimes...It's not important."

"Dave, take five." She was looking at the man who was looking at us.

"I don't work for you." He scowled, then moved on. Sulking off. I had won.

"It's not important," I went on. "But I'm here because..."

"Why are you here?" she batted her eyes. "Did you want to see me again?"

I breathed in.

"Did you-you know what happened to Dr. Thane, right?"

"Who's that?" She sounded genuine, but who could tell?

"Come on, Chip, I saw you in Century City."

"Oh yeah! We got a contractor's office out there. The Purple Line is going places, kiddo!"

"But you were in the same building. There was a fire," she shrugged. This was getting nowhere. I sighed and moved on. "Do you know where Mike is?"

She grabbed my fingers through the grid, intertwining them, excited. "Mike's your friend!"

"Yes, he is my best friend, and I'm trying to get in contact with him."

"Am I your friend too?" she giggled. "Can I be your *girrrrlfriend?!*"

I was both aroused and repulsed. A new look for me.

"What are you, 12?! Enough with that shit!" I stepped back. "A man is missing- a veteran is missing, and you people keep teasing your stupid little games!"

"Whoa, whoa," she put on a mock-offended voice. "'You people'?"

"Are you saying you're not people?"

"Good one, Trent!"

"Hey lady!" A brusque electrician from down below called up. "Are we going to get back to this or what!"

She comically rolled her eyes and sighed apologetically.

"I'm sorry. I'm on the clock. Let's talk later, yeah?"

"Sure thing, Chip." I didn't sound as stern and standoffish as I hoped. "You want to get some pancakes after work, talk about your evil boss?"

"I live in Echo Park. 415 Gittes Street."

"415 Gittes," I repeated.

"It's a house, not apartment. Come by around ten or so. We can hash it out."

"I'll be there."

She turned to go back to work and was already facing away from me when she casually threw in.

"Maybe we can fuck."

· · · · · · ·

9:58. Echo Park. I sat in my car, parked across from a little white bungalow in a sleepy neighborhood in Echo Park. Not too far from the actual park, where the little pond and the paddleboats. A pleasant area, but I knew this would be a dangerous night.

For my relationship so much as my life. Sure, I was burrowing further and further into this bizarre little sect with people unafraid to bust their own heads open and set fire to only tangentially connected vineyards. So yeah, I was sticking my head in the lion's mouth. But I was already there, right? I wasn't going to be any safer by sticking my head in the sand, or even leaving town. God only knows with "these people".

I was also worried Chip might try and seduce me. Hadn't she just said as much? She was such a peculiar young woman. So sunny yet unwholesome. On an intellectual level, I knew she was attractive, and I was not unaroused, but there was also something unmistakably uncanny about her, who could say. Yes, she was beguiling, but it was an invitation to a dalliance in the uncanny valley.

I hadn't told Lilith I was going, of course, which already felt like cheating. I sighed as I got out of the car, praying I wouldn't succumb to Chip's "charms", such as they were, and vowing that I would tell Lilith everything, in no uncertain terms, about this whole blasted journey. When it was over.

Whenever that was.

I walked up the porch and was already thrown off by the screen door. That's only a minor inconvenience, really, but you can't knock on it. She didn't have a doorbell either, so I guessed I would have to knock on it. Bang my knuckles against the metal siding to not make much sound, or against the stucco, which would scratch them up something fierce and also not make much noise.

Two seconds on her property and Chip had already made this awkward and unsettling.

Or was that me?

Anyway, I grunted and got ready to yes, knock against metal.

No need though, because the door opened, and PREGNANT SPIDER-MAN came strolling out.

You only think I'm making that up. But why would I?

Yes, someone in a Spider-Man costume just walked out of Chip's house. Which would have been disconcerting enough, even if the stomach wasn't bulging out (yet still contained by "his" friendly neighborhood red and blue). Distended? Beer belly? With child?

I didn't have time to ask (not that I wanted to), because without a word, the thin beast with his diminutive, almost skeletal frame, made it all the more disturbing. What was that? He/she/it passed me and left off into the night. Left me standing there, a warm, insufficient wind beating against my legs. The sound of an off-key flute somewhere in the distance playing a twisted version of "The Entertainer", with no ice cream in sight.

I was probably only standing there a moment before Chip appeared in the doorway, which was still open but behind the screen. She was poking her head in from the living room, perhaps just about to watch her friend go. Now she must see my handsome mug as well.

"Trent. Wow. Come in." Chip was wearing an odd blue dress at this point. Sky blue. Or arctic blue would be more accurate, as I would soon find out. It looked really cheap, like one of those Spirit Halloween costumes-which may be, after all, was revealed, exactly what it was. Her blonde hair was down and longer than I thought possible.

I pulled open the screen door and let myself in. I couldn't resist a little jab.

"Careful about inviting me in, Chip. You know what they say about vampires."

"What?" She wrinkled her nose. "You're not a vampire."

I looked around the place. Very tidy, and not sparsely populated. There was plenty of furniture, but it was all standard fare, and I couldn't really see her personality in the black upholstered couch and mahogany coffee table. It looked like a regular person lived here.

"No. But that's only because I haven't drunk blood. I think." I turned away from her to look at the bookshelf, which was filled with leather-bound texts of the Western classes from *Candide* to *Moby Dick*. "That's what somebody told me, anyway."

She threw her hands up in mock confusion. "What are you talking about, Trent?"

Her hands, by the way, were not empty. In her left, she had a small pair of scissors. Short, rounded blades with blue handles. Skissors. Kindergarten stuff. In her right, she held...a dark, pinkish blob. It looked like a fat little sliver of meat, but more gelatinous.

I know I didn't want to know, but I pointed at the object in question accusingly, without saying a word. She picked up my meaning.

"It's my tongue!" She waved it around, presenting it to my face. Indeed, the gummy confection, for so it must be, was tongue-shaped, and had even been crafted to have a similar texture to the human appendage.

"Is that...candy?"

"Yep!" She pushed it towards me, "You want a bite?"

I answered that with a frown, and then she put the tip in her mouth and bit it off. "It's cherry!"

I invited myself into the living room and slumped down on the couch.

"What did I walk in on?"

She sat down next to me. Too close. Still chewing her tongue.

"Just having some fun. We were making a video!"

I casually took the scissors out of her hand. I didn't want her to plunge such a blunt weapon into my thigh unprovoked. There was no telling with her. She did not object or offer any resistance, and in the same breath, I asked.

"What kind of video?"

She patted my arm rapidly so as I would share her excitement. "YouTube! It's called, FROZEN ELSA CUTS TONGUE, PREGNANT SPIDERMAN SPIES!"

You know, for kids.

Confusion. Revulsion. Incredulity. I screwed up my face, trying to think of a sane response, but all I came up with was:

"What?"

"So, Spider-Man wakes up," she told me, enthusiastically enthralled by her own narrative. "And he's confused because he's pregnant! So, he looks around- we'll throw in some of those sound effects when he scratches his head. He goes down the hall to ask his friend Elsa about it. But she left the bathroom door open, so that's his chance to peep on her when she's undressing. Heh heh." Her salacious laugh was creepy. Who would possibly be aroused by such a scenario? "Only she's not naked. She's cutting off her tongue!"

"That is so messed up!" I tried to contain my disgust. Right now, I was more puzzled than anything else. What the Hell was she talking about?

"No." She smiled dismissively. "Kids love it! It's funny! It's cute!"

"Chip, I don't know what kind of childhood you had, but that's some disturbing stuff. You're gonna traumatize kids like that."

"God, Trent, it's a PRANK! Elsa's pranking Spiderman. That's the whole point!"

"Elsa. So, you're the princess from Frozen?"

"Duh. Everybody knows that."

I looked at her dress, which was hardly Disneyworld quality.

"Yeah, Chip. It's so obvious that you have to call her "Frozen Elsa" in your video title.

"It helps with the search algorithms," she yawned and stretched back, then placed her legs on my lap. "Our last video got 80 million views."

"That can't be true."

"Oh sure. We're big in Russia and Vietnam. It helps that there's no dialogue. So, no language barrier. Kids everywhere can enjoy it!"

I looked down at her bare feet. Nails painted blue.

"Especially the ones with those nightmare fetishes."

"Nah, it's good clean fun," she said crossly, annoyed that anyone might find something unwholesome about bathroom peeping, bodily mutilation, and male pregnancy in beloved cartoon characters. "Maybe you're the one with your head in the gutter."

"Nonetheless." I patted her knees to get her attention. "That's not what I'm here about."

"I know. You didn't even know about this before."

I pushed Chip's legs off me and stood up. It wasn't proper to be touching her, and this was a confrontation, not a date. I would be faithful, and I would steel my resolve.

"What is this leading to, Chip?" I growled. "I want this to end."

"Somebody's grouchy."

"Just tell me. Please." I tried sincerity. Simplicity. "What is going on?"

"That's a broad question, Trent. How am I supposed to answer that?"

"Okay." I rubbed my forehead, irritated that I somehow knew less than when I arrived. Certainly was more confused. "Smaller questions. Specific. Where's Mike?"

"Haven't a clue." She was playing with the fray of her dress now. The question bored her.

"Why me?" I sighed. I knew this question was broad, even existential, but it had to be said. "What have I done to deserve this?"

She frowned, and she was serious this time.

"'Deserve', Trent?"

"I've tried to be a good person," talking to myself, talking to God, and not expecting much from Chip. "You know I go to church, pray. I confess my sins. I'm not a bad guy."

Chip groaned.

"Nobody ever said you were."

"Then why can't he just leave me alone?!" I whined. "This started when we were little kids! Why come back now?!"

In an instant, Chip was up on her feet and had struck me across the face, open palm. There was nothing preternatural about her hand, but it did hurt.

"Ow! Why did you hit me?!" I rubbed my cheek and wondered if that was a weird thing to say. Maybe I should have just cussed.

She folded her arms, cross.

"Because you're ungrateful! He's interested in you! Don't you think that's special?!"

"I think it's scary."

She rolled her eyes like I just didn't get it.

"Of course, it's scary. Everyone in the world is disturbed."

"You especially."

"Hush. But how many get his *special* treatment? Get to talk to him personally?"

"I don't know!" I spit back, angry that I was expected to welcome such supernatural harassment. "Mostly because I don't know who 'he' is! I came here to ask, and I still don't know anything else!"

"He is The King of Wax." She had her finger out at me and was scolding in the stereotypical school-marm fashion. "I told you that the very first time we met, Trent, and I haven't lied to you since."

"I appreciate your honesty," I conceded flatly.

"You should be flattered," she continued, matter-of-fact.

"In fact, I am," and as I was saying it, I realized it was true. "There is something devilishly exciting about it, I must admit. To be targeted by...such a sinister and powerful force. Makes me feel like the hero in some grand adventure."

"That's the spirit!" Her smile was perhaps patronizing like she was indulging a child's make-believe. "I'm sorry about your cheek." She reached out and touched my face, still a bit sore.

"It's okay," I mumbled, not wanting to dwell on it.

She kissed me where she hit me, very soft, small peck.

"All better?"

She was looking at me with beaming eyes, her hand on my shoulder. Waiting for me to close the gap.

I turned away. Her kiss was cold but not entirely unpleasant, but I had to end this now.

"I have a girlfriend."

"That doesn't mean you can't cheat on her."

"That is exactly what it means! You're in a relationship, you can't kiss, or, you know, with other people!"

"That's exactly what cheating is!"

She protested. "Once again, Chip, you are technically correct, but miss the point entirely. Who said I wanted to cheat?"

She slumped back down on the couch.

"Well you are here, aren't you?"

"Yes," I had to admit. "But I'm here for answers."

She sighed, impatient but accommodating.

"I'm listening."

"And who are you?"

"What?" She genuinely didn't understand the question.

"Well like, are you a human? Are you some sort of impish urban sprite?"

"That's crazy. What are you talking about?"

"Not the soda, Chip."

"I know you didn't mean the soda! But you're asking me if I'm some kind of pixie?!" She was amused and surprised, incredulous and only a little offended. I was reminded of Dr. Thane's office when his normal human reactions lulled me into a false sense of sanity.

"I just meant, you know, you're perky and you show up places, and there's something...off about you. No offense intended. I just want to know what I'm dealing with. You could be a spirit or some kind of robot...maybe just a hallucination, he's messing with my mind. Gaslighting me."

"Does he need to?! Are you even hearing yourself? Am I a robot?!"

I sighed. Sat on the arm of the couch. Next to her, but a safe distance.

"I'm sorry. It's been a weird month. So, you're just a human being."

"Do you want to see my bush?"

She didn't wait for an answer. Just raised her skirt and there it was. My gaze lingered a moment too long. Instant remorse coupled with disgust and arousal. The matching blonde patch above her lips sealed the deal. I was still looking where I shouldn't, but I could tell she was smirking. Rocking her legs back and forth. I finally looked away when she spread them completely.

"Fine. Dumb question. But where are you from?"

"Aurora, Illinois," she shrugged, acknowledging how inconsequential this was.

"How old are you?"

"Never ask a lady that question."

"But if you're a witch -a human witch, sure-you may have some delayed aging ability."

"I don't have superpowers, Trent." She rolled her eyes. "Would it help? Here..." She got up and walked out of the room. "Just a second."

I put my hands in my pockets. Alone in Chip's living room. Who knows what corner she was retreating to, or what armament she would return with?

A moment later, however, she was strolling back, little plastic card in hand.

"Here!" She thrust her driver's license into my hand. Her picture was a perfect likeness, frozen blue eyes, shark's grin and all.

"I hope that clears everything up." She glided across the room, doing a weird little dance. Spinning in a circle. Childish. "I'm just a normal girl."

"So you are, Miss Mayhew." That's right. Chip Solvang Mayhew. It was her name. "I'm sorry I doubted you."

She was hanging off the bookshelf, one hand grabbing on for dear life, the one reaching out to claim her identity like a kid trying to get the brass ring at the Merry-Go-Round.

"February '91." I handed the millennial her ID. "My Dad was in Desert Storm."

"My father was the manager of a donut shop. And a human being."

"Fair enough. Were you ever in a mental hospital?"

"Rude! But I know why you're asking. I didn't know Dr. Sourpuss before."

"But you know who I'm referring to."

"You gotta relax, Trent!" She threw up her hands, celebrating her own sunny disposition. "I'm your friend Chip. Just a normal human girl who works for the Metro brushes her teeth twice a day, and is in the inner circle of a glorious and terrible new awakening that will melt all in its path."

Where was this getting me?

"You didn't say *we* don't have superpowers." I pointed out, "You said *you* don't have superpowers."

"I don't, but that's okay. Probably be more of a bother. I just do what I want. The rest comes easy." She stood up. "Do you want some fruit juice?"

"Who is he?" I finally asked plainly, the question that needed to be asked. "Who is The King of Wax?!"

"I don't know." She smirked playfully. "I guess I've always been more interested in what he does than what he is."

"And what does he do?"

She giggled.

"You have no idea!"

I clenched my fists in frustration.

"There have to be some things you know for certain, even if your dumb crazy head hasn't asked the question."

"Oh, that's mean." She crossed her arms and pouted.

"You would know, for example, where you're from, and how long you've been with him, and...how did you start to work for this...King?"

Her face, more preternatural than ever, took on a dreamy, uncanny expression, and never was her smile a more haunting Jack-O-Lantern then when her eyes lit up.

"He came for me."

I stared at her, trying to be cold, but I felt a swell of pity. She was a human, still a young woman at that. I'm a Christian. I believe in redemption. Even for this twisted soul, it couldn't be too late.

"Why are you the way that you are?"

"You just asked the same question twice!" She suddenly kissed me on the lips, but I pushed her away.

"Come on, Chip. You don't have to do this, you know. You could just, leave, turn against him, fight back or just- be a good person! You don't have to do this."

"I want to."

I sighed. What was the point?

"I want to talk to him." Which was true intellectually, much as I feared.

"He wants to talk to you." She smiled. "Here, I wrote it down." She glided into the kitchen. "On the fridge."

She returned, looking at the yellow sticky note in her hand. "He knows you've been stalking him."

"I'm sure."

She furrowed her brow, trying to figure out the meaning behind the message.

"So, you all were...trying to find a drink or something?"

"It's a long story. I may write it down someday."

"I'd like that. You didn't check them all out, though?"

"No. After the Pick and Hammer, we got a new lead. And it panned out!"

"Lethally, yeah." She nodded. "But he's actually going to be at the place you didn't go to." She handed me the note.

"Donovan's Dive. Long Beach. Right." I looked up. "Thanks, Chip."

"You can just show up whenever. I think it's closed, and he'll know when you're coming."

"Fantastic." I sighed, stuffing the note in my pocket.

And we stood there, looking at each other. Chip was smiling wide and batting her eyes. Everything she did had the air of a Dr. Seuss coquette.

"So...." I trailed, uncertain. "I guess that's it."

"Trent," she snorted. "We know why you're here."

She pulled her dress over her head, and there she was. Smooth, milky-white skin. Butter blonde as above, so below. Her mammalian ludicrosities were small but pert. She was a perky woman, plainly visible now, and a highly excitable type. She was flush and ripe down there, drops of dew on a fleshy field.

I closed my eyes and took a breath. I didn't get an erection in that moment, because I had been semi-hard and testicles tingling ever since I arrived. Being in her alluring presence, alone with her in her home, had that effect. I had been raging since she kissed my cheek, and now I was on the edge.

"Alright." I kept my eyes closed, praying she'd get the message. "I'll...go see him then."

I stepped past her, ready to finally leave, but she was too quick and cunning. She blocked the doorway, displaying herself.

"Aren't you forgetting something?"

"Please."

"Don't you want to fuck me?"

I took another breath, frustrated with myself as much as her. That I could be predictable and seduced so easily.

"I don't think you'll understand or even believe me, but the answer is actually no. I'm not lying." Her eyes glanced, predictably, to my crotch. Fair point. "And you can see that I'm aroused. You know I've been staring at you, and I'm not I'm going to say I haven't been lusting. Of course, I lust for you Chip. You're a beautiful young woman-I mean, there's something off-putting about your appearance, and your persona-but when you want to be, you're really sexy."

"Aww."

"But the point is that even with my baser instincts being what they are, my higher functions...my mind, my conscience, my heart, my soul-doesn't want to have sex with you. And that's me. Yeah, I'm tempted, but this whole time I've been praying that I won't give in to temptation. So, it doesn't matter how much my body desires yours. What I want is...no."

She gave me a pensive stare.

"Who are you trying to convince?"

I walked around her.

"Just don't crash any trains."

She had her hands on her hips, faux-indignant as I exited.

"You only wish he was that predictable."

And I was out. I didn't look back. I did feel unfaithful, that coming here in the first place was a bad idea. But I hadn't consummated anything with Chip, and I got some important information for the next step. I just hoped Lilith would understand when I finally became a man and told her. Told her EVERYTHING.

As I was walking to my car, I heard the faint tune of a flute in the air. I turned back and Chip, still nude, was dancing in the doorway and singing a jaunty jingle.

"Always is always is always. As long as one is one. Deep in yourself for your father. All is none, all is none, all is one!"

Chapter 18: Corinthians

Chip had simply given me an address and told me to show up whenever. She had conveyed that the bar was closed for business and the fiend in question would arrive and announce himself whenever I choose to make that journey. I believed her. There was a curious sense of power in that. It wasn't an empowering power, of course, more like letting a condemned man select his method of execution. Or the hour, as it were. Come to think, it was rather insulting. Like he was continuing to toy with me. Biding his time. No rush. It was inevitable that we wrap this up eventually, so why not have a little more fun, torture the fellow some more, put him through mental agony by letting him decide when while he knows he cannot prevent its coming.

And yet I did have a choice. As I understood it, I could have just driven right from Chip's house to the bar and been met there. But that wasn't mandatory. The ball was in my court, and I wasn't sure how long I could prolong this ordeal. I certainly wasn't given an explicit deadline. Show up in three days or else. When is my homework due, Mr. King? Conceivably, I could just...not go there.

I had no delusions of avoidance, however. This could be put off indefinitely, but not eternally. It wasn't like it was going to just go away. Putting it off probably made it only worse. And the dread. I knew that the taunting would continue. Creepy phone calls in the middle of the night. Maybe more little tricks. I still wouldn't know where Mike was, and eventually, these people might threaten Lilith, which was absolutely unacceptable.

Jack Frost was an elemental force of nature, not a man. I couldn't just skip town, either. Thane was going on about the Pied Piper, stealing children in 13th Century German- a motif confirmed by Piebald. I doubt I could evade his grasp by moving back to Vermont or taking up Kevin on his Austin offer. Like

I was going to get away by getting away?

Not a chance. But I do think, in all his graciousness, that I would be allowed a few days to get my affairs in order.

•   •   •   •   •

I called my parents and told them I loved them. We exchanged pleasantries, and I told them I would visit them next week. I lied-or at least I thought I did, which means it was a lie.

I called my sister Darcy, currently on site on a dig in New Mexico.

"Hey Trent. What's up?" She was surprised to hear me, only mildly pleasantly.

"Yeah, I just wanted to see what's up. It's been a while."

"Cool. Yeah. What's up?"

"Oh, nothing much, just this and that. You know, still writing, still plugging away."

Opening with those kind of insubstantial banalities should give you an idea of the conversation we dragged out for a grand total of three minutes (0:2:46, actually, but whose phone was counting?) Sad, really. I expected this to be the last time we ever talked, and we said so little. Perhaps hoping to glean some comfort from the leavings of antiquated indigenous. I asked her about the petroglyphs. Same ancient, same ancient. As per usual, I tried to goad her into some sort of Erich von Daniken *Chariots of the God* or Ken Ham Young Earthism. Any aliens or dinosaurs on those rocks? I want to believe. She wasn't biting. Probably for the best. With my luck, she'd have excavated an antediluvian carving of a large man clad in yellow, surrounded by bees and the suggestion of unsettling pan flute. I could imagine a fat waxy smile which disturbed and allured even the primitive.

"Well, I better get back to it. Thanks for calling, little brother."

•   •   •   •   •

Agent Toastman had given me his card, and though I couldn't call in a favor, maybe there was one thing I could do.

I didn't want to leave a message but after several attempts.

"This is Special Agent Ted Toastman."

"Ted! Hi! Agent Toastman." I had a moment of cringe at my familiarity after he answered his phone with the formality of a desktop name plaque. "It's Trent Malloy." I cleared my throat to give myself time to think of what to say, even though I had rehearsed it thoroughly beforehand. "From the Dr. Victor Thane case.'

"I recall."

"You told me to let you know if I could recall any details, no matter how seemingly inconsequential."

"That is not exactly how I phrased it, but you are correct in the sentiment. I also surmise that is why you are calling."

"Yes."

"Go ahead."

"Well, you remember how I was telling you about...geez, Dr. Thane, and Pin's Brew and all that."

"You are speaking of the rare liqueur only found at a handful of bars in Los Angeles- one of which being The Pick and Hammer, the private psychiatrist's club of which Thane was a managing director."

"Yes. And that's what brought us there in the first place."

"I am tempted to dismiss this thread as wholly irrelevant, Trent, but I am curious as to where you are going. Where are you going?"

"Well, Mike and I visited his office...discussion of Pin's Brew...It came up that one of the other bars was called Donovan's Dive, in Long Beach." Well "it came up". I had used verbal ellipses to avoid a direct lie to the FBI. Just misdirection. Like a magician.

But he needed further elocution.

"What do you mean it came up?"

"Look, we were just talking casually about the drink...and it turns out that Donovan's Dive in Long Beach is one of the only other places that serves it. I don't know Victor Thane also was a partner in that bar or what..."

He wouldn't let me get away with trailing off.

"It would be easy enough to deduce if he said as much. Did he say he owned Donovan's Dive? Did he even mention it?"

I bit my lip. Do I dig myself in any deeper?

"No, Mike and I did our own research-before we met Thane, in fact. That's how we found him, remember? We liked the drink, so we wanted to try it at other bars. But I'm just thinking now-because we talked about it with him, the drink, and he had such an interest in it, maybe he also has connection to this other bar?"

"What is your obsession with this beverage?"

I wanted to tell him so much. I wanted to tell him everything.

"Just trying to help."

But I couldn't.

"Uh huh. I appreciate it, Trent, but I doubt there is a connection. It seems rather obscure, but I will not ignore it."

"Thank you."

"Is there anything else?"

I wanted him to save me.

"No. Just…I really hope you get your guy."

"I will let you know."

We said our goodbyes. Part of me was still holding out hope for the superagent like in my shows and in my dreams. But David Duchovny was a fictional character, and for now, it looked like I was on my own.

• • • • •

I had lunch with Lilith. It was this gourmet peanut butter and jelly restaurant in Beverly Hills. $8 for a fluffernutter. The world is a sick, fallen place, I know, and Los Angeles especially.

"What's next?" She picked at her Honeycomb Deluxe pensively, "A cereal bar?"

"They have one of those. In South Pasadena."

"Dude, we should totally go!"

"Had, I meant. They closed down."

"Boo."

She was in such good humor that day, so accessible, and yes, human, that I hated myself for the fact that I was still questioning her loyalties, that even now, eating PB and J on a sunny terrace, couldn't help wondering if she was in league with the enemy.

Obviously, I was the louse. I had come closer to cheating, and I was definitely closer to colluding with demons. I had gone to Chip's house, put myself in a position where she had gotten naked, and now I was going to willingly meet with the man in charge of all this? And I suspected Lilith?

Ridiculous. I should be ashamed. And I was.

But still…

And why? Because of her *name?* Or she had snake tattoos, so she was a snake, or on the side of the serpent?

"It's never going to work." She broke my chain of thought.

"What?"

She smirked and ran her finger along one of her sleeves. Nail on the cobra's tongue. "They're never going to come off, no matter how much you kiss."

She had caught me staring at her ink, once again, and I burned with embarrassment that she brought that up. Not so much that it was in public but that it was the first time she had ever mentioned it at all.

"That's, that's not really the point." I looked down. Not sure how to explain myself. Why did I like to kiss her tattoos? Well, the truth is that I wanted to lick them. And why? Remember that insatiable and futile appetite, not unlike hunger? Maybe it was the same dumb manifestation. Primal, as in primate. I see something that inflames my passions so much that when I actually have access when we're exploring each other's bodies, I desire to possess it, and the instinct is to taste.

But I hadn't done it yet. We had gone all the way, multiple times, but I kept myself restrained in that one area. I had kissed her arms and other painted areas (though not the uroboros on the back and not for lack of desire) tentatively but hadn't dared to run my tongue along their surface. I was afraid, of rejection and disgust. So even though she had given herself to me and I to her, I still hesitated to try what I most wanted, or even ask permission. That irresistible ink was one of her most comely features, one of the things that so drew me to her in the first place, but still, I hadn't consummated that aspect of my lust. This reticence was agonizing.

Yet she had noticed my kisses, the attention I paid to her body art, and was now calling me out on it.

"If you like tats so much, you should get some. You could rock 'em."

"No," I chuckled. I had henna-upped as Aldrich Killian a couple times, dragons on the chest, but that was temporary. "Me? Could you imagine? I-"

"Check it out!"

She was looking across the terrace. Under the veranda, Kirsten Dunst and her boyfriend/ fiancé Jesse Plemmons were sitting down, a tray stacked with goodies and two lime waters set down on their able.

"Huh." I tried to play down my excitement. "That's Kirsten Dunst."

"No shit, Sherlock. What do you think they're doing here?"

"Even movie stars gotta waste their money on delicious overpriced s'mores sandwiches."

"And they've got more to waste."

Kirsten was wearing sunglasses, but it was sunny so this might not be the transparently evasive technique celebrities used to barely conceal themselves in public. Jesse, who I knew from *Breaking Bad* and *Observe and Report*, wasn't wearing a baseball cap, and I respected that.

"Celebrities are so much better than real people."

I laughed but could tell part of her was serious.

"This is a new look on you, Lil." It was endearingly humanizing. "I've never seen you starstruck."

"Oh, total starfucker," she corrected me. "Are you kidding? Criss Angel came into the bar once, and I totally fucked his brains out in the lady's room," she pouted. "I wanted to anyway."

"He must have done some magic on you."

"He turned my pussy into a puddle. You gotta have some crushes, right?"

I shrugged, then gestured behind us with a tilt of my head.

"Really?" She smiled. "You wish that you had Jesse's girl?"

"Hey," I lowered my voice. The couple was a patio away, but still. "Mary Jane, you know?"

"You gotta thing for redheads?"

"Not really any more than any other hair group. But she had this real girl next girl quality, you know?" (Before that sexy movie sullied the term) "Like I could imagine her as a girl from my high school."

I surreptitiously glanced over. She was so pretty, even when she was doing something as unglamorous as an Elvis Presley (peanut butter and banana). Two of the best movies of the 2000s started with a still image of her face, you know. I could see why.

Peter had this arrestingly romantic description of Mary Jane in the first movie. He was telling her what Spider-Man told him, supposedly, as this was the only way he could declare his love.

When you look in her eye, and she's looking back in yours... everything... feels... not quite normal. Because you feel stronger and weaker at the same time. You feel excited and at the same time, terrified. The truth is... you don't know what you feel except you know what kind of man you want to be. It's as if you've reached the unreachable and you weren't ready for it.

Breathtaking. That's some *Summer of '42* romantic introspection there. Think about that, knowing what kind of man you want to be for the woman you wanted. But then I looked away from the girl on the screen to the girl in my life, and I knew who I preferred. Whatever else she was, Lilith was real.

I put my hand atop hers.

"Thanks, Lilith."

She seemed nonplussed by this sudden display of spontaneous appreciation.

"For what?"

"Oh, everything really. You're so great." I chuckled to mask a semi-serious approach to dip my toe in the water. "Even when I think you're evil."

"Evil?" she raised her eyebrows incredulously. I decided to change the subject. Lowering my voice, I came clean. About one thing, at least.

"And the truth is. About your tattoos. I don't look at them so much and kiss them because I want to get some of my own...But it's that they turn me on."

"Really?" She seemed to like that, which gave me hope.

"I...I kinda..." I lowered my eyes. She grabbed my hand encouragingly.

"Go on." She wanted to hear.

"I always wanted to, uh...lick them."

And there it was. The big confession. I glanced up, and she was not offended in the least. She was so casual, so "what's the big deal"?

"Why haven't you done it?"

"I did want to gross you out or anything."

"I think that sounds kinda hot. Let's try it."

So, we did.

·   ·   ·   ·   ·

And the next day I went to confession for what we did the night before. Reconciliation at the downtown cathedral in the morning, and then I would head over to Long Beach in the afternoon. A shot at Heaven before I went to Hell. TGIF!

After the routine laundry list of sins, I wanted a little extra spiritual guidance. Yet once again, I found myself unable to speak in anything more than vague generalities.

"...I swore. I used God's name in vain. I was resentful." I bit my lip. "I'm think I'm fighting demons, Father." I clarified because I knew what he was thinking. "I don't mean temptations. I mean material threats of a supernatural nature."

"Isn't that an oxymoron?"

"Well yeah, but no. I mean, angels can fall to Earth. They can do physical things. I mean, he could turn stones to bread, right?"

"You think you're fighting The Devil himself?"

"I don't know, maybe they're just men. With powers, possibly. Simon Magnus is the Bible. He was a magician. That's the whole thing, I don't know.

But I think I'm in danger."

"Have you talked to the police?"

"Oh yeah. Way back when it first started. That was practically 20 years ago. Didn't help much," I hesitated. "I going to meet these…maybe I can make a deal. It doesn't have to be so bad."

"'You cannot partake of the table of The Lord and of the table of demons'," he warned. "That's in first *Corinthians*. Whatever you're thinking of doing. Ask if this is what Jesus wants."

"It just…it's hard to see what I should do.

"Walk by faith and not by sight. That's in second *Corinthians*. You don't have to do this alone, you know."

I don't know what the priest thought of me. Probably I was weirding him out with all this talk of demons and magicians. But he was right. I just hoped I could take his advice.

• • • • •

Finally, right before I left for Long Beach, I called Mike. This was my last chance to reach him before Armageddon. I wasn't really expecting him to pick up,

"*This is Kripke: If you have something important to say, you won't need my invitation. If it's not worthwhile, save my time and your voice.*"

"Mike." I breathed in, unsure if he would ever hear this but wanting to put in the effort all the same. "It's Trent, of course. I don't know where you are, or what you're doing, or even if it's all my fault. I guess it is, probably. I pulled the thread too hard. But you know, you were there too, and we're in this together…and I'm glad we are. If I had to get tangled up in this evil, I'm glad it was with you. I just wanted to say, I'm sorry. Thank you, and I'm sorry. You know what for what. You've been my friend this whole wild ride…and I love you. God Bless. I really hope you're okay. I really, really hope you're okay."

There was an unpleasant click and a familiar voice affecting a cruel imitation of a mechanical pre-recording.

"Mike Kripke can't come to the phone right now, as he is occupied with other affairs of an odious and maddening nature. You know where to find him."

"Yeah." I grit my teeth, steeled my resolve, and hung up the phone because who was listening? "I do."

• • • • •

I turned to my Bible one last time before I left my apartment, to prepare for what you just can't prepare to.

Your opponent the devil is prowling around like a roaring lion, looking for someone to devour. (1 Peter 5:8)

So he was. And I was headed straight into the lion's den. I could only pray for the deliverance of Daniel.

Chapter 19: Long Live The King

I parked across the street. Wanted to keep my distance. I looked around at the parking regulations after I got out of my car. Wouldn't want to get a ticket. It's funny how pragmatic concerns hadn't totally fled my mind even in these circumstances. Survival instinct is funny like that.

Donovan's Dive was in an unimpressive, nondescript area of downtown Long Beach. It was a long, fat, and flat building about the size of a Red Robin with none of the charm. Forrest green exteriors with drab red roofing. The bar was sort of an island unto itself, sitting under the Blue Line metro overpass with nothing around it. There was a Walmart shopping center across the street, but this place was barren. The parking lot was empty. What a waste.

Gobackgobackgobackgoback. I kept on telling myself, but my feet wouldn't stop. I was being drawn as if by a magnet, by whatever malevolent forces were inside there. But it was my own free will. I couldn't stop myself. I had to see this through, and one way or another, it would all end this afternoon.

I clenched my jacket closer. Goosebumps on my arms. I was probably less cold than I felt, but I didn't know that. I felt an aching despair in my stomach as I stepped up to the curb and approached the door, and I realized that I had been feeling it for so long that it had settled-which is the worst thing of all. I had resigned myself to dread and depression. This was the world they had made, and now I was living in it.

I said a prayer. Gritted my teeth and donned my spiritual armor. I had thought about borrowing my Dad's gun, but what good would that have done?

Donovan's Dive hung in big wooden letters above the door. Nautical font, with a helm between the two words. I wondered idly who Donovan was. I imagined, briefly, a gruff but affable salty old dog, not unlike the Sea Captain from The Simpsons. Could he imagine what was being done in his good name?

In lieu of a knob, there was a long black iron handle to pull. It looked heavy and medieval. My first instinct was that it would be locked. It looked like a locked door. Barred shut. I hated locked doors. Denied access. Public pianos you weren't allowed to play. A hundred things to keep people out, and I hated them all.

In this case, however, I'd make an exception. I was praying it would be locked, and I hesitated before I reached out.

Why not listen to my internal ramblings? Why not simply…walk away? I actually laughed out loud at the simplicity of it. Status quo had got to go…or did it? Was the current situation really so unbearable? An unnatural animal corpse, a stray body part, frightening phone calls. That was surely preferable to annihilation. And, playing Devil's Advocate for the coward's path of least resistance, I had to admit, the further I went down this path, the worse it got. The eyeball in the drink that was absolutely inexcusable, and all involved owed Mike and me an apology. But if I had simply let dead cats lie, then the return of The Chandler, the bee in my phone, and the Death of La Cire could surely have been avoided, no? As shabby as this makes us sound, between field trip and library, I really had no such trouble until Mike came back into my life, and now that he was gone…I'm terrible, I know. But if I backed out completely, what would the reaction be? Let me live? Even if this continued as it had, I could cope, I'm sorry to say. Could I live with the idea that people who had met me but not me might be killed out of spite?

I could not. La Cire and Thane's blood might not be on my hands, but they were on my conscience. Besides, I was already here.

And the door wasn't locked. I pulled it open, and with only a moment to let the cool, dank air out, I walked inside.

What did I expect? The place was dimly lit and sparsely occupied, with stuffy, almost suffocating air. The stale smell of sour beer, old wood, and possibly urine penetrated my nostrils. It was a disagreeable first impression.

The bar was long and wet, in need of a good cleaning. Not a soul sat on one of the wobbly stools bar side, or in the booths in the back with the patchy red upholstery, or even at the stout barrels with manhole cover sixed tops they had in lieu of tables. This place was a miserable dump, and everyone knew it. That's why nobody was here.

Except the bartender. There he was, hunched over the end of the bar with his short, skeletal frame. He reminded me of The Crooked Old Man, but that's the wrong reference point. He was from legend, not nursery rhyme.

He was Piebald.

Which would explain why I was greeted with the inappropriately jaunty beat of *The Sailor's Hornpipe* as I walked in the door. His red and yellow Renaissance Faire garb clashed jarringly with the modern despair of the atmosphere, but he didn't care as he played his wooden pipe with a fervor that was paradoxically both jubilant and mechanical.

He didn't pay me any mind as I walked up to the bar and stood my ground. I couldn't see his eyes under his dandy green cap, complete with feather, but I gleaned he had a youthful, clean-shaven face with a handsome square jaw.

I tried to mask my fear by acting unimpressed. Bored and petulant, even.

"Are you it?" I wasn't sure if it was working. "Is this all?" I swept my arms around, gesturing to the shabby, empty establishment. I was both relieved and frustrated; no one else was here yet. I knew it was coming, and part of me just wanted it over with.

But I didn't want anyone else. Even this guy was too much. Unsettling. Alien yet familiar.

"Was that you? Earlier?" I asked.

He didn't say anything or even look at me, but he knew what I meant, as indicated by his playing the *Spider-Man* theme on his pipe.

"Yeah, I thought so." Which was only half true. First of all, I didn't even know what he was. Lilith's doll sprang to life? A living museum remnant, like Bowers, the Chandler? The myth himself? Earlier, I thought Piebald was only going to be a motif, the impish figure on the bottle and the doll in Lilith's bed causing an unnerving correlation. Now was I facing the man? Was he even a man? Was that old fairy tale true, and if it was, dear God, what was I up against? A figure that mythic and powerful and malevolent, and he was only the servant of a greater evil? I shuddered but tried to hide it.

"Can I ask what you are?" I shrugged as if it were a casual question. "Besides the spokesman for an obscure liqueur variety?" The attempt at levity didn't play. Not a peep. He had stopped the music. I was on pins and needles even before I arrived, and now it was unbearable.

"Listen, I don't want to sound impatient, but-"

He gestured behind him, to the row of bottles above the bar. He set a glass down before me. I gathered he was offering me a drink.

I stared at the empty glass. My order was obvious.

"PIMM'S Cup, please," I said loudly. "That's Pimm's, not Pin's- clear the wax out of your ears and get that through your skull. Oh, and hold the eyeball. Let's try to be civilized."

He nodded, seeming to agree.

"And I don't care if it's time to pay the piper. This is gratis. You all owe me about a billion dollars in personal anguish."

He tucked his pipe into his belt and diligently set to work. He made the cocktail properly, Pimm's No. 1, real 7UP, and the proper garnishes- that is cucumber, orange, mint spring. I kept my eyes on it, and there were no eyes in it.

He placed the cocktail in front of me. It looked absolutely perfect. I felt a little bad about ragging on the guy. Isn't that silly? But I felt the urge to apologize.

"Thank you." I raised the glass. "Cheers."

I took a sip. I never tasted anything sweeter. It was uncanny, as was everything that had ever happened.

Suddenly I felt a sharp pang of dread in the pit of my stomach, worse than anything I had experienced yet. I jumped away from the bar. What I was I thinking? I drank what he put before me!

Something was coming. I could feel it in the air, which was going staler by the second, as if all the freshness had been let out of the room, to be replaced by the faint smell of tobacco and moldy anxiety.

I looked away from the Piper. I bolted towards the exit, but it was too late. The door creaked open, frustratingly slowly with an irritating creak.

Mike stumbled in, looking all the worse for wear. His hair was tousled, and his skin was unusually pasty. He had a black eye, a busted lip, and he had been sweating profusely. He needed a shave and a shower. He was wearing the same clothes from two days ago, and the rings under his pale eyes told me he hadn't slept since.

"Mike! Geez! Thank-"

He wasn't alone, and he hadn't stumbled into the bar. He was pushed. Bowers hulked in after him, almost too big for his surroundings.

The Chandler's face was scared by third-degree burns, and his hair was singed off. I would have taken a perverse pleasure in his pain if I wasn't so disturbed by his appearance, which was now even more frightening. His beady little eyes were pinpoints surrounded by fat burnt flesh. He was hideous on the outside, at least, as he was within.

It was my less worthy and childish instinct to duck, to actually hide behind one of the bar stools, and I'm not proud to admit I gave into this shameful desire immediately. I had been so bold in Thane's office, but now that the monster had reappeared, I was powerless.

"Get up, Trent," Mike coughed out weakly as he slumped down at the bar, leaning against the wet surface without sitting down.

"He can stay where he is." Chandler slammed the door behind him and strolled over to the bar. He looked down at me scornfully. I regressed further. "Little boy."

And he was right. I felt like I was 12 again.

"Mike…" I whispered. "What happened?"

"No talking!" Chandler slammed his fat fist down on the bar. He turned to Piebald. "Mead!"

Piebald poured him a glass of that golden honey wine. Chandler picked it up and licked his lips. He raised the glass, but before he could drink…

"QUELL YOUR GULLET, CANDLEMAKER."

This was it. The boogeyman had arrived. I quaked. It had never happened. It was happening now. The people under the stairs had finally grabbed my foot. There was a skeleton in the shower. The monsters were out of my nightmares and into my life, and I could do absolutely nothing.

I didn't know where that voice was coming from, but it filled the air and rung in my ears. There was something warmly affectionate yet hollow, like a bell chiming through an empty cavern.

I shut my eyes as tight as they went. I was thinking, maybe if I clench tight enough, make myself as small as I felt, maybe he would pass me by, like a giant who doesn't bother to stomp on an anthill.

But it's never enough.

"Rise, boy."

It was a honey coated command, not a question, and I felt myself stand up, knees buckling, body shaking, eyes shut.

"Look at me!" It was a roar a thousand miles away from the silver tongue I heard before, yet disturbingly familiar, as if both inflections were different coasts of the same continent.

There he was.

THE KING OF WAX.

It was hard to discern his height. He seemed so tall, and his figure was so full, and when he stood over you, you instinctually shrunk back from his hulking posture. Yet his head was small, and he was so light on his feet that he gave off the air of a ballerina or a fairy.

From under his wide-brimmed Panama hat, his crown and halo, I could see a scalp of short, feathery hair. A blonde somewhere between honey and mucus. I suppose that was the point.

His skin was pale and jaundiced. It was a sickly, yellow effect. But he was not a man in ill-health. On the contrary, he exuded a sense of intimidating power and sturdiness. He could snap you like a twig.

He had a thick, square goatee ostensibly the same color of his hair, but it glistened. I saddened and disgusted myself when I couldn't help but think of Dennis Hopper in *River's Edge*. *I ate so much pussy in the 60s, my beard looked like a glazed donut.* It was a vulgar reference, but worse, why should my mind go to any reference? Even now? Was I so insulated, so filled with other people's content, that my experiences couldn't be wholly my own? For once, God, let me live my life, without comparison.

(Ironic that this sentiment should surface now, so near the end).

He wore no long flowing robes like I imagined a king. His prestige was in his swagger, his very aura. He wore a suit. The same suit, in fact...

That he was wearing...

That...

First time we met...

"Of course, we've crossed paths before," he drolled as if reading my mind and finding no surprises. "In your charmed life."

"Hi Trent!" Chip was standing beside him, and she looked so small, such a little girl, that I regretted even more ever being attracted to her. Even in her metro uniform, she looked like a kid playing dress-up. It was a Halloween costume. She was a child. But then maybe we all were next to him.

His hazel eyes gazed down at me, twinkling cruelly, like a Satanic Bing Crosby.

"In that position, you look as pitiful as you are." His voice was so soft yet loud, so authoritative yet casual, mellifluous yet belligerent, and from his demeanor, I finally understood that paradox Lilith had described. Truman Capote meets The Undertaker.

"Elderberry, jade, and sadness," I managed to whisper.

His leather shoes squeaked across the hard surface of the floor as he cut his way across the room and spread himself out in a bizarre slouch across two stools, next to The Chandler.

"Speak up. This is a crowded room, you know."

Mike's back was to the door, and his eyes were racing. Piebald. Chip. Chandler. The King of Wax. Me. Mike glanced down at me. His eyes narrowed. Was he thinking about bolting? I was. I probably would have.

In fact, I did. I looked away in shame as I gripped the leg of the stool tighter. Was that what this all had come to? Was I now being punished, at long last, for my cowardice as a child?

Mike was twitchy, but not indecisive. He kept his distance from Chandler, edging past his old enemy, and started to walk toward me.

"Come on, Trent, let's-"

With no effort but enormous force, The King of Wax raised his hand, and Mike walked face front into the back of it. The King's eyes were still on me. He hadn't even bothered to glance back at Mike, but he stopped him dead in his tracks, throwing him to the floor with a bloody nose with a mere wave.

"SPEAK," he commanded. "What was it you said?"

I looked over at Mike wiping his nose. I looked at the others. Chandler was staring into his mead, pouting, it seemed, that his lord had not allowed him to drink. Chip was bouncing from one foot to the other, goofy look on her face, awaiting further instruction. As was Piebald, who stood his ground, still as a statue.

I climbed up the stool and managed to get to the feet. I was on the other end of the bar, but still, far, far too close.

"I-I just wondered," my nose burnt, and my voice stammered. Where, God, was that swagger I brought into Thane's office? Mike had attempted to echo my bold, defiant exit there, but he was smacked down, and I could barely speak. "Was that you? W-who talked about 'Elderberry, jade, and sadness' Did you say that?"

"To whom?"

Then I almost cried of despair, because now I had brought her into the room. I assumed he already knew of her, and he did, but this was so maddening, this inability to separate the fervor of my thoughts from the plain reality. I assumed he knew all, did all, but what was I putting on the table?

Nobody. I mouthed, but no words came out. I licked my dry lips and tried to force air out. Nothing.

His lips curled up in a cruel grin. Lilith had been right. Too many teeth, too much gums. He put Chip to shame. He was the wax shark.

"Of course, I did. It was always me. Always has been, always will be."

"*Always*." The world felt dusty in my mouth as I raised myself, leaning on the stool. "Are you who I think you are?"

"And who do you think I am?"

"You know," I struggled to articulate my fears. "THE. Are you The Dev-"

I was interrupted by Chip giggling like a harpy. I had been intrigued, allured, and repelled by her in the past. She had had my pity, my desire, and my fear, but now I hated her in that moment. This wasn't funny, damn it. This was real.

The King laughed, a cruel, guttural noise, and then he yawned like a cat, twisting his head and manipulating his jaw further than I thought it could go.

When he opened his mouth, I could see the strands of yellow-white sticky clinging from top to bottom. Honey, wax, saliva, snot? I didn't know. It reminded me of a visual from all those videos I never should have watched, when she finished her job and showed us the results.

"Your fears are parochial, and your words are predictable," he chuckled through a mouth of scum. "You have no idea."

"Trent's a curious guy!" Chip was my side, her arm under mine.

"I didn't ask you to say anything," her master gently rebuked her. Chip's eyes went wide, and she let go. Shrunk back from me, cowed.

The King turned to Piebald. He rolled his hand in a gesture I could imagine Henry the VIII making to order more ale.

Piebald disappeared into the back, retreating into a door I hadn't even noticed.

"Don't you know?" The King licked his lips, looking at the space The Piper left behind. "Curiosity killed the cat?" he snickered, satisfied with his own obvious joke. He then cocked his head toward me. "And yet for all your curiosity, you are no nearer the truth than when you started."

"Yeah, then so why don't you tell us!" That was Mike, who had finished wiping his bloody nose and was now raising himself with his back against the wall. "If there's something you know, we don't, why don't you just fill us in?"

"I don't want to," he responded flatly, not glancing over to Mike.

Piebald returned, bottle of, you guessed it, in hand. He poured a glass of his brew, which the King greedily snatched away. He raised it.

"It's more fun if you don't know."

"Your fun is the least of my concerns," Mike seethed.

"And the most of mine," he returned. "Different people have different motives. You see?"

I walked on eggshells away from the bar, trying to avoid everyone, though I guess I was moving toward Chip's general vicinity.

"We don't know," I confessed. "And it seems the more we learn, the less we know."

"The first sensible thing you've ever said," he took a sip and then glanced at Chandler, annoyed. "Just drink already!"

The Chandler sucked down his mead greedily, like a thirsty ape.

"It's maddening," I went on, keeping my distance, "Because when we start to investigate, it just gets more confusing, and, it's like a nightmare that will not end, and I just want to wake-up!"

"Maybe you are," he mused with a cocky half-smile. "Dreaming."

"The Hell we are!" Mike shot. "This isn't a dream!"

"Are you sure?" The King asked pointedly. "Maybe wondering will keep you up at night."

"I'm not sure I'll ever sleep again," I shuddered.

"Truer words," he smacked his lips, relishing his drink. "Keeping you in the dark is my light."

"That won't work," Mike countered. "Because fear is driven by wonder, wonder by mystery. But a mystery without a solution is a waste of time. You think just because we don't know, we'll never know, and we'll always wonder. But if you preclude the possibility of ever answering, we cease to question. You cease to be an enigma and start to be a bother. Ambiguity is replaced by frustration, followed by dismissal." He spit on the floor.

"Rude!" Chip crossed her arms, indignant. Mike continued.

"All this toying is for nothing because we're not afraid. Just bored. You lose."

There was a moment of silence as everyone awaited The King's reaction.

"Petulant child," he mumbled. "WHEN DID I EVER SAY I WANTED YOU AFRAID?!" He said this as he sprung to his feet with a devilish speed and smashed his goblet with his bare hand, glass flying everywhere.

Deathly silence, again. We had seen a glimpse of this man, this monster's might. Chandler chuckled. Chip stood on her tippy-toes, watching The King walk towards Mike, eager to see what would happen.

Piebald started to play Greensleeves.

"Of course, I'm afraid of you." Mike stood his ground, but I could see he was shaking. "For now." Mike looked over at me, and I didn't know what he wanted. I was still shaking from The King's outburst. "But it won't last. Fear fades."

"Does it?" He grabbed Mike's hand, by the glove. Squeezed. Mike winced but did nothing but stare back at his tormentor defiantly. "How long have you been afraid of him?" And here he manipulated Mike's fingers to point at The Chandler. "He's done to your body these past two days what he's done to your mind the past 17 years. No son, fear doesn't fade. Nor does PAIN!" He snapped Mike's index finger, breaking and pushed him aside.

"Hey, leave him alone!" I heard myself shout, my instant gut reaction.

"We'll get to you." He didn't even glance back at me.

"Big man," Mike sneered, nursing his hand. "So, you know a few magic tricks, got a couple freak show slaves, and now you think you're the King? I guess it'd go to my head too. Fucking bitch."

"It's a common misapprehension that power corrupts. Power reveals," Mike was answered in a smooth, authoritative voice that knew what it was talking about. "Only the weak are manipulated so. That's why they're weak. So, no. It wouldn't go to your head, because you wouldn't have a head to go to. You in my shoes? The surge of power and authority would annihilate you," he quipped, almost like an afterthought, "probably be for the best."

"When will this end?" I asked, as his lectures were unbearable. He wasn't just hurting us. He was preaching as well. "This shouldn't happen! Are we in Hell already?!" I didn't know what I was saying, but I couldn't stand it.

"Your problem, Trent, is that you think you live in a world of implied moral order. You don't. There is no should or should not. There merely is. The Heaven and Hell nonsense comes from such rot. Two sides of the same coin I'm flipping. It's in my palm. As heads or tails just call me Lucifer-because that's the way you think. And that's easier for you." He pointed to Mike. "Your atheist friend has his own delusion. He thinks I'm the boogeyman. That all I want to do is scare you good children."

"Don't you?!" Mike cried out, "Because that's what you've done!" his voice quaked. He was near tears. "All my life...," he lowered his head, unable to go on or he would burst. I had never seen him so vulnerable.

And I knew what he was saying. Had he ever left the Chandler's shack? Had he ever been permitted to?

"Fear is boring. Fear is predictable. Fear is...simple," our tormentor went on. "I'm more interested in the unplaceably unsettling. The quietly disturbing. Not the goosebumps on your arm, nor the shivers down your spine, but the uneasiness in the pit of your stomach." I felt it now. He knew what he was talking about. "So, I diversify. I mess things up. A cat dead, or is it? An off-brand liqueur with a haunting logo." (Here he nodded at Piebald) "I play Mad Libs with the universe. One little change here or there and you're uneasy in a way you can't articulate. My work stays with you in a way that shock won't. You watch a video with a slasher with a knife?" He shrugged. "That may scare you for a minute. But a Disney princess pretending to eat the shit of a superhero? For kids?" Glanced at Chip. Piebald. Myself. "That stays with you."

"It does," I slowly admitted. "But I still don't see the reason why?"

"Exactly."

"Thane had a couple theories," I cautiously pointed out. "That you were the Erl-King or Jack Frost, or they're all the same thing..." And I thought about my reaction to the snowman raping Shannon Elizabeth, how sad and uncomfortable that made me, and realized it was exactly The King's purview.

"Pompous ass," his disdain clear. "I thank you for dispatching him."

"We didn't kill him!" I protested, staring at the fat man sitting at the bar who just had his mead refilled.

The King raised his hand, dismissing my objection.

"He's dead because of you, and the world is better for it."

"The first sensible thing you've ever said," Mike snapped. "Good riddance."

"This is not to say he was wrong." As if a clarification was in order. "I'm sure he told you nothing but the truth about the antics of our friend the Piper, raining frogs, dead Laotians. Certainly. But he didn't understand, and that was his problem, you see, he tried."

"But you're not supposed to understand." I nodded "Still, I did get some use out of Victor. As with all my disciples."

The King of Wax walked over to the Chandler. Mike stepped back. I noticed Mike had picked up one of the shards from the smashed glass. Earlier I noticed that breaking that glass with his bare hand did not draw blood from the great shifter, so I wasn't sure what Mike was planning. But I was afraid.

"Johnny Boy." The King stood over Bowers, slamming his hands on his shoulders too hard, but talking in a patronizing, patriarchal manner. "You had your fun."

"Fun," Mike repeated, seething with both hands behind his back. But he King wasn't looking at him.

"What disturbed you more, Trent? When you saw him burn your friend's hand, or when you realized he had been standing in his own piss and shit for three days?" With this, he reached down and grabbed the Chandler's crotch. Chandler winced but said nothing.

"My cowardice," I answered honestly. "That's what disturbed me. I left my buddy." I looked down. I didn't meet Mike's eyes. I don't even know if he was looking.

"Fair enough." He took his hands off Chandler and walked over to the bouncy girl awaiting him eagerly. "But how about our Chip?" He put his arm around her in a mockery of paternal affection, and she leaned into him. "Perfect, isn't she?"

"Who is this bitch?" Mike asked scornfully, but nobody paid him much mind.

"Desire and disgust are an intriguing blend, Trent." He was smirking at me. He reached into her shirt and grabbed her breast. Chip smiled bashfully.

"You want her, and you hate yourself for wanting her." He withdrew his hand and turned to her. "Take off your top, dear."

"Okey-dokey!"

He laughed, remarking, "You see? 'Okey-dokey' as she strips for your pleasure. As childish as she is alluring." He spanked her. She giggled. He pointed at me with a tone more matter-of-fact than accusatory. "You feel like a pedophile."

"She's 26."

"Yes. Even so."

The vest was on the floor and Chip finished unbuttoning her blue-collar shirt. She stood there now in a fuchsia bra with little bees on it. It was like something a middle school girl would wear.

"Give him your brassiere," The King commanded, hand around her, unhooking it in the back.

"Catch!" she threw at me, and I caught it, as is instinct when anything is thrown right at your face, no matter how soft the fabric and how warm from her skin. So, my shame is not that I caught it, but that I wanted to sniff it.

"You want them to fuck right here, your majesty?!" Mike stepped forward, breaking my distraction, God Bless him, and I dropped the bra. "'Cause we're wasting a lot of time!"

The King of Wax spun around slowly with uncanny mechanical grace, like a strange carousel, and faced the man with one glove.

"You imply your time has some worth. That you could be doing something more valuable right now."

"Plenty."

"Interfering with your students, professor? Drinking yourself into a stupor? Sitting in a parked car, trying to muster the courage to drive it off the cliff? This is the most valuable experience you've had in ten years. You won't live the same after this. Some gratitude is in order."

"For what?!" Mike spit out. "For your mind games, and postulating, and this grandiose bullshit? You talk up your own mystery, but it's easy. I know what you are. You're a bully with a God complex. I've seen guys like you all the time. They get a gun and a uniform and think they're king of the universe. So you can turn one booze to another, do this and that, and you have a couple freak followers. I don't care. You're still not in control like you say. You wanted to be in the shadows. But we found you, King. We exposed you."

The King's countenance darkened into a troubled and troubling scowl.

"You think anything that happened was without my permission? Could you be so foolish? I left you bread crumbs, and like good little puppies, you came right to my door."

"That's very easy to say." Mike shook his head. "But it's more of your bullshit. I saw those two jackasses in the office. Don't tell me that was part of your plan. Doctor Headcase is shouting at the Candleman. 'Kill them' 'No, they're not disturbed!'" Mike put on a mocking tone here, deliberately ignoring the Chandler growling in the corner. "Then one's dead, one's got a face that looks like it went through a flaming meat grinder." The Chandler slammed his fist down on the bar and bolted up, but The King shot him a look that sat him down before returning his attention to Mike.

"So, you doubt my power."

"The constraints of power are revealed by the restraints one puts on it himself," Mike countered. "Now you may claim to levitate or teach pigs to talk, but all I'm seeing is a series of petulant pranks. You're only amusing yourself. You have no powers of persuasion-that's why you have to recruit from the looney bin, and your man on the inside is burnt toast, so even that's gone."

"Go on." But it was not an affable invitation. More a threat.

And still, Mike continued.

"For something to be disturbing, it has to be deviant-that is from the norm, the path of expectations, and our sense of moral order-a premise you explicitly reject and thus contradict yourself. If there is no good or evil, then you cannot be evil, cannot be perverse, or disturbing. You pretend to act randomly, but in so is your greatest flaw-for the intentional lack of a pattern is itself a pattern. You're predictable because you try so hard to be unpredictable. Your claim of meaninglessness gives you meaning. We understand you because you've defined yourself by a rejection of understanding. There's something comforting about your attempt to destroy our comfort because you give a face to fears, an enemy to counter directly. You couldn't possibly be the abstract force of discomfiture, because by claiming your own agency you've personified your own negation. You're a walking contradiction, King. An oxymoron and a hypocrite of the highest order. By trying to tear down the wall of our sanity, you presuppose that wall exists, and thus strengthen it. If all we need to do to defeat you is to acknowledge you, then you've already lost."

It was an impressive speech, even if I didn't quite follow it. The King of Wax was silent for a moment, and I dared to hope he was defeated.

But sharply, pointedly, he retorted.

"And if I am so defeated, take your hand out of your pocket. Do it now."

Mike acquiesced. In his glove, he was holding a shard.

"What did you intend to do with so crude a rejoinder?"

Mike held up the glass, playing with it, letting it glisten in the light.

"I figured I might slash your face off. That ought to shut you up."

The King of Wax threw back his jacket, revealing a long revolver in a side holster. It looked like an old-fashioned model, and the grip was gold.

Mike whistled, surprised but unimpressed.

"And here I thought you were supposed to be a god."

"I never said that." He took his gun out of its holster.

"Still, a gun." Mike kept his smug act up. If it was an act. "Why your highness, I'm disappointed."

"Mike, shut up!" I yelled, more shrill than I intended. Whatever this was, whoever was holding the gun, it was a gun. There are some things that should shut you up no matter how proud you are or what lecture you're giving.

The King turned to me and poking the brim of his hat up with the barrel of his gun, he reminded me of a Kentucky colonel, just for a moment.

"Trent, everyone knows silver bullets kill werewolves. Do you know what gold bullets kill?"

I shook my head. He grinned and opened his mouth. In a sly magic trick, he was now holding a gold bullet between his teeth. He spit it out, and it fell directly into the barrel he had just spun open as if gravity itself was working for him.

"Everyone." He pointed the gun at me and for a moment my heart stopped.

Then he flipped the gun over and held it out to this side. He kept his eyes on me when he called, "Chip."

She diligently walked over, eyes gleaming.

"Shoot yourself in the head."

I wish I could say she hesitated. I wish I could say her smile faltered. That she opened her mouth and closed it, that even if she couldn't articulate an objection and put it forth into his face, that she wanted to. I wish I had seen a nanosecond of pause, even a hint of doubt in her eyes. I wish I could write her last words out, that she had had said something, anything, confirming in her final moments she was still a child of God on planet Earth.

She didn't though. Her expression didn't change, that creepy smile still plastered on her face to the end, and it all was over in an instant. Chip dead on the floor, bloody hole in her temple, and the gun was back in The King's hand, so quickly he had reached down in so fluid a motion that it hadn't even fallen from Chip's hand before he was twirling it around his finger, smelling the smoke.

I did notice Piebald's lip trembling though, for just a second, before he returned to polishing the bottle of brew. I'll always have that.

"GODDAMMIT!" Mike shouted impotently. The Chandler took this opportunity to reach over the bar and take a bottle of whiskey, which he gulped down greedily, face twitching.

"Oh." I tried to catch my breath. I walked towards Chip in a daze. "You didn't have to kill her."

"I didn't." His words rang hollow.

"You know what I mean." I was at her now. Her dead eyes still open, as was her mouth, never to speak again. I fell to my knees. "Please stop."

"Trent, get the fuck up." Mike was so cold. He claimed to understand everything, so where was he for me?

"Please. King of Wax. You don't have to...I can join you, or-"

He shook his head at me, in a quiet display of the cruelest pity I've ever known.

"You? Boy, whatever could I want with you?"

My surrender, then, was as meaningless as my early attempt at courage. As useless as anything I'd done on this Hellish adventure. I reached down and closed Chip's lids.

The King came forward and kicked me aside, gently, brushing me out of the way. He holstered his pistol and then swooped down and picked up Chip's prone body with little effort.

One of those barrels, I mentioned earlier? He went up to one and knocked off the cover with his elbow, revealing it to be full of boiling wax.

He held Chip upright in front of him like he was dancing with a giant Barbie. He kissed her on her brow, in an odd and unsettling show of affection.

"The raindrop falling from heaven is reunited with the sea that gave it birth," he said, lowering her into the wax. "She would have been a good woman if there had been someone to hand her a gun every minute of her life."

"Well, now we'll never know," I said quietly, closing my eyes and not knowing if he heard me. I'm sorry I didn't save her.

He pulled her out by her head. She was now statuesque, a human candle. A work of art.

"That wasn't so hard," he stated, looking over to the man who failed so horribly at that trade, let alone craft something like that. "Incompetent imbecile." He then let her sink back in and stuck his hand full into the boiling mixture. He took it out, unharmed, without blinking, and looked at it. "That wasn't so hot, either. You weakling."

We knew who he was talking to.

"The full measure of my power," that cruel, senseless person said, turning on Mike, who was wide-eyed and uneasy with shock himself now, "is not in those little tricks, but my ability to bend the will of men to my own. They obey my commands, whether they want to or not. Sometimes they know, sometimes they don't, sometimes they willfully try to defy. It's all the same in the end."

"The Hell it is." Mike was seething but tired. Where's the use?

The King of Wax opened the chamber and spit another gold bullet into the gun. He then presented it to Mike.

"You will kill for me."

"The Hell I will!"

The King gestured over to The Chandler, who stopped drinking, taking note.

"He made you," The King spoke as it was an indisputable truth. "And he started this. The last full gift of a son is to kill his father. Do it."

Mike shook his head but said nothing.

The King sighed and put the gun on the bar.

"Mike, kill John. Or John, kill Mike. It's all the same. My will either way."

He took a seat at the bar. I averted my eyes.

"And Piebald. Two more of you know what. One for me and one for Mr. Malloy." He looked over to me. "You'll want to watch this. Have a drink."

Piebald filled two glasses with the green brew.

"Leave the bottle," The King said to Piebald as he slid a glass my way. I caught it, just like a Western.

The Chandler's beady little eyes were darting back and forth between Mike and the gun. Mike picked it up, and pointed it at The King of Wax, right at the back of his skull.

"How about I kill you instead?"

The King sipped his beverage pensively, tacitly acknowledging the threat but not responding to it.

"A good king's work is never done." He winked at me with his left eye.

Which was the same eye, in fact, that he reached for. Without leaving his stool, pointing towards Mike, never mind the gun, and plucked out it out.

It all happened so quickly. In one fell swoop, he turned his long bony finger into a hook, and just scooped it out.

Mike was screaming. He had dropped the gun. I gagged but swallowed back vomit.

The King looked at the eye. Made a perverse contact with it, as if it was staring back.

"Will you look at that?"

He dropped the eyeball into the bottle of Pin's Brew and sealed it up before handing it to Piebald.

Yes, that.

"I would take advantage, John. While he's writhing like a wounded kitten. You have to take these opportunities when they come."

Chandler needed no further instruction. He picked his fat ass off the stool and scrambled for the gun. He had to bend over for it, but he was so grotesquely fat that it was a strain.

Mike was trying to stay on his foot, hand to his eye. Right to left. A diagonal line of pain and deformation. He saw what was going on though. He kicked the gun away from Chandler and charged right into him.

They were wrestling on the floor now, a grotesque, sloppy, stupid display. It was so clumsy and awkward to watch as if they were two middle-schoolers wrestling, rather than the monster and the boy he deformed, finally given the chance to fight back. Mike was bleeding, his socket exposed. He was clearly in a lot of pain. But it was no easy win for his old foe. Chandler was sweating and panting, so profusely, I thought he might have a heart attack.

The King of Wax was laughing mercilessly. Piebald was now wearing a satchel, a red silk bag of tricks-or maybe he had it all along, and he placed the bottle inside.

Chandler had Mike in a headlock, trying to choke him out. Mike was waving his hands around, trying to find the gun or a wayward shard. Chandler bit into his glove. Mike screamed out in pain.

I stood up. The King raised his hand, cautioning me to stay. What was I going to do anyway?

Mike elbowed Bowers in the chest and broke free as he struggled to catch his breath. Mike rolled over and had the gun in hand. He stood up, golden weapon pointed straight at the wheezing lunatic.

"You fat fuck," Mike gritted through the pain, the blood running down his face like tears in Hell. "I should have done this 17 years ago."

"Father, help me." The Chandler was looking over at The King, who did not look back.

"I'm not your father," he responded flatly.

"Shut up!" Mike struck Bowers across the face, clocking him with the gun. "You see that wax, you piece of shit?!" We all looked over to Chip's tomb. "That should be you in there! Now stand up!"

Bowers was catching his breath, his nose bleeding, looking down the barrel of his golden doom.

"Please don't make me."

"Stand. Up." And Mike was not to be defied.

With great effort, the man got to his feet, looking around for help that was not coming. Not from The King, anyway.

"Go!" Mike stuck the gun in his back and marched him over to the barrel, ignoring his blubbering.

"I don't want to do this. I'm sorry I hurt your hand. I'm sick. Ask Dr. Thane!"

Mike kicked him in the butt.

"We can't ask Dr. Thane because he's dead! You killed him!"

Bowers was facing the barrel, forced to stare into the goo. I could imagine the fumes of wax and Chip's flesh hitting him in the face, and it nauseated me.

"Please no!"

And then I knew what I could do.

"Mike." I stood up. "Don't."

He kept the gun pointed at Bowers' head, kept him bent over the barrel.

"Why the Hell not?"

Mike had one hand on the gun, the other to his eye. He wasn't looking at me.

But he could listen.

"Because it'll stay with you," I pleaded. "There's no going back from this."

"I don't want to go BACK!" Mike hit the Chandler in the back of his head. Only by keeping his hands on the edge of the barrel did he keep from falling in.

"So, don't. Move on."

"That's what I'm trying to do, Trent. I'm trying really hard to end this."

"Are we almost done?" The King said loudly, impatient. But I didn't have to answer him.

"Please, Mike." I stepped closer to him, away from The King, and towards my friend. "This won't end it. If you kill him, he'll haunt you the rest of your life."

Mike's hand was shaking.

"You don't-You don't know that."

"Get it over with," The King growled, but I ignored him.

I took another step toward Mike.

"I know guilt. I know shame. You know what I'm talking about. It follows you."

He finally looked up at me. One eye was bleeding, the other crying. Blood and tears.

"I...I need this. Trent, he took my childhood."

I reached the barrel. Bowers was such a pathetic, sobbing sight that I very nearly pitied him. But it was Mike, poor, dear Mike, with his pain and hatred and uncertainty, that was the most poignant thing of all.

I put my hand on the gun, gently lowering it.

"Don't let him take the rest."

Mike stepped back, breathing heavy. This was so hard.

Finally, he yelled out in anguish and tossed the gun into the yellow burning pitch.

"You're not worth it!" he screamed at the man who scarred him for life, but who wouldn't take his soul.

I breathed a sigh of relief and rapture. Mike walked over to the far end of the bar. He grabbed the bottle of whiskey Bowers had left behind and poured it over his open wound. Perhaps that would sanitize it, but I winced.

"What a disappointment," The King of Wax sighed, rising. He glided over to Bowers, who was sitting by the barrel, weeping.

"I'm sorry, father." he was on his knees, gripping The King's pants like a desperate child.

"Shhh, shhh. I know." It was obvious what was coming next, but there still was some final useless hope in Bowers's eyes as he looked up.

The King took Bowers's head in his hands. Pressed their brows together.

"I forgive you," he whispered.

Then he opened his mouth, pressed it to Bowers's and let loose an internal apocalypse of bees.

Bowers was squirming around on the floor now like an epileptic in a fit. He opened his mouth to scream, but buzzing horrors flew out. I could see them flying under his skin, stinging him internally, through his veins, in his skull. A body being eaten from within. It was excruciating to behold. His eyeballs bulged and finally exploded, and the swarm burst forth from his sockets. I stopped watching.

The bees picked and stung at the corpse on the floor. The King of Wax turned to Mike.

"You thought you could save him."

Mike shook his head, content he made the right decision.

"It wasn't about saving him."

"*No one dies like Gaston,*" I couldn't help but singing under my breath, remembering the hypocrisy of the earlier cop-out.

"Yes, yes, 'save yourself'" The King rolled his eyes. "Well, you won't even do that. The Sting or the Burn. You go either way."

He reached out his hand and threw a fireball at the door behind Mike. Then another at the back mirror. Two more at the booths in the back. He was turning this dive into a raging inferno, and our time was limited.

"This has become TIRESOME!" he moaned, stepping toward Mike and flicking some flames towards the ceiling. "Disturbed or not, you're at an end!"

He raised his hand with a fiery aplomb, getting ready for a fatal blast at Mike, who was standing, hand on the socket, unsure what to do next.

I saw my opportunity because I saw Mike eyeing the door every time The King looked at me. I should accept that, I guess. I slightly nodded as I made up my mind, willing Mike to take the opportunity while I had it. To exploit the monster's focus on me and leave me as I left him.

So, I ran over and grabbed The King of Wax's arm and held it off while I could.

"Mike, run now!"

"I'll get to you, insect!" But The King did not throw me away. Was I actually physically restraining him? I held his hand up under great strain. His arm was burning. With his other hand, he sought to swat me down, but I grabbed that too, and now we were wrestling, like Jacob and the Angel. He was so big and burly, so malevolent and powerful, and I was so meek. But it was working, I was keeping him from Mike, if only for precious moments, and I wanted Mike to have them. One final gift as the smoke rose and the flames crept up.

Mike was looking at us grunt and struggle, watching without saying a word.

"Mike, go." I looked back, and in that moment The King grabbed me by the wrists. He was burning me. He was hurting me. I closed my eyes, already misty from the smoke. "Run away like I did. I'm not tired of running away. I sleep with it. I've been doing it my whole life," I cried through smoky eyes and singed arms, pain and sadness meeting. "I left you. I'm running away from Lilith. I just can't..." I felt my own flesh burn up in the beast's cruel hands. I smelt it, and then everything was as it should be. Like it was just. "Can't STAY! JUST GO!"

The pressure on my hands relented. I heard a stumbling series of footsteps, the creak of the door swing open, a couple of coughs, and then nothing.

Mike had left. Without saying a word, he had left me.

I opened my eyes. I was looking at The King of Wax, an arrogant scowl on his visage. Flames were licking all around him, reflected off his livid brow. He narrowed his yellowish eyes.

And then he grinned, relishing my pain, Mike's abandonment, my fear, my suffering, my sadness. The blood I shed and the tears I wept. He disturbed me. He was happy.

"The Buddy System," he said simply.

He threw a massive fireball at the bar, and the glasses of liquor exploded. Piebald was at his king's side then.

"We have reached the mountainside." Hand on his shoulder, The King of Wax spoke to him, done with this game.

Piebald obeyed, playing a luminous melody I'd be remiss to call Heavenly, but that's what came to mind.

A door, pitch black like a tunnel, opened in the wall between them, and they walked through. To where, or when, I cannot say.

And then it was closed.

I rose to my feet, a mistake my trembling knees and weak constitution easily corrected. The smoke already blocked my path out and could not see my way to the door. My wrists bled in agony. My stupid lungs, weak with asthma as they had always been and overwhelmed now by blind evil, could barely muster the strength to cough. There was fire all around me. Maybe there always had been. Maybe there always would be- but at that moment I couldn't even fear Hell. I was so tired. Tired of fighting, tired of hurting, tired of being afraid. Sick to death of wax figures and harlequins, self-doubt, and one dumb mystery or inner disappointment after enough. Take it all. Half a dozen prayers raced through my head as I attempted to crawl across that hot floor, the start of an Our Father, the middle of an Act of Contrition, the end of a Hail Mary...

Now and at the Hour of Our Death, Amen.

So that was it, then I decided, with more resignation than bravery or fear. Thank you, God, for remembering Eckhart's lesson of the one sufficient prayer. I would accept it, because what choice did I have?

And because I am me, and references are a part of that, I turned to Panzram and *Midnight Meat Train* before it all went black.

Take me, Lord, let this world go, and I'll nose dive into whatever dreams may come, and see if that one is as lousy as this ball of wax and wickedness. I would die in a wretched pile of smoke and tears, I decided. It wouldn't matter if I died.

It was a foul world anyway.

Chapter 20: So Long, Swampman

Or was it?

I had surmised that it had been a matter of moments or minutes, 5 on the outside, between my passing out and the firefighters bursting in. About a quarter of an hour later, I awoke in the back of an ambulance. The paramedic, an irresistibly lovable Aryan named Scott, kept telling me I'm okay. He called me a superstar, champ. He asked me if I liked the Dodgers. I humored him. I wanted his smile.

My injuries were no big deal. Physically, anyway. I hadn't really inhaled too much smoke, and the burns on my wrists were only 1st degree. "1st and a half, really," Dr. Shapiro clarified. I'd be bandaged for a while, and I wasn't looking forward to the healing process, imagining a build-up of pus at some point that I couldn't help but popping, raw skin to follow...but that's for later.

After bandaging my wrists, she asked, "is there anyone you want us to call?"

"You mean my parents don't know?" I realized how small and sad that sounded as I said it. I didn't have an asthma attack in school. No one was going to pick me up from the principal's office. I was 29 years old and rescued from a burning bar over 100 miles away. Of course, they didn't know.

"We didn't know your emergency contact," Dr. Shapiro explained. "But if we-"

"No, no, it's okay," I shook off that brief, fleeting reminder that the safety of childhood was long gone. "Is, um, is Mike here?"

"He is." That was Agent Toastman, now standing in the doorway. "You'll be able to see him soon."

"Ted, wow!" I looked up. I wanted to go hug him, but Dr. Shapiro had just finished putting the tape on, and I didn't want to make any sudden moves. "It's ah, it's good to see you!"

"Likewise." He had crossed the distance and stuck out his hand, which he then withdrew, imagining a faux pas. "I am sorry. It must be very sensitive."

"Just don't grab me by the wrist too hard." I shook his hand, not too firm because he was keeping his distance, but it felt nice to have him there.

"So, how's Mike?" I asked, "is he going to be okay?"

Toastman took a gentle, delicate tone. He had impeccable bedside manner.

"I am sorry to say, they were unable to save his eye, but he is in stable condition, calm and lucid, without further injuries. Vision unaffected in his right eye, for example. It is a simplification, but phrase of comfort being what it is, I will tell you he is going to be okay."

That's debatable. And no surprise about the eye, of course. They couldn't even find it. I knew exactly where it was *when* it was going to have been.

"Oh, thank God."

"Indeed. You can go and see him shortly. Dr. Shapiro, was it?"

"Nora's fine." She smiled warmly. Such was the reaction of good people to Agent Toastman.

"I am sure she is. May Trent take leave of absence now, or was there anything else?"

She turned to me.

"Just keep it dry and clean. And stay away from burning buildings. You don't need to be sucking down any more smoke!"

A polite chuckle broke out.

"Terrific." Agent Toastman turned to me. "Trent, I will take you to Mike's room now. He should be getting out of ER soon enough, and we will see if you can visit. I imagine you two have a great deal to discuss."

"I imagine you, and I do as well."

He nodded slightly, not wanting to overwhelm me.

"I do have a few questions. Naturally, there is a lot to be sorted out, and if it would not be too much of a strain, I would like to talk to you. After you have visited your friend, of course."

"Not of course, not necessarily. If you don't mind, Ted." I leaned in. "I actually would prefer..."

"That we get the obligatory interrogation out of the way, so you can be free to relax with your friend without the burden of worrying about what you will tell the FBI in the back of your head?"

"Yeah."

"I understand completely. And yes, absolutely we can-we will do that."

I stood up.

"Great, so do we have to go down to the station, or?"

The Agent looked to the doctor.

"Could we-would you mind terribly giving us the room?"

"Of course. Feel better Trent." She smiled pleasantly and closed the door behind her.

He took the chair across from me, and I took a little pleasure in hearing that white paper crinkle as he sat.

"First of all," I asked, "maybe you could fill me in on what happened after I blacked out."

"Due to smoke inhalation, yes." He took out a small tape recorder. "Do you mind if I record this."

"By all means. So, I was just wondering, well, you're here now. Why?"

"To see you of course."

"But how did you know I was here? Uh, how did you get tipped off? Have Mike and I been on a watch list or something?"

"Nothing so worrisome. In fact, I was only responding to your very suggestion."

"Donovan's Dive?"

"The very same. You told me to look into it."

I smiled. He had listened.

"You thought it was irrelevant."

"That had been my initial impression, but recall what I have said about starting off with a premise. It did not take much time or energy to discover that the late Dr. Victor Thane was, in fact, the sole owner of Donovan's Dive. This research I could accomplish from my desk with my phone and laptop-from which I also encountered the curiosity that Dr. Thane was still paying property taxes on an establishment that had been closed for 17 years. The source of his depthless and seemingly inexplicable funds will no doubt be a case for the ladies and gentlemen in the Internal Revenue Service, but I was interested in the bar."

"So, you checked it out."

"I did not have a warrant or anything so formal, but I was curious, and as tenuous a lead as this might be, the revelation of such an exorbitant investment by the dead psychiatrist did raise an eyebrow. Anything odd concerning a man whose murder remains unsolved is worth further investigation. While formal inquiries were being processed, looking for fresh air and some in-person perspective, I drove out to see this Dive for myself."

I was on the verge of tears of joy.

"You were there."

"Indeed." He nodded simply, politely ignoring my rapture. "I had parked across the street and was observing the building from a distance. Unimpressive, to be frank. So, imagine my shock when Mike Kripke comes running out, minus an eye, a wall of flame behind him."

"You saw Mike?"

"He was coughing and delirious by the time I ran out to him. Bleeding profusely from the socket, of course. He kept pointing at the burning bar, screaming your name," Toastman coughed, moving on, "I called the fire department, and that was that."

"They wouldn't have gotten there fast enough," I realized. "It was you, wasn't it?" I was close to laughing, how happy that made me. "You pulled me out of the fire!"

Maybe he was my savior after all. One of them anyway.

He looked down, bashful and nonchalant.

"Well. Yes. There was not enough time to wait for the cavalry, so to speak. I ran in, came out with you, very quick. It really is not an episode necessary to dwell on."

"It's necessary to me, man."

"Hmm." He smiled, giving in. "Now how about you tell me what I need to know."

So, I told him. I told him the truth, and nothing but the truth, and pretty much all of it. I realized that I didn't actually have to lie to skim over those problematic and distracting supernatural details. As Agent Toastman said earlier, I could just say The King of Wax, for so he was known, was a cult leader. That he had ordered his fanatic to shoot herself in the head. After that, he dipped her directly into the wax. Then he ordered Mike and Bowers to fight after plucking Mike's eye out with his finger, which after, all is, physically possible. Mike spared Bowers on my plea, and then The King "released" bees onto his failed acolyte. I don't know how exactly he started the fire or how he and Piebald escaped, which was true on both accounts. As to the means of bee release, fire starting, and escape, Toastman seemed content to let forensics do the rest of the work. I had given him the meat.

He turned off the recorder after I had answered his final question. He frowned, then smiled, then shook his head. It was all too much. Much too much and it didn't make sense, and there was no way to look at it that made it any less loathsome or infuriating. Because the closer you got to this case, the more likely it was something else nasty would crawl up, a scream in the night, a "will this ever end"?

He put on a brave face, a pragmatic smile in front of all that confusion and disgust.

"It looks like I have got my work cut out for me."

"It would appear so," I stood up to shake his hand. "I'm sorry for throwing this all on your desk."

"It is what I do." He shook back vigorously, warmly now. "You have been very helpful, Trent."

I hoped that was true. I wanted to do for this man everything he had for me. I had even hoped, I don't know, maybe I could give him the fingerprints of the one who did this off my wrists. But they were just big amorphous burns, and I was past hoping he was a man who could be brought in so easily.

"So, what happens next?" I asked.

"Well, we have John Henry Bowers and Chip Mayhew to autopsy. They were in very strange states, understand. And put APBs out for...the others." He sounded exhausted with those details, and I didn't blame him.

Agent Toastman started for the door, then stopped in place. Shaking his head as if he could get all the bad stuff out. He still sounded more incredulous than horrified, as if he were looking at a Boschian train wreck from a distance.

"Bees. Human candle. Bars. Mental patients. The...The King of Wax. Tells a girl to kill herself and she does, without hesitation. What does all that mean?"

It's a question that still keeps me up at night. And here is what I said:

"That there is evil in the world."

He nodded.

"There's good too."

"I hope so." As he turned to leave, I stopped him. "Agent Toastman," he looked back. "Thank you for saving my life."

• • • • •

I didn't actually get to see Mike that day. It was running late by the time I finished up with Toastman, and they told it would be best if I came back tomorrow. Mike still needed work and of course a good night's sleep. They told me he was going to be perfectly fine (*not good as new*, I thought) and he was adjusting well.

I was disappointed that I had to come back, but I did find it interesting, the implication that Mike was already out of surgery. I had expected that he would be under the knife for hours and hours. But Mike's eye was completely gone. There was no fine-tuned delicate manner of reattaching optic nerves. They had a wound to treat. And seal up. It was over.

So, I went home and slept like a baby.

• • • • •

I came back the next day. I brought brownies. I don't know. I felt like I should bring something.

The Nurse, a kind young woman named Connie, possibly of Laotian descent, brought me to his room and told me to knock on the door.

"Come in."

I walked in and shut the door behind me.

It was a small room, cleanly kept and smelling of gardenias.

Mike looked rested. He sat up in bed reading a *Swamp Thing* comic book. His cheeks were ruddy, and his skin was flush. His wounds from Bowers's brutalization were already fading.

His left eye had a white surgical patch on it. Well, a wad of gauze held down with tape. He was no pirate.

On seeing me, Mike's lips curled up in an expression humans who haven't been through what we have generally considered a smile.

"Hey, Trent."

"Hey, Mike."

"You brought me brownies?"

I set them down on his bedside table. There was some space next to the flowers. I more than idly wondered who brought those, if he had anybody else worrying for him, or if it was just a nicety the hospital provided.

"I made them myself!"

"You lick the bowl?"

"You know I did."

Mike let the comic book rest on his chest.

"How about you pull up a seat there."

I did. I wasn't sure what we were supposed to say, but it felt like we were supposed to say something. An obligatory denouement. Like they have in movies. But I was so tired. I just wanted to skip it.

"How's your eye?" I instantly cringed at myself.

"I'm going to pretend I didn't hear you say that."

But it was in good humor. He could tell I was just trying to break the ice and that I immediately regretted opening that way.

So, I retreated, once more, into references and the innocuous.

"What are you reading there?" I pointed at this comic book. It looked colorful. Green, mostly.

"Hospital gift shop will blow your mind, my man." He handed to me, relived the conversation was lighting up, and we could move to safe subjects. "*Swamp Thing*!" he said this with a grin and a theatrical flourish. Kinda goofy, like he was relishing a childish artifact.

"Right on, man!" I took a look. The swamp was particularly vivid here, and I was impressed with how expressive they were able to make his face.

"I was always into that goofy shit. B-movie stuff. *Creature of the Black Lagoon*."

"Alan Moore had a good run on this one."

"Did he?"

"Yeah, he teamed Swamp Thing up with Superman. It was really cool."

"I don't know about all that. But it got me thinking. You know I was a phil prof, right?"

"What?"

"Philosophy professor."

"Oh. Yeah."

"Well, Associate Instructor. Didn't make full professor." (On account of...) "But I saw...ideas."

"Yeah?"

"Are you familiar with qualia?"

"Uh-uh."

"Qualia is an experience of the mind, relating to how it perceives and processes external stimuli."

"Hmm."

"But the thing about qualia is that it is subjective so that even though this is occurring in the physical world with objective phenomena, said experience is said to exist within one's own mind, and the question arises, what is real, what is it like? Is a thing itself or is it what we see it as?"

"You didn't lose me. You never had me."

"It's just the study of consciousness, Trent. Is it even real? Ouspensky said 'The greatest barrier to consciousness is the belief that one is already conscious'. But what does that mean, and is there any difference? What is sentience? Are mind and brain one? Is there something going on beyond your grey matter?"

"You know I believe."

"Yeah." He nodded. "But how do you know?" He didn't wait for an answer. He sat up and pointed at the comic.

"Swampman."

"Swamp Thing," I corrected, but I was in for a correction.

"No, this is something else. It just got me thinking. See there was this professor, Donald Davidson. Berkeley. And he had this idea. A thought experiment. Say a man is walking through the swamp. During a storm. A dark, unforgiving thunderstorm. He gets struck by lightning." Mike snapped his fingers. "Dead where he stands. But a minute later, lighting strikes twice. It hits the swamp, and it doesn't cause a fire or electrocute froggies. What this bolt does, is it rearranges molecules. Into an exact copy of the dead man. Right down to the atom. Head, fingers, knee, and toes. Hair, clothes, pocket protector. The whole shebang. And here's where it gets interesting. Because this bolt of electricity found its way across the universe to shake up some swamp matter in the exact shape of this poor sap a second before he got struck. Down to the brain cells. So, this...thing is standing there. In the swamp. And he doesn't know. Maybe he doesn't 'know' anything. Maybe he's just a pile of moss who looks like a man, going through the motions. And he goes through all the motions. He goes home. Eats dinner. Kisses the wife. Plays Horse with the son out by the garage. He acts the exact same way. Does all the same things. *Thinks* the same...if 'thinks' is even a thing. The guy's family, his friends, everybody he knew and loved, and cared about, they have no idea their man's decomposing in a swamp somewhere. They think this walking, talking pile of rearranged leaves and mud is the real thing. And who's to say he's not?"

I was stirred. It was just a thought experiment, but it was so poignant and haunting the way he said it.

"But he's not," I countered. "He's a different...thing. All the memories the man-the human person-might have had, everything he experienced, did with family. This swamp thing didn't do any of that. Just because he fooled them doesn't change reality, even if it's just fooled himself. He's an imposter whether he knows it or not."

"Yeah," Mike said dryly, "but how do you know?"

It was familiar, too.

"Wait, so you said a Berkeley professor came up with this?"

"Donald Davidson, yeah."

"When?"

"Late 80s, I think. Why?"

"Well cause that's exactly what happened!" I held up the comic, Swamp Thing taking on an ominous and mythic look in light of this discussion. "Kind of. In the early 80s. Alan Moore's reboot."

Mike reached for the book, and I handed it to him. He took a look.

"Looks like a swamp monster to me."

"Well it's obviously not that issue, and it's not the exact same thing. But Swamp Thing's whole thing was, originally, he was Dr. Alec Holland. He was a scientist, of course. I don't remember what kind. He's doing this experiment in the swamp, something goes wrong, and he's accidentally turned himself into...Swamp Thing."

"As he would."

"But...that's not what happened anymore. The way Alan Moore told the story, Holland was killed in that blast. His experiment went haywire, but it didn't mutate him into a swamp monster. He just died."

This confused Mike.

"So what's Swamp Thing then?"

"Swamp Thing was....I don't know exactly. A heap of moss and mud that came together, animated, and...absorbed the memories of Dr. Alec Holland."

"Oh." He got it.

"So that's the tragedy of the character. Swamp Thing's going around trying to find a 'cure', find some way to become human again...except he was never human in the first place. And when he finds out he's not Alec, he's just a, a weird chunk of nature...I don't think he knows how to live."

Mike nodded like he understood the feeling.

"Damn. That's sad. And VERY close. Swamp Person thinks he's the guy who died. When did Moore write this?"

"Early 80s. I don't know the exact date."

"Well either someone was inspired, or that's just some kind of cosmic coincidence."

"Like a lightning bolt arranging a mass of swamp into an exact copy of the man?"

"Hey, at least Davidson's swampman could go home and pretend nothing happened" he pointed to the comic book. "Moore's thing got a shit deal."

I laughed.

"But at least he found out," I pointed out. "It rips him up inside, and he's still an ugly pile of leaves, but now he can try to be the best Swamp Thing he can be. He doesn't have to live the rest of his life, thinking he's someone he's not."

Mike thought on that.

"But which would you prefer?"

I didn't have an answer. It was an interesting subject, but I felt we had to get to the point.

"So," I sighed. "I guess we should talk about it."

"Says who?"

He had a point, and I was momentarily disarmed. After all, the only one demanding closure was me.

"Well Mike, I've never known you to just let sleeping dogs lie."

"Or dead cats?"

"Or dead cats."

"Is that it, Trent? You blame me? I saw the cat and wouldn't let it be? I had to start asking questions after I saw that…" He coughed, not wanting to finish.

"No, no, no!" I corrected, apologetic. "If anything, it's my fault!" Objective analysis: Eh, not really. We were in it together, and if anything, he was more aggressive than I was. But I thought it was what he wanted to hear.

It wasn't.

"It's nobody's fault," he snapped, annoyed. "We all just played the hands we were dealt."

"House always wins," I responded somberly, whatever that meant.

"Anyway, I already told Agent Whitebread everything."

"Everything?" He saw my concerns and assuaged them.

"Everything within the realm of natural law and accepted scientific consensus. Left out the shooting fire and summoning bees. Said The King of Wax was some crazy guy. Which he is."

"If you say so."

"I didn't say he was 'just' some crazy guy."

Then a couple moments of awkward silence.

"Could you pass me one of those?" he asked, reaching for a brownie.

"Sure." He took a big bite, savored it.

"Mmm! Thanks Trent. You made these?"

"Yeah, I like 'em fudgy."

"Should have brought me some milk, too."

"Sorry."

"It's alright."

I breathed in. Nope. Couldn't just leave it at that.

"Are we really not going to say anything?"

"And what should we say?" He sat up and asked me pointedly. "You have any wisdom to impart? Accusations to make? Tell me Trent, what is supposed to be happening right now?"

I could understand his frustration.

"I just have so many questions left over."

He sighed, seeing my point.

"So do I. But neither of us have answers. And it seems like the more we find out, the less we know," he shook his head sadly. "I'm just tired of asking."

"He's still out there," I said this quietly. The room was so bright, right in the sun, but it was hard not to sound ominous.

"You sure about that?"

I nodded.

"Yeah. He and that...Piper. They just went out, this...I guess a portal or something, opened in the wall, shut behind them. I saw-"

"Yeah, you saw." His voice had a tangible bitterness now, but it was not directed at me. "You saw because you were there. To the end. I wasn't."

"Mike-"

"No. I wasn't." He closed his one remaining eye. "I ran out on you, man. I don't know why I did that."

"Because you were afraid, Mike!" I burst, at last sharing that with him. "You were afraid like I was, and you took the opportunity!"

"No."

"You ran out I like I ran out on you! You were paying me back! It's-it's just!"

"God damn you, Trent! It wasn't payback! You gave me the opportunity! You told me to run!"

"I know! I needed you to. I owed you that."

"You didn't owe me anything!" He was in anguish. "You were a little boy, Trent."

"So were you."

"But now we're grown-ups. And you were the one who stayed. You chose to stay, you made that sacrifice."

"It was shame, Mike. That's all that was."

"It was still a sacrifice. You knew what you were doing. And I abandoned you. And that wasn't payback and it sure as Hell wasn't just. I...I bitched out, man. I bitched out."

"He just ripped your eye out!" I felt impassioned to defend Mike's actions because otherwise, my own decision would carry no weight. Or maybe I just felt bad for him. "You were bleeding from the head! You think you were supposed to stay and fight?!"

"YES." He nodded vigorously. "YES! I see him with my other eye and give him Hell! He takes that out, I fight in the dark. One leg, I hop. Both, I fight him on my stumps. I crawl on the floor and gnaw at his heels. Every last inch of life, I stay to the bitter end. And if nothing else, if I can't do another fucking thing, the least I could do was die with you. You never leave a brother behind!"

"Or a buddy," I said flatly, finally, hoping to put this matter to rest. "I guess that makes us even."

"You think that's why he let you live?" Mike asked in a resigned voice. "Because we're *even*?" He put venom into the word.

"I don't know why he didn't stay to finish the job. Maybe he thought I was done for. I do know if it weren't for Ted, I'd be toast."

"He's a proper J. Edgar, him."

"Yeah. And now he's on the case."

Mike scoffed, perhaps louder and with more vitriol than proper.

"You really think he's gonna find, gonna *catch*...The King of Wax?"

"Not a chance."

"I'm through with that bastard," Mike sighed, knowing it was a surrender. "I'm not knocking on his door anymore."

"That's wise," I agreed, even though I know he didn't want me to.

"And if he keeps his distance, that's that." His tone darkened, not to fervor, but to despair. "He comes back to us...I don't know."

"He could have killed me, but he left. And that was the big showdown. I think we're done."

"So, he won." It wasn't a question. "He's still out there, doing his evil."

"Maybe." But I couldn't accept that. I couldn't let this story end that way. "But maybe we rattled his cage a little. Thane's gone so he won't be letting loose maniacs anymore. The King's lost some of his business, like the vineyard and Donovan's Dive. And Bowers...he's done his damage."

"Yeah," Mike nodded, trying to take what comfort he could from that. But he couldn't. "He sure did."

I wasn't sure what to say next. Mike's injury was still an elephant in the room, even now that we had the final confrontation with his abuser and he had suffered a more recent and devastating mutilation.

As if reading my thoughts, or at least on the same wavelength, Mike raised his right hand, staring at the glove. He held it up to bathe in the sunlight. Turn it over to see both sides. He made a fist, then he released it. He spread the fingers out and looked down at them, like a woman examining her nails.

"You know I've worn this thing for 17 years?"

"Yeah."

"You probably didn't notice, cause in middle school, high school, I wore two gloves. Matching set."

"We didn't hang out in middle school. Then you went to TJ, I went to Chantilly."

"Why was that, by the way?"

"Well it was a zoning thing, wasn't it? And Thomas Jefferson was a Governor's Magnet school, so-"

"No I mean, why didn't we hang out in Junior High? Why'd we stop being friends, Trent?"

I looked down. The question was *when?*

"Never mind." He knew the answer. "Anyway, after I graduated, I took the left glove off. Through college, teaching, basic-I got a special medical...I was always the guy with one glove."

"That was your style."

"And that's all it was. I was cultivating an image," he chuckled morosely. It was a small, dry laugh. "Some chicks thought it looked cool. Sexy even. A couple even wanted the finger." He raised his index finger. I got the picture. "Some kids thought it looked retarded. Some guys called me a fag. Mostly people think I do it for attention, and they're right. These days I might as well be wearing a fedora."

"It draws the eye," I admitted, but I wanted to be on his side. "But Mike, nobody, NOBODY has the right to judge you for that. You were 12 years old. And he-he *deformed* you."

"Dammit, Trent. What have I have I been talking about? And what do you think is under here?" He held up his glove, held it in my face. "You think I'm Skeletor or something?"

"I don't know. I didn't see how bad he got you."

Mike looked at me blankly.

Then he took his glove off.

His hand was pale, naturally, and his skin looked so soft and so clammy. A result of being kept away for so long. But it was not monstrous. Not by a long shot. The burning had left a pattern, but it was faint, and only around the edges. You had to be looking for it.

"He only held me under for a second. I think he got distracted when you ran. I pulled away from him, and then I was rolling around on the ground, crying my eyes out till they came for me. He went back into his shack, and just waited, I guess."

"Your hand looks fine," I said plainly. I thought about holding it, giving him any comfort and strength I had to give, but I couldn't muster that moment.

"Mom and Dad got me skin grafts in 7th grade. You can barely even tell anymore. But that's the point. I never needed...this."

He tossed the glove on the floor with little energy and no ceremony. I looked down on it. It looked so plain and insignificant. You'd think this would be some big cathartic moment, but he was so sad, so deflated, and he wasn't done.

"But this?" he pointed at his left socket. The wound was fresh, and the bandages were new. But that would pass, and he would wear a patch, or a prosthetic, or some other placeholder. And never again what he used to have. "This is real."

"Mike."

His voice started to crack.

"All those jokes and stares. The art school homo, the Michael Jackson. I owned that. That was my choice. I could take it off at anytime. But I thought it would make me...I was special." He attempted a smile there but couldn't quite make it. And now tears were starting to come from his one good eye, but that's not the one he touched. "This is for life. I can't ever-I didn't choose..."

He closed his eye, and we were silent for a while. There wasn't anything left to be said, because what could you say, and I got the feeling that it was okay to leave now. Or that's what I told myself, anyway.

"Well, I guess I should head out, let you rest up. I'm meeting Lilith at The Metronome."

"Ah," he attempted to smile. "So, you're still seeing that mamacita, the bartender."

"I hope so."

"*Te amo las chicas hermosa.*" His smile was whimsical and romantic in an almost forlorn way. "God Bless those Mexican girls."

"She's Cuban, or her parents were, but yeah."

Mike grabbed my hand. Holding me firm, looking me in the eye, imparting me wisdom with a charge.

"Be good to her, Trent. Be her everything."

His hand was clammy and shaking. Naked, it had been out of action for no short while, and I could feel it.

"I will."

He let go and sat back. He sighed, deflated and looking back. On everything, and most of all himself.

"I wish I could get a girl like that. Any."

"Maybe you should call Snow White," I said in good fun. "Be her Prince Charming."

He swatted at me playfully, grinning.

"Get the fuck out."

I rose. I guess that was it for now.

"What are you going to do next, Mike?"

He looked out the window, even though the blinds were drawn and there was nothing to see, and he grew distant.

"Oh, you know. This and that."

I didn't like the answer, but that was as good as I was going to get. I went for the door. He stopped me.

"Hey Trent."

I turned around.

"Yeah?"

"What if that happened to me?"

"What?"

"Swamp man type thing."

"Huh?"

"All those years ago." He put his hands behind his head, letting his mind wander to all those places we tend to go. "What if the real Mike Kripke melted in that pot? Just dissolved. Maybe Bowers was a better chandler than we thought because he pulled me out. The Human Candle."

Whenever he used to wink, it was always with his left eye.

"Thanks for being my buddy, Mike."

He gave me a goofy little salute, and then I walked out of the room, and the glove was still on the floor.

Chapter 21: Sometimes There's a Girl

I wasn't meeting Lilith at The Metronome. That was a lie. I don't know why I said that. The Metronome is not even a real place. I don't even know what it would be. A metronome's that weird back and forth clicky thing I guess some people used to help them fall asleep or time the beats of their instrument. Morgan Freeman had one in Se7en. Maybe if I had said "The Metrodome" that would make more sense, and maybe that's what Mike thought I said. But it still wasn't a real place.

As I was driving out to a bar in Highland Park, I tried to think what the Metrodome might be. "Metro" suggested metropolitan, and I'm not talking about Chip's urban transportation. I'm talking about something upscale, worldly, and refined, like Whit Stillman's movie. In some cities, they call the opera "the Met". And "dome", well that suggested a dome. I was picturing a planetarium. Maybe with a laser rock show. I saw my first laser rock show when I was three. Darcy never stopped teasing me about it, as I got scared and started to cry, and Dad had to take me out.

What scared me? I parked down the street from the bar and sat in my car, remembering. It was that giant red face, made of lasers. It looked so sharp, so spiky, so mad and mean. The eyes were huge and white and not shaped like human eyes. There was a weird grid across the face, like it was trying to burst out of a cage.

In later years I would realize this was Spider-Man. Please don't look too much into that. I guess I was disturbed by the image in a way I could not articulate. Could that be The King of Wax working his evil even then?

No, I decided. Of course, it wasn't him. So many things scare children, and we mustn't let that define us or stop us from revisiting in future years. I grew to become a huge Spider-Man fan. The Rami-Maguire collaborations are three of my favorite films. I fell in love with Mary Jane. I enjoy the comics, the cartoons, one of the video games, and the character in general. It was only years later did I connect the face that scared me to the superhero I adored, and by then I had outgrown the brief disturbance of single afternoon as a toddler for a lifetime of fandom.

And then that creep Piebald shows up as a pregnant Spider-Man doing unholy things with Frozen Elsa. That was sickening in an inexplicable way. And Chip, God rest her soul, may be gone, but those videos were still up. God knows who's putting these videos up, weird perverse stuff, ostensibly for kids, with the Joker and Ariel along for the ride, but they are getting views. Could I still like my friendly neighborhood web slinger like I had before?

Yes. Yes, I could, resolving myself with a smile as I closed my door and set out down the street. The disgusting, powerfully ominous figurehead who liked to orchestrate the unsettling would not take that from me. You're my friend, Peter. With great power comes great responsibility. I don't think that's something the villain of this story ever really understood.

Laser rock shows, I decided, reaching the door of La Cuevita, should be safe and happy for children. Like living museums.

Brad was working the bar with frosted tips. I wasn't sure I liked the fake blonde look on him or his sleeveless mesh shirt. I guess you don't know who Brad is, but that speaks to the larger truth that I haven't documented every single detail that transpired these eventful weeks. Yes, I did get to know Lilith and meet some of her friends.

Like Brad, the bartender.

Currently, he was hunched over the bar, engaged in a conversation with the sole occupant. It was day and early yet, and I hoped I would have some time with Lilith to myself so I could tell her all the things I desperately needed her to hear.

The thin gentleman at the bar was well dressed and self-amused. He appeared to be in his healthy 60s with a pencil thin mustache and a warm, funny voice.

"...It's not that I'm against it," he was saying, swirling his martini, "I don't know why anyone would be against gay adoption. Or any kind of adoption. If you ask me, Angelina's kids hit the lottery," he smiled, bemused. "Especially if she breastfeeds." He laughed.

I took my stand at the end of the bar, unseen.

"But you're saying..." Brad prodded.

"I just think it's so BORING. Why on Earth would we want to get domesticated? We used to be outlaws! We used our wits and fury to survive.

Now we want to get married and have babies? Isn't the entire point of being gay that we're not straight?"

"There is no 'point' to being gay," Brad rebuked. "It's your identity, you're born that way. It doesn't, you know, dictate your behavior. It's not a choice."

"Suit yourself," The Thin Man said drolly, lighting up a cigarette. Brad frowned.

"And of course, there's no smoking in the bar."

"Which is one of the most ridiculous things I've ever heard! How is anyone supposed to enjoy a drink without a smoke? This is a den of vice, isn't it? What next, we're not allowed to fuck in the bathroom?"

"You AREN'T allowed to fuck in the bathroom," Brad stated emphatically. "Now put it out," he added politely, "please."

"Looks like you're outnumbered, Brad," she came out of the back, cigarette in mouth, with a dull expression that spoke to a sleepless night. What was keeping her up? "Two to one."

"It's not a democracy." Brad began to polish a glass, annoyed. "It's the law."

"Maybe you should ask the owner," I piped in, by way of announcing myself and making an inquiry into a matter that should have been laid to rest.

Brad frowned like a man who didn't need such complication.

Lilith grinned, happy to see me and seeming to assume that my query was nothing more than an icebreaker.

"Out back, businessman." She hooked her finger into my shirt and pulled me towards the back.

It was a very familiar and endearing action. Playful and assuming an unspoken intimacy. I liked being pulled.

I should clarify at this point that Lilith and I were doing fine. Our relationship was suspiciously without conflict. When I told Mike, I hoped that I still had a girlfriend, that was speaking more to my trepidation about finally telling her anything, rather than any problems that had already surfaced. I know that in a traditional story structure, perhaps there would be a big argument at the end of the second act, a faux break-up, and now the reconciliation at the end. But it's not that kind of story. Part of the point, I guess, is that Lilith didn't have much to do with anything.

What I mean by that, is that if I were writing this story, Lilith would have figured in the climax. Of course, she would. Either my darkest fears about her nature would be confirmed, she comes out of the shadows as the most insidious minion. I had been infiltrated, played this entire time, and now the woman I loved would reveal herself as evil as her namesake-if not, in fact, that very same Lilith. Or else she would be a damsel in distress, of a sarcastic gloomy sort. My enemy would bring her before me, threaten her life. Perhaps make me choose between her and Mike, or else sacrifice myself. Yes, her presence at Donovan's Dive would have been quite dramatic.

And yet here she was, seemingly unaffected and of course oblivious of the recent weird horror. There was something oddly comforting in that, the idea that there still existed those blissfully ignorant of all that nasty business-the great majority of mankind, in fact-and that one of these happy people was with me now.

If I had to shatter that bliss and comfort in pursuit of the truth she deserved, so be it.

"Where you been, stranger?" she asked as we reached the empty patio. It was empty yet.

"Here and there. I-" I grabbed her cigarette suddenly and took a quick drag, impromptu and ill-advised. I don't know why I did that.

She looked at me, eyes wide but brow furrowed in an amused surprise, on the verge of chuckling.

"Okaaaay," she said without further comment.

"Yeah," I managed to avoid coughing. "I've been held up like crazy these past three days."

"Slave drivers at The Film Archive keeping you up at night?"

"Something like that."

"I wish you were around yesterday. I watched soooo much *Aggh!!! Real Monsters*! Nick Classic was running a marathon. And I smoked a couple bowls. Thug life."

"Sounds fun."

"You should try it."

"I never really liked that show. I mean that weird little guy with his eyes in his hands, and the walking black and white snake girl. It's...bizarre. And not in a good way."

"Can't quite put your finger on it?"

Was she suggesting...unplaceably disturbing?

"Are you doing that on purpose?" I didn't want the answer.

"What do you mean? And I was talking about the pot."

"I can't do that either. Asthma, you know."

"I know." She said that in a genuinely sympathetic tone and put her hand on my arm, comforting. "That's why I got you those edibles."

"Yeah. So that's something to think about. Getting high with you.

Watching Nicktoons."

"Well, which did you like?"

I shrugged, then.

"Doo doo doo do do do doo do, Doo doo doo do do do doo do, da da da da da da..." (That was me humming *Doug*, by the way)

"But you should seriously give the monsters another chance. They could surprise you."

That seemed as good a place to start as any.

"Lilith," I sighed, preparing myself. "I know I'm not going to like this." That was me doing Courage. "I also liked *Courage the Cowardly Dog*- but that's not the point. The point is, I've got to tell you something. I've got to tell you...everything, really."

"Should I be worried?" she raised an eyebrow. "You're not coming out to me?"

"What, of the closet? I wish it were that simple! But, yeah, you should be worried." I shook my head. "I'm trying to think where to begin here."

"How about you start at the beginning," she suggested. "And then when you get to the end, stop."

"Good advice...Okay. Did you...have you ever heard of those colonial villages? Living museums?"

And I told her everything.

I told her how Mike and I were friends, and more than that, we were buddies. I told her about the field trip back to colonial days, how everyone dressed and talked like history. I told her about the sick, disturbed man who sneaked into where he didn't belong. I told her about Mike's attitude and his madness. I told her I left my buddy behind while he was being mutilated, and how I carried that guilt for decades. The chance meeting in the library over H.P. Lovecat by way of Schrodinger. Meeting Mike again. I told her about Santa Monica, and the Pimm's turned Pin's with a grotesque garnish. I told her how Mike's Instagram investigation brought me here. I told her about her. It wasn't all recounting the finer points of a horror mystery. I opened up, at last, about my initial infatuation, how I couldn't keep my eyes off her, how my heart leapt every time she paid me a modicum of attention. She remembered Mike buying the whole bottle like he was a high roller, but now she knew the real reason. She gained new insight into what bottle she handed us. I detailed our trip to Deakins Porthouse in San Simeon and the compliance of poor doomed La Cire. How his list brought us to The Pick and Hammer, and therefore to Dr. Victor Thane, with his tales of Jack Frost and The Erl-King and the invitation I should have refused. I didn't go into every detail of his wax demonstration, but I did tell her about the return of the monster from our past, how Mike froze and I was able to affect a Lilithesque attitude of sarcasm and brashness that got us both out of there. I tried to remain detached and simply factual when I spoke of Thane's death, but my voice shook. I mentioned Agent Toastman. I admitted, with shame, my doubts and fears about Lilith herself to Lilith herself. How, in the light of all these infernal affairs, I wondered if she may have some insidious connection. Somewhere along the way was Chip, playful, inscrutable, mischievous Chip, who was as undeniably sexy as she was unfortunately doomed. A mad sprite who had my attention, my arousal, my disgust. With further shame, I was honest about our late rendezvous, and I didn't leave a single thing out. I thought total honesty there would be to my credit, but I felt small and ignoble as I went over it out loud. I came to the climax. Piebald was there-Lilith's own Piebald, the mascot from the bottle and possibly The Piper himself. Donovan's Dive turned into a bloody inferno. I told her about The King of Wax. I held back tears but couldn't keep from shuddering as I told of everything that when on in that awful confrontation. The King's gnawing accusations and disturbing philosophy of the quality of the disturbing. My fear, and Mike's too. Chip shot herself in the head on his command. He turned her into a human candle. No pity for the poor lost soul, just disdain for those of us who watched. He ripped out Mike's eye and put it in the bottle-that same bottle, I was sure, would be sent back in time. Mike and Bowers's fight. Mike got the upper hand, but I convinced him not to shoot. I didn't save the man though, screwed up as he was, so what pride was there? Bees and fire. The sting and the burn. I held off that hellish beast, as penance. I thought it was what I deserved, and Mike ran like I ran, as I told him to. This amused The King of Wax. He let me go and then he went. I surrendered to the smoke. I was saved, but what did my sacrifice mean? Mike had lost an eye, and I wasn't sure what he had gained, even as he left the glove on the floor.

And now here I was.

Lilith pursed her lips, processing that all, and it was a lot to process. She had been heroically restrained throughout the entire rambling recounting of the various horribles I have described to you in more vivid detail. I had resolved myself to plow right through, and as she did not interrupt, I never checked myself or digressed. I noted her reactions, silent though she was. Curiosity, incredulity, and amusement tempered with disgust were the flavors coloring her countenance, and I imagined she would have something to say when I was done. She was never bored, even though it was clear she wondered where this was going. There was a look of recognition when I got to Pin's Brew, and I could tell she saw the relevance of the stranger at the bar, especially when I described the man at the end as Truman Capote meets The Undertaker. She frowned a little when I told her about Chip, and by the time I was describing the terribly and deadly climax, her eyes were wide. She was not horrified. No, the time for horror had passed. But perhaps she was offended.

"So that's-that's…" I blew a stream of air out of my cheeks, deflating, exasperated.

"The truth," she said slowly, rolling her tongue over her lips, trying it out.

"Yes, the truth."

"And you're not lying. Or crazy. And it's not one of your fucking goofs."

"Not a goof."

"And you'd have to have some fucking vivid imagination to make a whole story around that guy who came into the bar, the one I told you about."

"You remember him."

"Guy like that, you don't forget. No matter how hard you try," she added scornfully.

"Yeah. And sorry about him-if I brought him into your life. Or maybe he was already here. His brew was anyway. Or maybe it's a chicken and egg type thing. I don't know. Who can tell?" I shook my head. "Still, I'm sorry."

"Stop apologizing, Trent. It's a very unattractive habit, and you do it way too much."

"S-right. Okay."

She put her hands on her hips, looking at me pointedly.

"And you didn't kiss her?" I was relieved that she was taking me seriously enough to pursue it, but I hoped we could move on.

"No. She kissed me, and it was only for a second, and I pushed her away and told her I have a girlfriend."

"I don't know if I ever authorized that term." My heart sank, but she smiled and gently grabbed my wrist. "But I like it."

"Thanks." My heart had risen again, higher than ever.

"But you touched her." Her tone was curious and only slightly accusatory, more matter of fact than anything else. "While she was naked."

"No, she hadn't taken her dress off yet. I pushed her away, on her shoulders. It wasn't cheating. But it was close. I shouldn't have been there in the first place. Opening myself up to that, temptation, you know…"

"Near occasion of sin," she remarked dryly. "Mike Pence was right."

"So, I apologize for that. Even though you don't like sorries. But there it is. A whole lot of messed up nightmares, and that's all I have to say."

"Trent, why are you telling me this?"

"Because it's over. I really, really want it to end. And I want to tell you the truth. Because you deserve it." I was looking at the ground now. Dirty asphalt with dead leaves and cigarette butts. "Even if you don't want anything to do with me afterward. The least I can do, and maybe it's not much, is just to tell you who you're with. And what problems he has."

"Hey." She lifted me up by my chin, and I was looking into her brown eyes again, more sensitive and empathetic than I had seen before, and she kissed me. "I believe you."

"Thank you."

"And I don't know what you feel so guilty about. All that shit doesn't sound like your fault, the way you told it."

"That's true. But blood on my hands? I don't know. I can't help but feel partially responsible for...some of it."

Was that true? I may never come to an answer. Not in this life anyway. Thane, La Cire and the fire victims, Chip, and Bowers. Would they still be here if I had left well enough alone? If I had told Mike to pound salt and minded my own business? I know it's a question I've asked before, and I'm sorry to repeat it. But it won't leave my thoughts, so it's bound to come up on the page as well.

"No." She shook her head. "You did nothing wrong."

"I'm happy to hear you say that." I smiled, even if it was artifice. Maybe everything would be okay.

"What's fucked up..." she took a harsher tone and threw her butt down, almost at my foot. "Is this demonic bullshit. What, you thought I was 'evil'? That I was 'in on it'? Grow up, kid!"

"Lilith, please. I know it was wrong."

"It was stupid and insulting. Fuck you!"

"It's just..." I was weary. "With everything going on, all the weird things that didn't make sense, I didn't know who to trust..."

"You trusted Mike," she said flat, sad, "but you couldn't trust me."

"That's right, I was wrong," It was a sorrowful, ugly fact. "Mike was an old friend."

"And I'm a new friend. You're supposed to trust me. Or what's the point?"

"The point is I trust you now," I said simply, "I should have from the beginning. I shouldn't let stupid things like the bar you work at or the doll you had-"

"Piebald." She was quietly defensive now. "From my abuelo." She slumped down, took a seat on the bench. "He had a puppet show. Back in Camagüey. Castro's people didn't like him. Some Commie bullshit. They closed his shop. Took his show. Even confiscated his puppets. Punch and Judy. Pepe The Bandit. Santa. That got on their nerves. Fuckers canceled Christmas. And my grandfather lost all of his felt children. Except Piebald. Saved him. Brought him here. Then he told me that story. A village infested with rodents. And not just rats. Bats, bugs, all sorts of filthies."

"Bees?" I asked quietly because I was seeing a new side to this story.

"Sure." She was distant, still remembering something bittersweet and not entirely gone. "Then the Piper came, and he played his tune. He got rid of the rats...but the monsters were still there. They lied to him. They said they'd pay him, but they didn't. They were dishonest and corrupt, and they kept doing the things they always did. That's why he took the children away. It wasn't revenge. They needed a better home. Otherwise, they'd grow up like the liars and thieves who raised them. Who abused them. Who had their power and did nothing good with it. So Piebald showed the kids a way out. He played the way to a better place...Where everything was strange and new."

"Lilith," I whispered. "That's beautiful."

"And what do you think I am?" She turned to me, accusingly. "You think I don't get it? That I'm not aware, I'm cultivating this image here? I know I act like a basic bitch. I'm sarcastic and wear too much black. But that's who I am, Trent. And that's – you know I'm not perfect. We're all trying to work things out. I wore a fucking dog collar for two months." She said this with an incredulous chuckle, and I joined in. "But I know what I'm doing. I'm not your Goth fuck doll."

I put my hand on her shoulder and looked her in the eye.

"I know. And I'm sorry if I ever-if I treated you like a fetish or a curiosity, or..." I scoffed. She was the realest person I knew. Funny how I didn't see that now. "Or a villain. There were just a lot things going on. But you were there, and I'm sorry I didn't appreciate you. I like you, Lilith. I should have said that."

She put her head on my shoulder, resting.

"I'm just...trying," she didn't say what. She didn't have to.

"We all are," I said softly, patting her hair. "I think we're going to be okay."

She sat up and looked me straight in the eye.

"So, don't tell me The Piper is evil. Do you dare tell me that." She was looking at me with fear and anger and most of all hurt, the pain that all was not right and that's your fault, and you don't know what to do. "My grandfather told that story. I used to tell it…" She shook her head. Not there yet. "What's so wrong about believing the children are in a better place?"

"Nothing," I was repeating now, holding her close and praying it true, because I needed it to be. "That's just coincidence they used that character. Or a perversion. That's what they do. These…people. They don't have anything of their own, so they have to corrupt, turn something wholesome into something depraved." A colonial village. Princess Elsa. Yes, Piebald. There it all was.

"And that's why they'll lose," Lilith said quietly, before adding, "in the end."

"Whenever that is," I added drly. Then we hugged.

Standing up, I came to the less supernatural but still difficult part of the conversation I'd been dreading.

"Speaking of perverts." I cringed. Smooth transition. "That is, perverting something that shouldn't be…" I closed my eyes and shook my head. "And it goes to what you were saying, not just being a-a fuck doll."

"Thanks?" She wasn't sure where this was going. I still wasn't facing her. Every word was like pulling teeth. "I don't think we should…have…sex…anymore."

She bolted up, shocked and annoyed. She grabbed my shoulder. "Trent, you look at me in the eye when you break up."

I turned around. I took her hands and faced her. Her palms to mine, fingers wrapped around her, it felt real, sincere, and so did her eyes.

"I'm not breaking up with you. It's the opposite if anything. I want to stay with you. I respect you. I want it to be good."

"Good?" She was nonplussed, but she didn't let go. "What, it wasn't good before?"

"It's been…wonderful. I want it all, every bit, and I don't want to feel guilty about it."

"Guilty?" She rubbed her brow, taking that in. "Why would you feel guilty?"

"I'm Catholic," I said simply, which really did put it all on the table

"Oh," her reaction was not scorn or dismay, but simple curiosity and understanding. "Well so am I, but nobody's ever called me out on it."

"Anyway, that's, that's what it is."

"Hmm." It wasn't quite sure what she was thinking. "How about everything but? You're still going down on me, boy?"

"Well I'd like to," I admitted out of the corner of my mouth. "But I think it's best to abstain from all, you know, sexual activity."

She crossed her arms, frowning.

"How lame. What's the point of having a girlfriend?"

It was a devastating thing to hear, especially when she turned away from me.

"That's a big question, Lilith. And I don't know what to tell you, except I'd like to find the answer."

After a loaded, inscrutable moment, she turned around.

"I'd like to find out too."

Then we kissed, and I couldn't stop smiling.

She was running her hand through my hair.

"So, this means you know I'm not really *that* Lilith, right?"

"Yeah. No desert demon here."

"Ooh. I like that nickname though. Desert Demon. Too bad it's kind of exactly the wrong message."

"Well, how about Diamond Lil?" I ran my finger along her arm, her painted skin.

She chuckled.

"Cause I'm hard as rock? Or just worth so much?"

"Diamond Lil was a superhero. She was part of Alpha Flight," I explained. "The team Wolverine was part of in Canada, before The X-Men. It was her skin, but more than that. Hard as diamond. Nothing could get past her. Not even cancer. She was the strongest, toughest babe around, and everyone knew it.

"Diamond Lil." She couldn't help but grinning in a wholesome, goofy way. "I like that." She looked at her phone. "It's too bad her break's up."

She headed for the door and beckoned me in.

"Come on, Detective. Let's get you something to wet your whistle."

"As long as it doesn't start with a P."

She stopped in the doorway, looking me in the eye with a playful smirk.

"Are you sure about this? No more blowjobs?"

"No." I nodded, smiling. Glad to have rejected, at long last, this point. "6th grade is over."

• • • • •

So that's about it for now. "It" being the story I've decided to tell, and "for now" being this moment. Naturally, quite a bit happened, before, during, and after. This is a selected series of events recounted through the lens of a very biased individual. But stories need bias, I daresay, and perhaps even an attempt at a detached, objective listing of these strange events would be all the more maddening. How does one connect the make-believe plantation in the year 2000 Virginia with the fire at a bar in Long Beach all those years later? There are people deceased, and their obituaries are risibly insufficient. The unexpected reunions, the senseless deaths, the eye in the bottle and the cry of the dead cat. These are facts sprinkled throughout a nightmare that needs more than facts. My voice is unmistakable, for I am the story, and the story is me, and without me, I don't know what you'd do with all this.

It was a weird, puzzling tale, that's for sure-or so it is from my perspective. It might not be a satisfying narrative when all is said and done. It's certainly not how I would write it. As I said, though the stakes were certainly high enough as it was, Lilith's presence in the climax would just make sense, as far as heroes and villains go. I would have liked to see more of Agent Toastman, especially if he was to become my FBI hero. I certainly wouldn't have passed out during his big moment. I also would have preferred a tighter conclusion, a more definitive defeat for The King of Wax. As much as it frightens me as a good person that he is still out there, it is also unsatisfying as a narrative that he got away, and I knew little more about him than when he started out.

My own hang-ups with reality aside, I can also see lingering questions on behalf of the reader. Such as, what happened to Lilith's daughter and was Mike stealing valor or what? Well, I hate to disappoint, and perhaps even an ounce of discretion seems ludicrous given everything else I've revealed. This is not to say I didn't find out the truth for myself, off the page, but I think I understand now.

Sometimes you don't get to know about the sex lives of Siamese twins, because it's their right not to tell you. And sometimes the whole thing still works even without that bit.

Sometimes the monsters that have haunted you your entire life show up again, scarier than ever. Sometimes the nightmares are real, and sometimes it looks like they're never going away.

But sometimes you have help. Sometimes a buddy comes back again, years after you thought he was gone for good, and you're as happy to see him as you are scared to see anything else. And sometimes, when the two of you are together, it's not so bad.

Sometimes you fight. Sometimes you run, but sometimes you stay.

Sometimes you pray. Sometimes you live. Sometimes you love. And sometimes you find you became a man somewhere along the way.

And sometimes Lilith is just a girl named Lilith.

The End

Acknowledgements

To properly thank everyone who made this happen would take an enormous amount of time and paper, and cannot be adequately explained briefly. I could write a book. And I did. With the help of those listed below, and I'm sure, many, many more. To anyone I might have missed, you have my apologies and my utmost gratitude.

With that in mind, thanks to:

God, accurately described as The Author of All Things.

Mom and Dad, Cora and Colonel Kevin Carmody, USMC, who have done more for me than I could ever say.

Black Rose Writing, for taking a chance on me.

Querytracker.net, for putting us in touch.

My cousin, Jessica Leake, for pointing me in the right direction.

Lesleh Donaldson and Paul Wolansky for the wonderful blurbs.

My brother Danny Carmody, and my cousin-in-law Nick Pitarra for those awesome drawings.

Franklin, Terry, and Kate at The Black List for giving me everything I needed to grow as a writer.

Elizabeth, Laura, Briauhnna, Zack, Charlie, and any other real people whose real lives I've taken bits and pieces from. Including Brian, Matthew, Aubrey, Truman, and The Undertaker, for serving, whether they know it or not, as character templates.

To the city of Los Angeles, a character in its own right. There are places in this novel that really do exist, either literally, spiritually, or both. See if you can find them, and make a story of your own!

To the prophet Isaiah, Descartes, Don McLean, George MacDonald, John Brancato, Michael Ferris, Tedi Sarafian, Ben Best, Jody Hill, Danny McBride,

Gale Ann Hurd, Nic Pizzolatto, Rashi, John Waters, Peter Jackson, Dan Wakefield, Clive Barker, Donald Davidson, Alan Moore, and all other creatives who have inspired me.

On the darker side, I must note the inspiration of Robert W. Chambers, Chris Claremont, John Byrne, Noah Hawley, Stephen King, and all kings and king-fearers.

My cousin David, because it was only after I finished this novel did I remember that when we were kids, he got me lost at the CoSi, the science museum in Columbus Ohio, where I burnt my finger in the hot wax of the candlemaking exhibit. In retrospect, that may have been a subconscious influence.

And finally, to you, dear reader. Thanks for everything.

Note From The Author

Word-of-mouth is crucial for any author to succeed. If you enjoyed the book, please leave a review online—anywhere you are able. Even if it's just a sentence or two. It would make all the difference and would be very much appreciated.

Thanks!
Brian

About the Author

Brian Carmody is the award-winning screenwriter of *The Batting Cage* and *Aunt*. He is an ardent fan of philosophy, noir, and Weird Fiction. He currently resides in Southern California. This is his first novel.

Thank you so much for reading one of our **Horror** novels.

If you enjoyed our book, please check out our recommended title for your next great read!

Doll House by John Hunt

"Scary, disturbing, creepy, suspenseful. It might be too intense for some people."

–Amazon Review

View other Black Rose Writing titles at
www.blackrosewriting.com/books and use promo code
PRINT to receive a **20% discount** when purchasing.